I PROMISE YOU

GRIM REAPER

SCARRED EXECUTIONERS
BOOK 2

LEXIE AXELSON

CONTENT WARNING

This book is intended for adult readers 18+.

This series is about *fictional* Navy SEALS.

This story contains content, themes and situations that may be triggering for some readers, such as grief, graphic violence, graphic murder, stalking, pregnancy, degradation, PTSD, sado-masochism, anal, breath play, CNC, rough, explicit sexual situations, near-death situations, graphic language, addiction, pregnancy trauma, pregnancy loss.

For a full list of content warnings, please visit the author's website. Your mental health matters.

https://lexieaxelson.com/

PLAYLIST

"No Words" by Cody Jinks
"Somewhere between I Love You and I'm Leavin'" by Cody Jinks
"Cast No Stones" by Cody Jinks
"Lust For Life" by Lana Del Rey, The Weeknd
"Art Deco" by Lana Del Rey
"Diet Mountain Dew" by Lana Del Rey
"Die For You" by The Weeknd, Ariana Grande
"Work Song" by Hozier
"Hopelessly Devoted To You" by Olivia Newton-John
"Bathroom" by Montell Fish
"Change" by Deftones
"Lonely Day" by System Of A Down
"Babydoll" by Ari Abdul
"Only Love Can Hurt Like This" by Paloma Faith
"Need You Now" by Lady A

1
———

KANE

Blood. It's...everywhere. On my hands, on my jeans, and even on my face. It's nothing new to me, but why does it feel like the first time?

Blood has never bothered me before; it's become a staple in my life. You'd think that being a special operator would have prepared me for this, but I can't seem to shake it out of my mind.

My pulse thunders rapidly and I flare my nostrils while every muscle in my body tenses up with no release in sight.

The way it spilled through my fingers as I tried to make it stop draining from Ari's body was persistent and inevitable, no matter how hard I tried.

I still tried to make it stop even though deep down, I knew...it might be too late.

Why wouldn't it stop?

No matter what I did or how hard I tried, more kept pouring out, her life leaving her with every drop on the floor.

When Grim took her from me, Ari's mother scrambled up, trying desperately to reach her daughter's lifeless body.

I'm holding Ari's mother in my arms as she wretchedly keeps trying to lunge for her daughter. I grabbed her before she could get too close, holding her tightly so she couldn't see what was happening.

She's screaming at me, hitting me, and I tighten my hold on her. I refuse to let her watch anymore. I force her to turn around. I lift her in my arms, turning her in the opposite direction of the horrifying sight before us.

She shouldn't see this. She doesn't *need* to see this. Ari's mother has been through enough.

I can't seem to take my eyes off of the girl I promised to protect. I *feel numb*, my ears ringing as the rest of the world fades around me. I forced my eyes closed, trying to calm the rising panic in my chest.

It's too much for me to bear. I've seen shit like this all the time on missions. I'm back home, and the darkness has followed me back here, too.

I can't watch this. I can't watch the girl I admire so profoundly die.

Grim is working compressions on her, using all his strength to keep her alive.

I wish it were me holding her instead; I let that thought go as quickly as it came; she's Grim's girl.

If she survives.

She *has* to survive.

Grim looks like he's lost his damn mind.

Every compression he makes on Ari's body has me wincing. His strength never wanes as he tries to get her heart beating again. He *has* to push on her chest with so much force that her bones almost break; it's the only way.

He's desperate to revive her; *I am desperate* for him to revive her.

I've never seen Grim so out of control before. He's always calm, collected, and composed. Lethal and *dangerous*.

I've never even thought the man could cry, as a tear falls down his face and lands on Ari's cheek.

His voice cracks as he repeats the same four sorrowful words repeatedly.

"Don't fall asleep, baby."

"Don't fall asleep, baby."

"Don't fall asleep, baby."

I repeat the words in my head, needing her to hear them, to listen to Grim, to *listen to us*.

His pleas for her to stay, to not leave him, caused an ache in my chest. She can't leave *me either*.

He keeps begging for her to wake up as if he can hear her, but Ari is too far gone.

I can't see how she or the baby will live through the night; nobody could survive that amount of blood loss.

I hadn't noticed I was crying until I blinked and felt the familiar warmth rolling down my cheeks.

Tears fall out of my eyes while I'm trying to contain Ari's mother as she consistently tries to grab her daughter. Meanwhile, also making sure Nora stays the fuck put.

Movement catches my peripheral, but Nora doesn't try it. I'm so grateful for small mercies; I don't think I could contain them both at the moment.

My attention goes back to the woman of my dreams, her boyfriend's frantic compressions, the only motion coming from her lifeless body.

We all have the proper training to do this.

Suddenly, that's when I see something I can't quite explain

from his profile. His eyes look like they flash a dark color, and I'm confused. Maybe the tears in my eyes are obstructing my vision, but I swear all I see is Grim's favorite color...black.

I try to get a better look at Grim, study him, questioning the need for glasses, or is the shock making me delusional? Then Ari's mom slaps my chest, deterring my vision from Grim to her.

"*Sueltame!* Let me go!"

She curses at me in Spanish.

"*Lo siento, Señora.*" I sigh as I tell her no, turning back to Grim, as he puts his fingers to Ari's neck, feeling for a pulse. He's hovering over her body, his face close to hers, as he releases a heavy exhale, as if he's been holding his breath this entire time.

"She's alive; she's breathing," he croaks out in a raspy voice.

I squint at him, trying to figure out what the fuck I just saw.

The door explodes open, footsteps thud, and everyone shouts. Paramedics rush through the door, followed by what looks like the entire police force.

They run toward Danny and, sure enough, they recognize Grim and I. A lot of the police officers are veterans themselves.

My captive on the other side of the room seems to think now is an excellent time to make her escape. It's almost enough to make me crack a smile.

No way in hell.

"Ma'am, stop running!" The police officers turn toward her, guns raised, shouting at her to stop. Two men tackle her to the ground before she's even across the room.

I'm not surprised they caught up to her quickly.

"*Sueltame!*" I whip my head back to Ari's mother as she slaps me across the face. *Fuck.*

My cheek burns from the collision as I finally release Ari's hysteric mother, stumbling away, and she runs to the paramedics working on her daughter.

They've got Ari on a stretcher; her mother backed off enough for them to do so.

The situation looks safer.

"*Mi hija, ayudenla, por favor!*" Mrs. Alvarez screams at the paramedics to save her daughter.

I can't believe this shit is happening.

I look toward Grim, his silence eerie throughout these past few moments. He studies one particular police officer, the look on his face making me nervous for the poor man.

His eyes burn holes into his name tag, and that's when I witness his transition into the side of him I only see on missions.

He grabs the police officer by the collar, towering over him, the veins in his hands protruding with wrath.

"You were the officer that was supposed to protect her. You were supposed to be working on this case, yet *you* did nothing about it."

Grim growls, his nostrils flaring, and it looks like he's about to commit his second murder of the day.

That's when I see it--*red*-so much red, seeping through the navy blue shirt plastered to Grim's chest.

This man's threshold for pain was impressive, yet unbelievable.

He stands there as if it were just another normal day. The lengths he'd go through for Ari were admirable, yet frightening.

"Grim!"

I snap him out of his blinded rage and his strangulation of the officer's neck. The poor guy shakes underneath his grasp, and his fear paralyzes his words to call for some assistance and salvation from his co-workers.

He won't find any.

Unsurprisingly, none of them try to intervene and spare his impending doom from Grim, and it's because Danny Rider will *always* have the upper hand. These men served their time in the military; their unwavering respect and his prestigious reputation mean they won't stop him from dulling out justice. He was a hero in the eyes of the United States and even more so here in Bloomings.

Grim looks at me, his glare sending waves of fury in my way.

"You're hurt, bro. Don't you feel it?" I point to my chest, then to his, trying to get him to look down and see where Shane stabbed him.

There's a tear in his shirt and a dark stain that trails to his waist.

I sway as reality and memory clash together.

The last time I saw him bleed like this is still fresh in my mind. The night we rescued Violet Redd, the grenade blast...he was fine; at least, he acted as if he were fine. I didn't notice until we flew back in the Chinook afterward. Red covered the back of his uniform as he bled from the shrapnel lodged in there.

I shake my head as I try to return to reality. The trauma of our shared past caught up to me in my moment of weakness.

He looks at his chest and blinks. If I thought I was covered in blood, Danny was showered in it.

"Sir, we need to get you treated." A paramedic surveys his wound and then gestures for Grim to follow him out of the house. He searches Grim for more injuries, worry clear in his eyes.

"I'm fine," he growls, finally letting go of the trembling police officer. The latter staggers back before he recollects himself and looks at Shane worriedly. He glances down at Shane's dead body before turning to Grim.

He wants to say something but grows more afraid and refrains.

Grim's eyes soften when he glances back at Ari, and pure agony spreads through his features. Two paramedics secure her onto the gurney.

"She's pregnant," he rasps. The paramedics stop moving any further, letting the information sink in.

"We'll do everything that we can. Are you the father?" a female paramedic asks him as she tries to keep a professional stature.

"Yes." He grabs Ari's hand, watching her with an intense expression of devotion. He narrows his brows as he intertwines his fingers with her lifeless ones. He firmly squeezes her hand and his eyebrows narrow, as if he's begging for her to squeeze his back.

"*Help them*, now," Grim demands.

"Come with us."

Danny walks next to the staff. His eyes never leave her, even though she's still asleep. I watch him, watch her, and I know he is ruined by her. The man is head over heels in love. The one man we all thought wasn't capable of giving himself to anyone. Ari has completely done him in for.

Her mother follows, too, and they go outside, leaving me alone with my thoughts.

I'm still inside the house and I feel like I'm going into some sort of shock.

I turn around to see Shane dead on the floor as police start their investigation. He's beaten to death, and Nora gets strolled away by two male cops in handcuffs. One cop on each side of her keeps their grip tight on her as they relay the Miranda rights. Nora is seething and I glare at her the entire time.

Pure evil motherfuckers.

Hurt people who have completely lost their way.

"Mind telling me what the fuck happened here? My partners are already getting Grim's statement, but I want to hear your side of the story."

I look at my hands, ignoring the police officer. They're covered in Ari's blood. It's dry already but still feels like the horror will be forever tattooed on my hands. I won't ever be able to look at my hands the same, knowing what just happened.

I need to be at the hospital. I need to be there when she wakes up, but I can't. Grim will see right through me and then...our friendship will be over.

Finally, I meet the older cop's eyes. His dark browns pierce through me, desperate to know my response. Wrinkles all over his face, his gut protrudes over his belt, and I try to speak, but I can't. Nothing comes out. All I can think about is Ari. How the fuck does he want me to speak right now?

"Son?" he asks again, and my brows arch. He repeats his question, and I can't find the strength to answer.

I swallow the tension I have in my heart. Watching my favorite nurse, not smiling, not talking, or moving...it did something to me.

Screw this, I can't hold back anymore. *I won't* hold back what I feel for her anymore. She might die and I refuse to lie to myself anymore. I love the girl. I love...her.

Always have.

She's with Grim, but I don't care. I've been patient and understanding and that hasn't gotten me anywhere. It's only gotten me in a shit place where I get to watch my best friend be consumed by her...

I'm done watching someone have the life I want with Ari.

I'm going to chase this feeling before it's too late.

"Hello? Mr. Slaughter?"

I blink fast, irritated. I take a deep breath to let all of my intrusive thoughts go to rest. My fists unclench, and I can finally gather myself and stop the spinning that's inside my head.

"Sorry...where do I start?"

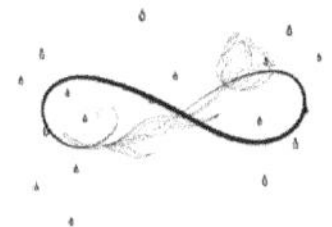

After being questioned by cops, they cleared Grim, Ari's mother, and me of any wrongdoing. It's almost midnight but I feel like I just woke up.

I stand in Ari's bedroom, looking at everything. It's decorated light and airy, like her personality. I feel like I'm intruding on her personal space, but I can't go to the hospital without showing my true feelings in public. If she wakes up, I need to tell her everything in private. So, for now, being in her bedroom is the closest I can get to her. I'll take it.

I can't be there for her just yet.

Staying here makes me feel like I'm with her, even though I'm not *really with her.*

I can't talk. I can't move. The only thing I can do is breathe and watch my phone for updates.

Grim texted me after I blew up his phone for Ari's status.

Finally, after a few hours, he answered, letting me know she's stable, but nothing else.

Relief cools the fire of hatred and anxiety I feel from the broken, worried possibility of never seeing her beautiful smile again.

I asked about their baby, but he hasn't responded.

It kills me not knowing what's happening to them.

I don't care if her baby is Grim's. If it doesn't work out with him, I would gladly take over and love her child like my own.

Grim is always gone. I'm about to get out of the Navy in a couple of months.

He's always been a selfish man, but I can see that he is slowly changing to be more for her...and I don't like it. It's selfish of me to not want him to be a better version of himself. He's changing to be more for her because that's what she deserves.

Still, I want it to be me.

I finally walk out of her bedroom fast.

I just need some fucking sleep...

Lopez will be giving me a ride back to my house. It's dark when I close her door.

A strong breeze refreshes the heat on my skin. It's getting colder. It's fall heading into winter.

I've been there since the beginning and yet Danny has the most incredible privilege to have kissed her... *Feel her. Take her.*

I slide into the car, slamming the door.

"Fuck, man, you're covered in blood... Is that—"

"Ari's blood?" I intervene for him, looking at him, aggravated.

He stills, looking at my face and then my hands, probably picturing what we went through.

"Yes," I finish, clicking on my seat belt.

He clears his throat awkwardly and reverses his car. Streetlights and porch lights flash and disappear across our faces as we drive away.

"What the fuck happened, man? How is she doing?"

I shake my head, looking at Ari's Bronco as he gets closer to the end of the street.

"I don't know."

The day I met her still feels fresh in my mind, like it was yesterday. I can't help it, but my mind drifts to the first day I laid eyes on her, knowing it felt forbidden.

December - The Day of Paul's Funeral
Bloomings, North Carolina

"This doesn't feel real," I rasp. My throat feels like there's a rock inside. No matter how many times I try to swallow it down, it's there, threatening to break me.

Paul is dead, and they finished putting him under the ground. I don't want to accept that we're burying one of our closest friends. It hurts so fucking much and to see the way everyone is taking his loss hurts me even more.

Two women sit by the closed casket. In my heart, I feel that Paul's girls, mother, and sister are the closest to it. I know it's them because they haven't stopped crying and they have the same long black hair. It's a different color than Paul's. Even so, I know it's them.

His mother holds onto the American flag presented to them by the Honor Guard. She's squeezing it tight underneath her knuckles while his little sister has her hands over her shoulder, soothing her. She's comforting her mother, who has lost her only son.

I'm sweating even though it's fucking cold. It's the middle of December and still, with the harsh, freezing winds, it isn't enough for my body to adapt. My emotions always get the best of me and I'm hot.

I feel defeated because I've never been the type to hold in my emotions.

Do I really want to keep doing this job? Do I really want to go to more funerals or end up attending my own, cold and dead, in my casket?

Rooker and Grim are both leaning on Grim's all-black F-250 truck. Grim has been drinking, training in the gym, and sharpening his shooting skills at the gun range since Paul died and hasn't been able to stop. Rooker has been doing the same thing except for drinking. Even though he's been heavily tempted to, his old lady won't let him.

While I've been playing soccer and getting lost in books, with a hint of liquor.

Grim has his hands in his pockets, and he's devastated...and he's hurting. He won't show it, but I'm his best friend. Paul was Grim's best friend, but Grim is mine. When I showed up as the new guy on the team a few years ago, he was cold and it felt like he wanted nothing to do with the new guy on the team.

Eventually, we grew close after a couple of deployments and barbecues at Rooker's house and he's taught me everything he knows.

I know when he's hurting. He's been different since the night Paul passed, and I don't blame him.

Grim fucking Reaper is what everyone calls him. He's the team leader, and we all have faith in the Navy's most merciless, dangerous asset. The most distinguished and secretive team in the military is led by my boss. Operator Grim is the number one special operator.

It's a team assembled by selecting only the best of the best

Navy SEALs, and Daniel Rider was chosen to be in the most stressful position any SEAL can be in.

We all have shed our sweat, blood, and tears and given up any chance at a normal everyday life at home. As long as we're special operators, it'll be anything but ordinary.

Fuck, I don't know how much more of this shit I can take.

"I've gotta go home. Noel wants me home before dinner so I can help her put our twins to sleep."

Despite Rooker being home for such a short amount of time, he's been disconnected from his family. He's been with Grim and me, ensuring we're not going to try to kill ourselves from a traumatic mission that killed Paul. I don't blame him. Sometimes, I regret choosing this as my career, and killing myself seems like an easy way out. Still, I couldn't do that to my parents.

Death can take any of us whenever it'd like, and we're flirting with the damn dark force whenever a deployment comes around and I'm pretty damn sure I'm not ready to wine and dine Death just yet.

"Danny?" Rooker interrupts Grim's intense trance. It's the first time I've ever heard Rooker call Grim by his first name.

He doesn't respond, but he looks at Rooker with stressed, puffy red eyes bleeding with sadness. He lifts his head, acknowledging him with a quick nod.

"Call me if you need anything," Rooker tells him while searching for his car keys in his pockets.

Danny turns away from him, grabbing a cigarette out of his pocket.

"I'm fine. Go home to your wife, rest, and spend time with your girls. I'm sure it won't be long until we're back on another mission." He lights a cigarette, and my heart drops at the mention of another deployment.

Another fucking deployment?

We just got back home.

Rooker walks away to find his car in the parking lot.

Grim's phone rings. He reaches into his pocket and sighs as he looks at the screensaver.

"Hello?" his deep voice responds professionally.

I look back at the crowd disappearing, and everyone who attended the service is now leaving.

"Yes, sir, I'm on my way. I can be there in thirty minutes."

Grim hangs up and turns to me with a stern look on his face. He wants to say something; I know it, but Grim never says much. He's quiet. He's always been that way, never truly shows emotions, and that's what makes him the most dangerous out of all of us. He's been in the Navy for so long that he's probably desensitized to feeling anything. He most likely can't feel shit, and I don't blame him.

"Admiral Ravenmore and other higher-ups called me in."

He's still like he's frozen, and he's staring at Paul's tombstone. He doesn't want to leave.

"Do they need us all to go in?" I ask.

He shakes his head, clenching his jaw.

"Hey man, just go. They've put him under already. Service is over," I encourage him.

"That's not it." He puts out his cigarette under his boot. "I feel like I need to say something to his family, and I just can't fucking find the words."

I nod, looking at the ground.

"No matter what you say, they won't like it," I murmur through heavy breaths, shrugging my shoulder.

He has every right to feel like he's at fault.

That mission haunts me. I can't imagine Grim.

When I reached Grim that night in Iraq, he was with Paul until he took his last breath.

He starts popping his knuckles and shakes his head.

"Let me know if you need anything, brother. I'm here for you," he tells me while unlocking his truck.

"And we're all here for each other," I finish for him, and for the first time in a while, he smirks.

It's a saying we all tell each other when shit gets rough and I'm glad it helped Grim feel a bit of relief.

He looks at the tombstone one last time and hops into his black truck.

Paul's mother was walking away with some family members comforting her, while his sister remained seated.

I'm hesitant to walk over, but I'm a bleeding heart and I can't help it.

Every stride on the ground has my heart pounding through my chest, and I can feel my deodorant wearing off from all the damn sweating.

I get closer to Paul's grieving sister and stand beside her with my hands in my pockets. She doesn't notice me standing in front of a smiling portrait of Paul, but oh, how I notice her.

She's fucking beautiful.

She's beautiful...and holy shit. Now I fully understand why Paul has kept her a secret from us.

I don't know her, but I'll give up everything I thought I loved to know everything about her.

"Paul Alvarez was a great man. I'm going to miss him." My voice comes out soft and welcoming.

Startled, she gazes at me as tears stream down her face. She quickly wipes them away like she's embarrassed. Her eyes trail to my chest, and she stares at the Navy trident with such hatred, but it doesn't bother me.

"Don't talk about him like that. Like you know him. You don't know him; you know nothing about my brother."

She's harsh and unforgiving, but it only intrigues me more.

"He was the best damn guitarist I've ever known. You could request any Mana song and he would play it for you. He also snored like a fifty-year-old man when he racked out and everyone knew to stay away from him when he ate something with dairy. Those farts of his were deadly." I scrunch my nose. It's my lame attempt to charm her.

She stops fiddling with the tissues in her hands and goes still. Her expression mellows as she looks at me, but she holds back a smile by biting her lip. She lets out a short laugh that almost sounds like a scoff.

I reach out for her hand to shake it.

"Kane Slaughter."

Her smile fades away quickly, and for a second there, I think she is going to slap my hand away or throw curse words my way... but she doesn't.

Finally, she takes my hand in hers and says in the sweetest, most angelic voice that makes me feel like I'm in definite trouble, "Ari Alvarez."

2

———

DANNY

Ari slowly breathes into a mask full of oxygen as the ambulance races to the nearest hospital, bypassing cars and running all the red lights. Each second that passes, I'm praying I get to see my girl open her eyes for me.

I'm watching her now like my life fucking depends on it. I look down at her torso as the medics attend to her wounds, exposing her stomach, and I'm going crazy on the inside.

There's complete, utter chaos burning every single cell within my blood, but on the outside...I'm calm and composed, as I usually am in these situations. My own parents trained me to be like this. An emotionless bastard since I was a child.

"Daniel, work comes before family, before friends...before love."

I grit my teeth as I remember his condescending belittlement as a little boy.

"As soon as you understand that work always comes first, son, you'll be a successful man like me."

My father's words ring into my head as I look at the woman who has me on my knees.

I despise him because look at me now.

I'm a fucked-up mess, but Ari and our baby... they've made me feel like I'm deserving of a family. Something I used to think was a curse.

I was just too gone and selfish to understand it.

But when I revealed every single dark shadow that plagued me, she did something that made me realize this world isn't such a terrible place to be in as I thought it was.

Even after I told her everything...

She stayed.

She stayed and accepted me, no questions asked.

Even when I told her about the day that haunts me and her.

One ghastly thought sits at the back of my head, knocking on my door, and I'm trying to block it out, but it's a real possibility I'm hoping never comes true.

Our baby not making it through this.

I keep thinking about our baby.

Please don't leave your mother and I.

Death has Shane now, but I refuse to let it consume our baby, too.

I wish our little one who holds a part of me and the woman who holds my heart hostage will also make it through this.

Our baby will make it through this.

Faith is a funny thing to me. I don't believe in it, but I believe in fate.

After all, fate kept bringing Ari to me when I tried to fight it.

This whole time since I met her, I wanted to protect her... from myself.

And that's when I feel a frigid breath on the back of my neck, sending icy prickles into every fiber of my bones, and my hair raises. Death is nearby, but he's not telling me a word *this time,* leaving me in a frantic state of hope.

Now you decide to not speak? Now you don't want to talk?

Fuck you.

But again...I'm only returned with pure silence, making every second I watch Ari asleep more painful.

One of the worst kinds of emotions to feel when you're hoping things go your way.

Hope is like fear in some ways. An emotion tethered by trauma.

False hope is as cruel as death.

I lick my lips as I watch my little angel breathe.

Her skin is pale, almost gray, but that's what happens when you literally meet my good friend because of all the blood she lost.

He hovered over her like the stalker that he is, eager to reap her up to Heaven, where I know she'll be in the afterlife.

I wouldn't let him take her from me.

I pleaded with Death because her soul isn't his.

Hell, it's not even hers–*it's mine.*

I will not live if she doesn't. I'll cut my own heart out of my fucking chest to join her in the afterlife. Even though I know I'm headed to Hell when it's my time with the number of lives I've already sent there.

Still...I won't ever let Ari escape me. I'm madly trapped beneath her wings.

Holding her into my arms as she bled out was all too hauntingly familiar, and all I kept thinking about was the night when we lost her brother, my best friend, Paul. My hands are stained with the blood I've spilled and taken. Paul slipped away to join Death and all I could do was watch the blood pour out of all of his wounds...just like my Ari.

To this day, I will forever regret not keeping the promise he made us *all do when he first asked for it.*

I've always been a selfish man, but not anymore.

I never knew what she looked like because I don't pry into my friends' lives.

Paul didn't have social media, and neither did I. I still don't. I prefer to keep my life private, as did Paul. We were alike in that sense.

Our conflicting work schedules made it hard for us to hang out when we were home simultaneously, but when we did, it sure was fucking fun. We'd been friends for five years, saving each other's asses occasionally.

When a man wielding a sword ambushed me, he saved my life. My attacker sliced my back, but Paul put a bullet through his head before he could do more. Now, it's a scar. The first scar Ari noticed when I took her to my house the first time.

The ambulance swerved sharply and everyone inside was thrown off balance. My instincts kicked in right away, and I held onto my girl so she would stay safe from swaying, but the vehicle regained control and rushed to the ER. I can see the red sign awaiting our arrival.

I finally feel the pain from where I was stabbed in the chest. It throbs and burns. Shane's weak attempt to redeem himself, but it's just another scratch truthfully.

I quickly give myself a once-over. He only cut through muscle. I'll be fine like I always am.

I look at her short hair and get lost in the strands of it. The color of her hair is so black; it's almost obsidian, and her soft velvet hair reminds me of the dark, unforgiving night I met Death for the first time.

Where my journey of guilt began. In Iraq. The mission that

killed my brother. The ultimate decision that caused Paul's death and left me with self-blame.

"It's colder than Grim's heart up here. This beanie isn't doing shit for me." Rooker's teeth chatter, and white puffs of air loom as he breathes the words out.

And here we fucking go. Let the banter begin.

I shake my head, clenching my jaw.

He's not lying; we're all freezing our balls off.

"Remember that time we went fishing, bro?" Paul looks back at Kane over his shoulder, then turns to Lopez. "What I would do to be back in Florida on a warm and sandy beach. Grim and Cobra didn't catch shit that day!" Paul jokes with the cowboy from Texas, as our boots crush twigs underneath our boots, high into the mountains of Iraq.

It's dark, but our night vision eyewear allows us to see. It's cloudy, and the moon has betrayed us. We have nothing to guide us through the night but our equipment.

We are in the middle of fucking nowhere with no other civilian in sight, and it gives us a small window to talk before it's time to get to work.

"How could I forget? You lost my favorite fishing rod, dick," I spit, walking over a log and clutching my rifle tight in my hand.

"It's not my fault the fish chose me over you. They just like me better, just like the women," he delivers it like an overconfident remark, and I don't need to look at him to know he's smiling ear to ear, antagonizing me.

He's always fucking with me because I'm the only one on the team who hasn't committed to any girl. I don't do relationships. I don't have the fucking time to entertain a girl back home long enough to keep her. I don't want to. It's pointless.

I'm never home anyway, so what's the purpose?

I like having work as my number one priority and nothing and no one else.

I roll my eyes.

"It's also not my fault a fucking shark ripped it out of my hands." Paul lets out a harsh breath as he continues, as if he's having a hard time keeping up. We've been hiking around fifteen miles now, but we can't stop. We're already so close to our destination.

The number one terrorist on the list awaits his doom, and we're gladly going to bring it to him.

He executed an attack on one of the US embassies, killing ten contracted workers, chopping their heads off, and hanging them on spikes.

That didn't sit well with our country, so...they brought another mission to my team and we eagerly accepted it.

"I should've thrown you in the water, giving them more to eat." I smirk, refraining a laugh from escaping my throat as I think of that sunny day in Florida. It was a four-day weekend and the boys and I wreaked havoc in Miami and bar-hopped for three straight nights. It wasn't El Devine, but it was fun.

"The longest recorded sniper kill was achieved by a new Navy SEAL. Did you hear about it? Nobody even thought it was possible, but this guy made a fucking headshot from football fields away. Fucking insane. Admiral Ravenmore was impressed enough, and they're in talks to add him to our team," Kane shares with us,

getting between Paul and me, huffing through his difficulty to even out his breathing.

He's captured my full attention and piqued my interest.

I glance over at him, raising a brow, and I see drops of sweat fall off his eyelash. My Reaper mask doesn't stop me from showing my emotion. My eyes say it all.

"No fucking way. What's his name?" Rooker asks, re-adjusting his rifle over his shoulder on my right.

"His name is Hannibal. His Operator name is—" Something tweaks in the distance, interrupting Kane from talking further. It sounds like a branch breaking...a branch breaking under someone's foot. It sounds like a threat.

We all grow quiet in less than a second. We all lock our lips tight, and we stop moving. Our teams go rigid, holding our rifles up to our eyes, ready to engage.

We crouch, and I search for any life that may threaten ours.

I wave my hand over my side, motioning them to follow me, but I'm the first to do a quick scan of evaluation.

I sharpen my gaze, looking at everything in my sight, and that's when I see the culprit.

I see an eight-point buck, thick rugged antlers, and bright green eyes glow, glistening right back into my vision as I shine my light on him.

I scoff, lifting my lips into a curve on one side, and my sharp canines brush over my bottom lip as I squint.

A fucking deer.

I drop my rifle and relax my shoulders.

I let out a sigh of relief as it gallops away, disappearing into thick trees. I stand tall, re-adjusting my posture and running my hand through my beard, over my mask. It's a fucking habit.

We don't have to engage in a fight just yet. One of the worst things that could happen is getting caught off guard and ambushed.

"All clear," I whisper into the mics.

I move forward a few steps in front of the teams and instruct them not to follow me.

"I'm going to do some recon."

"Roger that," my team whispers, synchronized, acknowledging me.

I walk for about a minute, pushing through thorny bushes and broken branches.

My shoulders bear the weight of my wandering mind. Everyone depends on me to get us through this.

I felt a strange sensation prickle on my neck, like freezing air blowing on me, which I have never experienced before. It sends goosebumps all over my skin, and I turn my head, expecting to see Paul messing with me. I'm already preparing myself to condemn him because he's going against my orders. I told him to stay put with the rest of the team. He knows when to separate foolishness from work.

I turn my head around to be met with no one. I narrow my brows, confused, when I see that I'm alone and Paul is far away from me, talking to Kane and Lopez.

I shake my head, shrugging my shoulders.

Am I going fucking crazy? It felt like someone was breathing on my damn neck.

I need a cigarette.

I continue to move forward, stepping on small rocks underneath my boots, and that's when I notice we've reached our destination.

We're at the edge of a fucking cliff.

I look down. The tip of my boot is off the ledge as I look down. We're hundreds of feet into the air. If we fall, we'll die an instant death with our brains splattered across the floor, coming home in a closed casket.

Dirt and small molecular rocks fall off when I drag my foot back. I look into the distance. Wrath sparks into every single vein coursing toward my heart when I see a fucking army of the terrorists we've been looking for, but they're not sleeping, no.

Fuckers are wide awake, and it looks like they're planning something. They're all gathered around each other as if they're attending some meeting.

They all have their attention on one man, and my eyes light up like the Fourth of July.

I quickly grab my rifle, peeking through the scope, and sure enough, it's him.

Omar stands tall, unaware his chest is right in the middle of my crosshairs. Our number one target.

He's pacing back and forth as he speaks to his own army of a team that has followed in his footsteps.

My lungs constrict, and I'm eager to pull the trigger. I want to watch the bullet pierce his monstrous, evil body, making him fall to the ground like he deserves and take another soul. Our intelligence got it right, causing my eyes to darken as I celebrate internally.

But I can't pull the trigger.

I can't endanger my team's lives by instigating chaos and a potentially deadly battle if I kill him. Unfortunately, it's too far off a shot. We need to get closer and pick a better, safer area to execute the mission.

Rooker walks and stands to my right, looking the same way as I am through his rifle. I look at him through my mask, and I can sense his body language shift and go rigid when he sees Omar through his scope.

He looks up from his scope and his eyes crinkle with celebration, a sadistic grin underneath his mask.

"Bullshitting is over, boys. We're here." I smile wickedly into the mic, the words rolling off my tongue smooth like whiskey.

3

———

ARI

Darkness. I'm in a pool of dark shadows and I know something isn't right, but I don't remember how I got here.

My hands feel heavy. My head is pounding and my thoughts are scrambling.

Why am I so thirsty?

I swallow, trying to quench the ache for water, and my throat feels dry and *sore*...like I was intubated. Surgical patients tell me these are the symptoms they experience when they wake up. Wait, does this mean what I think?

Why do I feel like a surgical patient?

This can't be good.

My eyes remain shut, no matter how hard I try to flutter them open.

Where am I?

I must concentrate. I'm conscious; I know that much. I have to listen and focus on regaining myself.

That's when I hear it.

The sound of beeping from a monitor fills my ears. I've spent way too much time in a hospital to know that's where I lie and the beeping is coming from my vitals.

I'm enveloped in nothing but black and I try again to pry my eyes open, but fail miserably. I know I'm in my body, but still, it doesn't feel like my own.

Frustration grows, and I try moving my head, but again...*nothing.*

I can do this. I can do this.

Is this sleep paralysis?

Oh, no. If this is sleep paralysis...

Panic courses through my throat, small whimpers being forced through my teeth. It's like my spirit is banging against walls of a closed room with no door to escape. Fear rises in my chest, and my heart pounds as I grow frantic.

I've experienced sleep paralysis multiple nights, and it only started when Paul died...and it's terrifying. Your mind is awake, but your body feels paralyzed.

Nope, I refuse to let my body stay in this state.

I try to regain consciousness and attempt to move again.

The muscles in my fingers twitch.

Success.

As my fingers twitch, I can feel them moving across something and I'm concentrating so hard, trying to block out the sleep that consumes me. Soft blankets underneath my fingertips.

I'm in a bed?

"Her heart rate is rising. She's waking up."

Danny.

I hear him. My brother's best friend. My heart flutters at the sound of his husky, weary voice. I'm immediately drawn to him.

It's my Danny.

I'm desperate to wake up immediately.

With each breath I draw in, pain greets me. Something in my lower abdomen is causing me discomfort, and I groan. My high-pitched groan reverberates through my chest, and I realize I'm that much closer to waking up.

Okay...why does my chest feel like it's broken?

How is that even possible?

Cold hospital air burns through my nostrils as I weakly attempt another breath in through my nose and there it is again.

Pain.

Ouch.

What the hell is that? It shouldn't feel like someone hit my chest with a sledgehammer, over and over again.

My chest feels incredibly sore with each breath I take.

What the hell happened to me?

The last thing I remember is-is...pain.

Shane's attack. Nora. A knife plunged into me. My mother on the floor.

Shane's dark brown eyes looked heavily dilated, staring at me with so much hatred, I could feel his own pain fill me like fire, scorching the light I had in my heart.

My baby.

And then I remember a frigid breath on my neck, whispering sickening words into my ear—the *Grim Reaper*.

And that gives me just enough fear to break free from the chains my mind has me in.

I gasp for air as I shoot up from the hospital bed. My hands go straight for the railing to support my weak energy. I sit up, breathing hard, and feel my blood pressure drop, making me more disoriented. I'm no longer trapped in my body. My eyes explode open, and *I am in a hospital bed.*

I was right. White is all I see.

White bed sheets, white lights, and two pale faces.

Danny and my mother stare back at me. Their pale reflections are the only thing I see before I'm dropping back down on the bed, weak, my head hitting the pillow, and I wince.

The jolt of my body has me dizzy and lightheaded, but it doesn't stop me from trying to breathe harder.

Danny grabs my hand and holds it tight. His familiar texture on mine makes me feel safe, like he always does.

"You're awake," Danny says in a comforting voice, forcing a small desirable smile with relief washed all over him to see me conscious, but there's something more behind his eyes, *something terrible.*

"*Mija*! Oh *mija*." My mom swarms me and envelopes me in her arms. She pulls me into her chest and I'm confused.

I let her hug me, but I don't feel comfortable enough to hold her back.

I feel like I'm going numb. I blink hastily, touching my chest where it hurts, then my stomach, with perplexed fingers.

Where is Shane?

Oh no, is he somewhere close by?

Wasn't I at my mother's house?

I move away from her, retreating my hand from Danny's hold at the same time. An IV is stuck into my other arm. It moves as my hands go to palm my lower abdomen. I can feel the confusion and anger building up inside of me, and I'm tempted to scream.

"Where is he?!" I shout out manically, looking around the room and into the hallways, dreading to see his face come after me again.

"Ari, it's okay. He's not here, and neither is Nora. You're safe."

Danny stands from his chair with purpose, getting closer to me. He tightens his grip over the railing of my bed.

"My baby." I blink rapidly, looking around the room, then back to my stomach. "Is our baby okay?" I ask, my voice cracking.

I tilt my head upward, meeting Danny's gaze with my trembling lips, and eyes that beg for good news, and he clenches his jaw. He holds a cold stare, and I'm swallowing another dry bump in my throat. *He looks guilty.* After what feels like an eternity, his expression morphs from guilty to stoic.

"Tell me!" I shout at them for answers, fisting my hand and I pummel the bed impatiently. I look at him and then at my worried mother, who holds her hand in front of her mouth like she wants to speak but can't.

Then she shakes her head frantically, her bangs moving back and forth across her creased forehead.

"*Mija.* You lost too much blood. You've been asleep for days. *Te moristes....*" My mother cuts in, telling me that I died. Her voice shakes like she can't believe her own words. She can't look at me, so she looks down at her feet. She's an absolute worried mess. Her hair is tied up in a messy ponytail as she holds her cardigan close to her body, trying to comfort herself. I know my mother and she does this when she's anxious.

A bandage is plastered across her forehead. The same spot where I saw her bleed when I found her passed out on the floor. She looks stressed and frantic. She can't look me in the eye, and I know this is bad.

I died?

"What?" I cry out. My eyes search for Danny's and my mom's, demanding them to answer my question about my baby. I look down at my stomach, but I can't see anything. I'm in a hospital gown. I palm my stomach and something feels fresh with pain.

"You died, *mija*. And...and..." she cries, not letting herself finish.

I tremble as the words roll out of her mouth. My eyes widen and I can feel my eyes water full throttle.

Danny looks like he hasn't slept in forever. His eyes are sad and his dark sandy blond hair I love so much is shaggy. He runs his palm through his beard, weary.

"But my baby?" I croak. A tear drops falls down my cheeks, passing my lips.

"Our baby didn't make it." Danny looks straight into my eyes and I think I'm about to faint.

No.

"What?" I glare at him with anger, and he meets my stare with his own softened blue eyes.

This is a bad dream. It has to be.

How could those words fall out of his mouth and he's not breaking?

He's lying.

"You're lying! You're fucking lying to me!" I rock my head violently, looking at my belly, clutching it as if that would help turn back time.

"You promised me you would never lie to me, Danny! How could you say that?" Tears fall out like a monsoon, and Danny frowns. As he leans in to touch my cheek, I push his hands away and they smack against him loudly.

"No! Don't you dare touch me!" I bellow at him as I cry harder, tears pouring out of me as my eyebrows grasp together. "I won't accept this!"

I rip the bed sheets, tearing them away from me so they're no longer covering my waist, and I lift my hospital gown desperately.

"*Mija*, stop," my mother begs from the corner of the room with a gasp.

I sob, hyperventilating, my entire dream of becoming a mother ripped away from me when I see a slash like a C-section scar. It's red, swollen, and fresh.

No, no, no.

Shane took away my baby from me?

I'm not going to be a mother anymore?

I feel like I stop breathing for a second and I close my eyes, trying to figure out a way to make this feel like I'm hallucinating. I rub my belly with my hands over my scar, like I used to do when Danny was away on his deployment. My lonely nights weren't so lonely because of our baby. It was my way of holding my future, even though it was still months away until I met her or him. I prayed and envisioned the way I would get to say hello for the first time, with my hands on their fingers with a precious blue or pink onesie, repeatedly on those lonely nights. I've witnessed many deliveries in the hospital. I had the privilege to watch newborns curl their tiny hands around their mother's pinky or index fingers, whispering hello's to their cooing newborn as they lay on their chest, bonding together.

"Please don't tell me I don't get to say hello to our baby, Danny. Please."

I can't look at him. I shut my eyes tight, rubbing my hand over my belly.

Silence envelops the room, and I'm spiraling.

I tip my head back, looking at the white blinding lights in the ceiling, causing me to inhale sharply. I squeeze my eyelids closed again, as if that will help relieve the despair I feel in my chest.

"Oh." I cry out and I hyperventilate as I remember just how painful a sharp blade feels. My chest hurts, and I feel like the more breaths I suck in, the more I drown in my own sadness. And I can't stop trying to breathe. I can't stop gasping for air. I feel like I'm going to suffocate even though I'm not under water and my blood pressure rises to dangerous limits. Tears gush down my face, my throat stings, and a panic attack ensues, consuming my heart and soul.

Then Danny moves, lifting his legs and gets into bed with me. He's stone-cold and emotionless while I'm a wreck. I push him away from me, my hands going for his shoulders first.

"No!" I reject him with disdain laced in my tone, but he refuses to let me push him away.

He lies on his side, and he pulls me into his chest, trying to comfort me.

Shane and Nora killed my baby, and they almost killed me.

I'm having a hard time wrapping my head around the reality as Danny kisses the top of my head soothingly.

Something inside of me breaks. A crack in my soul and humanity. I thrash with possessed anger.

Danny wraps his arms around me protectively even as I scream and hit his chest with my fists.

"No! No! No! You're lying!" I'm hysterical, and my voice lowers with crescendoing sobs.

I want to get away from everyone. I feel like I need to take out my anger on something and someone.

Danny tightens his grip on me harder and breathes into my hair. My mother sobs silently as she watches me fall apart into his arms.

The trauma from the attack is all too much, and I'm furious

with everyone. My mother. *Danny.* I feel like he's the one to blame for everything that has happened this year.

I can't help it, and it might be wrong. It might even be selfish, but I blame him for everything.

"My baby! Not my baby!" I yell and bawl against Danny's arms. I'm using all my strength to fight against his hardened muscles until I finally surrender to him. I give in to my need to feel the pain instead of trying to fight away from it, and I'm crying into his chest, clutching onto him like it's my last few minutes on this earth. I give up trying to push him away and let him hold me. My mouth is open as I wail my broken heart away.

This feels a little like déjà vu.

A mother losing her child. Something I thought would never happen to me.

I sound like my mother.

I sound like my mother when she lost my brother. When those two uniformed men showed up at our door.

All of my thoughts sink in and that's when I feel an ugly emotion pulse through me.

I resent this military life with all my heart as I try to catch my breath.

I can't control myself. This pain is more excruciating than a stab wound. I'm grieving uncontrollably, and I can feel a dull pain where I was attacked by Shane and Nora. My side, my back, and my lower abdomen feel sharpened with raw pain, stinging like needles.

"Baby, you're going to rip open your stitches," he tries to console me by holding me tighter, protectively creating a haven enclosed inside of his arms. "Focus on my voice." He tells me as his deep voice softens, and it's helping me relax slowly...bit by bit. More tears escape from my eyes as his strong, large hands snake through my hair. "I'm sorry, Ari. I'm so fucking sorry. Cry, hit me as hard as you can, scream at me, hate me. I can take it. What *I can't take* is you opening your stitches and bleeding again."

A nurse bursts through the door with syringes in his hand. His emotions are written all over his face, and he looks terrified or broken for me, or maybe both. He must be new because that's one of the first things you learn in patient care. Control your face.

I don't care if the whole hospital can hear my cries... I just lost my baby.

"We have a sedative for her," he starts in a shaky voice, but Danny doesn't let him finish as I continue to mourn and shed heavy tears in his chest.

"Get the fuck out. She doesn't need it," he snarls at him, ordering him to leave, downright explosive, before turning back and kissing my cheek as I hold on to him tighter. I stop thrashing, but I'm still breathing hard as I try to let the news sink in when I don't want it to.

My mom goes full mama bear on the nurse and starts cursing at him in Spanish, demanding him to give us space and shooing him out of our room. She follows the nurse out and closes the door behind her, slamming it shut.

We sit on the hospital bed while I focus on slowing my breathing. The scent I love so much, *Danny's scent*, slowly anchors my hysteria away, grounding me. We sit there, and my sniffling is the only thing we can hear for the next ten minutes, but he doesn't stop holding me. After a few long moments, he lifts my chin to see him like he always does, and the familiarity of his version of love warms me.

I'm sure I look horrifying, snot running down my nose and reddened eyes, but I don't care.

"The doctors said you lost too much blood. There was

nothing they could do to save our baby," his deep voice murmurs, and I can tell as each word leaves his mouth, it's painful for him.

I rub my nose with my knuckles and blink.

"So, they cut me open? While I was asleep?" I whisper.

"Yes." Devastation flickers across his eyes as he tightens his jaw.

That explains the dull pain I feel below my stomach.

"How long have I been out?" I ask, dreading the answer.

He brushes my hair out of my face, tucking it behind my ear. He does the same on the other side, watching me intensely.

"Three days."

Oh my gosh.

"Shane? Nora?" I shiver when their names leave my mouth. Their manic faces reappear in my eyes, and I hold on to Danny tighter.

"Shane is dead. Nora's in jail."

"H-how? You killed him?"

He nods.

"He can't hurt you anymore. *They* can't hurt you anymore. As long as I'm around, no one will hurt you again, I promise you."

I'm still staring at his chest, but I finally meet his blue eyes. Those beautiful light blue irises I could get lost in forever. Danny makes me feel safe *always*. My panic attack slowly fades away as he holds me in his arms, and I let all the events settle into my foggy brain. I thought I had died because I swear I saw my brother so vividly. His guitar playing our favorite song.

"I saw Paul," I mumble.

"You saw Paul?" Danny asks.

The beeping on the monitor speeds up, along with the beat of my heart.

"I saw him. He was playing his guitar," I breathe out as I search for any reaction from Danny...but nothing. He's not giving me anything. But when I stare at his eyes longer, I have another flashback. A flashback of what I last saw before I went drowning in pure black shadows.

His eyes transformed to black. The Grim Reaper tattoo he had on his body spoke in a demonic voice that sent shivers down my spine.

I break away from his gaze, afraid of the hallucination. *Afraid of Danny.*

"What's wrong?"

"Nothing...I just—"

Should I tell him what I saw?

Will he think I'm crazy?

"I just don't know how I'm alive," I confess. It's the truth, not the entire truth.

"It doesn't matter, baby. Look at me."

I tilt my head upward, tears escaping me again, and I wonder when I'll ever stop fucking crying.

He shakes his head, wiping them away with his hand. "You're still here. You're alive and you're not going anywhere. I've got you, Ari." I purse my lips and I watch his eyebrows pinch together as he declares himself to me. "I've got you for the rest of my life. I'm not going anywhere. I promise you."

4
___

ARI

I'm staring at the food my mother just prepared while the sounds of spoons colliding with plates are the only thing that fills the tension in the room.

It's one of my favorite dishes tonight. My mom made it, hoping it would get me to eat.

Albondigas.

Meatball soup with red rice and potatoes.

All I can do is stare at the reddish soup, watching the heat seep into the air above from how freshly cooked it is. It smells incredibly appetizing, but the misery I feel stops me from enjoying anything anymore.

I can't keep my eyes off my plate. My stomach growls, and saliva fills my mouth, but why can't I move? Why can't I eat these days or have an appetite?

It's because...I'm too broken.

My baby should be kicking excitedly as the smell of dinner fills my nostrils. I should feel some signal in my stomach from my baby dancing, eager to eat with kicks against my flesh, but...nothing, and it makes me angry. I tighten my hold on the spoon, staring at the meatballs, unable to blink.

Sometimes, I feel like I have phantom kicks, but then reality sets in, and I want to scream.

We're in my small dining room area in front of my kitchen. I moved straight into my new home I had applied to before Danny got back home. When I confessed my pregnancy to my mother, I also applied for houses to rent that day.

When I left the hospital, I spent the first few nights at my mother's house, too afraid to leave her by herself until it was time to move into my small cottage home.

It was time for me to set boundaries with my mother.

Danny and my mother have been spending more time together recently, and it comforted me knowing they're creating a relationship. They never got a chance to get to know one another.

"*Mija*, your food is going to get cold. You need to eat." My mom looks up from her seat with a spoonful of red rice in her hands an inch from her mouth.

She looks at me, up and down, as if she's waiting for me to fall apart on the table.

I'm empty but agitated. I don't mean to seem ungrateful for my mother's help the past few weeks, but my anxiety and depression won't let me eat, and it's pissing me off. I can't eat like I used to. It frustrates me, just like it frustrates her.

She gives me a look of concern. Danny wipes his mouth with a napkin, and I know he can sense my unease.

He clears his throat before putting the napkin down next to his bowl of soup.

"Wow, Mrs. Alvarez, you've truly outdone yourself. This is my first time eating something like this, I might just finish the rest of what's left in that pot." He distracts her with a charming smile and stops her from continuing to hover over me, and I shoot him a grateful smile.

She shifts in her seat, quirks her brows at him, and laughs.

"I wouldn't doubt it. You're a big guy. Almost like *mi hijo*, Paul. My son was very tall. He took after his father in that way." She puts another spoonful of a meatball into her mouth as she reminisces about Paul. I grimace internally at the mention of my father.

Then my heart sinks at the mention of the two men that no longer inhabit my life.

Will I ever be able to move on from not having my best friend?

"Please, call me Karolina," she tells him and then swallows her food.

I take a deep breath as the loneliness slithers into my stomach, and I'm tempted to go back into my room and just lie there until I cry myself to sleep.

I sleep with Danny's gifts in my hands every night. The same gifts thrown to the floor when he rescued me from Shane and Nora. The newborn onesie he tried to surprise me with before I got attacked.

I hold a cherished onesie tightly in my hands as I drift off to sleep. The shoes that Kane bought sit on my nightstand...they are the last things I see before I let the darkness take over me.

Every. Single. Night.

These past few weeks have been hell. I'm still trying to get all of my stuff moved in while I battle my issues. With the help of his team, Danny has moved most of my things. I'm grateful for Kane, Lopez, and Rooker. Danny was not happy when he found out I was going to move into my own place. He wanted me to move in to his house instead and even offered to pay for the rent until the contract was over. But I refused, and he respected my decision.

I haven't been able to smile in a long time; it feels like forever.

I don't want to be around anyone until I'm ready. I stayed away even though his team helped out, I would leave the house with my mom. I haven't seen them since before I was attacked. I've kept myself hidden from anyone who wasn't Danny or my mom. I haven't seen my friends or any of my other family members.

"Thank you, Mom, for coming over and making us dinner." I force myself to take a bite of food. I do it for her because if I don't show her I'm capable of eating, she won't leave. I refuse to let her worry about her remaining child. It isn't healthy for a woman in her fifties to worry non-stop.

Fake my strength for her *again...* I have to.

"Yes, thank you, Karolina. We both appreciate your help. Mexican food has always been my favorite," Danny says as he finishes the last bite on his plate. "This Horchata is amazing. Please show us how to make it." He reaches for the sweet cinnamon drink and holds it to his lips.

Horchata is one of my favorite drinks.

"Oh, Ari knows how to make it," she exclaims with a big smile, looking at me proudly. "Do you know I've taught her every recipe I know since she was a child?"

I've always looked up to my mother.

"Really? I knew I liked her." He winks at me, his blue eyes meeting mine as he drinks. He's trying to cheer me up, and it does for a split second. His magnetic charm makes it hard to deny him anything.

A blip of fire consumes me when he gives me a comforting smile.

The ends of my mouth curve slightly, returning his warmth. I appreciate the effort my boyfriend and mother are making to help me feel better, but I want to be alone. Even though I know it'll just be more damaging to myself in the end.

Still, I want to process this alone.

"So, when do you go back to work? I understand that you're in special operations, just like my Paul was. You were close friends with him, but we never saw you around." My mother shifts the mood quickly. It almost sounds like a scolding, and I grow tense at how intrusive she's become.

My eyebrows raise as I catch onto her. I know what she's doing. She's going full mama bear on him, bombarding him with questions since they never properly got to know one another.

I came back from Iraq, pregnant, and she has the right to question him as if he's a threat to my future, but I trust Danny and can make my own choices.

"Mama, *por favor*," I denounce her respectfully. I chew faster before I swallow.

She looks at me with an innocent expression, shrugging her shoulders like she doesn't understand why I would be upset, but she knows she's prying hard. I don't want Danny to feel uncomfortable.

"It's okay, Ari." He rubs his beard, and I know bringing up Paul only brings him pain, but he's very good at not showing his emotions. This time, he doesn't stiffen at the mention of my brother. He's relaxed, and that is something new.

"Yes, I'll be going back to work soon. I'm a SEAL, just like Paul was." He looks at my mother, and he's stony-faced but not upset.

"I will forever owe you an apology for not sharing my condolences with you when he died. There's no excuse for that, so I won't try to give you one. Usually..." He clears his throat, getting lost in his memories. "Paul would come to my house or Kane's.

We're also on different teams, ma'am, so sometimes when I'm home, he probably wasn't. Or we would both be deployed at the same time."

My mom relaxes her shoulders.

"Yes, my son was always busy."

"I didn't know who Ari was. I knew he had his mother and sister waiting for him at home...but Paul was very private about his life, like I am with mine. We both had that in common."

My mom grabs his hand, giving him a comforting squeeze for a couple of seconds and then lets go.

"This year has been tough for Ari and I...with Shane...the baby..." she breathes out before grabbing another spoonful of soup.

I can't take it. I don't want to talk about how much this year has changed me in good and bad ways. I can feel my frustration and anger as the events of losing my baby and almost dying flood my mind like a hurricane.

The mention of my baby hits me like a lightning strike of dread. I will not pretend that I'm okay anymore tonight.

I'm not.

I stand from my chair, grabbing my plate and spoon. Scrambling to get away from everyone. I can feel Danny and my mom watching my back as I stomp away. The last thing I saw was Danny at a loss for words, and he broke his gaze and looked at the table instead.

"Ari Natalia! Finish your dinner," my mother scolds me, her eyes widening with authority.

I've already made my way to the kitchen, stopping in front of the sink. I'm not turning back now.

"*Estoy cansada,*" I tell her I'm tired, tightening my grip on my spoon right before I drop it into the sink. I retreat to my bedroom, opening the door slowly, and I can feel an anxiety attack rising more and more.

I remove my clothes, replacing them with an all-black pajama set—a short sleeve with shorts. I can hear Danny and my mother's voice, but it's muffled and I can't quite hear what exactly they're talking about.

It's only seven at night. I have no motivation to do anything. I lost my baby.

What am I supposed to do now? Move on?

How the hell am I supposed to do that?

I grab the newborn onesie from my bed like I always do before I toss the blankets over me.

Scrunching it into my hands tight, I settle into my pillow on my side and stare at the cute unisex newborn shoes Kane got.

He has always been there for me, although I haven't seen him since I was attacked. Danny's and Kane's faces hovering over me were the last moments I remember before I passed out unwillingly.

Fuck Shane. And Fuck Nora.

Fuck. Everything.

Finally...my breathing evens out, an anchor of numbness replaces my anxiety, and I'm slowly blinking into a slumber of drowning sleep as my pillow grows wet with tears.

5

———

DANNY

I sigh, popping each finger in my knuckles. I can feel the tension in the room between Ari and her mother. It saddens me to watch her drained from everything. She lost our baby and almost lost her life.

I watch Ari retreat to her bedroom until she closes the door. The loud door slam sends her mother flinching her shoulders.

I lick my lips and stare at the empty bowl before me.

I give Ari the space she deserves and needs. She hasn't been the same since they attacked her, and it kills me.

"She needs time," I say, reaching for my pack of smokes in the pocket of my pants. I put my plate together to take to the sink so I can step outside for a smoke.

I've been at a loss since I watched my little angel's life slip away from me, literally.

I'm forever changed, and it's because Ari did that to me. She saved me from myself and I'm determined to *save her from herself.*

I won't ever fail her, and that's a promise. Starting with my fucking drinking. I haven't gotten drunk since the night of our fight and I never will again.

"She needs God. She needs to come back to the church with me." Karolina's voice cracks as she holds back the sobs with her napkin.

I admire her faith in God. I respect it. Even if my beliefs are different.

I'm not sure what I believe in.

Paul was extremely devoted to his religion, just like his mother is.

"Danny...promise me you're going to take care of my daughter?" She looks at me with watery eyes, begging for an answer.

That's an easy promise. A promise that was sealed eternally when I first laid my eyes on her at El Devine.

"I promise you I will always take care of her." It's an oath I made the day Paul asked me to.

Something twitches in my chest and it has me internally struggling with the anxiety I usually push away with alcohol, but I stopped doing that recently. I'm determined to fight for Ari, even if it means going back on everything I had once sought out for myself.

"*Senora*, can I ask you something?" I blurt out.

6

———

ARI

The shower hits my head as I coddle myself. I'm sitting in my bathtub, watching the water hit the tub. I'm holding my knees close to my chest, shaking from the cold.

I managed to move into a little cottage home right after we left the hospital, deep into North Carolina woods, and I was growing used to it. A big milestone achieved, but I couldn't celebrate it.

My scars are still reddish-purple since they're still so fresh. Shane will always haunt me. Even though he's dead, he's left his mark on my body, and I resent it.

My mind has traveled to the darkest places since my near-death experience. I haven't been eating. I've been sleeping more than usual and having nightmares where I wake up in the middle of the night sweating, and my heart thunders against my bones.

Danny hasn't tried touching me. He hasn't tried to push me to do anything even though a part of me wants him to, but I know myself too well... I'm not ready. He knows it.

We both know it.

It's been two months since my attack, and I will have to start work again. Although Danny wants me to stay home so I can recover longer. He's offered to take care of me in every which way I need, and that means everything to me.

He means everything to me.

He also doesn't want to let me out of his sight. He's been sleeping at my place every night, holding me when I wake with my terrors.

A part of me is angry at Danny. I was angry at him because I didn't know who else to blame.

I'm angry at the world.

Angry at myself.

I have a huge part in everything that's happened this year.

I went against my religion, the views I treasured so much. I have sinned more than I should have this year, and maybe that's why I sit here, *numb* with self-doubt, grieving my brother and child.

Is God punishing me?

I gave myself to Danny because a part of me didn't believe in God anymore after Paul died. My view of Catholicism changed after his death because why would God let this happen to a man like him?

I wanted to explore.

What does Ari want?

The day I met Danny...it felt like fate, and I couldn't resist the sinfully handsome man in front of me. I was eager to join him in his world and unveil the new era I wanted to evolve into.

A woman unafraid of the consequences.

Now, I feel like God has punished me deeply for indulging in the temptations I craved deep down inside me.

Now look at me.

My shower curtains open, and I don't even flinch. I know who it is. Even though I had locked the doors to my house, Danny has a key. He's been at work all day, and it's late at night.

I feel a blip of happiness whenever he's around because I know that I'll be okay. I know he wouldn't let anyone or anything hurt me. I love him so much, but I haven't been myself lately. I can't greet him. My head doesn't turn, and my tongue doesn't move. My grief paralyzing me, forcing me to keep watching the water go down the drain in circles.

"Baby, the water is freezing." He's shocked when he realizes I'm bathing in devastatingly cold water, and he moves fast when he discovers I'm soaking in it. He reaches over and shifts the temperature to warmer quickly. Turning the metal knob with determination, I hear his hands grasping it tight, and the metal squeaks.

My eyes never leave the bottom of the tub. I shift my vision slightly, watching the water crash against the floor, hearing it splatter harshly. I've lost myself completely in these emotions, anchoring me down since the attack. At this moment, I can feel nothing but pain from losing myself.

I'm trembling from the cold and don't have the energy to care. My body is full of goosebumps and raised hair follicles. My hands and feet are purple, and shaking from the cold water I've been bathing in for the past forty-five minutes, but I don't care enough to help myself.

I don't care about a lot of things lately. I can't feel anything either.

I still shake as I hold my knees to my chest, naked. My hardened nipples graze my knees.

"D-did y-you k-know?" I ask, emotionless, my teeth chattering through every word I've forced out from the piercing cold that fills me. My jaw was tempted to lock on itself completely. My body shakes as I clench my arms on both sides, digging my nails into my skin.

"Know what, Ari?" He's concerned, and this is a new side of Danny. He's changed so much in amazing ways since I first met him. He has let himself be vulnerable around me. He finally let me into his world. Still, I feel too damaged, too traumatized to enjoy our growing relationship. I'm so proud of the man he's becoming. I knew he had this side of him all along, hidden under layers of darkness. That's why I fell so hard, blindly.

I turn to him. He's dressed in black—a black sweater, dark jeans, and boots.

It's December, just a few days away from my birthday...and Paul's death anniversary, and I'm bathing in freezing water, yet I still can't feel anything...but *pain.*

Finally, I'm able to croak out with a broken voice.

"Y-you w-were r-right, Danny." I stare straight into his weary eyes now, slowly blinking through heavy, soaked eyelashes, and he has his full attention on me. I frown, looking at his chest moving up and down with each deep, slow breath he takes, my lips shaking, and my eyes squint through the water, hitting my face.

He's apprehensive.

His face is blurry as the shower water and tears corrupt my vision, but I can still see him, *see through him.*

"It was a boy." I cry loudly, sucking in the air as my voice twitches with despair. "We had a son." My voice cracks, and I inhale another deep breath after the last word leaves my mouth. My eyebrows narrow at him restlessly. An attack of pure agony and desperation unfolds throughout my body like wildfire, and there's no fucking stopping it.

"Ari," Danny consoles me, his voice deep and concerned. He

leans forward, steps into the shower with me, and positions himself behind me, slowly and carefully. He's still fully clothed and sits in the tub with me. I'm crying uncontrollably into my knees while he pulls me toward him between his legs. He's getting himself all wet; his clothes get soaked in seconds. As he holds me, I drag my hands around his dampening black shirt.

He strokes my wet hair, and I hug him tight.

I discovered our baby's gender at the hospital before I was discharged, but I never said a word. I needed time to process everything, and finding out I had a son was another blow to what could have been. The little family we were supposed to have.

When Danny left to shower at home and face the curiosity of his parents about how they didn't know he had a girlfriend, nevertheless *a pregnant one*, I asked the doctors to let me *see him*. Hold the baby I lost. I've been holding it inside all this time and can't do it anymore.

I'll never get to hold my son as he coos in my hands, scrunching his butt out as all newborns do when they stretch.

This hurts so much.

"We had a *son*," I repeat, holding Danny tighter until I can't breathe. I claw my hands into his shirt, looking for some release from this unbearable pain. When will it stop? *What did I do to deserve this?*

He consoles me, rubbing my arms, embracing me closer, and kissing my cheek. It's rare, but I'm growing used to it.

"I don't have a baby inside of me anymore. I used to say good morning to him every day, but now I can't. I have to grieve for my brother and now my son, too?!" I shout. "This isn't fair, Danny. Why is this happening? Please make it stop." I protest to God, no longer speaking to Danny. I yell at the ceiling as if he can hear my declarations.

"Everything will be okay, Ari. I know it's not right now...but someday, everything will be okay, I promise you."

53

7

———

DANNY

Ari fell asleep on my chest in the bathtub after asking me the same questions over and over again.

"Why Danny? Why us? Why our baby?"

I carried her naked body, dried her up, and clothed her in her favorite pajamas. She's now in bed, sleeping harder than I've ever seen her do.

Nothing has ever made me feel like this.

No one has.

I fear nothing.

I'm calm, collected, quiet even.

But seeing my little angel like this...*it kills me.*

Something's different about me. Something inside me has changed, but I don't resent it this time.

I welcome it.

I'm leaning in the doorway, watching her. My arms are crossed against my chest, one leg over the other, watching her take slow, deep, and steady breaths.

If I had only killed Shane the night before he and Nora

attacked her, Ari would still be pregnant. She would still be carrying our son. And she wouldn't have had to go through this darkness.

Ari's mother would be okay.

She begged me not to go that night. She begged me to stay the night I discovered he had continued to screw with her.

I'll always do what she asks because she is my weakness. There's not a thing I wouldn't do for her. I'll cross every fucking line, I'll break all the rules, I'll drown in her love.

I'll die for her.

Still...

I will never forgive myself for not getting to Shane sooner. First, Paul, and now this?

When I killed Shane, the police cleared me of any wrongdoing after a thorough investigation, and I wasn't charged. However, Nora will be imprisoned for the rest of her life.

Our son is gone, and I feel like pieces of me are forever gone with him. I thought I didn't want kids.

I thought I would be a horrible father. I also didn't want to raise them in a fucked-up world like this. Evil people like Shane lurk here, and he took away our innocent child.

I didn't want kids because I felt it was even more selfish of me to put them through an absent father. I will be absent because of my job. I'm always doing shit that could kill or injure me physically.

I'm already disturbed mentally.

But my God, how I wanted my son.

I wanted to be a father to the little boy we lost.

I'll forever regret the night I exposed classified information to Ari about her brother's death.

But not because I broke the rules.

Not because I told her the truth she deserved to know.

Because of the shit I said.

For the first time in my life, I reacted to emotions that night, something *I never do*. I reacted because of the drunken rage I had bottled up inside. I told her things...all the things that permanently pull at my sanity.

And now, I will make it up to her every day of my life. From the moment I wake until the day Death comes to collect my soul.

If I'm going to be a father, there's no other woman in this world I want to have a child with besides my little angel.

Our baby was a blessing I didn't know I needed or deserved.

I had a blip of happiness watching Ari grow into a woman who carried a part of me and her inside her.

Every time I think of that day, I'm angry with myself and have the urge to drink again, empty every whiskey bottle I own in my house until I can't feel anything.

But I'm learning to stay away from drowning in alcohol. I promised Ari I would control myself and intend to keep that promise. I'm still a whiskey man, but I would control the amounts I consume.

I've fallen for her. I'm obsessed with keeping her safe, and I'll make sure of it for the rest of my days.

I brush my hand through my beard, deep into my thoughts, still watching her sleep. She's underneath her light sage green blankets, and she looks comfortable. I'm about to climb into bed with her, but I wanted to burn one outside before joining her. I reach into my pockets, holding my pack of cigarettes, hesitant to pull them out.

She's helped heal my traumas...

I feel like a new man, and it's because of her.

She is my safe haven. She is the sanctuary I didn't see coming.

My chest tightens with unwavering pain as the moment I found out my child was gone catches up to me, and there's no escaping it...no whiskey to fog it away, and it consumes me.

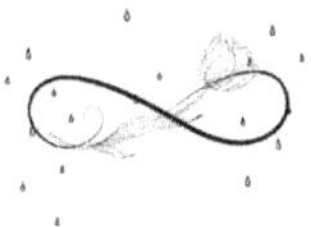

I sit alone in the waiting room, and I can't stay still.

I loathe hospitals. The cold temperature makes it feel unwelcoming; the atmosphere is full of dread, the environment chaotic.

The only reason I like them now is because Ari works in one, and when I step into the one she works at, I get to see her in her cute little scrubs, helping people.

Saving them.

I rejected any treatment until I discovered Ari would be okay. There's no way in hell I'm letting any other doctor or nurse touch me without knowing her condition. Ari's mom was being evaluated still, but so far she was okay—nothing too serious.

My knee bounces with unease. Every second feels like an hour, and I keep checking my watch as if that would make time pass by faster.

Kane keeps blowing up my phone, text after text, so I shut it off. I squeeze the off button on the side of my phone so hard it turns off in seconds and shove it back into my pocket.

I can't think. I can't move. I can't even fucking breathe because I'm not holding her in my arms, watching the eyes I love so much sparkle.

I knew she fell hard for me when we first met...and now she's all I think about, from the moment I wake up until the second I fall asleep, all I see is her.

I will set the whole world on fire if she dies on me.

There is no me without her.

She has my pathetic, blackened soul wrapped around her wings.

And there's no coming back from this.

A tap on my shoulder makes me flinch, and I stand from my chair like it's vital.

I turn around to meet the trauma doctor who's treating Ari.

His expression is weightless.

Nothing behind a cold stare, and I can't fucking tell what his following words will be.

My heart is pounding, and I grow impatient the longer he deadpans.

"Mr. Rider." His voice is unemotional.

"Tell me she's alive." I demand him to give me the answer I need to live.

"She's alive." His voice is crisp and concise, as if he's purposefully speaking every word thoroughly to ensure I understand the situation.

When he says that, my whole body transits to relief. I heave out a heavy exhale and relax my shoulders.

"She will be able to recover fully, although we don't know when she will wake up. Could be in a few hours, could even be days."

"Days?"

He nods.

"I need to see her. I need to see her now." I step forward, headed toward the room I last saw her in, not caring if he stops me. No one will stop me from being there for her and our baby.

He grabs my arm, and I tense up my bicep, looking at him with murderous eyes.

If he thinks—

"She's not in her room, Mr. Rider." He lets go of my arm, and I raise my brow.

"What the fuck do you mean?" I snarl.

"She's still in surgery...she—" He clears his throat and softens his tone, finally revealing some emotion, and I'm bracing myself.

This can't mean...

"The baby did not survive. Too much blood loss. She's in surgery so we can deliver your son...I-I'm sorry for your loss." Each word that comes out of his mouth is sharp, cutting me more profoundly than the scars on my body ever did...leaving me in shock. There are no words that I'm able to form, and my brows narrow furiously as the hospital gets tuned out, slowly. I rub my temples, shaking my head.

My son...I have a boy.

"He's gone?" I choke out, trying to stop the lump in my throat from forming.

I'm breathing, but I feel like I just died.

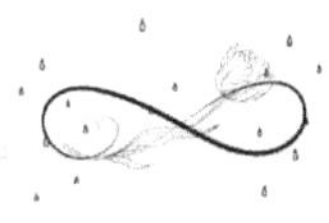

My phone buzzes in my pocket, making the memory vanish as quickly as it was triggered. I stand straight, leaning forward and take my eyes off my little angel.

I took a leave of absence after everything went down. I still have some time left before it's back to deployments, long work-days, and missions.

It's the first time I've done that...the first time in years that I've taken a leave of absence. Work has always been my only priority, but not anymore.

I take my phone out of my pocket and see it's from the team. The group chat is going off again, and I know it's bad news if it won't stop. I take a deep breath before I read the texts.

Rooker: Sorry to disrupt your leave like this, but Admiral Ravenmore wants all executioners on a Face Cam right now. It's important.

Shit.

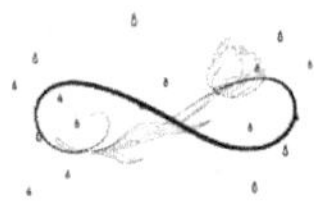

I open up my laptop in Ari's living room. I set down my thin black device on her wooden coffee table. Her house is a one-floor-only cottage home a few miles from mine. I helped her move everything into her home, even though I insisted she stay at my place. Lately, my little angel has become so fragile I'm afraid if I touch her, she'll have an anxiety attack. I don't want to push her for more until she's ready, even though I'm dying to feel her the way I desire to.

I've wanted to devour her every single day and night, but can't bring myself to do it. My way of loving her in the bedroom hasn't changed, and I know she's not ready.

I'll be patiently waiting until the time is right.

I hop into the group call, and everyone's already waiting for me.

Admiral Ravenmore, Rooker, Kane, and Lopez sit in their homes, each with a different background.

Admiral Ravenmore speaks first. "Grim, we're pleased to see you're doing okay. My condolences."

I grind my teeth, and my soul blackens with anger. He hasn't called once or texted me personally to express any empathy. He only cares if I'm alive and ready to return to work.

I look down at the coffee table and grab my glass of whiskey I had poured myself before I jumped into the call. I take a sip, giving him a nod of acknowledgment.

"How's Ari doing?" Kane asks.

My eyebrows raise at the mention of my girl's name, and I already want to cut throats.

I look at Kane through the screen; he's eager to know the answer, fidgeting in his chair.

"She's doing the best she can right now." I look away from the screen as I pop my fingers. "I don't want to talk about this. Please respect our privacy," I demand through my rugged demeanor.

"Say no more," Admiral interrupts.

Kane's expression stutters and his face drops. He thinks I don't know…but I do.

"Well, boys, I called you in tonight because we're receiving threats. Gravely, dangerous impending threats that the Navy doesn't take lightly. That the President of the United States takes very seriously. It's top secret, and you guys have special clearance to this information because it specifically deals with your entire team," Admiral Ravenmore says. "Remember the mission the night Paul died?"

We nod.

"Yes, sir," Rooker tells him.

"The number one most wanted man on the terrorist list who escaped that night has come back to haunt us."

I freeze in my chair.

"What the fuck? Forgive me, Sir, for the profanity, but…what the fuck?" Lopez asks.

"How?" Kane asks.

"Well, sons, there's another thing. Remember the mission where Damon Hawk was found dead in Iraq?" Ravenmore continues, and I can feel myself dreading the information.

"Grim Reaper, here, killed his only son that night. The man you killed when you engaged in hand-to-hand combat? That was him. That was his only son, so he's doing everything he can to avenge his death." He shifts in his seat nonchalantly and intertwines his fingers. "He's been gathering an entire army and threatening to find you. He is even putting a bounty on your head. A hundred million dollars if someone kills the Grim Reaper. They've got their nickname for you. They *want to kill Death*, they say. They say they want to kill the one that looks like the reaper."

"I'd love to see them try." I smirk wickedly. I place the glass between my lips, letting my favorite amber poison roll down my throat. They think they can kill me; well, that's just too fucking cute.

"Hooyah," Rooker roars in agreement, getting anxious in his seat.

"So what does this all mean?" Kane asks.

"It means they want to bring the war to us, son. Intel has got a hold of some disturbing information. They're already lurking inside the United States looking for you, Grim. Stay alert. I need the team to stay grounded in North Carolina in case of more threats. Only need-to-know personnel know about these threats because we don't want to cause a panic in this country."

"Holy shit, it's that serious?" Lopez exclaims.

"I'm dead serious, son. They're out to get all of you, specifically Grim and anyone that stands in their way."

"Operations have changed to stateside for the time being. Is that what you're saying?" I ask.

"Exactly. No out-of-the-country deployments for now. This team has been granted special clearance for CONUS operations. But, Grim, there's more."

More? How much more could there be?

"Make sure you keep your family close when you can, but also express the seriousness of their discretion. Stay close to them whenever you're not at work. These evil motherfuckers won't hesitate to use the ones you love and care about the most to get to you. *To find you.*"

I look around, making sure Ari can't hear any of this. She doesn't need more stress added to her plate right now...because of my job.

"I know, Sir. I know how this all works. You don't need to tell me twice." I clench my jaw. I'm coming off rude, but I know how this protocol works. I've been in for fifteen years already.

I look at my phone, turning it on to look at my screensaver. It's a picture of Ari and me on the Black Hawk helicopter. I took a photo of us before it took off. She was in her scrubs, cuddled against me, her hand on my chest, smiling brightly. It's my favorite picture of her.

This means they'll be coming after my family...they'll be coming after my little angel.

I won't be able to keep this secret with me forever. But if my silence about the dangers at hand can help her worry less, then I'll keep it to myself. *I'll* worry about it. I've carried weight like this on my shoulders my entire life. I need to take care of her...in the ways that I know how.

"One more thing, boys," Admiral Ravenmore continues to spill information, and I wonder when this meeting will fucking end.

I need to make sure I'm in her bed because it's not a matter of *"if"* Ari wakes up with a night terror; it's *when*. I need to be there, so she knows I'm never leaving her again. I will be there to console her back to sleep, feeling her heartbeat against my chest until she's okay again.

"Daegan Hannibal, Operator Creature, will be a new asset to the team, Executioners. Welcome him with open arms."

Rooker's eyes widen, and it looks like he just saw a ghost.

"Creature? You're talking about the SEAL that broke records for distance. The deadliest sniper in the entire military?" Lopez blurts out with an ecstatic tone. I look at his side of the camera, and he shifts in his seat, elated with a huge grin. The cowboy from Texas jolts with curiosity like a fan, but I'm impassive. Another team member I'm in charge of...*responsible for.*

"Yes. That's exactly who I mean. He's...*special,* to say the least. He's a little off, but nonetheless, he shows immense promise. He doesn't say or talk much, but he always places the job and mission first, so I expect him to thrive. He always does in every situation he's been put in."

"With all due respect, Sir, I'm still on leave and need to go, so let's cut to the chase," I interrupt, looking straight at Ravenmore's green, dull eyes, tightening my lips. He's unbothered by my honesty, and at this point, almost fifteen years in, he's not surprised. I'm in no mood nor interested in getting to know Creature's backstory. This is just another operator attached to my team. I can bother with the details later.

"When does this take effect?" I start to pack my cigarettes against my thigh.

"Immediately," Ravenmore replies.

8
———

ARI

"I'm glad you're doing better, Ari. You've had the worst possible year. I won't be leaving for vacation again anytime soon," Emilia says while hugging me.

We're all at my house having a girls' night before I have to start work again. It's been two months since the attack and I feel weird. Like I'm not entirely healed. I keep having nightmares of a Grim Reaper whispering the same eerie words to me almost every night. I still haven't told Danny anything.

"At least he's dead now and can't hurt you again," Meredith chimes in.

"Danny killed him," I murmur.

"Damn. A man that literally would kill for you. He's a keeper." She raises her eyebrows, shrugging her shoulders in awe.

"He is." I purse my lips, the emotions getting to me. I feel like I'm about to fall apart again. I bounce my foot up and down, holding my blanket tighter.

"What is it, sweetie?" Emilia grips my shoulder.

They turn toward me, and I feel like I'm about to explode and let my intrusive thoughts win.

"I love him. I'm so fucking in love with him," I confess with a tear falling out of my eye.

"That's a good thing, sweetie, don't cry," Emilia says.

I shake my head. Guilt creeps into my chest. I'm so in love with him even though he hasn't said it. He doesn't have to...but still. I'd like to hear those three words from the man who infuriates me.

"I'm also incredibly angry with him."

"What? Why?" Meredith flinches, her tone baffled.

I look around my living room for the right words to say.

Danny was called into work for an emergency. His leave had just ended, and the military wasted no time jam-packing his schedule. They canceled his deployment for unknown reasons that he couldn't tell me.

"This might be wrong of me, but I just feel like maybe he shouldn't have started a war with Shane. Maybe this wouldn't have happened if he hadn't met Nora?"

I look at them with widened eyes, confused by my admission. I'm hurt, angry because I keep replaying what I could have done for my baby to remain alive. "It's all my fault or maybe it's his."

"*Or maybe* it's no one's fault. Not his, not yours. Girl, don't do that. Please don't do that to yourself and don't do that to him. He was protecting you that night at El Devine. This might be harsh, but I don't care. I'm your best friend, and you need to listen to me sometimes even though I can be a dumb ass myself. Would things have turned out differently if Paul was still here? Because he would have *killed* Shane that night at El Devine. And it would have been Paul starting a war."

Emilia studies me. She's looking at me to see if I'll break, but I won't. I won't ever break again. I won't ever let another man or woman hurt me again.

"You're right. I know, but there's something else." I sigh.

Meredith's eyes pop open, gawking at me as if I just slapped the side of her head.

"Oh God, like what?" Meredith shouts, annoyed, smacking her teeth and narrowing her brows at me. Her wine glass jolts, and it almost spills over.

We sit silently for a few seconds when a smile pulls at my lips, curving into a smirk.

A laugh escapes me uncontrollably through every breath that leaves my body, and then Emilia joins in, laughing harder.

"Like damn, how much more could there be?! Like, fuck. Your whole life sounds like a thriller movie lately," Meredith complains through smiles.

"I know, I know...but the thing is, I can't help but feel like he's keeping something from me. Like a secret."

"You think he's cheating on you? That fucking bastard—" I cut Emilia off before her mind travels to the worst.

"No! That's not it!" I cut in, covering Emilia's mouth.

I trust Danny in that way. I trust him with my entire life. He would never cheat on me or betray me.

"Then what is it?" Emilia puts her hand on her waist impatiently.

I lick my lips, unsure of how to say it. I'm not ready to talk about my near-death experience. I'm not prepared to talk about losing my son. And I am not willing to talk about the hallucination just yet.

"I don't know, but I will find out."

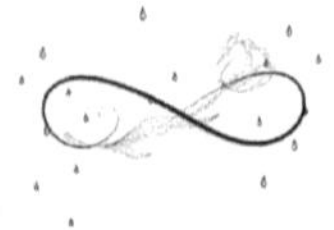

It's eleven at night, and I'm playing fucking soccer while listening to Mana on my earphones.

My little cottage house sits on three acres of land. It doesn't come with a fence. Thick trees and bushes surround my new home, like a cabin in the woods, and it's cozy.

Danny hasn't returned home from work. He said he would as soon as he could leave but that something horrible was unfolding and he would fill me in in the morning. He said he'd probably come back at three a.m.

I can't sleep when he's not home. I've grown so used to being in his arms, falling asleep in them every night, that I felt like I had to distract myself from the depression that threatened to take over me every day.

Danny set up a net between two trees in my backyard so I could play whenever I felt up to it. It's my first time trying it out, and he built it just right.

It's dark, the night freezing, and I can see my breath as I breathe heavily into the icy crisp air. My birthday is tomorrow, followed by Paul's death anniversary soon.

I'm wearing a jacket and thin sports leggings that hug my legs. Perfect to run around in and kick a soccer ball.

My feet crunch over frozen sparkling ice that has taken over my entire lawn. That happens in the winter in North Carolina sometimes.

I feel relief knowing I can do things like this again. When Shane was alive, I feared for my life every day. I was on edge every second and now I'm starting to feel free again, but he took something from me. Something I've dreamed about since I was a little girl. To become a mother.

Danny and I haven't talked about it too much. It's too painful for me, but I do want children again, even though I'm not ready to have sex just yet. Maybe I'll revisit the possibility of getting pregnant later.

The thought of losing my baby sends my anger boiling hard, ready to burst through.

"He's not capable of love." Nora's voice echoes in my head, loud and clear. Her vicious words are a reminder of the man I'm in love with. Flashes of her broken soul like a slideshow, take over me.

My nostrils flare, and I scrunch my nose when the memories of Shane and Nora stabbing me return. A thick blade appears, waving back and forth in front of my face, inside my body...

Hot air runs through my nose, and I kick my soccer ball so hard that I miss the net, hitting the tree's thick bark instead. It spirals out of control, striking right back so fast I move out of the way just in time and it flies behind me.

It lands in a tall man's hands. Hands that aren't Danny's but are familiar.

It's Kane.

I squint at him, ensuring he's actually there, and sure enough, it's him. He stands tall in a dark gray beanie and a black leather jacket, with a playful expression. He looks good...I shake myself out of that thought.

What the hell is he doing here?

I pull out my earphones and look around, worried. Is he here with Danny? Is he back home?

"Hey there, what'd the soccer ball ever do to you?" he says with a welcoming, heartwarming smile.

"Kane... I-I, uh, what are you doing here?"

He walks toward me, and I'm still shocked, even a little scared, so I take a step back. I'm extra cautious nowadays.

I'm thrown off by the sudden visitation.

How does he know where I live?

I don't take surprises like this too well since I experienced a horrific stalker like Shane.

With every stride he takes, getting closer to me, I swallow. I swear I feel a spark in my chest and internally refrain from feeling anything more.

He towers over me, handing me back the ball. I grab it from him, but it does something when our hands touch. I didn't mean for our fingers to collide. I try to pry the ball back from his hands, but he gives my hand a tiny squeeze before he lets go of it.

He clears his throat, looking down at me.

"I couldn't sleep. I haven't seen you since..." he trails off.

"Since I almost died?" I finish for him.

He swallows nervously, and I watch his Adam's apple bob up and down.

"Well, not almost. You *did* die."

I let out a heavy breath. I don't want to revisit this.

"So you thought you could stalk me instead because you couldn't sleep? How do you even know where I live?"

He lets out a sigh.

"I helped move all your stuff in, remember?"

I had already forgotten. Everything has been a fog since I lost my baby.

God, I'm losing it.

"Right..."

"Ari. We made a promise. All the guys did. Paul's team and Grim's. Rooker, Danny, and I. We all promised Paul we would watch over you if he died. Didn't Danny tell you that?"

This is the first time I've heard this. Danny told me he made a promise but never said what or to whom.

Danny hasn't told me a lot of things.

I shake my head, leaning on my hip and dropping the ball.

"A promise?"

He nods.

"Damn it, Paul."

"Hey, he was just trying to be a protective older brother. You can't fault him for that," Kane defends him.

I shake my head, lost in thought. It definitely sounds like something Paul would do.

"So then, where's Rooker? He's not going to show up at my house in the middle of the night, too, is he?"

He chuckles. It's deep and—

Crap, I can't be thinking these things.

"Nope. At least, I don't think so."

"So, then what? What kind of guy shows up at my house in the middle of the night if not a stalker?" I sit in the grass, getting comfortable, crossing my legs.

He walks closer and then sits next to me.

"Someone who cares about you deeply." He gives me another delightful smile. His shoulder brushes against me, and I have to force myself to look away from him. The way he's looking at me... it's the way Danny looks at me. And darn it. I miss when Danny looks at me like this because it means seconds later, he would end up deep inside of me, and we'd devastatingly devour each other...*for hours.*

"Look, I know I shouldn't be here, but I don't get much out

of Danny. The man keeps shit inside. He won't tell me how you guys are *really* doing. So, I thought I'd check up on you. The middle of the night isn't the best time, so please forgive me, but I needed to see with my own eyes that you're okay."

I scoff, rolling my eyes. I'm bitter, but I don't care.

"Well, I'm not. I'm not okay, but maybe I will be with time."

Kane licks his lips, nodding his head, and looks away from me. We both grow silent, and I'm at a loss for words. My hands grow cold since I'm no longer moving around. He shouldn't be here. This is wrong. If Danny finds out he's here, I'm pretty damn sure he wouldn't like it.

"Why aren't you at work...with Danny?"

His dark blue gaze pierces me, then flicks to my lips. I suck in a breath when I watch him *watch me*. Finally, he grabs the ball from my hands and stands.

"Admiral Ravenmore only wanted Grim to come in tonight. When you're the most distinguished lethal man with the most kill count in the entire United States military, and I'm talking all branches combined, the work just never stops. There's always going to be work that needs to get done. Work that not just anybody can do."

I raise my eyebrows. I mean, I knew Danny had impacted the military community, but damn. This explains a lot. It gives me an insight into everything he's been through. But I know this is just one reason for all of his darkness.

Constant deployments?

Constant missions?

Constant death?

This is what he only knows.

"How long has he been in?" I ask, standing too.

Kane looks at me like he wants to bite his tongue, but continues, anyway.

"Since he was eighteen."

My mouth gapes open.

"That's absolutely insane. Eighteen years old?"

"Yeah, I've known Danny for years now. I met him about six years ago. He has taught me a lot. I'm a better SEAL because of him. I will always have respect for him. Though…I'm amazed he hasn't gotten out yet. I'm damn ready to pull the plug after my contract ends in a few months."

"You are?" I'm shocked at his admission. Danny has told me time and time again his job comes first before anything or anyone else. Kane is the complete opposite of Danny. Danny loves his job. It's what he enjoys. From what I know about him, being a Navy SEAL is where he thrives.

Kane nods, dropping the soccer ball on the ground. He steps on it with one foot, holding it in place.

"All of this shit, Ari…" He stops and shakes his head as he looks at the stars in the sky. "Can I be honest with you?" he pleads.

"Of course."

He sighs, letting out a breath, and I can see the vapor from his warmth linger in the air as he turns back. He looks like he's hurting. He's always been there for me since Paul passed, so it's the least I can do for him.

"All of these missions, seeing the lengths evil wars can bring. It's getting to me." He lets out a short, sarcastic laugh that disguises his true feelings. "Sometimes, I just lose myself in random moments. I'll find myself just staring at the wall, thinking about my past deployments for a while, not realizing an hour has been wasted…staring at a fucking wall."

I bite the inside of my lip. It gets to Danny, too, and that's why he drinks. He promised me he wouldn't get drunk again, and I believe him. He keeps proving that to me every single day. He hasn't gotten drunk since the night he confessed the details of Paul's death.

"Talk to someone then, Kane. Talk to someone in psychiatry, a therapist even. They have a lot of resources and options at the hospital I'm working at on base."

He shrugs and stands in silence, watching me.

"I think I would just like to play soccer with you for a bit, if that's okay?"

This feels wrong, but I try not to read more into this. I'm just playing soccer with one of Paul's best friends. Danny's teammate. At midnight.

What could go wrong?

I shrug, and my body jolts forward, kicking the ball from underneath his massive foot, dribbling it to the soccer net.

"Sure, but you're going to get your butt kicked by someone a whole foot shorter than you."

"**G**OAL!" Kane shouts into the air as he runs away from the net, dramatically.

It's about midnight now and I've forgotten all about my trauma for the past hour and it felt amazing.

We've been playing one versus one, and I'm getting tired finally.

Kane kicked the ball into the goal, surpassing me.

I roll my eyes at his ego, trying to catch my breath. My throat and lungs hurt from breathing in the cold air so much that it burns. I pull the ball out of the net. He's way faster than me, taller, and has longer legs. Of course, I'm going to lose against him.

He's lifted his shirt over his head like all professional players do when they score a goal and I'm met with a six-pack of abs. My eyes trail down from his perfectly defined abdomen muscles down to the V covered in a patch of dark hair that leads to...

I mentally slap myself.

He pulls his shirt back down and I unglue my eyes from him.

"Whatever. Don't flatter yourself, Mr. Slaughter." I have to stop myself from flashing a smile. I know I'm being a sore loser, but again, I wear my heart on my sleeve, not caring if he can see how competitive I can be sometimes.

I walk toward my porch, leaving the area where I lost myself in an intense game against a SEAL. Kane follows me with a smug look, grabbing his leather jacket from the grass and throwing it over his shoulder.

"For someone so tiny, you're a sore loser."

"I am not!" I lie through a high-pitched defensive tone.

I bite the side of my cheek, pouting.

"You are, but it's okay. It's cute."

My heart pounds with complication as I sit on the wooden steps leading to my front door and hold the ball onto my lap. My heart rate is all over the place from all the back-and-forth running, or it could *also* be from the man who's always been there for me since Paul's funeral.

He needs to stop saying these things, yet I can't seem to stop him from doing so.

He sits next to me, and I scooch further away from him, making sure there's distance between us. Kane has never been shy about his interest in taking our relationship to the next level, but I've never wanted to take it further. I was heavy in grieving. I was freshly single from an abusive relationship and now? I'm with a man I'm so in love with yet unsure of the truths I know he's hiding from me.

And Kane is close friends with Danny. It's wrong...

"Ari, I really admire how strong you are. No matter what you go through, you manage to always push through."

My heart skips a beat as those profound words leave his mouth. He can't be saying these things to me because I know he wants more from me. I can feel it. A cold breeze brushes through us, making me shudder as I hold the ball.

"Thank you. I appreciate that. I really do. I can't thank you enough for always being there whenever you could when Paul died. It means a lot to my mother and I. I just needed a break from everything."

I give him a friendly smile and turn toward him. But it's a mistake because now he looks at me intensely, and I can't move. I haven't been kissed on the mouth in over a month. Danny has been giving me the space I need, and I'm so grateful for it, but at this moment. I'm about to lose control. Kane has engraved a special place in my heart because of his consistency throughout my grieving.

"I'm always going to be here for you." Kane leans closer, and I stop breathing as his face approaches mine. He's looking at my lips...and so I look at his.

I fucking miss kissing so severely. I miss the feeling of losing myself to someone. I miss losing myself when my lips crash devastatingly onto Danny's with impenetrable lust. I miss the surface of my heart erupting into a fire of craze that could never be put out.

I miss it so much.

I miss all of these things.

I close my eyes and let myself get lost in this forbidden feeling, but I don't lean in. I trust myself. I know what I want and this isn't it. I know what I have to do.

I can feel his body heat now, so I shut my eyes even tighter and frown. When I open my eyes, his breath hits my lips. He's so close to kissing me.

This is not who I miss.

I miss Danny. I don't want this from Kane. I crave the man who takes my breath away with just one look.

I'm not doing this. I'm not a liar.

I let my head fall, leaning away from Kane's lips.

A low groan escapes him as his body clenches. The air transforms into bitter tension. We were about to kiss, and he knows it.

We both know it.

"This is wrong. I'm sorry. You shouldn't be here," I tell Kane as I stand, getting away from him fast.

What am I doing?

He sits silently, staring where I used to sit on the steps as I walk away. He's not moving, but his body language tells me he's hurt.

But I'm angry with him for pushing the limits with me. He's never done this before; it's taking me by surprise. He's always been a shoulder my mother and I could lean on after my brother's passing. But this? This was something new...and I'm conflicted. Because I love him for that. But...I'm with Danny.

"Good night, Mr. Slaughter." The guilt begins to eat me alive with each step I take.

What is wrong with me?

I walk toward my front door quickly. I feel terrible. This isn't like me. It was a weak moment rooted in vulnerability and trauma. Yes...that's what it was. It *has to be.*

I grab the door handle, about to swing it open. It opens slightly, but my movements fall short when Kane stops me from running away.

He grabs my hand in his big, rough hands and grips me hard, then slams the door shut, and fire pricks into every single vein, boiling when I hear it close.

"You're right, Ari Alvarez, I shouldn't be here." His voice is deep and full of ecstasy, almost seducing. "But I don't care anymore," Kane adds, his tone full of momentousness.

I feel like whatever he's about to say will end his friendship with Danny forever. His dark blue eyes are searching for something more from me urgently. I turn away from his eyes and look at his hand wrapped around mine.

His big hand swallows mine whole, and I try to retrieve myself from his grasp, but he holds on tighter.

"I need to say something, and I'm going to say it once and never again."

I lift my chin to face him at his persistence. I'm enveloped with pure curiosity. It isn't like him to be so authoritative around me.

"I'm in love with you. I've always been in love with you since the first time I saw you. I've been keeping my distance, but I can't anymore. And I need you to know this."

There it is, his blatant, simple yet catastrophic confession I knew was coming one day. I assumed that he wouldn't ever come truly clean about his feelings after he saw me with Danny at the beach.

A tear falls out of my eye as he confesses his feelings. I feel completely torn in two. I don't want to lose Kane—he's too important.

"I'm all in, Ari. I'd leave the fucking military for you. Danny might not want children, but I want it. I want it all. I want babies, a marriage, I want...*you*."

Why is he doing this? Why now?

"Kane, I—" What the hell does he want me to say to that? This is not okay, but somewhere deep down in my heart, I know he might be the better man for me. He's soft and sunny. While Danny is dark and full of demons he didn't ask for. He was thrown into it by his parents. Thrown into the fire and forced to learn how to adapt to being burned daily.

Still, I can't surpass the fact Danny has changed me in good ways, too.

Even if his love for me has been challenging, he's taught me many things about myself and has helped me grow into the woman I am today.

"I just don't know what you want me to say, Kane," I whisper.

"Don't say anything. I just need you to know." He closes the distance between us even more now. He lifts his arm and palms the side of my front door. His lips are on my ear, causing my skin to quiver and my lungs to stop at a standstill.

"I'm all in. I know you're with him now. Don't get me wrong, Grim is my best friend. He's my brother. He started to change slowly this past year, and it all makes sense now that I know it's because of you."

A cold breeze whips our way, sending the tips of our noses freezing and my bangs brush over my eyes.

Kane moves them away, forcing me to look at him.

"You're good for him, but maybe you need someone who's good for you." He gives me that same dashing, warm, dorky smile and drops his hand to his waist. He finally leans away from me as he whispers, "I'm willing to be whatever you need me to be when I'm with you in any way that I can. No matter what, I made a promise, and I've kept it since day one. I'm all in, Ari Alvarez."

Another tear falls down my cheeks.

I'm fucking confused and overwhelmed.

"Damn it, Kane, shut up," I murmur, fighting so damn hard not to slap him.

Kane scoffs, followed by a smirk.

Then he gives me a dark expression that intensifies, and it's a look I've never recognized before. When I think of Kane, I think of the steamy, dorky guy that's always happy.

"You've just crossed a line. Nothing will be the same after this." I shake my head slowly, disappointed.

I can see the moonlight reflecting through his eyes as he finally softens his appearance and wipes my tears away. His touch sends flutters throughout my stomach.

He can't be doing this to me. I push his hand away, taking a step back.

"I know. That's the point," he replies.

I narrow my eyes, not wanting to decipher more.

"Sweet dreams, Ari." His jaw sets tight, and he releases my hand. This is a side of him that I've never seen before. It's so dark and yet...so intriguing.

Before he turns around, his dark blue eyes linger on my lips a little longer. Flustered doesn't even begin to describe the way my chest feels. It's on fire.

Shit.

It's been too long since I've felt Danny.

Then Kane turns around finally and retreats to his bike. He slides his arms into his leather jacket, throwing it on as he disappears behind the thick trees that surround the front of my house. The entire time, it feels like the world is in slow motion.

I'm in love with a man named Daniel Rider.

And yet, I can't help but feel like there could be something more there with Kane Slaughter. Because he just showed me he's capable of saying those three words, but Danny still hasn't, which is disappointing after all we've been through.

10

ARI

I'm engulfed in dark shadows again. Paul plays the guitar to Mana and I'm watching him in the dark on his bed. Every time I see my big brother, I'm always happy. He visits me only in my dreams, but this time, it's different. I don't feel bliss this time. I only feel dread.

Paul plays the guitar, and he's not smiling. He's frowning as he plays aggressively. Then I see something. Something eerie and familiar.

The Grim Reaper slowly creeps up behind his back, appearing above his shoulders, and I see a hand with no flesh, just bones, creeping over his chest, grabbing him.

I can feel my heart beating so hard that it hurts.

Danny's exact tattoo appears behind my brother, and I try to yell, but nothing comes out. I try to warn him, but no scream leaves my constricted, dry throat.

Then the Grim Reaper turns to me with an insidious expression and smiles viciously, revealing a skull face.

"Time. Waits. For. No. One."

The same demonic voice comes from the Grim Reaper. The same voice I heard as I slowly slipped into unconsciousness when Shane and Nora killed me.

That's when I feel a cold, freezing breath down my neck, and a sensation that something is sitting on my chest, pressing hard while shivers strike all my bones and I'm sinking further down a hole of fear.

"Nooooo!" I am finally able to scream as the dark visions vanish away.

I jolt upright in my dark room, breathing hard, trying to escape the nightmare.

I cry into my hands, and my front door swings open.

It's Danny.

He's covered in camo paint all over his face. His uniform is riddled with equipment, and a gun is holstered at his waist.

The last time I saw him like this was when he was my patient in Iraq.

His massive frame swallows the entire doorway and when I look at him, butterflies I thought had long flown away come back full circle for a short moment, and I want that feeling to stay.

Why does seeing him like this scare me yet intrigue me more?

I hate that this has been a recurring thing since my attack. I feel embarrassed my boyfriend has to continuously see me like this. Even though, with every waking terror, he's there...he's always there, making me feel safe. Like nothing else matters. I retreat back into my hands, where I continue to whimper.

He's back home but the feelings from the nightmare continue to haunt my mind.

"Baby, what's wrong?" He sits beside me on the edge of the bed and grabs my shoulders. The bed sinks underneath his massive frame while he's hovering over me protectively.

"What took you so long?" I shout, angry. I'm being unfair, but I can't help it. I hate being alone after everything I've been through. I can't stand being alone. I know Shane's dead, but Nora is not. What if she comes back for me?

What if Shane's spirit still haunts me and that's why I'm having these nightmares?

"Ari, I left when I could. I just got home when I heard you screaming. Are you having another nightmare?" he asks, rubbing my back.

I nod.

"Come here," he orders softly.

I climb on top of him, straddling him on the bed. He holds me back tight and I can smell cigarettes mixed with his cologne, and leather seats...all over him. It smells familiar.

It smells *good*.

"They won't stop, Danny. It won't fucking stop. I dream the same thing over and over again," I exclaim as a panic attack unfolds. I'm breathing hard, sucking in breath after breath, but it's useless.

I sob against his neck, his dog tags against my cheek.

His body grows tense. He loosens his grip around my body.

"What do you dream about?" He lifts my chin to face him.

I look at him again; the light blue irises flash with concern, and he looks drained. It seems like he's already been through one hell of a night, and I'm adding more to it.

I bite my lip as he narrows his eyes, pleading for me to tell him what I dream about.

I won't let the trauma we've both been through derail our relationship. I will bottle it up. I refuse to let silly hallucinations take over me completely.

"It's nothing, I'll be okay."

He holds me and doesn't stop soothing my back. His hands snake under my shirt, and I feel his calloused palms all over my back, rubbing me up and down until, finally, the anxiety attack subsides.

"It's not nothing. Tell me."

I shake my head, refusing.

I don't want to tell him how weak I am. I'm already showing him that.

I soak in every second of being in his arms like they'll shield me from any more anxiety attacks.

As soon as I feel okay again, I get off his lap and sit beside him. I love that he doesn't pry further. Our waists touch each other at the sides. My gaze changes from looking at his beautiful ocean eyes to his soft lips.

I need him. *I need all of him.*

I want to taste his tongue that's been tainted by his cigarettes. I want him to completely devour me like he used to, even if that means it comes with pain.

I just need to feel *something.*

And that's what Danny does to me.

He makes me feel alive even though I feel wilted on the inside.

He catches my gaze, deciphering my need for him, and then stands, walking toward my bathroom door.

I'm left devastated, as the rejections hits me harder than it should.

I don't want him away from me. He's been so patient with me.

The sex is world-shattering. I think of the moment we gave into each other for the first time...it was relentless, complex, and rough. I saw the outcome of what we did to each other in his barracks room. He fucked me so hard that the headboard made cracks and dents into his wall.

I miss it.

"I'm going to take a quick shower. I'll come back to bed when I'm done." He sighs, tired. "I knew this was how it would be when I started to work again. It never stops." He shakes his head once, scoffing. He stops at the doorway, shrugging his shoulders, and I can hear his upper back pop as he stretches his muscles and spine.

"What did you need to tell me? Why did they cancel your deployment? What did the Admiral want from you so suddenly?" I blurt out.

He turns to me, and he's stuck in his thoughts. He purses his lips, and I know that I've asked him something that's classified. I'm pushing him for more. I need to get inside his head. He's hesitant, quiet, and rigid. But then he smiles when he looks me in the eyes. The way his lips slowly form into a stressed, crooked smirk makes my heart stop for a blip in time.

God, I swear his smile alone makes me flush throughout my bloodstream. Bliss simmers in my veins. It sends my eyes blinking fast and fluttering so quickly, struggling to stay attached to his blue eyes gazing at mine.

Then he walks over to me.

Is he going to give in?

He kneels, kissing my cheek, softly brushing my skin, and every fiber on my body jumps, electrocuted with heat. His beard prickles into mine and I bite the inside of my cheek, missing the way it feels between my thighs. I close my eyes tight as his lips linger for a second longer on my skin and then he pulls away, leaving me begging for more. The emotions sparked detrimentally from passion anchor down so fast to my stomach.

"Happy birthday, my little angel," he tells me against my cheek, his voice vibrating through my ears, and I'm disoriented from the clash of his touch.

Of course, he knows it's my birthday. I didn't have to say a word.

"We can talk about the details of work another day. Today is your day," he continues.

Maybe I can use this day to my advantage.

"It is my day," I repeat.

He cups the left side of my face into his hand, and a low, deep groan releases from his throat. I open my eyes when I hear the familiar lustful sound, and I meet his darkened ones and I know this look too well. He wants me just as badly as I want him. Our faces are so close to touching, I can smell his intoxicating scent. His beautiful face is enveloped with face paint, and I am so attracted to it.

"The day we crossed paths was the day my world became worth living in."

He brushes his finger across my bottom lip, and the need to truly *feel him* haunts me harder.

Damn it, he can't say these things and then not expect it to not go any further between us?

He walks back toward my bathroom door. He pulls off all his equipment from his uniform and then places it on the dresser individually. After his vest is off, he tucks his fingers underneath his shirt, throwing it over his head, undressing. His well-trained and defined back muscles are on display, and I'm blushing hard when I see his back tattoo. I rub my thighs together, hoping it helps.

"I have a surprise for the birthday girl when you leave work."

My eyebrows raise.

"Oh God. The last time you told me that, I was in a helicopter, unstrapped."

He smirks followed by a laugh.

I want him so badly, but he thinks I'm not ready, and he's probably right.

He places his shirt in the hamper, and I look at my clock on the nightstand. It's three in the morning, and I refuse to go back to sleep, knowing I might dream of the Grim Reaper.

"You haven't *really* touched me, Danny. You haven't even kissed me since the attack."

His body goes still. Is it still with desire? Or still, because I've called him out on something we have refused to discuss? We dismiss the elephant in the room that lingers every day.

It's like my words struck a sensitive chord inside his soul, and my candor paralyzes him.

He looks back at me. His expressionless face infuriates me as it usually does. I can't read him anymore and that frustrates me. The light from my lamp illuminates the profile of his beautiful face and I can see the scar on his lip.

"No, I haven't. Because once I kiss you, I know myself too well." He clenches his jaw. "If I kiss you, Ari, there's no stopping me. I won't be able to control my need to completely consume you...and we both know what *that* exactly means, my little angel."

11

ARI

I went back to sleep after Danny returned from the shower last night. I went from tossing and turning to instant relaxation when he got into bed with me, his arm over my waist.

It feels weird to be back at work. It feels strange to be known as the girl who was attacked and lost her baby. The baby I kept a secret from everyone.

I'm still working in the trauma unit, and the ER is full of people. Sailors, marines, and their families impatiently wait to be seen. I hear chatter between the medical staff, pagers going off, and the hospital phone ringing constantly.

I hug my cardigan that's thrown over my scrubs tighter. My body struggles to adjust from the cold weather outside to the heated hospital.

As soon as I walk through the emergency doors, my heart stops, and I'm met with a familiar co-worker across from me by the nurses' station.

Lori.

I stop in my tracks and look at my close friend, who stands tall before me, just as stunned as I am. I'm about to start tearing up when she closes the distance and hugs me.

"Ari!" she says as she collides with me.

"Lori!" I exclaim back with a smile. "I knew you were coming back, but why didn't you tell me you were here already?" I push her shoulder playfully.

"I'm sorry! When I got back, my girlfriend and I went to Hawaii for a few weeks. I just returned a few days ago. My bad, my bad." She holds her hands up like she's surrendering.

"I'm so glad you're here."

She immediately acknowledges my pain even through the credible facade I'm putting on, like a mask.

"I heard what happened," she murmurs. "I'm so sorry."

I shake my head while doctors pass us by frantically.

"I'm getting better."

"Okay." She sighs, not believing the lie I just told her.

"Okay," I whisper.

"The gang's back together and I couldn't be happier," Lori says, hugging me closer to her body.

"I know..." I swallow the rock in my throat. "It just feels weird. Like I shouldn't be here; I should be home, crying my eyes out, mourning my brother and baby, but I think I need this. I need to be at work helping people."

"And that's totally fine. Do you need to cry? I'll cry with you. Do you need to eat a mountain of chocolate and pizza? I'll eat it all with you. Do you need to scream at the world? I'll scream as loud as I can until I lose my voice."

My lips lift into a small smile.

"I've got you, girl," Lori tells me, elbowing me playfully.

"Thank you, Lori. How's Doctor Diaz?" I ask while making my way toward the nurses' station, clocking in for my shift.

"He's fine. He's still there in Iraq. But he should be coming back to the States soon. I wish every doctor was like him. Now we're stuck with the grumpy Doctor Reese."

I don't recognize that name. Have I been gone that long that Doctor Golds left? I knew he was about to retire, but I've recently been distracted by my chaotic life to keep up.

"Who?"

"Doctor Reese? The new attending that started last week? He's a terror to be around. He's always pissed off. You could do everything right, and he'll still find a way to be mad at you."

I look over the list of patients in the ER. The list is long. I'm in for a busy night, but maybe this is what I need. I need to keep my mind distracted from the sadness that wants to drag me down further.

"Great," I mutter, walking toward the coffee station, in need to fuel my body with vast amounts of caffeine to get me through my first day back, and Lori follows me.

My mind trails to the past as I remember my time in Iraq. Being around Lori triggers that. I had a bigger purpose in my life there. I saved so many lives, including one of my brother's friends. I also discovered parts of myself I thought never existed inside of me because of a man named Danny Rider. He showed me a lot about myself. Pushing my boundaries, fracturing the shell I hid behind all my life. The first time I ever surrendered myself to someone. I only have good memories of that place, except for the few I have of Shane.

His cold, distant black eyes make me panic whenever I think about him.

Maybe if I distract myself with work, I won't fall deeper into this depression: the constant heartache, grief, and loss.

When I received news my brother died, it was in North Carolina.

When I got attacked, it was here...in North Carolina.

When I lost my baby...it was here *at home*.

I may run away from my problems, but this time, I will never apologize for putting myself first.

"That's enough gossiping, you two." Someone's rugged glacial voice cuts our conversation short. I flip over to see him, and he's staring knives at the both of us.

"Doctor Reese." Lori crosses her arms defensively.

"Sorry, sir. Won't happen again," I apologize.

I say I'm sorry because the last thing I want to do is piss my new boss off. I refuse to get on his bad side on my first day back. I'm a people pleaser, it's just who I am. I can't help it sometimes.

"We weren't *gossiping*, doctor. We're talking about work," Lori snaps back, fearless. Her tone of voice was professional, but I'm internally rooting for her.

I love that she never takes shit from anyone, including our new grumpy doctor in charge of us.

"Either way, get back to work." He closes his binder, unbothered by Lori's defense. "There's a patient that got out of surgery about a week ago, Ms. Alvarez. She's in room one." He looks at me with an icy glare. "Please get her to walk. The faster she walks, the faster she can get discharged."

"Yes, sir."

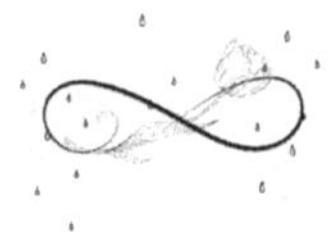

After waves of patients poured in, I finally could eat my lunch. Or rather, stuff it down quickly. I had almost forgotten to take my break. I was too busy caring for my patients and ensuring I had the correct medications and dosages.

It's already been one hell of a shift, and I'm still not halfway through it.

I review my patient's chart, taking in every detail of her case and history before walking in as usual. I look through the glass to see a young woman with long black hair flipping through the TV channels with the small plastic remote in her hands. She doesn't notice me yet, but I can see the cast on her ankle.

I had surgery not too long ago...

I hate what comes *after*. It's a long journey to recovery. Not everything fixes or heals with surgery. Some things take time.

I finally entered the room with the physical therapist at my side.

"Hello, Ms. Salem." I walk over to her side, and she turns toward me, startled by my greeting. "We're here to help you start walking. How are you feeling today? Any pain?" I ask, gripping the armrest and looking at the monitor.

Her blood pressure and oxygen levels are normal, and so is her heart rate.

So far, so good.

At first, she seems puzzled by me, but then she eyes me so intensely I'm lost.

"Look, I know why you guys are here, and I'm telling you, I'm not ready right now. I won't walk; I just had surgery a week ago," she complains, crossing her hands over her chest.

I frown at her refusal. I have to get her to walk out of this bed. The longer she sits for hours, the more she's prone to blood clots.

"Ms. Salem, this is Mr. Cameron, our amazing physical therapist. We have to get you to walk, at least for five minutes, and then we'll leave you alone, I promise," I request with an encouraging smile.

Mr. Cameron's shoulders sag. He usually wants them to walk more than just five minutes, but this was my best attempt to help her.

"We shouldn't push her so much. Let's start with baby steps," I whisper, trying to keep my voice low.

"No. I'm not ready." Ms. Salem fusses, protesting, unbothered. She shakes her head violently, her black hair jittering.

Mr. Cameron sighs, frustrated with impatience, crossing his arms disapprovingly.

Before we walked in, he informed me she had been fighting her required therapy every time he tried to help her.

I clear my throat, my vision piercing him for his attention, demanding it. I place my hand in front of him, motioning for him to stop, mouthing the words, *I've got this.*

"What are you watching?" I ask, walking toward her.

I have to help her, but in ways that don't seem unemotional or cold or treat her as if she's just another patient.

This poor woman needs to be treated with understanding and fortitude. If I were in her place with no family or friends to help me get through surgery or to learn how to walk again, I'd want at least one person to *understand me.*

I know this young woman hasn't had any visitors since she checked into the hospital with a broken ankle severed so severely she needed emergency surgery to fix it, or she would have had an amputation.

She looks at me with overwhelming disgust before rolling her eyes and returning to the television.

"It's a movie...a sad one."

"Oh...what's it about?" I grab a chair and sit beside her bed. Mr. Cameron watches us, disgruntled.

"It's about a girl..." She coughs to conceal her voice breaking. "It's just a movie." She doesn't want to talk, but that doesn't stop me from trying. She's closed off; it reminds me of the new version of myself.

"Tell me. I've never seen this one," I tell her. The actress in the movie is crying on a tombstone, and I'm already intrigued. She's kneeling on the floor, bawling, clutching her chest, struggling to breathe.

"It's...about a sister who lost her older brother in a car crash," she deadpans, still not bothering to look at me. But then I noticed the ache pricking at her throat when she said '*crash*'. "It's my favorite movie now...now that I lost my older brother earlier this year the same way." She stares at her fingers, massaging them nervously. "He was my best friend. I don't have a lot of family that cared for me, but *he did*. He was like a second dad to me." She whispers to the point where I almost can't hear her.

The monitor beeps louder, and the grief contorts on her face. She's breathing slowly but harder—her heart rate spikes, signaling a panic attack. I'm an expert at detecting those these days and a complete failure at dissolving my own.

Paul was everything to my mother and I. He was the foundation that kept our family together.

"I know what that kind of pain feels like," I concede as I look at the girl who continues to cry for her brother in the movie.

"Don't pretend to know what pain looks like," Ms. Salem snaps at me, her voice rising. "Don't pretend to act like you can relate to me. You're a pretty girl, probably a successful nurse in her twenties." Her eyes scan me up and down like she's reading me. "I'm sure you have a hot boyfriend obsessed with you. I know girls like you. You probably have a sheltered life with possibilities handed to you. You don't know what struggle is like. You don't know what losing your brother in a crash is like. So please...*stop pretending.*" She spits her words, full of hatred.

She doesn't know that my brother is dead and that I grieved for my baby soon after, and that's okay.

I'm pretending to be all right.

I'm pretending to be fine when I'm not.

I have to because that's what I need to do.

I swallow the sorrow that fills my stomach when the thoughts of grief seep into me. I swear I can feel my baby kick inside me as the anguish slithers in my chest again, constricting my lungs.

I take a deep breath and close my eyes tight for a split second, regaining stability.

"I lost my brother too...not long ago," I confess. "I looked up to him my entire life, and then..." I sigh. "Then he was gone in a split second. It was like he was here and then—" I bite my lip as I lose myself further. "He was...gone."

The last encounter with Paul flashes through my head like a movie. It's blurry but the emotions are still crystal clear...like it was yesterday.

He was leaving our house for his deployment. His fifth one, and he was excited to be with all his teammates after a weekend of partying with friends outside of the house.

Even though we lived separate lives, our love for each other never bottomed. Our bond is imperishable.

I never was worried about him leaving for deployments. *Never.*

Because he always came back home. He always kept his promise to us. I was too naïve back then to think he would return in a casket.

I clear my throat, stopping the giant rock from growing. The short memory of him waving at my mother and me through the driver's seat in his Bronco. His aviator sunglasses on, one hand on the steering wheel as he blasted Mana into his car. Him driving to base...vanishes when Mr. Cameron clears his throat, snapping me out of my reverie of the fall morning a year ago.

"But I do know that our big brothers wouldn't want us to keep going like this. I'm sure your big brother would want you to try to walk for him." I smile at her, and she finally looks back at me, her dark brown eyes watery with grief, and I offer her my hand.

She looks at my hand and then back at me.

She wipes her tears as Mr. Cameron meets me at my hip, his hands intertwined, ready to help.

"Fine, just five minutes."

12
—

ARI

There's only one more hour left on my shift and I can say I survived my first day back.

All I have to do is deliver their results and discharge them with medication. So far, their tests have come back negative. I look at the following patients on my care list, and one of the names seems familiar.

Rooker, A.

I don't know many Rookers, but if it isn't Enzo Rooker, Danny's close friend, who could it be?

I walk into the room and I see a woman with her child. They are asleep on the bed, cuddled against each other.

As I approach her, her cell phone on her side lights up brightly. I freeze in my tracks when I realize what her wallpaper is. It looks like a family of four, a happy, wide-eyed Enzo Rooker with his wife and two daughters.

This is Rooker's wife.

Holy shit.

I shouldn't be surprised. All service members and their families get treated on base for the most part.

She flutters her eyes open slowly when her phone buzzes with text messages. She lets out a deep breath, stretching her arms upward, and I give her a comforting smile.

"Sorry, I fell asleep. It's been a while since anybody has seen me," she rasps, yawning. She stretches her arms over her head.

"I'm so sorry about that. I'm Ari. I have your daughter's test results. How is she feeling?"

"Ari? Like Ari Alvarez? Paul's sister? Danny's girlfriend?"

Her questions jump at me one after another in shock, ignoring that I told her I had her daughter's results.

"Yes, yes, and yes." I smile.

"Wow, the woman that tied down Danny Rider. I feared that man would always live the bachelor life and never settle down," she jokes, crossing her arms.

I laugh as I grab a stool and sit next to her.

"I'm just as shocked as you are."

"Huh." She bobs her head as if she's impressed. "Well..." She looks at her sleeping daughter, pushing her hair out of her face. She has red hair and freckles on her nose.

She's adorable.

"Her fever broke about ten minutes ago after she was swabbed for the flu."

"That's excellent news!" I exclaim. "She's good to go home. The results came back negative. She doesn't have strep or the flu. It's probably just a virus that has to take its course. Tylenol for the fevers and make sure she's getting lots of fluids and rest."

"Well, that's a relief. She'll probably be better in a few days then. Enzo told me I overreact, but I can't help it. Whenever they get sick, I freak out."

"That's understandable. I would be the same way..." My heart sinks when those last few words leave my mouth. I clear my throat; my smile disappears and I try to push the thoughts of losing my baby deep into the back of my head.

It takes me back to the day I went to the doctor's office for the first time, alone because Danny was on deployment and my mother still didn't know.

Maybe I wasn't ready to come back to work.

Noel notices the awkward shift in my behavior and changes the subject.

"Enzo and I met in a bar, just like you and Danny." She stands, grabbing her purse.

Noel has short brown hair, slight silver hair poking from the root, and hazel eyes. She's taller than me.

"You did? Which bar? It wasn't El Devine, was it?" A small laugh escapes me as I roll my eyes, expecting her to refuse.

"It was. It was my bachelorette party." She blushes, raising her brows and shrugging as if the memories are now hitting her. After ten years, Noel still blushes as she thinks of the day she met her husband.

"No way. Wait, your bachelorette party? Like you were engaged to someone else at the time?" I try to control my face.

What a ballsy move.

"I know, I know. I'm not a slut, I promise. Or maybe I was. I don't even know anymore. We've been together ten years already."

She lets herself get lost in the recollection. She stares at the ceiling and lets her feet hang over the bed.

"I literally had my engagement ring on my finger when he came up. I had a shirt that said *bride to be*, and that still didn't stop him. I had *I'm taken* written all over me. But Navy SEALS are stubborn as hell, which I'm sure you've realized by now." She finally looks at me, shaking her head with a giddy curve of a smile.

"Danny Rider? Stubborn? No way," I say sarcastically as the blue-eyed operator enters my vision. The night I saw him drinking alone at El Devine in his baseball cap, I should have noticed he was a broken soul then, but I didn't. I was too mesmerized by his presence.

"I think you're with the most stubborn one out of them all. Danny is...he really isn't bad like I know he thinks he is. He is the most giving, even if he won't admit or see it in himself. I will say this. I've never seen him so consumed by anything or anyone in his life that wasn't his job."

Butterflies swirl in my stomach.

"How long have you known Danny?" The way she talks about him, I feel like she's known him her entire life.

"As long as I've known my husband. Almost ten years." She sighs.

I purse my lips.

"Enzo is wise, the peacemaker of the team. He holds everyone together when the morale is low. I love that about my husband. He tries to keep the team from killing each other when times get tough. Kane is the golden retriever, sensitive yet intense when he needs to be. And Lopez...well, he's the youngest one out of the group and has a lot of growing up to do, but as far as I know, he's a goofball. A Mexican cowboy from Texas."

She knows them all so well. I only genuinely know Danny and Kane. Lopez and Rooker are mysteries.

Wait, she's been a military spouse *for ten years*?

"You've been living this military lifestyle of constant deployments for ten years?"

I've only been with Danny for a few months, and it's all too much. The constant worry, the anxiety I feel whenever I look at my front door. I can't handle it.

"Yeah, ten years have flown by. It's funny because I told him the night we met I didn't ever see myself being tied down to a man in the military. Yet he charmed me as soon as I looked into his hazel eyes. I told him," she lifts her index finger, "one, I'm with someone already. Two, I will never date a military man. And you know what he did?"

"Oh, Lord, what did that man do?" My eyes circle in curiosity.

"He said, 'One, I don't care—engaged ain't official. And two, you won't date one, but, baby girl, you'll marry one after tonight.'"

Damn.

I clap my hands, raising my eyebrows, fighting the curve of my lips.

"So, he whisked me away from my girlfriends. We talked and danced all night until El Devine closed. I've never connected with a man so fast. I felt like crap because I should have felt guilty about it, but I didn't at the end of the night. I ended it with my ex-fiancé the next day."

"Is that usually how it goes with these men? Fast-paced?"

"Honestly, it's cliché, but yes. But I think it's for a good reason. These men who serve our country are almost always gone, depending on the type of job they have, of course, but this life is hard and it makes you appreciate every second you have together because you don't know when it'll be your last. I think that's why things tend to be more fast-paced."

I'm just sitting in this chair, soaking every word Noel shares with me. I don't know if I want to be with someone who's always gone.

I know I want Danny, though.

The Navy will always have the upper hand in our relationship, demanding his skills and taking time away from our normal life at home.

"You don't know if they'll be gone on training, missions, deployments. It's hard on the wives, especially our children. I've been begging him to leave the Navy, but it's an argument I won't win. He almost died this last time." She chokes up and takes a deep breath, closing her eyes. She massages her brows with her fingers before collecting her emotions.

"I've come to accept he's retiring in the Navy. It only took me ten years to accept it."

She opens her eyes and looks at me with a comforting smile.

"Thank you, Ari."

"What for?"

"Enzo told me Paul's little sister helped save his life in Iraq. You gave me my husband back, alive. Thank you. I don't know what I would do without him. He's my other half."

She looks at me straight into my brown eyes, and I feel a wave of confidence in my skills.

"I will be forever grateful to you for that." She nods, crossing her arms over her chest.

"I don't blame you for feeling that way. I've only been with Danny for less than a year, and I'm already intimidated by his schedule. I-I'm not sure I can do this. I'm not sure if I can continue being worried like this. Especially after my brother's death. This life is hard, just like you said."

She relaxes her posture by lying back in the hospital bed, studying me. I have to gather her discharge paperwork before she can leave.

"Your feelings are completely valid..." She pauses, intertwining her fingers and relaxing them on her lap. "But I'll tell you something." She bites the inside of her cheek.

"Yes?"

"If you leave Danny, it'll destroy him. He loves you. That man is so in love with you; he's in dire cavernous trouble with how he feels about you."

I can't help it, but even Noel can say those three words for Danny, and he still hasn't.

He has told me time and time again he isn't a man of words, but a man of actions. He doesn't have to say it. I know the way he feels about me. At least, that's what I tell myself.

I clear my throat.

"Well, Noel, I will be back with your discharge paperwork so you can get home to your other baby and husband," I tell her as I reach for the doors.

"Thank you, Ari."

I give her a nod in response, flashing a smile, and walk toward the nurses' station.

I palm my lower belly, feeling that same pit of anxiety I've been trying to escape.

"You'll never guess what case I'm working on right now." Lori drops her clipboard on the counter desk and rubs her eyes, frustrated.

"Oh no, you need help?" I offer.

"No, I'll be fine."

"Then what is it?"

She looks at me, furrowing her brows so hard, trying not to laugh.

"A Mason jar got stuck somewhere."

"What? Like where?"

"Somewhere the sun doesn't shine."

I gasp, holding my hands over my mouth. This is the first time I've heard about this.

"Like...in the bu—"

She cuts me off, placing her head on the counter so I can't see her anymore.

"Yes," she squeaks through a heavy breath.

Her forehead rests on her forearms as she squats down, stretching as a frustrated groan releases.

"How did it not break?" I ask, lowering my voice closer to her ears. Well...this is a first.

She lifts her head so her chin rests on her forearms, pieces of hair land on her face, and she blows air from her mouth to clear them away.

"By the grace of God."

13

———

ARI

My feet ache, my back hurts, and the scars I carry on my stomach still hurt.

It's been two months, and I can still feel the wounds like I was stabbed yesterday. I think it will take me forever to heal from this...even longer mentally. It's seven at night and the sky has multiple shades of purple, pink, orange, and blue. I have a beautiful view of the sky as I make the drive home.

Lori was right. Doctor Reese was an absolute pain to be around. I miss Doctor Golds. She was a fantastic doctor and now we're stuck with the Grinch. He's very picky with his version of protocols and scheduling. It was ridiculous. He even tried to keep me past my scheduled hours and go over time today, but Lori quickly stepped in, reminding him it was my birthday, so he let me go.

Nothing too crazy happened today at work. There were no code strokes, nobody died, and everyone who came in was discharged or hospitalized.

Everyone lived, so it's a good day.

I haven't heard any phone calls from my mom wishing me a happy birthday and I find it odd. She never forgets my birthday. I haven't spent too much time with my mom since the attack. I've been self-isolating, but not entirely.

Danny's been there since I was hospitalized and he's been there through my night terrors. He killed my abuser and sent the other one to prison.

Every night around three in the morning, I wake up screaming, a Grim Reaper freshly haunting my mind, and Danny is quick to hold me until my anxiety attacks subside.

I'm in love with him, but something else fucks with my head, and it's our future. Our future remains uncertain. I'm unsure if I want to be with someone who's always gone. I'm unsure I want to be with someone who might not come home alive. I don't want to be stuck waiting for any man or worrying about him.

I'm not being fair. Or am I?

I lost my brother to the same job Danny holds so high.

It's not like he's just choosing to be gone. He has an obligation to the Navy. To his work that has been engraved into him since he was a child by his parents.

Danny puts his life on the line every day at work. He saves people and kills people.

What if I'm too broken to enjoy our growing relationship? What if I'm too fucked up to be loved now?

I'm about five minutes from my house and haven't heard from Danny either. I wasn't sure if he'd be stuck working late or if he had any other plans.

I pull into my house, and my stomach drops when I realize Danny's not there.

I park my car and look at myself in the mirror. I have my usual day-to-day makeup on, and my short, straight black hair falls past my shoulders now. It's growing back slowly.

When I make it to the door, I tilt my head to the side, confused when I realize it's already open and soft music's playing in the background.

My eyebrows quirk when I realize the music sounds so familiar. It's one of Danny's and my favorite songs by Cody Jinks.

I get anxious with excitement. I push the door forward as sweat nervously unfolds inside my clothes. As I swing open the door entirely, it slowly reveals Danny standing in all-black clothing with flowers in his hands.

I inspect the rest of my home to find a big group of familiar faces beaming happily at me. My living room is full of our family and friends. Lit candles surround my floor, along with pink balloons.

"No Words" by Cody Jinks plays and my world stops. Especially when I see the 6 foot 6 Navy SEAL holding the brightest pink tulips I'd ever seen. Those big hands, which I love so much, curl gently around the flowers.

Mr. Danny Rider looks flustered when my eyes lock on to his mesmerizing blue ones. I don't think I've ever seen Danny blush until tonight.

My mother, Emilia, Harry, and Meredith stand to his left behind him, and Danny's entire team is on the right side, behind him.

Kane looks at me with a beer in his hands, and a hardened gaze, and I turn away so fast. The last time I saw him was bittersweet. He tried to kiss me.

Rooker stands tall next to his beautiful wife, and two twin daughters hold on to him with giddy smiles.

Lopez stands next to Zeke and...Violet?!

I'm left completely speechless. My eyes get glossy and tears pour out of me as I gasp. I palm my face with my hands on both cheeks. I look over all the bright faces in the room and break into soft giggles.

He did this all for me?

"Happy Birthday!" they shout simultaneously.

"Oh my gosh..." I murmur, excited.

Danny walks over to me. He pulls me into his chest and lifts my chin. People clap behind him and I swear I can hear Lopez whistling loud.

The man that I love to hate smirks sinfully. I know this look.

He's going to kiss me for the first time in a while. I close my eyes and tiptoe to meet his height more easily, bracing myself for the anticipated clash.

When his lips meet mine, I cry even harder. He moves against me, slow, soft, and patient. Butterflies thrash inside my stomach, and fire ignites between us as his lips suck mine.

A quiet groan escapes his throat, and only I can hear it.

"Surprise." He smiles against my lips and heat explodes inside of my chest.

"You did all this for me?" I whisper against his beard.

I reach for the flowers, but he tugs them away before I can touch them.

He shrugs at the same time his devilish smirk resurfaces on his beautiful face.

"Maybe. Or maybe we share the same birthday and these flowers are for me."

I roll my eyes at him, pushing him away from me. He laughs as I purse my lips together, trying to control the mess of emotions that threaten to complicate my birthday celebration.

"I know your birthday is March 27th."

This means so much. This was the grandest of gestures. I've been isolating myself from everyone for the past month and seeing the people I care about come together at once feels so good. He locks his lips with mine again and I get lost in him, forgetting where we are. He does that to me.

"Oh, get a room already! I want to drink without having to look over my shoulder to see if your tongues are down each other's throats," Meredith shouts, crossing her arms with a wine-glass in her hand.

Everyone bursts into laughter, but not my mom. She's conservative as ever still and rolls her eyes, shaking her head disapprovingly at Meredith's outburst.

I step aside from Danny and glare at her. Everyone approaches us ecstatically. Violet drags me by my arm into the center of my living room and hugs me tight. It feels great to be reunited with one of my patients. A patient that has turned into a close friend of mine.

Happy birthday wishes pour out of everyone's mouths, and I'm trying to engage in every conversation thrown at me left and right.

I look over Emilia's shoulder, and Danny stands with a glass of whiskey. He lifts the glass to his lips and winks.

I mouth the words *thank you* to him, and I'm smiling so hard my cheeks are cramping.

For the first time since the attack, I'm happy.

I'm okay.

14

———

ARI

We're sitting on my couch in the living room.

Danny, Kane, Rooker, Lopez, and Zeke stand outside on my front porch. Danny and Rooker are smoking ciga-rettes, as they're all deep into a conversation. I'm watching them through the large window that allows me to see my front yard. It's my favorite place in the house to relax and read books when I have a view like that.

"Violet, I still can't believe you're here. How the hell are you?" I ask her. Violet has healed, at least physically. I'm not sure about the battles she has to endure mentally.

"I'm doing better." She sighs, drinking a sip of her beer.

"And you're here with Zeke?"

I see the way they look at each other. There is definitely some-thing going on.

She nods.

"He has helped me in a lot of ways. We're friends," she murmurs while taking another swig of her beer, and I know there's something more than she's letting on. As she drinks more,

111

she looks through the living room window. The blinds are pushed up entirely, and my dark green curtains are pushed on either side.

Nobody looks at someone like that if there isn't intimacy being shared.

I want to bring up Damon, but how? I want to share my condolences. Her story broke my heart, and I prayed for his return every night. Knowing the outcome *kills me.*

I don't want to imagine what it's doing to her.

"I'm sorry about your baby." Violet turns to me with a glimpse of sadness in her eyes.

I stiffen when she mentions my son.

The thought of looking down at my c-section scar makes me cringe. I don't want to talk about it. I'm instantly angry, curling my fingers on my scrub top, but I know it isn't fair. She didn't do anything.

I can't think of the child I lost because a part of me *blames myself.*

Maybe I should have put Shane in jail way sooner and not let our history or his upbringing affect my judgment. I was stupid. So fucking stupid to think he was not capable of murdering me.

Then another part of me...

Blames Danny.

As I turn away from Violet, I drink some of the sangria he made me. I give her a quick nod in acknowledgment.

I look out the window and find Kane's attention on me. The organ inside my chest skips a beat as a wave of guilt washes over my mind.

He flares his nostrils, biting down. I can see that his jaw flexes when he watches me, but it's short-lived. Then he looks back to Lopez.

I break away from him so quickly before anyone can notice

the glance we shared. I look around to see if anyone caught that and realize I'm in the clear. Rooker pats Danny on the back like he's proud of him, and I wonder what they're talking about.

I need to tell Danny about Kane's confession, and I will tonight.

It isn't right. I know it isn't right. A small part of me thinks about Kane, but I'm too overwhelmed with grief to give it any more thought. He will always have a special place in my heart, but he's starting to blur those lines. I'm barely holding on. All I know is that I care about him. How couldn't I?

He's always been sunshine.

"All right, girls... I'm going to shoot my shot with Mr. Slaughter over there. Wish me luck." Meredith gets off my couch and starts going out the front door. Something small slithers through my emotions when she begins her conquest to Kane... and I wouldn't say I like it.

I shrug it off.

"You don't need it. Go, get him, girl," Emilia eggs her on playfully.

I fake a smile as I turn back to Violet. "You're out of the military now?"

"Technically, yes, but I just couldn't do it anymore. I feel like I don't have a place there anymore. It feels meaningless now that Damon is gone," Violet whispers and chokes up when his name leaves her shaky lips. She looks away from me and stares at the floor.

"I might join again when I feel like I'm ready."

There are no words. I have no words to give because there aren't any.

She twirls her beer in her hand as I embrace her. I place my hand on her shoulder comfortingly before I let her go.

"So I'm going to ask you again."

My eyebrows raise.

"Have you ever experienced love at first sight?"

She asked me this when we first met in Iraq.

She gives me a playful smile, like she already knows the answer to her own question. She looks at Danny through the window and then back to me, giddy.

I turn my gaze to Danny. His dark blond hair is styled and combed the way I love it. Zeke and Rooker also roar with laughter, drinking more of their beers down. He's smiling, laughing, and looks more at peace than I've ever seen him. Before he revealed the gruesome details about my brother's death, he was killing himself slowly with alcohol. His confession about feeling responsible for his death haunted him. And now?

He's happier.

Shitty things keep getting thrown into our lives, but Danny has been making sure that I'm always okay since the attack. He's been taking care of me, putting me first. He even took a leave of absence and used up all his free days.

We're healing each other.

Small white flurries of fog escape from their mouths as they laugh. I feel relief that Danny has been able to stay strong for the both of us. He hasn't spent time with his team since the attack like this.

Heat swarms my cheeks and chest.

"Love at first sight with Grim Reaper...the deadliest special operator in the entire military? I'm impressed. I was always told he had a heart of ice and skills of a cold-blooded killer, incapable of committing to anything more than his career." She tries again.

"Yes...yes, it was love at first sight. At least for me, it was." I smile, biting my lip as I remember when he told me he didn't dance at El Devine. We haven't said those three words to each other, but *he* doesn't have to. He shows it enough. He isn't a man of words like he told me once before. He's a man of action. A clip of nostalgia plays in my head when I remember wearing my cowboy boots, ordering a daiquiri while a mysterious tattooed man wearing a black hat watched me.

"That night at El Devine changed my life forever. I knew I loved him then and I know I love him now."

KANE

"Oh fuck, Kane!" she moans my name, and I smirk without mercy, intensifying each stroke, deep and unforgiving. The sounds of our skin slapping against each other make me want to come even faster. But I want to enjoy this. I want to soak in every fucking second because I've wanted to do this since the day I met Ari.

I'm fucking her hard, fast, and desperate. I have her bent over, and her short, dark hair is sprawled over her back.

I push her face deeper into the pillow with my hand, rough but gentle enough not to hurt her. I'm muffling her sounds and cries. No distractions. I don't need to hear her voice. I need to get lost in my mind instead.

I'm savoring every second, releasing the built-up tension from the woman of my dreams.

I close my eyes, and a deep groan releases from my throat as I get lost in my thoughts even more.

I finally reach my climax when I see her beautiful face, and my thrusts slow down as everything comes to a standstill. I'm breathing heavily, sweat dripping down my chest as I face the ceiling, eyes shut tight as I finish coming. I needed this. It was good, but...not good enough.

A smile reaches my face when Ari's beautiful brown eyes come into my head, and I feel a bit of relief come off my shoulder. The weight of watching the one you admire continuously breaks your heart.

But then the fantasy sinks deep, disappearing when Meredith interrupts my thoughts.

"That was fun," she purrs seductively.

I pull out of her quickly, grinding my teeth when I realize my imagination is just that—a fantasy in my head.

My body was here, but my mind was trapped somewhere else in Ari's beauty.

I should feel guilty, but I don't.

I fucked Meredith, Ari's best friend, and all the while, I was picturing Ari instead.

Her hair, her voice, her body.

Danny is one lucky motherfucker.

If I can't have Ari, I have to do something else, *someone else* to distract me from the heartache it is to watch the one you want, the one you're deeply in love with, be with someone else.

I'd rather take a dozen bullets to my chest than continue watching Ari kiss him.

Danny doesn't deserve her. He's my best friend, but he's not her match. He's ruthless...whereas she's kind, sweet, fragile. A goddess in my eyes. She needs to be handled gently and with care.

I pull the condom off myself and sit on the edge of the bed, keeping my distance from Meredith. I can feel the bed shift when she moves closer, and I stiffen. She doesn't make me feel even a fraction of what Ari does to me.

I'm done hiding my feelings for her. It's been bottling up for a year now, and I feel like if I don't do something to try to move on, I'll be lost.

Danny's my best friend. He'll kill me if he discovers I told Ari I'm in love with her. I would be lying if I said I'm not afraid of him or scared of the things he'll do when he finds out, *but I am.*

I've seen just how dangerous and sadistic this man can be when he needs to be. That's why he's called Grim fucking Reaper.

I stare out Meredith's window, the moonlight shining through, leaving hints of blue rays. I brush my black hair back, letting out a sigh.

I left Ari's party early because I needed to. It *fucking hurts* to be around them. Watching someone you're in love with be with someone else is torture.

I feel Meredith's hands start at my mid-back and she moves them up, trailing her fingers on my skin, over my shoulders, and down to the front of my chest.

She kisses my neck slowly three times before I can feel her lips on my ear. "Let's do that again." She murmurs lustfully.

The bliss I felt after getting lost in my fantasy sinks down even further. I gently take her hands off of me.

I walk away from her bed and throw the used condom in her trash can that lies in the corner of her room.

I'm quiet and trying to disguise the fact that I feel no connection with Meredith. She's kneeling on the bed, naked, playing with her hair, hoping I'll give in to her request.

Her deep-toned skin and amber eyes are enchanting. Still, I feel like no one compares to the sweetheart that's Ari Alvarez, and I resent it. I resent the sweetheart who's forbidden.

"I'm sorry, Meredith, but I've gotta go. I have to work early in the morning, in about four hours, actually." I reject her as I pull my jeans back on, sliding in one foot at a time.

It's not a lie. I did have to go back home. Work never stops.

She frowns and sits, covering herself with her blankets as I button my jeans.

"Oh...okay, I get it," Meredith says, disappointed.

I've hurt her feelings. I get it, I know, but this will take me some time. I want to take this slow. Maybe I can move on with Meredith.

Could carrying on with her help me through this?

"This was fun. I'll call you tomorrow." I lean in closer to her, shirtless. My hands are on each side of Meredith's waist, the bed sinking as the muscles in my triceps constrict as I close in the distance.

Her eyes light up with hope as I peck on her cheek. There's no emotion to it. There's no emotion because they're all somewhere else...all for Ari.

Fuck, I'm an asshole.

I want her so badly, but Meredith and I hit it off well at her birthday party. She's outspoken and wild—the total opposite of Ari. I didn't know this was the way my night was going to turn out. I hadn't planned it to, but I'm glad it did. It's been a minute since I had a girlfriend. I don't want a girlfriend just yet. I'm waiting until I'm certain of the next girl...because I want to make sure my next one will be future wife.

Meredith smiles. Her smooth skin glows as she blushes. I back away from her, grab my shoes and finish dressing.

I need to move on...so I slept with Meredith. I need to try at least, right?

"You better." Meredith bites her bottom lip before lying on her pillow.

I wink at her as I throw on my shirt. She lives far from my house, so I have a long way home.

I almost didn't give in, but I'm having the worst case of blue balls since I've been home from Iraq.

Nothing will relieve it, truly, unless it's from my favorite nurse.

I walk out of Meredith's house, quickly greeted by the December winds.

Fuck, it's cold.

I start jogging as another harsh wind makes my hair fall into my eyes. As soon as I get home, I'm turning on the heater and knocking out.

I'm halfway to my motorcycle when my phone rings.

Fuck. I don't have to look at it to know it's work. I'm not surprised that I'm getting alerts this late at night; it always comes at the oddest hours. Another mission...another deployment.

My contract will be up soon, and I'm counting down the days now because I don't want to end up like Paul. I stop on the frozen grass, my boots crunch, and I take my phone out.

16

ARI

Saying goodbye to my friends was harder than I thought. I was so happy to see them celebrate another year of life with me. I almost didn't make it to this day.

Soon, I'll be making a trip to my brother's tombstone to talk to him, to catch him up on how much of a rollercoaster my life has been since he's passed. Also, to reassure him of how much I love his Bronco and that I take it to get deep cleaned monthly. I wonder if he'll teach his nephew how to play guitar in heaven and if it'll be a Sublime tune or Mana.

God, how this fucking hurts.

"Good night, Mom. Thank you for coming." She squeezes me tight, and I hold my breath for a second.

"Happy birthday again, *mija*. I'm happy to see you're doing better."

"Thanks, Mom."

My mom helped me clean up the house after almost everyone was gone.

Danny still chats with Lopez and Zeke on the front porch.

They both begged him to keep drinking longer, but he refused. He hasn't gotten drunk since that one night when he confessed everything to me and I'm so proud of him.

I know he has a long way to go, but it's a start.

"It's because of Danny, isn't it? He hasn't left your side through it all, has he?" she asks, holding my hands in hers.

I watch my possessive Navy SEAL give Lopez a brotherly hug. I wonder what they're talking about. I study Lopez's mouth, trying to read his lips and decipher his words.

I'm cleaning up leftover dishes in the kitchen. I'm incredibly exhausted, but it was so worth it.

Finally, I'm able to make out some words along the lines of, *"I look up to you, man."*

I break away from eavesdropping. I shouldn't pry, but I admire how much everyone looks for guidance through Danny.

Lopez is the youngest one at around twenty-five.

"Ma..." I still get uncomfortable talking about my life with my boyfriend or anything regarding our relationship.

I hug my mother goodnight.

She leaves my house and bids Danny, Lopez and Zeke farewell before walking to her car.

I'm yawning through every motion as I clean the leftover dishes. Tonight was so much fun. I reunited with all my friends and family...all because of Danny.

For the first time in a long time, I've forgotten about the trauma I've been through this entire year, and I can't thank him enough.

From losing Paul, going to Iraq as a civilian contracted nurse, to falling for my brother's best friend, to getting pregnant and losing our baby so violently in one fucking year...

Tonight was a breath of fresh air and it felt good to forget I was broken, even if it was for only a few hours.

I finish with the last dish and glance over to the front of my house, looking through my windows.

Zeke has left with Violet, leaving only Lopez and Danny, and they're smoking, sitting on the chairs on the front porch, deep in a conversation.

I don't want to bother him. I want him to enjoy his time with his friends as well. I feel like today was much needed for the both of us.

I take a deep breath and shut the faucet off, drying my hands with a kitchen towel. I'm tired, my muscles ache, my mind running miles per hour with uncertainty and I can't shake that something is missing...

Will I ever be whole again?

I shut the kitchen lights off and walk into the dark hallway. I don't even make it to the first door when my phone buzzes against my thigh from inside my pocket.

I think Meredith forgot something. She always does, but I remember doing a quick sweep after everyone left and didn't see anything.

My fingers search for my phone in my pocket, my fingers gripping it when I touch the cold plastic phone cover in the dark. I take it out, *not expecting* to see the name reflect on my screen saver.

> Kane: Happy birthday to my favorite nurse.
> Good night, Ari Alvarez.

I re-read the text repeatedly at least five times.

I blush red, my fingers flick with hot nerves but I don't respond. He didn't speak one word to me tonight but he decided a text is more fitting? What does he expect me to say?

Knowing there are feelings behind his words...it isn't right.

I turn my phone off and touch my lips like a gasp will escape my throat. My fingertips console the bewilderment I feel on top of my lips.

I won't entertain Kane.

He left my party early with Meredith, hand in hand, lust glowing in their eyes. She kissed his neck as they left my front porch. It doesn't take a scientist to know what they must be up to tonight...so why is he texting me?

I push out thoughts of Kane and keep walking in the dark, my feet thudding against the floor softly. Each step I take has me puzzled. I'm about to open the door to my bedroom but decide against it. I palm my wooden door like I'm about to push it forward, but I can't go through with it. I don't want to go to sleep just yet. I don't want to cry myself to sleep like I usually do every night, fearing that Nora will be outside my window twirling a knife like a game. I don't want to drift to sleep, terrified I'll be dreaming of my brother's guitar.

I used to enjoy hearing that song; it used to be good nostalgia for our childhood memories, but now it's an ominous sound that has me quivering with trepidation.

I don't want to see my brother anymore, at least not right now. If I hear his guitar, it only means Death is nearby, and that's...that's terrifying.

I head toward my office room instead.

Since Danny refuses to let me out of his sight, I turned an extra room into a place of work for us.

I walk into the room, and instead of turning on the room lights, I reach for the lamp in the corner of the wooden table.

I turn the little black dial until it clicks twice, soft yellow light illuminating the room, revealing a cozy space.

It's small but welcoming.

I have my diplomas from high school and college and my RN certification perfectly framed, exhibiting my accomplishments on one side of a wall.

Danny made a shadow box of our son's beanie, a picture of his little feet blackened prints, and a 'Future Navy SEAL' onesie inside. It hangs on another side of a wall, displayed perfectly in the middle. It's the first thing I see against the light blue colored walls, and it makes me happy. Danny is good at those things. He's exceptional at building things, doing handy work around the house, and always taking out the trash for me.

He said he didn't want to be a father but he had bought him a crib, clothes, and a guitar so he could follow in Paul's footsteps. Even then, he knew it would be a boy. After I told him we were pregnant, he did all that the morning after.

Now, all of it sits inside storage.

I stare at the shadow box. I feel like I'm watching what should have been my future hang on the wall instead of living it. It does something to me. I'm in a trance, my thoughts running wild and I feel something twitch inside me.

It's an ugly, sickening, unfamiliar darkness I don't recognize. I've never felt it before.

Instead of feeling sad...I'm angry. I don't want to feel this pain anymore. I refuse to let Shane win.

My fists clench at my sides, and everything stings. I'm going through the stages of grief all over again.

"Ari."

Danny's shielding voice interrupts my lucid thoughts, but not enough to make me move my eyes.

"Yes?"

"Everything okay?"

I glare at the wall, tearing my gaze away from the frame, refusing to answer his question.

I look down at the floor, my eyes pacing nervously against the hardwood floors.

"Look at me," he demands, and I take a few seconds before I give in to him.

I turn around and a tear escapes me. It rolls down my cheek, fast moving against my lips.

"I need to forget," I concede with a harsh tone that breaks at the end. I swallow the growing edge in my throat, looking at the man I love deeply towering over me.

"Forget?" His jaw clenches as he lifts his hand, tucking a piece of my hair behind my ears, but he doesn't stop there. He caresses one side of my face with his palm, his thumb brushing against my cheek soothingly.

I close my eyes, relishing every second he touches me before he pulls away like he has been since the attack. He refuses to touch me these days, *really touch me*...and I resent it.

"I need to forget the bad. I don't want to feel like this anymore. I don't want to remember anything," I breathe painfully. "Danny...it's still my birthday," I whisper as another tear falls down my cheek, through closed eyelids, and I tighten them harder until I've given it all my strength and it burns.

He stops caressing me, about to retreat from my face, but I grab his hand softly, stopping him.

"Help me forget a little longer," I plead, my eyebrows pinching desperately as I inhale scathingly, narrowing my eyes at him.

Danny's face hardens and his whole body goes rigid at my request. With his other hand, he brushes his hand through his dark blonde hair, contemplating. His blue eyes darken, and I step closer, daring him.

"I won't be able to control myself with you."

"Then don't. I don't want you to," I tell him, and he finally moves his hand again, his thumb brushing my bottom lip, and he hums dauntingly.

I feel like my words struck him so profoundly because it's a look he gave me before when it was my first time.

I can sense his unease when his jaw contorts, as if he's lost in his thoughts.

He closes his eyes as more tears fall down my cheeks. He leans down, and I can feel his cool breath, scented woodsy, rebellion, and whiskey.

Danny's scent alone has me aching for his touch.

His lips brush across mine, softly at first. His beard tickles my chin and I can't help but love when it does that.

Everything about him, every little thing, will always draw me to him.

He dangerously grabs the back of my hair, pulling it as his tongue demands entrance inside. I grant him immediate access and return with my own.

His kisses feel different than ever before, and I can't quite put the words to describe him, but he has me breathless, panting. The arousal that pulses with need won't stop and it just gets stronger when he squeezes my ass, pulling my waist closer to him, feeling *him*.

He's hard with anticipation and greed.

"I'll help you forget everything..." He grabs me aggressively by my waist, pushing me against the desk, and my heart skips a beat from his voracious need. "But me." He turns me around hard, fast, and determined.

He lifts me high in the air, my feet leave the floor, and I'm in the air for a second or two before he sits my ass on the desk.

I start to breathe heavily with anticipation. Danny looks like a beast who hasn't been fed in years.

He pulls down my scrub pants fast, deliberately, until they're on the floor. Goosebumps pebble over my skin.

I'm already wet, ready, I'm so fucking ready.

Make me forget Danny. Make me forget all the darkness that keeps threatening to destroy us both all year.

"I won't ever let you forget how fucking much I worship you."

I need him. I miss him. I miss when he can't stop devouring me, even if it comes with his sadism.

He palms his hands on either side of me on the desk and kisses my lips roughly, with need, and there's nothing in this world that can stop him.

"I've missed you," I breathe through our feral kisses.

He crashes himself against me, his tongue slipping in momentarily before he pulls back, but barely. He smirks against my lips, and his growl sends me a whirlwind of adrenaline.

We're both in a frenzy to feel each other.

"You miss getting fucked by me, baby?" His voice is deep and beguiling. He kisses me one last time before one of his hands goes to my throat. My eyes widen with lust, watching the dangerous, forbidden man who begged me to stay away from him, fierce with need. He grips my throat hard, choking me; the last breath I held escapes me like a gasp.

"Y-Yes." I push that one word out when I realize the pain he promised me has returned. I never thought this would become a part of me...but Danny showed me it was a revelation hidden...a part of me that I will always welcome, unashamed.

He showed me it was always there within me like a candle, waiting to be lit by the right man.

I'm naked from the waist down, and he hums sinfully. His eyes trail down from my eyes, my lips, my breasts, and then my bare core.

He loosens his grip when he sees I'm ready for him to claim me the way we both yearn for, like we need this to survive.

"I want to pretend I'm okay just a little longer," I murmur through his chokehold. "Like the past two months didn't happen. Like I'm still me."

He hesitates, and I can see that he's debating to take me the way he truly desires, and I feel like he's going to stop.

"Don't you dare treat me like I'm broken tonight," I taunt him. "At least just for right now."

He deadpans but then quickly shifts into the man who has always intimidated me with one look, taking my breath away.

He won't treat me like I'm fragile and I'm internally burning with anticipation as I read his body language.

He's back.

He kneels, his lips hovering over my clit, and I bite my lip anxiously. I haven't felt this intimacy from him for what feels like years and I think I might die if he doesn't act soon.

I want to cherish this moment. Avoid every single dark thought that has been eating me alive since I lost my baby.

Since Shane and Nora scarred me forever.

"I don't deserve you, but I'm keeping you anyway," he tells me as he inserts two fingers in, slowly making me arch my back from the unexpected entrance.

His fingers go in deeper, moving in and out. My nipples harden through my scrubs, and I whimper with pleasure as I feel his familiarity.

The way he glides through me sends me into euphoria.

Forget.

All I want to do is forget.

This seems like the perfect way to feel like I'm still me and not battered with trauma.

Sliding in and out, he murmurs, "Baby, you're so wet and I haven't even started."

Then his fingers disappear, and I'm left conflicted.

I'm breathing heavily, panting hard with lust. His lips brush against my clit and then I feel it. A moan escapes me, loud, when I feel his tongue at my slit, he stops at my clit, touching it, and a bolt of nirvana strikes me. My head falls back, and I swallow the screams.

"Your cunt is only mine to taste, to fuck, to break."

"Please," I beg, closing my eyes shut tight.

Then he towers over me again, and I'm confused.

"Stop teas—"

"I know it's been a while, but don't forget who you've missed, Ari. Do I need to remind you of the way I like to fuck? Who exactly owns this cunt?" My eyes circle when I feel his lips on mine again, moving ferociously, and then he pulls my hair tight, and I gasp against his lips. "Let me see you cry for me, baby."

I don't want him to stop.

He tilts my head back so I'm looking at the ceiling. My neck is exposed as he hovers over it.

"Say it, Ari. Who does this cunt belong to? I want to hear you scream it." His breath lingers on my neck.

His fingers tighten against my scalp, pulling hard again, and I squint from the pain. But it doesn't hurt. What hurts more is the fact that he stopped kissing me.

"It belongs to you," I tell him through ragged breaths.

He pulls again a third time and a harsh moan escapes my lips, and I tighten my legs wrapped around his waist in response, pulling the front of him until his bulge against my heat.

I miss his monstrous size.

"Scream my name," he demands, his mouth against my ear. My clit pulsates with need.

"Danny!" I scream loud, but it comes out like a high-pitched moan.

He rests his forehead on the side of my head, satisfied.

"That's right, baby. It's all mine." His tongue trails the skin on my neck to the side of my cheek. Then he lets my hair go, and he's back down between my legs. "My little angel cries so pretty." He lifts my legs over his shoulders, so now my calves are on each side of his face and then he devours me to the point of seeing golden sparkles. I close my eyes and the grandest of smiles reach my face.

He's so magnetic. My heart is beating, pounding hard for him. His beard pricks the side of my thighs and damn how I missed that.

He's fucking me with his tongue and playing with my clit with his fingers so right, so good.

My elbows are the only thing keeping me from collapsing from the orgasm, threatening to obliterate me with each flick and stroke of his tongue and finger. He removes his fingers and replaces them with his mouth instead.

He takes my entire clit into his mouth and sucks on it.

Oh... God.

Each suck has me close to riding his face.

"Oh..."

Then, he bites down on it so precisely that instead of pain, my back arches from the intense pleasure.

My entire body shakes from that one nibble, and I scream.

"Oh fuck, Danny! I'm about to finish."

I snake my hands through his hair, pushing his face down harder onto my clit, and he smiles against my pussy.

"No, you're not. I didn't allow you to finish just yet, little angel." He stands, retracting his mouth.

He steps closer until his waist is between my thighs instead of his mouth. He rips open my scrub top, exposing the skin on my chest and bra. It had buttons that started from my collarbones down to my midsection on my abdomen, but they're long gone now. The buttons dislodge into the air, falling onto the floor, and my breasts jump up and down from the sudden exposure.

Danny stiffens; his blue eyes drawn to my chest. He's captivated by my bare breasts and then he pulls my bra down to my ribs to where my boobs are out of my bra, spilling over.

Then his hands are at my neck, gripping me hard, squeezing me tight like a necklace. Every one of his fingers wraps around my neck, tight, but I can still breathe just fine.

"You'll shatter all over my cock when you finish the first time. The first of many to come for the rest of the night."

"Yes, please."

His hands are still choking my neck when I feel his lips command my mouth. We lose ourselves in each other. Our kisses don't stop; they're fast erotic, and then his tongue dominates mine. I can taste myself on his tongue.

He always wins.

I reach for his belt. I pull it out so fast from his waist, throwing it to the floor when it escapes every loop on his waistband. He still has his all-black shirt on. With one hand still on my neck, choking me, the other pulls down his slacks just enough to expose his massive, thick cock. He strokes himself a few times, positioning the head of his cock right at my entrance.

"Fuck me, Danny," I rasp.

I look up at his beautiful face. He narrows his brows at me and he looks handsome as hell when he looks at me like this. His blue eyes overflow with ecstasy.

Then he pushes the first inches of his length inside me, and I moan, gasping for air and screaming at the intrusion.

"Damn it, Danny, I don't think I'll ever be able to get used to you." I almost try to scooch away from him, but he holds on to me tighter, his fingers digging more into my skin.

"My handprints will be carved into your body by the time I'm done with you," he growls, not missing one beat.

Why do I love it so much when he grips me tight?

It hurts too good.

I'm not used to him anymore. I almost forgot how it feels to have him inside me, stretching me so much to the point I bleed. He hasn't even pushed his entire length inside me yet and an orgasm almost overcomes me.

I try to move myself in a better position, but he secures me tighter, pulling me toward him as he's forcing me to take more of him.

I moan loudly as I swallow my fate.

"It hurts."

"Good. You've always been able to take it. I'm not going to stop until I've claimed what's mine." He groans deep through his broad, muscular chest and then smiles as he watches his cock move deeper inside me. The waistband of his pants is below his dick, hugging his thick, tensed thighs.

"I warned you. Once I start, there's no stopping me from making my little angel fall from heaven on my cock."

I'm trapped. There's no stopping Danny's need to feel me tonight...and I wouldn't have it any other way.

"Fuck." He snarls. As I feel myself continuously drip for him.

I blush when I see that he grinds his teeth impatiently. He's about to lose control, and I'm more than ready.

"Don't hold back," I dare through his chokehold.

He smirks as a wave of exhilaration possesses his body.

"Never have, never fucking will."

Then he ultimately enters, and my head falls back.

My nipples harden from the pleasure and I don't want this ever to end.

He's not soft, he's not gentle, he's unforgiving. Relentlessly fucking me harder and harder. It's so hard that my breasts bounce with each deep, rough stroke. He's pounding me so hard I could fall off the desk. But he holds my body in place with his large hand wrapped around my neck.

I'm close. *Way too close.*

The short hair on my face, breasts, and palms bounce up and down from each strong thrust that sends me up in the air before he pulls us back onto the desk greedily.

"Yes," I shriek with lust. The sensation of having him inside me makes me lose myself, silently begging him for more.

The desk moves underneath me, thundering as the friction beneath the wood scratches at the floor.

It collides with the wall hard and rough, making each thrust of Danny's hips known. Marks and dents appear when his thrusts become more violent.

We're about to break the desk.

Then, the most detrimental sound chime sounds between our skin slapping.

His phone rings, and I almost roll my eyes in annoyance.

For the love of God.

He slows his thrusts, groaning in frustration.

He can't ever miss a call or a text because of his role on the team. Then he pulls out his phone from his pants that are just below his groin, to read the caller ID. He sighs, frustratedly pissed off. Someone is calling him, ending our first time together since the attack.

I hate his job so much at this moment.

He answers the phone, still inside me.

"Hello?" He clenches his jaw tight, looking away from me. One of his hands lets go of me, and I watch him, disappointed. He shifts his wrist vehemently to look at his watch straight forward and not slanted. He looks at the time above his cuff impatiently. His demeanor changes for a second.

"Now? Tonight?" he asks, his brows pinching together, staring at his watch.

I jolt, trying to push myself off of him.

It's such fantastic timing.

I'm midway off him when he puts his phone on his shoulder, muffling the mic and grabbing me angrily.

"Where do you think you're going? You're not going anywhere," he growls, narrowing his eyes at me.

I bite my lip and I don't dare move anymore.

He picks up his pace as he places his phone back on his ear, and I grab a hold of my breasts with one hand for balance.

"Yup, message received," Danny tells the caller, his tone emotionless and rugged.

Then, another deep, harsh thrust. And another and another until he's full-blown breaking my body.

I'm going to come.

He feels so good. His cock hits all the right spots.

But before I come, I am going to make him regret taking this phone call.

I remove his hand from my neck and bring his thumb to my mouth, licking it first, then I place it right above my bottom teeth, then I slowly place the top of my tongue on his like I would the tip of his cock.

His blue eyes light up like he first saw me naked in Iraq, I've got his attention now. I raise my brows at my small victory.

"Yeah, I-I'm listening." He stutters his words and I smirk in satisfaction as he thrusts inside me. He glares at me, shaking his head as a devilish grin tugs at the side of his lips. My eyes widen innocently at him, and I shrug my shoulders.

My mouth closes on his thumb, and I suck on him hard, moving it in and out of my mouth as he fucks me.

He stops his thrusts. He's breathing hard when he realizes what I'm doing.

"I'll be right there." Then he hangs up, scowling, throwing his phone on the desk hard. I wouldn't be surprised if it cracked from how hard he threw it.

He's leaving? *Don't they have other Navy SEALS to bother?!*

"Oh, Ari. You're playing games. You know, I always win."

He turns me around so fast. My ass is off the desk and I'm on my toes. My palms rest on the counter and I curl my fingers at the edge of the desk to stabilize myself. He has me bent over with my ass on his cock, and I'm biting my lip.

"The birthday girl needs to be punished for that." He snarls behind my ear.

Then a hard slap echoes against my ass, and I yelp from the collision. His hands grip my waist on both sides of my hips, hard and tight, positioning me the way he wants. I know the bruises will reflect in the morning.

"I don't know what you're talking about—" He doesn't let

me finish. Another slap on my ass cuts me off, and it burns, and then he's inside me again.

My eyes roll to the back when I feel the deep, fast thrusts, and then I'm shattering when he hits a spot deep inside of me.

"Oh God!" I shout, curling my fingers into my palms against the desk. And I squeeze my hands into fists as the orgasm implodes every single vein with fire. Every nerve flares with sparks of dark euphoric pleasure, and I feel like I'm floating. I moan his name over and over again, but he doesn't let up.

Slap.

Slap.

Slap.

Another harsh slap on my ass as he goes in deeper.

"God can't hear you, little angel. My name is the only one you will ever cry out for."

His pace races with greedy speed, followed by a loud monstrosity of a groan.

He squeezes my thighs to the point another moan escapes me. My hands go to his, tightening around his wrist, scratching his skin as he thrusts like he can't get enough. He inflicted havoc on me like a built-up craving and I was his release.

He's filling me up with his come again, fierce and never-ending voracity. He's making sure I take it all in. I enjoy every second of this devastatingly amazing dark reunion.

He pulls out of me, and everything slowly falls past my inner thighs.

He's watching everything flow on my skin, dripping down, and he hums with satisfaction, pushing some of the fluid back inside me. He licks his lips, then reaches for his pants.

"You know I'm on birth control," I breathe. "I'm on the pill," I admit, trying to recover from my bliss.

"For now," he replies, pulling his pants up.

Heat swirls into my chest. Does this mean what I think it means?

Would he be open to the thought of being a dad again?

He grabs me, turning me around gently. I'm no longer bent over. Instead, I'm standing as tall as my short frame allows me to. I tip-toe when I realize he's changed his demeanor. He's smoother, careful, and slow—the complete opposite of moments ago.

He kisses me with so much passion it sends butterflies through my stomach.

Best birthday ever.

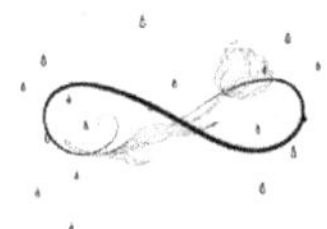

My front door swings open, cold winds blow through and it causes me to shiver. Danny hesitates at the door.

What is it about this man in a military uniform with camo paint on that has me disoriented with lust?

It feels like the time he left me in Iraq. When he went on his mission for Damon and it took me back. I don't want him to leave.

The familiar dreadful emotion of worry and anxiety swirls in my stomach.

The devastating reminder he could end up in a casket like Paul haunts me. It will forever haunt me. I don't like watching him leave because then I'll be sleeping alone to deal with the Grim Reaper visiting me when I sleep, and the constant worry of my boyfriend's safe return.

I can't tell him about Kane now. He needs a clear headspace. I don't need Danny and Kane to get into disagreements when they work on the same team. The thought of his confession hindering their friendship and work... I don't want to imagine them fighting, or worse, while they're out on a mission.

"I'll make it up to you when I get back." Danny stands in the doorway, tucking a knife into his vest. He's in the uniform he uses for his missions with a substantial tan-colored bag slung over his shoulder.

"I hate this," I complain, hugging my velvet, silk sleeping gown to my body to keep warm. I have the heater on, yet I'm still shivering from the cold weather.

"I know."

"Sometimes, I wish I could change my past so my future wouldn't be so hard to live in." I don't know why I said it. It was an intrusive thought. I look up at Danny, my eyes bleeding for comfort. "Are there things you would change about your past?"

He shakes his head.

"I wouldn't...because my past led me to you."

Fuck, I could melt. His past held a lot of darkness, and he still wouldn't change it?

I lean on one side of my hip, biting the inside of my cheek.

"Danny?"

"Yes?"

"I just want to tell you that I'm proud of you. I've noticed the way you've begun to change. I may not love your job, but I love that you try to save everyone you can. And I want to thank you."

"For what?"

"For being the only man in my life that hasn't left me."

"I'm sorry this job takes so much out of me. I'm doing my best not to let it consume everything and anything left of my humanity, but you have everything to do with that. I'm a better man because of you. So, thank you."

"Where are you going? When are you coming back?"

He's silent. That's an answer all on its own. He either can't tell me, or he doesn't know.

Then he smiles. It's a smile that tries to disguise what he's feeling. He feels guilty. Something I wasn't used to seeing. This is the first time I've seen him feel bad about leaving me. That's...*new.*

He drops his bag in the doorway. I stroll toward him, and he closes the distance before I get to the door. He takes two steps forward and grabs me.

He cups both sides of my face and kisses me slowly. Fire fuels every vein that pumps to and from my heart when he touches me. I'm weak when he kisses me. *I'm weak when he looks at me.*

"I'll see you soon." He smiles against my lips before planting another soft kiss on them, and butterflies flutter. My hands find his and I gently squeeze.

I smile, finally opening my eyes to see his light blue ones.

"See you soon."

17

———

DANNY

What a ballsy decision these terrorists have made. It's even more insane to think they can bring this war to us. But oh, how I love their enthusiasm to take me out. I love how they think they can kill me. It's just making this that much more fun.

I get to reap souls.

The thrill of seeing life drain from evil people, sending their souls to my good old friend, Death, is what I thrive on.

And I always win.

Still, I'm upset they ruined my little angel's birthday. I'll be gone for a while because of their need to kill me. This was supposed to be Ari's day, and they took that from me and her.

I will enjoy every moment I get my hands on them and make them regret starting this bounty they have for my head.

I. Can't. Fucking. Wait.

It's the middle of the night and we're about to breach a little house in the middle of nowhere in Georgia. They're just hours away from where I live. They found us fast; our primary mission tonight is to discover how they could get this information quickly.

They're sloppy already and have revealed how evil they can be. They came out on military intelligence's radar when they caused quite a stir at a local bar in town when a couple of women reported being assaulted and raped to the police.

They're dead men.

"Creature, you comfortable up there?"

Operator Creature.

Admiral Ravenmore wasn't lying about him.

Daegan Hannibal, age thirty-five, has dark hair, and tall, built, gray eyes and wears a black mask like the rest of us, except he never takes his off after being captured. No one knows what hides beneath the right side of his face, but rumors say he's scarred horrifically. He's partially blind in his right eye, yet he never misses a shot. He refused to talk about it when he was a prisoner of war. No one knows how he got his injuries, and he doesn't talk about it, nor am I too intrigued to ask. As long as he carries his weight and executes a job well done; I don't give a fuck about his personal life.

The man refused to take a leave of absence when he returned home and was assigned to my team immediately.

He might be more insane than I am.

Creature hides behind a tree somewhere in the distance on a hill, looking for any movement, watching us all like a hawk in the shadows, anticipating.

"Another day in paradise, Reaper," he murmurs with a low chuckle.

"Roger that," I reply.

I'm the first to enter. We don't explode through a wall this time.

It's more calculated. We want to enter like ghosts that go through walls; I love the challenge. I take out my knife, cutting through the mesh screen. It's a one-floor house on a ranch.

I make sure my lovely knife always stays sharp.

I spent the whole night sharpening it on the drive here. Thinking of all the ways I will use it on these motherfuckers. They have no idea what they're doing knocking on my door.

Rooker, Lopez, and Kane follow me behind.

We're all geared up head to toe, night goggles strapped on tight. Our faces are covered in camouflage paint. And, of course, our masks. Each one of us wears a mask on missions.

"They want to kill Death, they say. The one that wears the reaper mask, they say."

Admiral Ravenmore's voice plays in my head vividly and viciously, like a broken record.

They want to hunt me?

I'm fucking game.

I open the window quietly, not making any sound. The noise of the cold wind drowns out our footsteps.

We enter the living room, and I let Rooker take the lead for the first time in a long time. It's a tactic we discussed on the way here. I want to see how it goes. I want to see if there's even a slight chance I'll be able to walk away from this life to join Ari in a civilian one, and the only way that's happening is if Rooker shows me I can pass the torch to him.

The thought of breaking away from my career was never even a thought. A year ago, I wouldn't believe where I stand right now.

Danny Rider, captivated by a sweet little soul named Ari, wondering about the possibility of leaving the Navy.

We're quiet, holding our rifles tight, night vision goggles on, walking through the house.

Our boots quietly step on the floors, and I'm in a different state of mind—the mind of a killer. Death is in my head and he's excited.

Hell, so am I.

This is the part of the job I hated yet thrived in.

We don't know how many of these criminals are here, but we figure it out as we go.

The house has a basement that I'm aware of. It's perfect for questioning and housing more people. There are probably more of these assholes down there.

Rooker is in front of me and we're ready to capture, but if they engage us first, it's lights out for them.

Then I smell my sweet little angel. Her sweet perfume that has me always so intrigued to *taste her*. It fills my nose and spreads everywhere.

It's only been a few days, and I already miss her.

I need to push her out of my mind even though she's invaded every part of it devastatingly.

I can't fuck up, I must stay focused, or it means my team's life or *mine.*

Suddenly, I see something on the right side of Rooker through my night vision. A gun sticking out of a hallway to his right.

A dead man, walking.

It's a pistol pointed straight at his head. I react. The only thing you *have* to do in these situations. Spend one fraction of a second too long in thought, too long in decision-making, and you've sealed your fate. You are hammering the nail in your own coffin.

You hesitate, you die.

You think too hard, you're dead.

Something I've been slowly teaching Ari. I've been giving her lessons on self-defense ever since she was attacked, teaching her my ways to defend herself and how to shoot a gun if it ever came to it.

I grab the handle of my knife tucked into my kit. It slips out of its case like it always does. I flick it fast and quickly, aiming for his arm.

The sound of a knife pierces through his bones, puncturing him to the wall.

Target hit.

I'm not surprised. I never miss with my knife.

His gun gets tossed into the air from the forceful impaling, steamrolling the bullet to shoot the ceiling instead of Rooker's head.

The man completely misses Rooker—a man saved.

Rooker flinches, bewildered, when he realizes what happened. He catches his breath before turning his rifle on the threat.

"You just saved my life for the thousandth time." He huffs a short, grateful laugh.

But I'm emotionless.

I don't feel shit.

Rooker puts his finger on the trigger, getting closer to him, ready to eliminate the threat, but I stop him.

I motion for him to stop. He nods in recognition. He's always been my right-hand man. He knows every single one of my moves.

I stalk toward the man with fast, long strides, my boots hitting the ground hard, making deep thuds.

He's mine.

He can't die, though. We need information.

"Fucking shit!" the man yells in pain, panicked, staring at his wounded arm. My knife hit his arm so fast, deep, and forcefully that he's pinned to the wall. The blade is holding him there like a hostage.

I smirk in satisfaction when I hear him cry out in pain. I love it when they do. He was about to kill one of my brothers.

It's pitch black. Little light illuminates the room, but I know he can see me. Rooker shines a light on him and he watches me, instantly growing pale. He keeps trying to grab the handle out of his arm. His speed at detangling himself from the knife increases the closer I get to him. But he fails and winces every time he pulls, and there's no outrunning me.

The blade pierces his flesh every time he tries to bolt, attempting to untether.

I'm close now, looking down at him, amused at his pathetic attempts. Even if he frees himself, he will never truly escape.

He shakes when he realizes I'm here with his incoming doom. Sweat has broken out all over his forehead, and little sniffles whimper out of him.

"It's you." He inhales sharply, his eyes circling so big I can see every little vein in his eyes.

I scoff.

I get in the man's face, squatting.

"You're Death. You're...you're the one who killed Omar's son, you're—"

He's quivering, sweating, and trying to swallow his trembling saliva through shaky, fearful breaths. His words barely come out of his mouth as he stutters on each word.

"Death got your tongue?" I look down at him eagerly.

"Grim Reaper."

I clap my hands, congratulating him, sinisterly. All lasers from my team's weapons are pointed at him from behind me.

"Ready to sing for us?"

"I'm not telling you shit."

He reaches for another gun tucked into his pocket and tries to aim it at me, but I'm fast. I grab his wrist and twist it so hard he drops the gun, and his bones break. I kick the gun to Rooker, the pistol gliding across the floors and he stomps on it.

Then footsteps surround us all, loud and heavy. I turn to Rooker and he returns my gaze with a delighted shrug.

An electrocution of adrenaline shoots through me. "Let the fun begin, boys," I roar with amusement.

Two men charge me. One has a gun, and the other a machete.

Rooker shoots the man with the gun straight in the head. I pull my favorite knife from the man's arm and wall. A blood-curdling scream escapes from him. I throw the man wielding a machete up against the wall with one arm as he screams at me. He charges me with impressive speed, but it's not enough to get me.

I stab him in the neck, and he drops the machete. He scratches at my hands, and I let him go. He ends up on the floor, hitting it hard, red splatters everywhere, even getting some on my boots. Fuck me, I just bought these. Death smiles as he hovers over the man scrambling for life, doing his best to hang on.

But I'm not done.

The man with the broken wrist scrambles for the machete dropped to the floor now that he is a free man. I watch him grinning behind my mask at his enthusiasm.

He really thinks he can escape us. How tragic.

Kane steps forward, pulling out his pistol to shoot his hand, but a sharp, loud bang sends the man's hand exploding, and blood explodes all over us. At first, I can't figure out what the fuck just happened. If Kane didn't pull the trigger, then who...?

The front window to the house had shattered simultaneously when the man's hand ruptured.

Ah, that makes sense.

"Creature, you almost fucking shot me, asshole! I know you're new, but what the fuck!" Kane unleashes his fury at Daegan through the mic, and I smirk as Kane shudders from the unexpected shot.

"Don't get your panties in a twist, Bane. *I never miss.*" Creature's voice vibrates in our ears sinisterly as he reloads his sniper.

"Nice," I compliment Creature. He does make a great addition to our team, after all. I stare at the man's hand marked with a deep, wide hole in it. He squirms, roaring in anger as if the louder he gets, the more it'll help ease the pain.

"Grim, there's more of these fuckers in the basement," Lopez shouts from the corner of the room.

18

———

DANNY

Five men sit tight, strapped and bound to a chair. It's a dark room, and they only have one small light from a lamp that Lopez turned on. It illuminates them like a Broadway show. They're the entertainment for the night.

This mission wasn't what I was expecting. I caught myself hoping for a quick return to my angel in a day or two so I could make it up to her by having her sit on my face, devouring her until she shattered into clouds of bliss. *Wishful thinking.* It looks like this might drag out for weeks. Delta and the local police will show up soon to do their own investigative work.

"I'm the nice one. Please give me the answers. We all know how this ends tonight, right? With you finally giving in."

"Suck my dick," one of them says, spitting at Rooker, but he misses horribly. His saliva lands next to his feet. Rooker gives him a wicked grin. Even though he's masked, I can see it.

I'm in the corner of the room, leaning against a wall in the dark with one of my boots pressed against a coffee table, sharpening my knife quietly, anxiously. Maybe I won't have to get involved. But the sadistic parts of me hope I can get in on the fun.

They still don't know I'm here. I'm Death's shadow tonight. I'm no longer Danny.

"This ends with you guys revealing who your friend is. Show us, Mr. Death, and you all will be rich men." The man seethes with hatred.

Lopez laughs as he circles them like a shark.

Kane stands there watching, a hand on his hip, fingers on his rifle.

"You don't want to ask for the Reaper, son," Rooker warns them with a wicked smile. Rooker is doing a fantastic job. I'm feeling more confident about my possible decision to leave the military. I'll leave this life even if it used to mean everything to me. It is no longer that.

Ari is everything. Her happiness is everything to me. I put her in danger when I wear this uniform, and I don't think I can do this anymore.

"I'm not scared of him. Come on, you guys will be million-aires. Tell us where he is, and I'll tell my bossman to spare you and your family's lives." He snaps his teeth. "I know you're Cobra." He points to Rooker and then points to Kane.

"And you're Bane."

Kane holds onto his rifle tighter with anger.

Now I'm seething. If they fuck with me, that's fine. In fact, I encourage it. They fuck with my brothers; they will repent soon.

"What's your name? Let me help you. I encourage you to talk to me instead." Rooker points to himself, his fingers uncurling with mercy.

Good. Because they won't get that from me.

"I'm the nice one. But you're pushing my buttons. Are you

sure you're not scared of the Reaper? He isn't a man who grants mercy, but I am." Rooker gets in the man's face, and two start quivering with fear.

"We know more about you guys than you think. Rumor has it Mr. Death has a little girlfriend. And you have a wife and two daughters." Rooker stands, clenching his fists, as one of the guys doles out information. He's about to lose his control, and I don't blame him, but we can't touch them.

Do they know about his girls? Do they know about mine, or are they bluffing?

The thought of them getting their hands on her infuriates my veins. I see red and the Grim Reaper's icy breath touches my neck. No one will ever lay a finger on her. They'll be six feet under the ground if they even breathe the same air as her.

"Fuck no, we're not scared of him. Nothing scares us," another terrorist chimes in, and they laugh.

It's my turn to laugh—loud, deep, husky, and wickedly. My roar of laughter interrupts the thickened, intense silence.

Everyone in the room turns to where my sinister, deep, rusty laugh came from. Now they have my full attention, and they will regret it.

Rooker sighs in defeat, letting his head fall and shaking it, disappointed at the captured criminals.

"Tsk, tsk, tsk," Rooker mocks them before he stands up. He crosses his arms, joining Kane.

I light a cigarette in the corner of the room. Sparks light up my face in the dark—once, twice, three times in the dark—before the fire finally burns on the tip of my cigarette.

Marlboro.

I breathe it in, letting my lungs settle the smoke. I hold it there for a couple of seconds. Then I push it out into the air.

I walk over to them slowly. With each step I take on the wooden floors in the dark, my boots make a loud, resounding thud.

They squint at me, trying to find me, and then I enter the spotlight that illuminates them. I'm towering over them, flinging my cigarette next to the guys' feet, sighing as I place my hands over my knees as I squat.

His pants, where his groin is, darken.

Motherfucker pissed himself.

I shake my head, smiling underneath my mask, and get into the man's face. My eyes circle more significantly with wrath as my smile fades, snapping my teeth, disappointed.

"Ask and you shall receive."

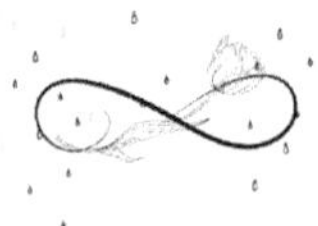

Delta showed up an hour later and didn't get much out of them tonight. We don't know how these fuckers got information on our families. I sit in the basement, worried.

Do they really know about Ari? Do they know about Rooker's wife and daughters?

But how?

I'm sitting on a chair in the dark basement, twirling my knife in my hand. I don't feel like Ari is safe, and with what happened with Shane, I can't risk losing her. My world only makes sense because she's a part of it.

The need to take my phone out and text her overwhelms me. I feel like I need to check on her. I don't know when I'll be home, but I know I need her to tell me she's okay. I wonder if her nightmares are still haunting her, and I feel hopeless not being there to comfort her until she falls back asleep.

Ari has me wrapped around her wings, and I'm the one who's in fucking trouble.

Our journey isn't your typical one, but it was a wild road up to this point. Our relationship has been complicated since the start, but the longer she stays in my life, the more I can feel myself becoming the man I didn't know existed and the man she needs me to be.

A man capable of change.

A man...utterly obsessed with the sweetest soul.

"What's going on?" Rooker asks, walking down the steps.

I shake my head, frustrated, as I pocket my phone.

"Not here. We can talk more when we get back to base," I whisper, unsure if the house is bugged. I don't want to mention Ari or Noel giving these bastards more fuel to use against us.

"Grim, there's more. I came down here to get you. You need to see this."

My eyebrows raise as something sinks deep into the pit of my stomach. It isn't good—this feeling of bad omens burns through my mind.

"Where?" I follow Rooker up the stairs from the basement. Instead of telling me, Rooker has me follow him.

He leads me into the hallway. We're moving over dead bodies, one after one, my boots thud against the floor.

All the lights are still on and special operators and police raid the house, taking pictures of the scene and collecting evidence.

The room he leads me into has my heart breaking.

A group of young children, crying, hugging each other for comfort. They're huddling together like penguins trying to disappear into the walls. Their eyes are full of confusion, loss, and fear.

Lopez and other guys from Delta console them, getting them water to drink and asking them questions like what their favorite color is or their favorite cartoon to distract them from their reality.

"You guys are going home, all of you. You're safe now. We're not going to hurt you. We're in the military," Lopez ensures that they shouldn't be afraid of us. He looks at them, one by one, observing their responses.

"It looks like this house wasn't only to house terrorists. These kids were going to be trafficked." Rooker crosses his arms against his puffed-out chest.

Wrath blinds my vision. Fire implodes underneath my skin and my chest aches, watching these innocent souls captured and forced to see what we fight against daily.

The evil in this world just won't ever fucking stop.

"We just saved about twenty kids tonight," Kane adds next to me, and I think about my son that I lost. My son that should be in Ari's belly growing.

A huge lump in my throat forms and I have to clear my throat hard as I stare at these poor kids.

Shit.

"Get them back to base...safe. Admiral Ravenmore needs to know about this," I order my team. I glance at the small children with distress.

Knowing I lost my son...this hits harder than usual. I can't imagine how the parents of these abducted kids are feeling right now. I would go fucking crazy. Burning the whole world down until I found my son.

As I'm about to walk out, a little boy, who looks about five, takes off running. Lopez doesn't try to stop him. As soon as he reaches me, he crashes against my thigh and holds onto my legs like he's trying to hang on a raft in the ocean for dear life.

He tugs on my pants, and I give him my undivided attention.

"Excuse me, mister," he says through sobs, tugging on my pants again, and my heart anchors down into a pool of sadness, hearing his plea. Even through such a traumatic, dark experience, he's polite.

He has the same features as Ari. Tan skin, black hair. I can't help but imagine our son may have come out with these same features.

"What's up, little man?" I squat, so we're now face to face.

"I want to see my daddy and mommy. Please, mister."

"I promise you, you'll be with them soon. We're taking you to a safe place where those bad guys will never see you again."

"Can I ask more questions?"

"Yes, little man?"

"What's your name? You look a little scary."

I can't tell him my real name. I'll give him the short version.

"Grim."

"That's a funny name."

"It is, isn't it?"

"Are you a superhero?"

"No, little man, I'm a SEAL." I ruffle his hair playfully, and he giggles. "You're safe now, you all are. You're going home."

He stops giggling when the words of sanctuary register for him. Then he throws his little body around my shoulder, hugging me hard. At first, I go still. I don't have too many interactions with children. But I interact with the little guy as if he was my son.

I hug the boy back, patting his little back.

"You're not a seal—that's an animal," he tells me, puzzled.

"Not that kind of SEAL." I break away from the hug, ruffling his black hair again. "I work for the Navy."

He beams, amused, observing me for a few seconds. "I want to be just like you when I grow up...a SEAL." He sniffles. He wipes his tears away with his little hand.

If I'm not already fucking broken, I am now.

I take off my mask. My face is still covered in camo paint with green, black, and brown layers, so I'm not worried about my identity being exposed.

I toss it over to the little boy, and his eyes light up like a Christmas tree. His brown eyes glimmer with joy through the holes of the front.

The disguise is too big for his little head, but he holds it into place with his hands, so it stops swaying.

"You already are a superhero."

19

———

ARI

Life is a lovely lie.

Those words come back full force with a demonic presence.

"You fucking slut! I can't believe you fucked him."

I can feel a sharp, dull pain in my back. Smiling like a maniac, Nora twirls a thick blade in her hands like it's a game. I'm trapped, and no one is here to save me.

All the memories come back, flashing one after the other repeatedly. It's one of those nightmares where you try to open your mouth to scream, only for eerie silence to follow. That nightmare where you try hard to run but feel like your feet sink lower to the ground in slow motion.

I can see Shane hovering over me again, trying to rape me. Watching his possessed eyes send dread curling through my chest like an explosion of fear.

I wake up from my nightmare, springing my body up, so I sit on my bed and scream into my dark, empty bedroom. I grip my bed sheets, curling them into my hands, searching for Danny, only to remember he's not home yet.

"No!" I shout. I blink fast, trying to escape the horrid fog desperately, trying to end the suffering I endured while I was asleep. I swallow as heavy breaths leave my lungs.

I palm my stomach and close my eyes tight, and that's when I notice my body is coated with sweat all over. As I try to steady my breathing, I pull the covers off to cool down. The adrenaline pokes at my chest, so unforgiving that I cry harder.

When will these terrors end?

Danny isn't home yet. It's been weeks now since my birthday party.

I look at my nightstand and check the time. Please don't let it be three in the morning.

I tap it with one of my fingers, lifting it so it's visible. The white light radiates off my phone, beaconing my face and bed.

Fear cripples my skin, and the hairs on my neck rise when I read the time.

3:33 a.m.

Why am I constantly waking up around 3 in the morning?

When will I stop dreaming of Danny's tattoo?

Then I see his name on my phone. It's a missed text message.

My chest fills with gratitude upon reading it.

> Danny: I miss you.

He's okay...he's alive. I can fall back asleep knowing he's safe.

Clutching my phone tight, in the middle of the night, with both my hands...I feel less alone knowing he's thinking of me. I respond to his text and shut it off, placing it beside me on the bed. I lie back down on my pillow, rubbing my belly gently in circles.

I hope wherever he is, it's not too far away, and he manages to avoid getting blown up or shot.

The amount of change Danny has made to make sure I know that I'm the number one priority now in his life has me more in love with him.

I look at the background of my screen, and I stare at my sinfully handsome man, who's trouble and magnetic all into one unbreakable soul.

It's a picture of us when he took me on my first helicopter ride. That night was one of the wildest adventures I've ever had in my entire life. I'm unable to look at a helicopter the same anymore. It was the first night I discovered the darkness that lives inside me. He broke my shell, and the ways he did weren't fluffy. He did warn me beforehand and I'm glad he didn't ease me into his world. He didn't change that part of himself for me...and I don't want him to. Instead, I let his emotions claim me in a way that was greedy and impatient.

He was unpredictable, always leaving me wanting more.

He's sadistic, but I wouldn't change that about him. If it weren't for him, I would still be playing pretend with my mother and myself.

Danny has been through so fucking much and I peeled back the secrecy surrounding his trauma, one layer at a time. One by one this past year, it wasn't easy; it was even a bit toxic, but I accepted him. It explains why he is the way he is and I'll do it over and over again.

I head toward my kitchen to fetch water. My throat is dry and since I can't sleep, I might as well hydrate. I walk through my hallway and it doesn't take long before I'm opening my pantry. My living room is dark—the only origin of light is the microwave light. I always leave it on at night.

My mom customarily left a kitchen light on, and I followed in her footsteps when I moved into my home.

Then I hear something hit my door, and it takes all of my concentration to distinguish if it was a tree branch falling from the strong winds outside or...a person knocking on my door. I close the pantry door slowly, trying not to make any noise. As soon as a click follows, I place the bottled water on the counter and I walk out of the kitchen.

Every step toward my front door has my body crippled with fear; watching the shadows of trees sway in the wind through my curtains has me questioning my need to investigate.

The only people that would stalk or hurt me can't hurt me anymore.

Shane is dead.

Shane is dead.

He can't hurt me.

Nora is in jail.

I tip-toe, looking through the peephole. I keep myself balanced on my toes, giving myself a boost. Looking through the tiny circular window, I see...nothing.

Then a ghastly cold brush of air cradles the side of my face, demanding my attention.

How did the wind blow into me if I'm inside my house?

I look to my left to investigate the source of the foreign element.

Then I see my curtains flow like they're being blown.

A window is open.

What the hell? I don't remember lifting it, and Danny would never leave the house unlocked.

Before making sudden movements, I clutch my phone tight before I check my security cameras. My fingers shake as I scroll from side to side on my phone screen, searching for my app. My breathing is enhanced with panic, but my eyebrows narrow when I don't see any notifications.

No alerts, no sign of break-in attempts, nothing.

My rigid body goes relaxed with solace. If there's no sign of an intruder, I'm okay...*right?*

My bones creak in my feet with each step I take, getting closer to my window.

The crisp air is still flowing like a fan against me, and my whole body shivers the more I get closer to the window. The temperature causes goosebumps to explode upright, and I hug myself.

I quickly pull down my window, locking it, as one last gush of ice wind freezes my skin.

The screen is still there, untouched.

Screw this. I'm going back to bed. This is the last thing I need right now.

I go back to the kitchen, finally grabbing what I came for. I swallow the room-temperature water until the water bottle is halfway empty.

I need to rest more before I go into today's constantly busy shift.

Today was going to be another day of work. A twelve-hour shift in the ER awaited me in just four hours and...I was excited.

I wondered what types of cases awaited me today in a few hours and I'm hoping I avoid sex injury cases, and I silently prayed no Special Operator would be in a bed, barely hanging onto life. Honestly, I hope *no one* dies today or is struggling to hang on.

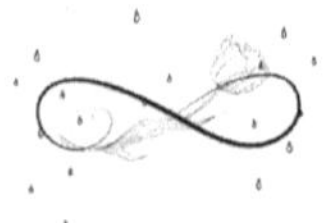

I stop by my mother's house after work because today is not just another day.

Today was the day my brother was killed in action from a mission gone wrong. It was a day that changed my path in life. I was going to be a pediatric nurse. After he passed, it was a decision I made without any hesitation.

I will honor my brother for the rest of my life, helping men and women like him. If I can prevent a mother or a sister from losing their son or brother, I'll do it forever, as long as my body will let me.

Grief is a pain that won't ever let up. A pain that will follow Mother, Danny, and me no matter what, but the amount of detrimental sorrow would vary.

Grief comes in waves and storms that crash into us whenever something pushes it.

It could be a memory, it could be a holiday...or it could be *a song.*

After giving it three knocks, I walk into my mother's house, and she responds swiftly.

"Come in!" she shouts from the inside, but her voice is far away.

She knows it's me. She still has the security system set up. Danny ensures they're always charged and running because my mom asked him to help her keep up with those things since she's alone. I also help out, but I think it makes me fall even more in love with Danny, knowing he makes an incredible effort to keep his promise to my brother.

I walk into the living room, and the air is warm, contrasting the freezing weather outside. A peppermint Christmas-scented candle fills the room, and my mom has decorated the Christmas tree...without me?

Every year since I was old enough to speak and walk, I would help put up her tree and decorate each branch with sparkling red and golden ornaments.

I stare at the tree, finished from top to bottom with nostalgia. I remove my jacket, admiring it like a little girl again. I always thought a Christmas tree held magic as a child.

I smile at the twinkling golden lights as I recount every time Paul would help us, although it was more of a mom-and-daughter thing. Most of the time, he would be in his room getting lost in virtual worlds on his computer, practicing his guitar or even skate-boarding outside.

I let my jacket fall onto the couch cushion, folded in half. I pull the sleeves of my white sweater over my thumbs as I walk deeper into the house, looking for her.

I walk into her bedroom first, thinking I'd find her there since she's not in the living room. This was about the same time she'd watch her routine novellas. It's empty and I knit my brows together, perplexed.

Where could she be at this time of day?

Then it dawns on me, and my chest tightens with melancholy. I take a deep breath and prepare for what I will walk into.

I close the door to her bedroom, gripping the doorknob tightly but closing it softly.

I turn around and my breathing quickens with each careful

step as I coat myself with strength before opening the door to Paul's bedroom.

Light shines from the cracks underneath the door, and I softly bite the insides of my cheek.

I push it open. My feet feel heavy purposefully because I don't want to see my mom upset. I can't bear to hear her cry.

Paul's sublime poster is the first thing I see. Sublime was one of his favorite bands and the first song he learned to play the guitar was "Santeria".

Mom's clutching his uniform while sitting at the edge of his bed.

She's not crying, she's...*okay.*

The rest of the bed is littered with photographs. Pictures of my brother as a baby until he reached his thirties are scattered everywhere, but my mom has herself intact.

"Ma, you put up the Christmas tree without me?" I act appalled, joking with her to lighten the mood even more. I put my hands on my hips, further dramatizing my comments.

She returns my gaze with a smile.

I walk over and drop next to her, grabbing a photo.

"Sorry, *mija,* you're just always busy. I couldn't wait any longer. I didn't want to bother you because you work a lot, and I just wanted to give you space while you recover. I'm trying something new." She sighs, putting Paul's uniform top in a hanger. She stands, walking to his closet.

"I appreciate that, Mom, but Danny left a while ago. He left for work and I'm alone at my house, so you'll see more of me around. I'll be the one invading your space this time," I jest, slapping my hands on my thighs and shrugging my shoulders.

"You're always welcome." She hangs his uniform up and turns around.

I place the picture of Paul playing his guitar on the bed and return her stare.

"*Mi hijo...*" She sighs. Her face says she's all right but her eyes are stressed. "I don't want to believe it's already been one year."

"I know, Mom."

"He had so much to live for."

"I know, Mom," I repeat, looking back at other photos on the bed, looking for any with Danny and sure enough, there's one with his entire team and Danny's. My eyes light up when I see the man that infuriates me. A smile spreads across my face like an instant reaction. They're all on a deployment, covered in face paint and holding their rifles. I never recognized him before. The man was always there but not there, *if that makes sense.* I search for more pictures of Danny with my brother but don't see anymore, then something catches my eye.

It's a photo I've never seen before. I study the unknown woman in the picture.

She's beautiful.

Of course, Paul doesn't let us into his private world. Of course, I had to find out he had a ton of friends I didn't know about that cared about him *after he passed.*

"Ma, who's this?" I ask, lifting the picture so she can see it.

She walks over to me, grabbing her reading glasses. After adjusting it onto her nose, she skims it.

"I have no idea, but she's pretty." She collects the other photos from the bed, ideally placing them together. "I was going through his nightstand, and I know I shouldn't have, but I couldn't help it. I feel like I have to clean his room and organize his things...even though I know he's not alive. A part of me doesn't want to believe it still. I clean it because it still feels like a bad dream. Like he's going to come home any day, walking through that door in his uniform, and—" She inhales a sorrowful breath. "I just want him to come home to a clean room. To know I'm still here, still waiting for him to return...no matter what. I won't give up on him."

I stand, tears threatening to escape as I rub her shoulders, hoping it'll prevent us both from breaking down.

"Mom, we will see him again, I promise you. We haven't given up on him...but when it's our time, we're going to see him again, and when that time comes, we're all going to have dinner together, catching up on our past adventures or whatever it is that people do in heaven. But right now, we have to *live for him*. No matter what, because that's exactly what he would want."

This makes my mom finally cry, but she's still okay. She smiles as she wipes away one escaped tear.

"You have a lot of explaining to do when he finds out you've been driving his car," she teases through stressed laughs.

I roll my eyes, smirking.

"I know."

"Did you stop by his grave today? I went early this morning. Left him his favorite candies, pulparindos." She tells me, putting the photos back into the drawer neatly on his nightstand.

"I did."

She looks at me for a few seconds, hoping I'd open up to her more about my visitation, but I want to keep it short.

"Good."

20

KANE

All I want to do is be home, away from all this darkness. Open a bottle of Tito's vodka and go to sleep. Maybe I should hit up Meredith again when the mission is over. I need to run away from how I crave Ari all the time. Ever since she was attacked, this protective need has only worsened, and I don't know what to do with it but be there...as a friend.

"Get some sleep. You only have twenty-four hours. Cobra and I are staying on base to return all the children safely to their families. Tex, Bane, and Creature. Please go home. I expect you all back here after you get your beauty sleep," Grim orders us.

We're in a conference room for our last brief of the night. The mission was successfully carried out and there's another one that follows. Although we still don't know where they're getting their information from and that's bugging us all out.

I shrug, sighing. I take off my mask and throw it into my rucksack.

"I don't sleep. I'm already beautiful, can't you tell?" Creature's wicked voice says. His bright gray eyes burn holes into Grim sarcastically.

He never takes off his black mask. We all wear the same one, but he doesn't take his off. Not since he was a prisoner of war. No one knows what happened to his face except the doctors who worked on him.

Grim scoffs out a chuckle.

"Look, man, go home. I'll call you if I need you guys back here early." He rubs his beard, taking out his phone.

"Are you sure? You know I'll stay, I don't mind," I ask one last time through tired eyes. It's been almost two days without sleep and my body feels like it's not my own anymore.

I sneak a peek across the table from where I'm standing in front of him.

That's when I see *Angel* as the contact name.

I know that's what he calls her. He's texting Ari.

I have to take a deep breath to relax the tension, hoping it'll erase my sullen frown.

Fire burns through me, and I have to clear my throat from the jealousy. A sting pops through my jaw when I realize I'm locking it too hard. She's not mine. She's my friend...a friend that I'm hopelessly in love with.

Fuck, this sucks.

"*Buenas noches*, ladies. You ain't gotta tell me twice," Texas says through a smirk while he takes off his mask. His black wavy hair is ruffled up, playing with a toothpick in his teeth. He grabs his camouflage ball cap, with the Texas flag displayed in the center of it, from his bag, placing it on his head before walking out.

"All right, Grim, just let me know if I have to come back." I yawn, straightening my back before swinging my rucksack over my shoulders as I exit the conference room.

Then Creature follows behind, and Rooker and Grim are left alone. As soon as we leave, the Admiral walks into the building. He's dressed casually in sweatpants and a dark navy-blue shirt.

He tilts his head, acknowledging us, as he swings the entrance door to the building open.

"Good job tonight, boys. Get some rest."

Creature and I nod in his direction. He makes his way into the conference room with Grim and Cobra without another word. In some ways, the admiral is just like Danny, always serious and never knows when to stop working.

The December air is cold and fresh. The temperature is still manageable. My combat boots thud over frozen grass, the moon lighting up my all-black bike.

I throw on my bike helmet and start it. The engine rumbles and I race out of the parking lot.

The wind hits me like waves as I drive. The Red Hot Chilli Peppers play through the system as I speed my way home.

It's around three in the morning and there's hardly any traffic. I exit base, passing by the gate guards, going down the empty highway.

When I get off the highway, I stop at a red light and plant my feet back on the ground, waiting for it to turn green. I stare at the lights and feel my eyes growing heavier.

I'm so fucking tired...I hadn't realized it when I was at work, but now it's taking over me like a drug. I shake my head to wake myself up.

Finally, it turns green, and I shake my body as a cold shiver runs down my back.

I need to get home and rack out; my date with vodka would have to be postponed.

As soon as I accelerate, I don't even pass the other side of the intersection.

Before I realize what's happening, my world spins like a carnival ride at the local fair. I feel a harsh impact, and I'm off my bike, my body and bike floored, scraping and skidding on the road.

I roar in agony as I feel a burning sensation through my body, over my clothes.

Sharp pain shoots through my nerves, and I feel like I was just hit by a car. It felt like I was gutted in the stomach, making it hard to breathe, and the last thing I heard before the devastating impact was tires screeching.

There's broken glass everywhere and my bike sits next to me.

As the adrenaline courses through my veins, I'm scared to move. I just got hit by a car and I don't know the extent of my injuries.

I keep reminding myself to stay calm as I take off my broken helmet with trembling hands. The glass in it has shattered and I can feel one of my eyes swelling already, as if I'm about to have a black eye.

I blink three times, hoping it'll make everything stop spinning. My vision is solid, and I'm good to fucking go.

"Holy shit," I groan.

I'm alive...

I'm still alive.

I don't know how, but I'm thanking God for that, but my solace is short-lived.

I throw my helmet to the side as I lie on my back, trying to catch my breath. I can hear someone walking toward me, but why aren't they apologizing? Why aren't they freaking out like any other average person who hits someone in an accident?

They hike over the glass and broken motorcycle parts, and I try to sit up to greet the person who just hit me with their car.

I'm halfway up before a heavy boot is pressed on my chest and I'm pinned to the ground.

"What the fuck!" I growl and grab onto their feet, ready to twist it off me.

The man's face is covered in a white mask, and he's tall. He looks like someone who just robbed a bank and used a beanie as a disguise. With holes cut into his eyes and nose. He wears all black and there's something behind those troubled, dark eyes.

This was done on purpose. Another one of the terrorists hit men standing before me.

I'm fucked.

My training kicks in and I'm about to throw him to the ground, when he pulls out a gun, aiming straight at my face.

"We're going to send your good friend, Death, a message." His finger touches the trigger and my heart pounds. I can hear it through the ringing in my ears. He's going to kill me.

"Fuck you," I spit.

The man tilts his head to the side mockingly. He pushes the barrel between my brows, and I can feel the cold gun metal touch my skin.

This is the end.

"Revenge is the sweetest form of war, Bane," he hisses. He knows my operator name. "All the executioners will pa—"

He doesn't finish. A suppressed gunshot tweaks into my ears and I flinch, shutting my eyes tight as blood splatters all over me, sending the hitman lifeless. I watch him flop to the ground, on top of the broken glass, and I rub the blood off my eyes.

That was a close call.

The gun in his hands falls to the ground with him and I look around to see who the fuck saved my life.

Who the fuck just splattered his brains all over me?

Creature steps into my view. His gray eyes squint at me with pity and I can tell he holds a bored expression underneath his mask.

"He talked too much." He shrugs with his pistol, which has a silencer on it. He tucks it back into his belt as we look down at the hitman. "Now the messenger is the message—how poetic." Creature tells me, followed by a roar of laughter.

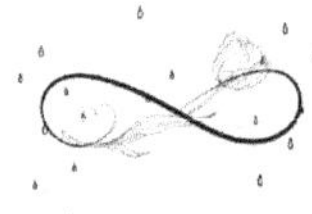

I lie on a bed on base after getting checked out by our medic assigned to the team. Creature apparently was watching me. He noticed I was being tailed outside headquarters as we both left. So instead of him going straight home, he followed and let me get hit by the fucking car.

He said it was because he wanted to make sure it was a hitman. And that he thought it was funny to see me get scared.

Asshole.

They refused to take me to the hospital. It would mean absolute chaos for us and the mission would be compromised.

After a long list of checks and tests, I'm cleared, albeit with a black eye and a few cuts on my face.

My body has been bruised good, one eye swollen, but... I'm alive.

"No word of this gets out, Kane. Not one fucking word. We

don't need to alert the public of these criminals. You know the protocol," Admiral orders me from the door.

"But, Sir, Paul's sister deserves to know what's going on."

"Excuse me?"

"I just think we should start telling our loved ones."

"Know your fucking place, Slaughter. If we start telling civilians about what's going on, it'll be a shit show."

"So we're just going to keep fucking pretending that—"

"Do you need to be put on restricted leave, son, behind a desk so you can learn how to shut your fucking mouth when speaking to an officer?" he threatens, his green eyes darkening with condescension.

"No. No, Sir."

"We have this under control. If we have to bring in Delta, then that's what we'll do, but as of right now, I believe this is a war we can win. So...after tonight, it's back to work. Report to Grim." Then he slams the door shut, pissed off, leaving me alone with my thoughts.

I throw my head back onto the pillow, running my hand through my hair. I squeeze my swollen eyes shut tight when I think about getting a rental until I can get it back from the shop. I'm hoping I don't have to buy another bike.

Fuck.

It was my favorite motorcycle and now it's headed to the shop for repairs.

"I can't wait to get out," I mumble as the group chat buzzes repeatedly.

Another text chimes in from Meredith.

A small smile spreads across my face, but deep down inside the sick, selfish parts of me, I wish it was my favorite nurse...Ari Alvarez.

I go to her contact name and click on it...tempted.

So fucking tempted to hit the call button, desperate to hear her voice.

I can't help it. I feel like I'm hitting a new low in my life, searching for the only comfort I fantasize about. Black hair...a girl that loves to play soccer and help heal people, and has the prettiest brown eyes I've ever seen. I haven't been the same since Paul died, the recent deployment from Iraq, and now this?

I just think I need her to be the angel in my life, too.

21

———

ARI

It's a slow shift for once. This week has been overflowing with patients of all kinds. Military families that their usual provider dismissed led to our lobby full of misdiagnoses.

Marines and sailors still in their uniforms came in with injuries sustained from training or just from the usual typical work day.

A wrong decision could lead them to a chopped-off finger or broken bones. More cases of PTSD flooded my list of patients, making my heart bleed with empathy.

I will always look at the broken souls with abundant compassion and respect.

Hurt souls that have lost their way didn't mean they could never be found. It just meant they needed one person to notice they were suffocating, to rescue them from their self-inflicted drowning.

If I could be that one pair of arms and ears, I'd always do it with no hesitation or questions asked.

I see what this career can do to some men and women. I saw what it has done to my Danny, yet he still has stayed strong and, most importantly, *alive.*

He has so much responsibility on his shoulders it's no wonder his favorite pick of self-loathing and poison would be whiskey.

I'm proud of how much he's changed into a better man for *himself.*

The clacking of keyboards and groans deriving from pain from the patients loom into the air as I walk the hallways back to the nurses' desk.

I hug my jacket closer to my body and wince when I accidentally touch where Nora stabbed me.

I flinch when my fingertips touch the purple scars over my scrubs.

Even though most of it has healed, this wound will forever be *fresh* to the touch—a ghastly eternal reminder of the doom I faced that day.

The day my baby and I *died.*

And yet, I'm still here, but my son isn't.

A dark part of me wishes I hadn't lived. Is it dark, though?

Is it dark to want to be with my baby that I never got to kiss? Never got to watch Danny and I cradle what our love created?

I'm shaken away from those thoughts like a cloud poofing away from the ominous world I throw myself in whenever something triggers that memory.

Heavy footsteps behind me were followed by a comforting, soft voice from the nurse who took me under her wing when I first got to Iraq.

With every step I take, my muscles and joints are strained with the bit of energy I have left.

"Girl, you're coming with me to Hawaii one of these days. It's so fucking beautiful there," Lori reminds me of the vacation she took with her girlfriend.

"So I've heard and only seen it in photos."

"By the way, we never got to talk..."

I furrow my brows as I look at her.

"Tsk. Tsk. Tsk. Those hickeys were not from Doctor Diaz. They were from Rider. Please catch me up on that part of your life."

I roll my eyes, fighting the blush.

"Well...yes. Yes, they were," I concede, defeated.

"Hmm, why didn't you tell me?"

"Because I didn't know what we were. Plus, I was still processing what was going on between us."

"Dude, talking about relationships brewing when we were in Iraq... I have some fucking hot tea about our favorite Doctor Diaz."

"Oh my gosh, spill it! Tell me." I look around, making sure no one can hear us.

"His wife cheated on him while he was still in Iraq!"

"No!"

"Bitch, yes!"

"That man gives so much to be cheated on." I frown, leaning on one side of my hip.

"Yeah, I know. He's the kindest person I've ever met. The best doctor I've ever worked for. Some people can't handle the long distance and the time apart."

A wave of guilt crashes into my chest when she says it. Because when I came back to North Carolina while Danny was still deployed, it sucked. It was so hard. His absence made me question our relationship, and he almost felt like a ghost from our zero communication.

Clouds of doubt hover over my mind. The love I have in my heart for Danny is unwavering, but this lifestyle is lonely.

It ate me up inside, worrying about him when he was in Iraq, mainly because of what happened to Violet and Damon...*my brother.*

I swore off military men, only to get deeply wrapped up in one.

Each day that went by without him felt weird.

"How did Stacy handle you being away for so long?"

Lori shrugs and sighs as she fills her mug with coffee.

"This isn't something new to her. Of course, in the beginning, it was hard for both of us...but she trusts me, and I trust her. Next year, we're planning on getting married."

"Oh my gosh, Lori, stop. You're going to make me cry," I shriek with happiness, pushing her shoulders playfully. I've always been a hopeless romantic. The thought of marriage seemed just that, a thought. Does Danny even believe in marriage if he can't say those three words I long to hear?

If I had to guess, probably not.

"Don't cry. Fuck, I should've chosen my words more carefully. I'm sor—" Lori picks up on my emotions that I've been trying too hard to bury, at least when I'm at work.

"Don't be!" I wave my hands in front of me, hectically. "I'm truly happy for you. I'm not upset, I promise. I'm just so excited for you."

"Thank you," she murmurs, biting away her smile.

"And, of course, you're going to be my maid of honor. No excuses!" She waves her index finger back and forth.

"Really?"

"Yup. Oh, by the way... I don't mean to change the subject,

but before we get called back to work and I forget, Violet wasn't the only prisoner of war case. We had another after you left."

"Oh no! Wait, how did I not hear about that?"

"Why would you hear about that? Sometimes, shit gets buried deep so the media doesn't get their hands on it. I wish it were like that all the time. People deserve privacy. For example, with Violet. I'm sure her story being all over the news was difficult for her to deal with."

"You're right."

"This time, it was another Navy SEAL. He was captured and tortured, but he ended up escaping. He saved himself."

"Wow. Is he okay?" I've never heard of that before.

"I treated him for a few days before returning home. What they did to him was so evil..." She pauses, shaking her head as she recounts the memories. "Half of his face is a mystery. I didn't get to see it. Only Doctor Diaz did and he didn't say what he saw. One eye is almost entirely blind. He didn't talk at all. 'Yes' and 'no' were the only amount of communication he used. He didn't like to communicate, so that made treating him vexatious. He was a bit *off* the entire time we treated him. I thought it was because of all the trauma he went through...but apparently not. One of his friends said he has always been like that even before he was a prisoner of war."

"Oh, poor guy. I'm surprised Danny's team wasn't called in for his extraction."

"To my knowledge, his team was requested, but this happened when..." She trails off, looking to see if she crossed a line, but I nod for her to go on.

"When all that happened with Shane, Danny turned it down. And so his team refused to go in without him, so they called in guys from the Army. Some guys from Delta, but they were already too late since the guy had escaped." She shrugs. "They were able to find him and bring him back to base, though."

"What's his name?"

"Daegan."

I open my mouth to ask what his operator name is, but we're interrupted ruthlessly.

"Here's Ms. Alvarez." I turn around to meet Dr. Reese. His silver hair is brushed back. Every single strand is completely hardened with product, shiny even. Not one single strand is out of place.

But he's not alone. A handsome, tall man grins back at me mischievously. There's nothing warm about the way he looks at me. He has familiar facial features.

He looks like—

"Lori, I have a patient in Room 3 that needs to be prepped for surgery now."

Lori purses her lips together, violently annoyed, and forces a smile. Her green eyes shine with frustration.

"Of course. I'll be on my way." She grabs her cup of coffee and walks away.

"I'll leave you two alone." Dr. Reese glances back at the mysterious man. "Looking forward to our Saturday golf with the other group of veterans."

The man smiles in agreement, shaking his hand.

"Always a joy, Reese."

The doctor pats his shoulder in a brotherly gesture and walks away, leaving me alone.

What the hell is going on?

Is he in Human Resources?

"I'm sorry, but do I know you?" I squint at him, trying to figure him out. Did I miss something when I came back to work?

A meeting with new hires? I'm usually really good at remembering faces, and this man has a face I wouldn't easily forget.

"Ah, so this is my son's girlfriend. The one who has made a severe impact on his life." His tone is welcoming, yet something behind his grin says otherwise.

"You're Danny's dad?"

"My name is Damian Rider. Daniel Rider is my only child. My only son. The most lethal operator in military history."

Why is he talking about him like that's his only identity? Like that is what Danny only is to him?

"I am aware of that."

"Is there a place we can speak more privately?" His question sounds more like an order.

"Umm..."

The break room?

No, there will be too many people.

I look for the closest room possible, anxious to hear what he has to say. The fact that he came to my job to talk with no warnings or heads-up intrigues me.

"There's an empty hospital room we don't usually use for patients. It's being remodeled. We can talk there."

His lips curve into a devilish grin, satisfied with my answer.

"Lead the way." He bows, throwing his hand in front of him.

It doesn't take long until we reach Room 12. It sits at the very end of a hall, far from the chaos that is the ER. It hasn't been used in weeks.

One cleanly made bed with fresh sheets sits in the middle. A sink with a mirror. And a counter with a faucet and napkins in a corner.

Your typical hospital room.

Damian closes the door behind him, sending me into a slight jump of nerves.

I don't think I like this...at all.

"So you're dating my son."

I nod. He doesn't waste any time getting right into what he came here for.

"Grim Reaper is what everyone calls him, and they call him that for excellent reasons, Ms. Alvarez."

He walks by me, his shoes clacking with each step as he passes. I step away, creating distance between us.

The aura he gives me isn't good. I can feel the tension he's trying to hide underneath his expensive suit and tie.

He looks out the window at the courtyard, pulling the blinds down, then turns around.

"You know he's more than just a Navy SEAL, right?" I can't help but feel protective of him. With the insight Danny has given me about his father, I almost want to curse at him.

I've only been in the same room with Damian for less than a minute, and I can see why their relationship is so estranged.

This man radiates a frozen hell and not in a good way.

He scoffs, chuckling as he shakes his head.

"You don't get it. A woman like you will never get it."

"Excuse me? What's a woman like me?" I narrow my eyes,

seething inwardly, and can already tell this conversation will be atrocious.

He doesn't answer. Instead, he smiles sardonically.

"I've been made aware that Danny was to be a father but unfortunately, the fetus passed away."

He did not just call my baby *a fetus.*

"Fetus?!" I shout, appalled. I hold my stomach, protecting my baby's honor.

"You mean *your grandchild,*" I spit, holding back tears fueled by venomous wrath. I look around to see if anyone can hear this man's ridiculous, outrageous words, but the door is closed and we're far from the nurses' station.

"He doesn't need to be distracted by unplanned or rather premeditated pregnancies to trap him."

Is he really accusing me of this?

"What? Do you think I tried to trap Danny?" This is my first time meeting anyone from my boyfriend's family, and I never thought it would go this way. "You don't know me. You don't know our relationship. I love your son with all of my heart. I would do anything for him."

"How do you know about our billion-dollar fortune? My businesses? Who told you? That must be why the relationship started and went so fast."

My mouth gawks open. Each word that leaves this man's mouth has me concerned.

"My son has a reputation to withhold, and you threaten that, Ms. Alvarez."

"My name is Ari," I interject.

"I don't think I need to learn how to say your name since you won't be a part of my son's life anymore. I don't need to bother with minor details."

"I don't need this. I don't need to be belittled by you. I love Danny, and I don't need to explain what we have together with you."

"My son has a couple of years left to give from completing his twenty years of a polished military record and career, and I'll be damned to see him throw it away over you, over a fucking nurse."

Yup, and that's my cue to walk out of here.

"Goodbye, Damian."

He snaps his teeth.

"I'm not finished."

"But I am," I spit, turning around to leave.

"You step out of that door, Ari, and I'll be making some calls regarding your position at this hospital. I was a SEAL once, just like Danny, a highly respected veteran," he drawls, his jaw twitching with stipulation. I grab the doorknob, just slightly about to flee the sapping energy he radiates through me like a drain.

I stop when the threat of losing my job rings loud and makes me hesitate.

"Unfortunately, my son isn't quite just like me." His large, veiny hand enters my personal space when he clenches the door right underneath his fingertips, gripping it harshly. I step away from him, retreating to the other side of the room.

"I blame my wife for that. She makes room for weakness and I don't have time for that. I can separate my love life from what needs to get done. I've taught him that, you know, work will always come first. Devote your life to work and that's what makes a successful man." He readjusts the collar at his neck, looking down at me with a fake façade. His body is collected and composed, but his eyes scream at me with disgust.

"Do you want him to throw away all of his hard work? If you

say you love him, show him that you love him by putting him first before your own needs, Ms. Alvarez. Don't let him throw away his career after all his hard work and sacrifice. It seems to me you can't handle this military spouse life, anyway. He deploys a lot. He already had to take a long leave of absence to be by your side when he had never done that before."

"We lost our child! I died in his arms! I can't believe I have to justify this for you."

Still, he holds his ground, stony-faced.

"How sad. I pity you," I blurt out.

"Why's that?"

"Your son is more than just a special operator, Mr. Rider. He's giving. He's strong. He loves to paint, build things, and help others. He's the strongest man I've ever known. He's intelligent, and he knows how to take care of me. He would've made an amazing father."

"That's very kind of you...maybe even a little naïve. Still, Ms. Alvarez." His eyes pierce through my own like an arrow. "You don't belong in this world. This military world has already eaten you up, chewed you, and spat you out, leaving practically nothing behind."

So, he does keep tabs on his son.

"Your brother. A fallen sailor, right? A fallen brother?"

I open my mouth, but he doesn't let me finish. His treacherous words keep going.

"Navy SEAL...what was his name?" Damian taps his jaw sarcastically. "Paul Alvarez. What a shame, my condolences."

Now my blood is boiling. No wonder Danny doesn't speak to this man.

"Don't talk about him," I say, with hatred pouring out of me like acid.

"I'm just saying. After all that you've been through, I understand you, Ari. I fully understand why you second-guess your ability to be with someone in the military. It's not for everyone, and it certainly isn't for you."

Did he overhear my conversation with Lori? Has he been stalking Danny and me like a creep?

"I suggest you stop talking to her before you lose the ability to do so." My eyes pop open when I realize who it is. "Tread your next words carefully when you speak to the mother of my child." Danny's tone deepens harshly behind me. I turn around, pivoting my feet in the middle of the hostile relationship between the two.

He's back.

The built-up anger I have slowly subsides briefly when I see him standing by the door. He's in his uniform still, a dark brown shirt with camo pants and his favorite knife on his waist.

It feels like a fireball of utter affection is bludgeoning me when I hear his protective, familiar contention.

I face Danny, whose stature is anything but kind or welcoming toward his father.

Damian's eyes soften for half a second but then light back up like a flame, burning holes into his son.

They both look so much and act alike when angry.

"Hello, son." Damian's tone shifts to a defensive, authoritative, as if to assert himself over Danny.

Before I can get to breathe in some vengeance, he continues while Danny burns holes through him.

"Haven't seen you in a while. I was just—"

"You were just leaving." Danny stalks two steps forward, each step sending a threatening message.

"Come on, don't get offended, son. I just wanted to meet Ms.

Alvarez. Make sure she got a proper welcome into the Rider family."

"Her name is Ari Natalia. If you disrespect her again, it'll be the last time you ever utter the word *family*. It's the one thing you were not successful at keeping, Damian. Or do you need me to remind you of your failures?" He takes another threatening step forward. His gaze sharpened with edge. I think he's referencing the affair he had.

My lips flatten with anticipation. The madness between them is waiting to unfold with one wrong word or sudden movement.

This isn't happening. Sweat begins to coat my skin as Danny's hands ball into tight fists. I haven't seen Danny this angry since that one night he revealed Paul's death. I'm afraid of what he'll do.

"She doesn't need anything from you. You've never cared about my personal life, and she is *my life now*."

Damian glares at me before turning back to Danny with a forced smile.

"You've changed."

"Leave, Damian. Or I'll be the one making calls to have you barred from this hospital."

Each word pummels Damian's ego and I find it hard to relax my shoulders from the pure tension.

"Daniel, what's with the hostility? I haven't seen you in months and this is what I get? Why haven't you called your mother since you've returned home?"

"I've been busy." He's cold and curt.

Damian shakes his head, grinning ear to ear like this was a game of chess. He walks toward the door, brushing by Danny with no fidget in his step.

He walks out the door but stops before turning the corner. Danny watches him like a hawk the entire time.

"By the way, son, she is not a mother...not anymore."

It felt like I was stabbed in my heart when those words left Damian's mouth, and I felt enraged to the point where I wanted to slap his face.

My spirit shatters into a million pieces at his parting words. *He didn't just say that. How could he be so cruel?*

Danny goes full-blown rigid. His eyes darken with anger. His breathing escalates, and I can tell he will not be doing so much *talking* anymore and he's about to do something else.

I rush toward him, practically leaping to his side. My heart stops in my chest. I won't let him and his father further destroy each other.

"Hey!" I grab his shoulder and intertwine my fingers with his. "It's not worth it. Stay," I plead with him as Damian leaves us alone. He closes the door behind him with a soft click.

Danny looks different from the last time I saw him. He has camo paint still smudged all over his face, like it's worn off.

"Now I know why you don't speak to him. I'm so sorry, Danny. Just know I'm here for you...always." My heart breaks knowing that that heartless monster raised Danny. I can't imagine what his childhood was like, living under the same roof as Damian.

He relaxes underneath my fingers.

"Don't be sorry." He walks around me and closes the curtains behind me, shielding us with another border of privacy.

He cups my face with both hands aggressively, kissing me hard, and I melt. He forces me to tread backward until I feel my back hit the wall.

"It's been too long..." he breathes against me. I'm instantly thrown off, but so turned on. I've missed him so much, too.

"Grim. Lock it up, let's go." Rooker's authoritative voice snaps me out of our passionate seclusion. He bangs on the door three times, purposefully hard and fast, and my eyes bulge open when I realize we're not alone.

"Oh my God, Danny! Rooker is here?! Is your whole team here?" I hiss, keeping my voice low, my cheeks burning with embarrassment. The door is unlocked. The curtains only give us a thin layer of privacy if it gets swung open.

I perk up to meet Danny's sinful grin as my sudden swell of internal shame amuses him.

"They are."

His eyes almost closed, calm and collected, unbothered, smirking like he's about to devour me completely, and there's no stopping him.

"Make something up," he demands before he goes to my neck, biting it hard, ricocheting a moan to escape from my lips.

"I...uh, I'm administering him fluids, he's umm...he's—" He bites again, his teeth sinking into my skin. I moan, resting my head against the wall. I close my eyes and face the ceiling. Then, Danny starts to suck on my neck. His fingers slide down into my waistband, and I swear I stop breathing...and then I gasp when I feel him touch my throbbing heat, which bolts a sharp spark inside me and spreads like a wildfire.

I'm in trouble.

"Dehydrated!" I squeak out just as he kisses my lips, miraculously keeping my voice professional and less hasty, like I'm not just getting felt up by my boyfriend in a hospital room. I kiss him back hard, leaving little nibbles on his bottom lip as I do and I grip on to his hair, pulling him closer.

He doesn't stop, his movements don't quit, and his tongue, God, his tongue, continues to move inside me...he *knows how to work my body.*

Rooker scoffs and walks away, chuckling.

He's not stupid. He knows what we're doing, but either way...he gets the message and his footsteps thud away. There's no fucking IV bag in here, either way he leaves us alone, buying us time.

"You're going to get me fired, Danny," I complain about the possible outcome if I get caught. Especially if it's from Doctor Reese. My new boss has zero patience, and I can't imagine what he'll do if he finds out I'm skipping work. He ignores my warnings and slides his fingers inside me.

"Already wet for me, baby," he groans in satisfaction. "Stop being so scared." He pulls on my hair.

"The only way you're leaving this room is full of my come."

23

DANNY

The fire inside me has ignited, and only her cunt can put it out.

I missed her.

I've missed this.

"This was the longest mission of my life," I whisper into her ear.

Screw this. I will fuck her like it's my last day on this earth. I don't care if we're in a hospital room; I'm taking full fucking advantage of having one small window to see her again. I've been deprived of her taste, and I'm a starved man, determined to empty my lust inside her.

We returned to base at the Admiral's request before we're back out doing God knows what.

"Fuck, baby, I've missed you." I grip her jaw, forcing my tongue down her throat and groan in satisfaction when she reciprocates with equal fervor, dancing with mine. My insanity will boil over if I don't get her naked and feel her soft skin against mine in the next few seconds.

"I missed you t—" She tries to grab my face, but instead, holds onto my shoulder when I lift her off the ground, securing her legs around me right before I slam her firmly against the hospital room wall.

If this is what it's like to be sick with her love, I never want to be cured.

Taking care of her will be the end of me.

I've been on edge, unable to relax since I left for the mission. That's when I realize that I have to tell her that I'm leaving again after I'm done showing her the level of insanity she puts me through... what her soul continues to do to me.

A foreign anchor of guilt weighs me down. I've never felt this before, but for the first time in my career as a SEAL, I dread knowing I must leave my little angel behind again.

She doesn't know what's been happening behind the scenes...she doesn't know the mission that killed her brother continues to haunt us persistently.

But I promise myself it will all be taken care of so we can finally move on without having to look over our shoulders ever again.

She doesn't need to know. My girl has been through enough. I don't want her to be afraid. Her night terrors are slowly letting up, barely.

I've been watching over Ari. Her healing journey has just hit a stable point, and I don't want to taint it with the evil lurking in our shadows.

I can't tell her, but I don't want to lie to her either. I'll do whatever it takes to protect her from any more pain...even if that means not disclosing the current situation.

I want to tell her. God, I want to tell her everything.

But if I can keep her focused solely on healing from the attack, from the loss of our baby, shielded from the chaos that I will hold on my shoulders for the both of us.

I need her to be whole again.

I'll always be the asshole in her story with open arms to protect her. I'll be the villain if that means she stays shielded from evil.

I want her to wake up every morning unafraid, and if she knows the truth, I don't know how she'll react.

I snap out of my thoughts when she smiles at me, and every time she does that, I swear my world stops.

She's the only light in my life, and I intend on making sure she always shines bright for the rest of our lives.

I scoff with a smirk before I plant another kiss on her full lips.

I need to feel her voluminous tits underneath my hands, and I need them now.

I snake my hands underneath her scrub top. Her skin erupts in goosebumps and then I find her hardened nipples, and my cock jerks when I thumb her nipples. I can feel my uniform grow tighter. I palm her breast hard and it fills my hand like they were fucking made for me and only me to suck on...*to fuck*.

"Danny," she moans against my lips, but it drives me even more crazy, my stomach clenching with desire and greed.

I grind my pulsing cock against her throbbing cunt. Even through her scrubs, I know she's longing for me.

I'll be the only man she'll ever moan for, and that's a fucking promise.

"Does our situation feel familiar, baby?" I squeeze her breasts again, and she gasps.

The way she tried to tease me in Iraq only got her choked against the wall, her fragile throat beneath my hands as we kissed.

One of my favorite memories of my little angel comes back to me, sending me into euphoria.

"Doesn't ring a bell," she whispers, panting hard, her vision pinned to my lips.

"Did you just sass me, Ari?" I taunt, my tone threatening. Another boundary to fracture and I will.

I will be her firsts and lasts and that's an unbreakable vow of mine.

Ari goes rigid like she did something bad, because she did. She's flicked on the wild switch, the fucked-up parts of me dangerously waiting for me to inflict pain on her.

She swallows, unable to answer.

"Let me remind you what happens when you disobey my commandments, little angel." I grin wickedly, ready to play the games I always win. "Your tits are exquisite. But they would look even more heavenly with my dick in between them."

"Now, get on your knees and let me fuck those tits."

I drop her to her feet, gently. Ari's cheeks blush bright pink as she registers what I'm about to do to her. She bites her bottom lip, her front teeth digging into them.

I can't wait to make her bleed again.

I tower over, my palm on the wall, waiting as she adjusts her on her knees.

She looks so fucking cute in her scrubs...but she looks even more sexy without them on.

"I just want to finish what you started in Iraq," she confesses, her eyes dilating as she throws her scrub top over her head, flinging it behind me on the hospital bed.

"Careful what you wish for." I pull on her ponytail, causing her beautiful dark black hair to dislodge from the hair tie. I will make a mess of her, the way I've been waiting to, longing to since I left her on her birthday.

She clenches her thighs together, probably to satisfy the need to feel me. And I will satisfy her like I always do...after I'm done punishing her.

This whole hospital will know just who she fucking belongs to after I'm done with her.

No one would dare fire her, knowing she's mine. But mostly because of how hard she's worked to earn her position here. I wouldn't allow it—*over my dead body*.

The sounds of hospital chatter, phones ringing, and monitors beeping should be enough to swallow the sounds I'm about to force out of her mouth.

My hand grips the back of her head, pulling from the roots of her hair, and a harsh breath escapes her mouth when I force her eyes on me.

She smiles, glaring daggers at me. Her brown eyes sparkle like they always do. I'll never take for granted the way they come alive when she sees me.

She reaches for her back, her fingers quickly unhooking her light pink bra and her tits bounce when they're free. The way they move up and down...

Fuck, I need to taste them. They're luscious tear drops waiting to be sucked on, and I will take them into my mouth after I fuck them. Her light nude brown shade nipples are perfectly pointed.

Fuck, I'm in trouble.

I lick my lips, letting her hair go to rip off my belt. I can't undress—it's a damn hassle to put my gear back on—but I don't need it all off to make her scream.

I loosen the bolts on my belt, ultimately loosening the waistband.

"I'm going to claim those, too, finally." I jerk my forehead, insinuating for her to grab her perfect tits together. I pull down my pants just enough for my cock to appear. I fist myself, stroking it as Ari grabs her tits, pushing them together, creating the perfect entrance.

Then she reaches for my cock, licking the precum with a flick of her tongue, and every single blood vessel inside my body explodes with anticipation.

She cleans up the dripping liquid from the head of my dick, and I groan. She knows how to push every one of my buttons to have me on my knees.

"Just a taste," she purrs, giving my tip a teasing suck, hollowing her cheeks, and I have to hold on to her hair again to stop myself from fucking her throat.

Seeing how much I've corrupted her, breaking the shell her darkest fantasies were hiding behind, makes me happy to see her give in unashamed.

"You've missed this? Choking on me, didn't you?"

"Yes," she rasps.

I don't waste any more time. These moments are so precious. I don't know when I'll see her again after this, and I don't want to keep her too long from her patients, but I will claim her, fuck what's mine before I have to leave.

She's always been so obedient, so submissive, so good.

"I can't believe I'm doing this." She shakes her head, fighting back a smile. "You're the devil."

I grip her jaw tight, rubbing my thumb across her lips. I hum, enchanted.

"I'll try not to drag you to hell, baby. Now, take your punishment and spit on my dick." She gawks at me, shocked by my demands, but does she stop? She keeps looking at the curtains that shield our situation even though the door is closed with no glass windows.

Rooker's doing me a favor and most likely guarding the door. A favor that I will soon have to pay up with a pack of beers.

She spits on my length.

Fuck.

"That's my good girl."

I thrust my hips between her tits.

I'm relentless, passionate, fucking them with urgency. Her eyes look forever tethered to my size, watching me like it's her first time again.

Technically, it's another first for her. I'll fuck every part of her body if she lets me.

The peak is already close.

This is what she does. It's been too long without feeling her. I always think about her when I have those small windows to myself on the job.

I want to come all over her tits, and I want to watch her watch me, spread myself on her, and mark her, but I have other plans for how I want to finish.

She rubs her tits up and down, groping my dick to match my movements.

I need to be inside of her. I need to feel how her pussy clenches down on me when I break her.

"I need to feel your sweet cunt around my dick when you come." I pull out of her chest, pulsing for her. I yank her up by both of her hands, and she stands, gasping with excitement.

"You don't need these, don't ever wear panties again. Your

beautiful cunt should never be hidden from me." I grip the thin material of her underwear, tearing it off of her quickly.

She flushes when she sees them drop in two pieces, torn seamlessly.

I pick her up, carrying her like a feather.

I love that she's so short.

I push her up against the wall again, breathing heavily, and my chest constricts when I watch her so flustered with arousal. She's dripping down her thighs already.

"Someone might walk in here! They'll hear us!" She pants into my ear, frantic.

I smirk, leaning closer to her cheeks. I tuck a part of her hair behind her ear.

"Good."

"Danny..."

"You worry about the wrong things, Ari. Just worry about trying not to scream when I fuck your brains out against this wall."

I take one of her tits into my mouth, sucking it, caressing it in my hand. I fling my tongue around just before I bite on it, and she reaches underneath my shirt, scratching my back in response.

I growl from pleasure. The pain she inflicts on me is ruthless with how she makes me feel...

She's probably broken through my skin, and I don't mind bleeding for her. I'll bleed for her any day.

"I need..."

"Tell me what you need." I position myself at her entrance, lifting her higher against the wall.

"I need you inside me...now," she breathes, shaking, her fingers digging deeper into my skin.

I push into her and she moans into my shoulder, holding onto me, her arms hooking themselves on my back tighter.

"Mmm..." she whimpers as I push more of myself into her tight cunt. She won't ever get used to my size, just like I won't ever get used to how her insides feel.

Her eyes roll back, and she throws her head back, resting it on the wall. I savor every second she looks like this when I'm deep inside her. I want to go deeper. I need to.

I don't care if I can't. I'll make it possible. My good girl can take it.

"No one has made me feel so out of control, like you. What you do to me is brutal," I growl while burying my face into her neck, biting into her skin. Her scent is heavenly, so sweet and airy, and I know it's not just her perfume...it's her.

She's so seductive, without even trying.

I grab onto her waist, pulling her more onto me so I can drive my cock inside deeper.

Ari watches my cock slip in and out of her. She bites her lip, her back hitting the wall each time I thrust harder. "That's right, baby, watch me fuck you because this is the only cock that will ever be inside you for as long as you live."

She's right. I have been dehydrated. I need to be refueled by her cunt. By her love.

This was the moment I realized that I'd never be the same operator...or man again.

I need Ari in more ways than she thinks.

I need her to survive.

"Oh!"

"My filthy girl, you are mine forever. There is no one else but me. Do you understand?"

I pound her harder and harder and fuck I'm about to climax. I watch her wince with each aggressive greedy pull when I grip her waist closer to me making sure she takes every single inch of my dick.

She looks stunned when I change the pace to a more painful need to finish. She grabs a hold of my dog tags for balance, hooking one of her hands around the metal, closing her eyes tight.

"Good, hold on to something because I don't plan on letting up...at all."

I grab her jaw, tightening my fingers and forcing her to look at me.

Her mouth gapes open, and she pants hard, her entire body jolting up and down.

I don't ever want to stop railing her.

"Say it."

"There will never ever be anyone else but you, Danny." She moans, her breasts writhing as I fuck her and I can feel her hardened nipples graze my chest when I lean in to kiss her, biting her lip, stretching it with my teeth, pulling it back, like I always do.

And then I hit a certain spot inside of her, letting her bottom lip go, when I force myself deeper than I thought possible, only leaving my balls outside of her cunt.

She stifles her moans against my neck, forcing herself to keep quiet. She clenches down on me, and I fucking lose it. I lose all control and I'm filling her up, resting my forehead against hers, clenching my jaw so hard I can hear myself grinding my teeth with pure heavenly satisfaction.

We both come together in our deep ocean of endearment.

I make sure I empty every single drop of myself inside her, my thrusting slows down, keeping my promise of her leaving this room, full of my markings, *full of my come.*

She's exhausted, her arm muscles trembling, twitching around my dog tags. I continue to fill her up, and then I finally pull out when it's the last thing I want to do, but I have to get back to work.

Finally, she lets my dog tags go. Her hand trails down my uniform top before she rests her face on my chest as I continue to hold her up against the wall.

I let her catch her breath, not daring to set her down just yet. Savoring a few more seconds having her on my chest.

Then I bite her lip, ripping it with my teeth just enough for her to wear red. She sucks in a breath from the pain. Salacity overwhelms me, and I'm hard again. I suck on her lip. She looks at me when I'm done and she looks almost dazed from the explosive sex.

"You bleed so fucking sweet."

"You're insane," she rasps.

"For you," I mumble as I brush my hand through her hair.

"I don't want you to leave. Is that selfish of me?" she asks through fast breathing.

"It isn't."

I'm not tired one bit. I could fuck her for hours if I got the chance, and I will as soon as work slows down and I get to be home again for more than a few fucking hours.

I set her down, and she retrieves her clothes as I fix my own.

She's a fucking goddess. An angel walking this earth and I'll never get enough of her. I continue to watch her like a diamond that glistens just by existing.

I'm never letting her go.

"I swear if I get fired..." she says, pulling her scrub top over.

"You won't." I tuck in my dog tags back inside my shirt.

Every patient needs a nurse like her. Every doctor, every hospital needs a nurse like her. A kind soul like my Ari.

We clean ourselves up, and she frantically tries to un-wrinkle her clothes.

She's so cute. Adorable, even. She worries too much.

She reaches for her underwear, but I snatch it from her hands and put it into my pocket.

"They're torn, anyway."

She blushes red while fixing her hair again in a tight ponytail while I buckle my belt on. And then I experience a pure warm, genuine destruction of a feeling entering my chest and it causes a reaction out of me.

I smile the biggest I ever have in my life and I have to look away from her when I realize what's happening to me. I look away, ungluing my eyes from her beautiful black hair, when she tucks the last pieces of hair into her hair tie. I pull away because I'm tempted.

I'm tempted to say things...say words I've never said before to anybody.

My phone buzzes in my pocket, throwing me out of my element. I pull out my cellphone as Ari continues to recollect herself behind me. I'm still facing the wall, looking at my phone in annoyance—back to fucking reality.

Rooker: Another mission, Grim. We gotta go.

I read the text, Rooker holding me accountable for my team, reminding me a job still needs to get done.

I throw it back into my pocket and exhale.

Time to go.

"Did something happen again when you were away?" Ari asks me from behind, and I stiffen. I can't tell her anything, at least no details. She wants me to open up to her, and I don't blame her. If I was in her position and she kept leaving me all the time, I'd want to know everything.

So I decide to open up just a smidge of what I've been dealing with, keeping shit still classified.

"Yeah...it's not anything good...to say the least."

"It never is good..." She holds me from behind, giving me a hug. "Open up to me, please."

Fuck, how am I ever supposed to say no to her?

I don't think I'll ever be able to tell my girl no ever again.

"It involves children. That's all I can say." I grab her hands, pulling them off of me, slowly.

I start to disassociate myself from her. *I have to.* The stress of the next mission tugs at my concentration. I'm already entering a state of mind where I don't feel anything, a state of mind where I'm focused on solely keeping people alive.

"I don't want us to keep any secrets between us."

I freeze.

Because even though I'm not lying to her, I feel like I am when I refrain from giving her all the details. But it's not only because I want to protect her...it's because I can't.

"There's something I think I should tell you. Maybe I'm overreacting and...maybe I'm even going a little crazy, but I don't want to keep things from you. I did that with Shane, but I won't do it again."

"What is it?" I ask.

She thinks I don't know that Kane visited her when I was called in to work, but I do, and I'm still waiting for her to tell me about it. I want to kill him for going behind my back and visiting her in the middle of the night.

He was one of Paul's best friends, too, and he'd made a promise.

We all did.

But I will engrave it into his head that the promise made to Paul is my responsibility now, no one else's.

And I will.

She looks up from the floor, finally mustering up the courage to let me in.

She should never keep secrets from me again...she should've told me about what Shane was doing to her right away. She should have told me that she was pregnant *sooner.*

I push these thoughts out of my head.

"The other night, my window was open. I don't remember opening it, and I doubt you left it that way. And then another day...my room felt out of place, like someone was there, as if someone went through my things."

I inhale, tension building in my shoulders.

"I check the cameras, you know that, right? I check them all the time. Zeke checks them, the security company checks them. They're being monitored twenty-four-seven. No one has been at the house, and if someone has, I'd know about it. The security company knows about it and watches for intrusions when I can't."

She looks up at me like she's waiting for me to say more.

"Come here." I pull her in, tucking her under my arm.

I lean down as she tiptoes to reach my lips.

I kiss her hard and fast; it's short, but it's long enough to feel myself getting hard again.

She's my obsession and my newest addiction, but this time, I don't want to be saved from it.

I kiss her one last time. Savoring this final moment I have with her before I leave because the reaper is calling my name, reminding me of the man I have to be in just a few moments.

"You take my breath away."

I smirk in response, smiling against her lips.

"By the way, you're my date to the upcoming military ball."

"What? When?"

"It's next week. I already bought you a dress. It's in your closet, hiding in a box. I placed it in there before I left."

"Okay then."

"I'll see you soon, little angel."

"See you soon."

I turn around, throwing the curtains to the side. I make sure she's fully clothed before I open the door, my whole body way more relaxed than when I walked in.

She's looking herself over in the mirror when I take my last glance at her, fixing her hair.

So fucking beautiful. She's making it hard to leave.

Then I walk out of the door, ready to get back to fucking work.

I crack my neck side to side as I walk down the hall. I spot the entire team at the end of the hallway, lost in conversation. Rooker stands closer to the room I walked out of, guarding it.

Kane and Hannibal stand there awkwardly. Kane tries to say something to Daegan, but he gives a haunting glare back at Kane. Kane gets the message and shifts off the wall with his boot, walking away from him. Then I spot Lopez. He's talking to a nurse, and it looks like he's trying to woo her with his charm as he palms the wall, leaning on it, hovering over her, grinning. He plays with her hair as she blushes, her dimples deepening on her cheeks. I'm not surprised he holds this reputation.

I roll my eyes, but I can't get upset... I'd be a hypocrite.

I just fucked my girlfriend in a hospital room against a wall a few minutes ago.

Rooker straightens his posture from leaning against the wall. He was on his phone, typing away, probably checking on Noel and his daughters. But when he spots me getting close, he tucks his phone away.

"Dehydrated, huh?" His voice is laced with playful accusation.

I walk past him, not bothering to stop, ready to leave the hospital, and he follows my steps, matching my speed.

"Severely parched... I almost had to be admitted." I smirk, shrugging my shoulders, loosening the knots in my back with my sways.

"Right, and I'm having the shits. Do I have to get admitted, too?" He sighs, shaking his head.

He knows I'm spitting bullshit, but he doesn't pry further. Rooker is the one I'm closest to, constantly calling me and the team out on their shit.

"I don't know, man. I hear having the shits can lead to dehydration. Do you want to stop by Noel's so she can...rehydrate you?" I raise a brow, pushing his buttons. "You guys live on base, right? We can stop by for five minutes."

He rolls his eyes. "I don't know about five minutes," he mumbles under his breath.

"You're right. What was I thinking? Three minutes is your limit." I roar with laughter before he pushes my shoulder, pissed off.

"Asshole."

We finally catch up with the team and I watch Hannibal play with a 6.5mm Creedmoor bullet in his hands, twirling it between each finger as I get closer.

"Let's go, boys," I order them as I turn further down the hall-way, and everyone follows. I can hear Lopez from behind me, bidding his farewells to his new flavor of the week.

24

———

ARI

I can't believe what I did with Danny in this room. My reflection reveals messed up sex hair, a swollen lip, and clammy skin.

Butterflies take flight as I remember when his beautiful teeth had my lips stretched out like a strip of candy. And I wonder when I'll see him again even though he just left.

My hair is still visibly out of place, even though I've tried everything to make it look like I didn't get fucked against a wall by a very much starved, deprived man.

My muscles tremble from holding onto him, and I can still feel what he left inside me. I make a mental note to clean myself up before I go back to work.

The height difference is not a disadvantage...not one bit. It's a freaking blessing with the way this man tackles and folds me into the positions he craves.

Is there any part of me that he hasn't fucked already?

I'm sure he'll think of something, or maybe he even has other positions in mind we haven't done yet. He'd have a long list of other forbidden public places he'd like to venture into that could potentially get me killed or even fired.

I squeeze my thighs when I remember his cock between my breasts.

He could make me come with just the tip of his dick inside of me, and I almost did, but when he pushed more of himself in me, hitting that one spot that sent me into a world where I only saw gold stars...I came.

The sex with him gets better and better.

I've got to push these thoughts out of my head. I need to focus on getting through the rest of the day without thinking about what we did in this room. Or the empty hole in my heart that weighs on me whenever he has to leave.

I hold my wrist up, looking at my watch, and that's when I realize I had spent almost an hour not working. My eyes bulge, and my heart sinks with disappointment in myself. I lost track of time because I was too busy with two Rider men.

Damian and Danny.

If I thought Danny was cold-hearted...his father won by a landslide. I never want to be around that man again. Danny intervened just in time. Who knows how badly that could have escalated?

Then I was *"re-hydrating"* my boyfriend.

I drop my arm and rush out the door, looking for any missed text messages from Lori through my watch. My feet scurry out of the room, my shoes squeaking against the tiles. My watch vibrates with an alert. I hold it up, but then I hit something hard, bumping into a man's chest.

"Oh, I'm so sorry! I should've been paying attention to where I was going," I ramble, but a pair of familiar hands stop me.

Kane.

"It's okay, Ari. It's just me," Kane reassures me with a hard look, rubbing my shoulders. I meet his dark blue eyes, and that's when I realize I've been caught. His eyes scream, *I know what you just did in there.*

I want to run away now.

He looks like he was in a terrible fight or a car crash. He has little cuts and bruises under one eye. I want to reach out and touch him, ask him what happened, but the words get stuck in my throat.

"Sorry about that. I need to get back to work before my boss and co-workers kill me," I apologize again, waiting for him to let me go. I lick my swollen bottom lip from where Danny bit me. Crap, it's so obvious. He doesn't let go of me right away. Instead, he studies me a few seconds longer, pursing his lips when he watches my own.

Then he scoffs when he sees the blood on my tongue.

"I'm sure they won't," he says casually, releasing his grip on me.

"What are you doing here? Don't you have to go? Danny just left, didn't he?" I ask, looking around.

"Exactly. I do have to go. But not without saying goodbye to my favorite nurse, Paul's little sister."

I take in his blackened eye and grab his wrist softly.

"Kane, what happened to you? Are you okay?"

"I'm great," sarcasm evident, and I glare at him, crossing my arms.

"Kane...don't tell me I have to worry about you too?! Have you been looked at yet? Is that why you're here?" I shake my head. "Danny told me you guys are leaving on another mission..." My voice breaks because I constantly worry about Danny's return.

Even Kane's. I feel like I've grown attached and invested in every man on Danny's team.

I pray for them all to come home safe to their families.

"Yes, I'm fine...and of course. This job never stops, but we should be back soon." He sighs, running a hand through his dark hair. His eyes pierce mine with intensity. He doesn't flash his cheesy, warm smile I'm accustomed to. He reads me like a book, taking notice that I'm basically begging him for something positive to say. His brows raise and he flashes me a forced grin, exposing his perfect teeth. "But it's okay, Ari, don't worry. We will stop these guys before they can lay a finger on you or us. They won't even get a chance to get within walking distance of you. We won't allow it."

My hands drop to my sides in anguish, my shoulders stiffen and I watch Kane's face drop into shock, a frown replacing the million-dollar smile. I look around us, over my shoulder, at the thought of Shane breathing down my neck again. I shudder as chills rapidly spread across my skin, and my knees begin to buckle.

"What did you just say?"

Kane looks taken aback. He jerks his head, pinching his brows together, matching my confused expression.

Lori enters from behind him, leaning over his frame to the side at the end of the hallway, waving her arms to catch my attention.

"Where have you been?" she mouths.

She points to her watch hysterically, but I ignore her. I lean forward, blocking her out of my vision with Kane's frame.

"Grim didn't tell you?" Kane says.

I shake my head vehemently. "He didn't tell me what?"

"I thought he would tell you something like this." He looks away from me, nervously running his hand through his dark hair.

It doesn't sit well with me, but I still vouch for Danny's heart. Maybe there's more to the story... perhaps he just forgot?

"Tell me, Kane. Tell me right now."

He looks around, and it seems like he's searching for some privacy. Or maybe he's making sure the Admiral doesn't come grab him by the neck.

"Fuck it, you deserve to know." He leans into my ear, whispering, his breath sending more shivers up my spine. I'm paralyzed, waiting for him to spill. "People are after Grim. The same people that killed your brother."

This can't be happening.

I gasp, bringing my hand to my mouth. My stomach turns into a thousand knots, my world spins, and nausea grips me tight.

"What the fuck are you talking about?" I push him away, my palm firmly against his vest. The force manages to make his over six-foot frame take a step back. He tries to grab my hands to stop me, his fingers attempting to curl with mine. His lips flatten when I pull my hands out of his grasp.

"How is this possible?"

"Grim has a fucking bounty on his head. We're all at risk. They won't stop at anything to have us dead, the whole team, specifically Grim. They'll even hurt you if it means they can capture him. If it means they can hit him where he'll hurt the most, and that's you, Ari."

The blood drains from my face. My vision blurs immediately with fear, black clouding the edges. Suddenly, my hearing goes to silence, and the only thing I can hear is my heart drumming against my neck.

They want to kill Danny?

Teary-eyed, I tremble, my lips quivering for a response.

My heart begins to race harder and I flinch when Kane calls out for me, snapping me out of the spiral violently.

Teardrops streak down faster onto my cheeks, falling on my scrubs, and I can't blink. I can't move...all I can do is breathe.

It just won't ever end, will it?

If what Kane's saying is true, that means Danny has been keeping things from me when I've repeatedly warned him to let me in. That means...*he's been lying to me.*

We can't possibly move on with each other when things are still hidden.

My eyes shake side to side, searching for relief in Kane's dark blue eyes, hoping this is all just a bad dream again. Maybe if I close my eyes, I'll wake up pregnant at Danny's ranch like I did after Emilia's wedding.

After such an amazing moment when we shared such a serene reunion underneath the moonlight and waves crashing against the shore.

But when I blink and open my eyes again, I'm met with a softened Kane Slaughter, and I'm still in the same hallway of this freezing hospital.

It's not a dream. It's my horrid reality.

Danny's integrity has been fractured.

Someone is after my boyfriend. Someone who will go to great lengths to hurt me just to get to him.

Shane is gone, Nora's in jail.

Now, there's someone else out to hurt me?

"I don't want you to worry. I know this is the last thing you want to hear right now, but you have one of the best security systems installed in your home and it's encouraged by the Admiral that you continue to live your life normally. We got this. We got...*you.*"

I laugh, rolling my eyes.

"Live my life normally? Really, Kane? Has there been anything about my life that has been normal lately?"

He swallows and looks away from me like he can't bear to see me like this.

I have nothing more to say to him.

I resent their jobs.

I hate this lifestyle.

I'm over having to look over my shoulders constantly. I'm over my boyfriend leaving me all the time. I'm done having to wait for his return constantly. Having to put my plans on hold because I can't get out of bed some days because all I think about is him. The worry that clouds the back of my mind when he isn't near me, sleeping next to me, holding me.

I'm over it.

I need to take care of my patients.

"Well, gee, thanks." I brush past him, my shoulder grazing against him. I'm coming off rude, but this time, I want to and I don't care. "Thanks for letting me know, but I've got to get back to work," I snap, wiping away more tears from my eyes.

"Ari, wait." He grabs my forearm, his fingers pressing against my skin, pleading for me to stop.

I discover things I need to know by Kane *again*. First my brother's death, and now this? I find out by his teammate and not the man that always makes me feel safe, the man I've fallen in love with mindlessly.

I twist out of his grasp and jog away, continuously drying the waterfall of sorrow that pours down my eyes.

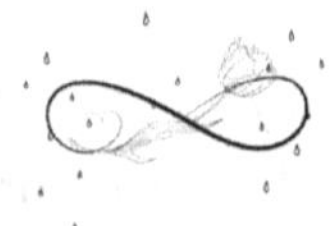

I have to stop by Ms. Salem's room before I go home for the day to check if she's made any progress with her recovery.

Apparently, Doctor Reese was aware of Damian and Danny stopping by to see me, so he let it slide, which was odd.

Lori told me Doctor Reese was a family friend of the Riders. There's no way in hell he doesn't have some connection with them because that's the only reason I still have my job. No yelling, no scolding or belittling came from Doctor Reese when I returned.

I don't know when I'll see Danny again, but this is the first time I don't want to be around him.

I'm livid and broken; betrayal burns through my bones, and I don't know what I'll do if I see him.

How could he keep this from me?

How could he not tell me after everything we've been through?

After Damian's horrid welcoming, and then Kane's revelation a second time...

I'm just...angry.

I walk into Ms. Salem's room, and she's going through a magazine, her legs underneath the blankets as if already tucked in for the night.

It's getting late, and she's my last patient.

"Hi, Ms. Salem. How did physical therapy go?" I look over her vitals, ensuring her blood pressure and oxygen levels are stable.

I can go home knowing my last patient is on her way to sleep. At least this is one part of my day I don't have to worry about.

Her dark brown eyes look tired, and she yawns, stretching her arms over her head.

"It went well. I didn't curse at him this time. He's actually cute now that we've gotten past our initial tension." She wags her eyebrows up and down before shooting me a giddy smile.

I chuckle, and it feels good to forget my harsh reality, even for a couple of seconds.

"Although I walked for a few minutes, but the pain was unbearable for some odd reason." She shrugs, reaching for her ankle over the covers. "So they're keeping me here longer to try to find out why and if the surgery had any post-operative complications."

"Oh no. I'm so sorry about that."

"Ehh, it's okay. I get to spend more time with the cute physical therapist." She blushes, lying back on the bed and crossing her arms. She looks at the ceiling as if she's daydreaming.

"There we go. Think of the positive. Always try to remember that," I say, checking my watch.

She catches on, shifting in the bed.

"I know that look. I used to have a boyfriend, too. Who is he and what has he done to you?" she playfully teases, but my hackles rise.

"It's nothing, Ms. Salem. Please get some rest and I'll see you when I come back for my next shift." I force a smile, pivoting toward the door, but she stops me.

"I guess we have more in common than I thought. I used to have boyfriend troubles all the time. He was a cop...always leaving me and kind of an asshole."

"Yeah, men..." I shake my head. Danny is kind of an asshole, but an asshole that I'll be forever tethered to.

An asshole I'm in love with.

"First, we bond over losing our loved ones, and now? Boy problems." She taps her jaw, and my emotion cracks when I think of the siblings we lost.

"Men are trash. That's why I'm single." She shrugs nonchalantly, looking away from me and back to her magazine.

My lips curve.

"Not all of them are, though." I instantly think of Kane and how he's always been good and kind despite his occasionally over-stepping, which is quite overwhelming. Like today.

"Whatever. In my mind, they all are."

"Good night, Ms. Salem."

"Good night, Ari, and remember, you're too beautiful to be sad."

Waving goodbye with a smile, I close the door to her room and take a sigh of relief. Last patient of the day is stable and in good spirits. The best way to end a shift.

25

———

ARI

Something wakes me up during the night, but I don't know what.

I'm on my stomach, face down on my pillow. I graze my hand over to the empty side of the bed, and my chest sinks to the pit of my stomach.

He's still not home. He's not home...in my bed because I've distanced myself from him. *Because he's still fucking working...*

I haven't answered his calls or texts.

He doesn't blow up my phone, though. He only reaches out to me at the oddest hours, sometimes late at night or around three in the morning, wishing me sweet dreams.

But he knows.

He knows I'm purposefully ignoring him.

He knows there's something wrong because he stopped trying to get a hold of me. There haven't been any more missed alerts from him, and he should be back any day from his mission because the military ball is in a week, and we were supposed to go together.

Not anymore.

I'm still going because Violet will be there with Zeke, and she begged me to go to it since it's her last night in town before she has to return to Texas.

I continued my daily routine, not letting the uncertainty of my relationship with Danny alter my mood and work. I made sure my mother was okay by calling her first thing in the morning as I got ready for work. I pushed through the long hours of sick patients and a grumpy boss. I would play soccer for a few hours after I made myself dinner with music blasting through my headphones until I was so tired and covered in sweat. Even through the freezing winter winds, I was able to exhaust myself and overheat.

Unsurprisingly, Danny missed Christmas. It should have been our first Christmas together. I wanted to watch his face light up when he saw that I bought him a new rifle he's been eyeing. The uncertainty only grew more after that.

I spent the holiday with my mother a few days prior. Eating posole every Christmas was a tradition. She would make it for my brother and I. I helped her make it while we listened to Christmas music, and talked about our New Year's plans. We finished the night off with a homemade blueberry pie I freshly baked from scratch, topped with ice cream.

I couldn't help but feel like something was missing, and it took my happiness away. The ability to feel grateful for another day was difficult because of Danny's absence. His absence leaves a hole in my heart and a weight on my shoulders.

Would it be like this for the next few years that he's in the Navy?

Spending holidays without him? Not a phone call? Not even a text?

We opened up our cliché Santa Claus wrapped gifts. I got her a new watch that tracks her fitness goals. She talked about wanting to stay in shape and wanted some more motivation when she took her afternoon walks to the park, earlier this year.

She knitted me a blanket.

So here I am again, after another long shift at the hospital. I stopped by my mother's place after for dinner. This time she made green spaghetti with chicken. She hadn't made it in a while because it was hard for her. It was one of Paul's favorite dishes, but this just meant she is starting to accept he was gone. Another leap in a good direction.

I drove home after I helped my mom clean up. After we finished eating, I washed the dishes, said goodbye, and headed back to my place.

Even the weather is different tonight.

It's dark and rainy. It makes me reminisce about the night Danny took me to his house for our first date.

My phone starts to ring, interrupting the radio. My windshield wipers aren't the only thing I hear anymore; instead, Danny's phone number spreads across the display screen in the center of my car.

Two options stare back at me, and I hit the red one.

It grows quiet except for the thunder and unforgiving rain that explodes on the glass. The winds threaten to sway my vehicle. I drive by the thick trees surrounding my cottage home, eager to get into bed and sleep. I cry myself to sleep like I usually do every night since Kane's revelation.

Nowadays, I sleep next to the Glock that Danny bought and trained me to use—waking up several times during the night because my anxiety gets the best of me.

Even though Shane is dead and Nora is in jail, I still wake up, clutching my non-existent baby bump as the Grim Reaper lingers in my head.

And then...my life turns sour again. I have the incredible shit end of the stick because now I get to worry about evil people that want to hurt me...to get to Danny.

I can't believe I'm thinking this, but Damian might be right.

Fuck him and his ego. And fuck him for the way he treated Danny and his mother.

But the bastard might be right, and I hate that.

This life is *hard.*

This military world has already eaten you up, chewed you, and spat you out, leaving practically nothing behind.

It's not for everyone. It isn't for you.

Those words stung and left a bitter taste...Is he right?

Danny still has a few years left before he retires, and I'm not sure if I'll be strong enough to support him and watch him leave me *over and over again.*

Fully aware he might not come back home to me.

When Kane almost kissed me, promising me things like a family and about the possibility of leaving the military, it did something to me. It made me realize that I want those things.

I want all of those things and more.

But not with Kane.

I want it all with Danny Rider.

It's getting dark. Purple and blue shades barely illuminate the sky, and the raindrops from the rainstorm bang louder.

That's when I catch Danny on my porch, sitting with his head hanging down on a bench he built for us. He carries a bouquet of flowers in his hands, dressed in all black.

Tulips.

Pink tulips dangle from his big hands. As I drive to park next to his truck, I swallow the rock in my throat. His betrayal weighs heavily on my spirit, and I don't know what will pour out of my mouth when I walk out of this car.

All I know is that this should have never come from Kane. I wanted transparency from Danny, and I've told him this repeatedly. I've set my standards high after Shane, and I will not lower them or apologize for it.

I turn off my brother's Bronco with a heavy sigh as I stare at the speedometer, and the engine transitions to silence. Thunder rumbles in the distance, rain drops blur my windshield and I can't see anything clearly anymore.

My hands shake as I pull my keys out of the ignition.

I open the door, and the rain hasn't let up. In fact, it just got worse. Freezing water hits me hard as I step out. I plant my running shoes into puddles of water, getting them soaked through until I feel water in my socks. I take a deep breath and close the car door.

My hair and uniform get drenched right away, and my skin explodes with goosebumps.

It's so cold.

My thoughts are already scrambled as Danny stands from my porch and walks into the rain to get to me.

My heart breaks because the closer he gets to me, I know the wall I've built has shattered into irretrievable pieces, and Danny will unfortunately get cut by them. From breaking my vows to God to losing my best friend and my baby in the same shitty year, I'm letting this entire year's trauma affect me now.

We stand there in the rain, our bodies facing each other, but my eyes linger on the ground. I still can't look at him just yet because once I do, I feel like I'll want to let him bury himself inside me. A part of me wants to keep pretending. Like our paths are fine, and I should give in to the dangerous lust we hold for each other until the sun comes up.

But I refuse.

"You've been ignoring my calls." Danny breaks the icy silence first. He deadpans, his tone unreadable, and I can't tell if he's sad, mad, or disappointed. "Are you okay?" He leans forward, taking one step closer, but I don't answer. "Let's go inside and talk." He offers his hand for me to take, and I push it away.

"No."

"Ari."

"Why didn't you tell me?" I tilt my head up, glaring at him through the harsh rain hitting us both. My black hair sways from the wind and his dark blond hair is wet and shaggy. His light blue eyes darken, and his jaw tightens.

"Tell you what?" He takes another step closer, but it sends me another step back, creating a distance between us so I can say what I need to say without his magnetic, sinful attraction to alter my strength.

"Why didn't you tell me that the same people responsible for my brother's death are after you...after us?" He goes rigid, his grip on the bouquet intensifies, and his knuckles turn white. "Why are they after you, Danny? I know you've never been in a serious relationship before, but this is definitely something you warn your girlfriend about."

My bangs drip with rain, and Danny rubs his hand through his beard, looking away from me.

"Who told you?"

"It doesn't matter."

"You're right. Why am I asking? I already know who it was." His deep voice concedes with a grimace.

"It doesn't matter. I've told you time and time again. No more secrets, and you still can't do it."

"Ari, it's a little hypocritical of you, don't you think?"

I'm taken aback. I narrow my eyes in confusion at his accusation.

"No more secrets, but you still haven't told me about Kane's visitation."

My heart sinks, and I had already forgotten about that because nothing happened. Kane has always visited me and kept his promise to my brother. Visiting me in the middle of the night was something out of the norm, but still, he has always been there since Paul died, even though I never gave him any attention. I acknowledged his efforts, but that was all it was. I never carried personal conversations with him since I was too busy grieving and studying in the past.

Lightning strikes in the distance, flashing Danny's face with light shades of white, like a flashlight.

"I didn't tell you because I didn't want to create an unnecessary rift between the two of you." I wave my hand defensively. "You guys work together, you guys are friends, on the same team, and I won't add more fuel to a fire that doesn't need to be ignited. It's silly, pointless, and *innocent*."

He squints through the rain. The water has completely flooded his clothing, accentuating every muscle underneath his black shirt.

He sighs.

"I didn't tell you *to protect you*. You don't need to worry about the bullshit that my job holds. Nothing has happened so far. My team and I are taking care of it, and if that means you can focus on rebuilding yourself without having to worry about things you shouldn't, then I'll be the fucking bad guy in your story."

"Really?" I squeak, my scrubs feeling heavy on my body now. It's fair, but at the same time, it's dishonesty.

My eyes sting and grow heavy with anguish. I look away from his beautiful face to muster more courage to say what I need to.

"I don't trust you anymore," I tell him brokenly. It almost comes out like a whisper, but I know he heard me. "Your father was right. I'm only going to hold you back."

"He's not right about anything, Ari. He's a narcissist."

"But...your job...this constant feeling that Death surrounds us like it has a permanent hold on me and the ominous darkness of it reminding me that it did its damage on my soul. It echoes over and over again in the depths of my mind. I can't do it anymore, Danny." I suck in air because I feel like I'm suffocating. My voice pitches high with despair. "You are no good for me. I... I need time alone. We need time apart." I say sternly. "You're poison to me."

He stops breathing, and so do I when the words leave my mouth.

Do I mean it? Do I really mean this?

Danny pales, as if I just shot an arrow through his heart. His face falls, jaw clenching hard as he straightens his back. He steps away from me, turning around slightly and rubbing his chin.

"You're always gone, anyway. I'm always alone." I feel like I have to tell him these things. For one, it's the fucking truth. And second, maybe I can make him hate me this time around. Maybe it'll help him realize I've been a complication all along like he said I was.

"I won't let you leave me, Ari. Grant me mercy by putting a bullet in my head, then. Because I'd rather die than live in a world where someone else has your soul and not me."

I'm inflamed with anger, and I charge over to him. I push his shoulder, but he doesn't flinch.

"Just please go! Leave!" I point to his truck menacingly. "Leave like you always do. Leave now! Before I say things." I scream.

The rain picks up harder, and the pouring water patters the surface of our skin.

He looks up at me and furrows his eyebrows. He's in pain as my words leave my mouth.

"No. Just say it, Ari, stop being so fucking scared all the time. Stop being so fucking weak."

Now, I've pushed him too far for the first time, and a part of me regrets it. Maybe I'm being unfair...or maybe I've just hit my limit with lies and the horrid events I've been through this year.

The words sting, and a lump grows more in my throat. Anger makes my body tremble, and I grow hot as fire blows out of my mouth like a dragon with my words.

"All right, Grim Reaper." I spit. "Your name fits you perfectly because so much death surrounds you. Everyone around you dies! I will not be a part o-of—" I stutter. "—of this curse that surrounds you."

Danny's jaw clenches harder, and I can't tell if he's shocked from the different side of me that has unlocked or hurt because my words are getting to him, but I don't care. For the first time, I don't care if my anger hurts someone else. I want him to feel what I feel. I want him to be angry with me. I want him to hurt like me.

"Everyone dies around you. I almost did. Our baby died." I pause and palm my lower stomach where I used to hold our child, taking in a deep breath, before continuing, "Damon." I didn't mean to bring up the hostage, but the thoughts keep pouring into wounded words. "My own brother died around you."

Then he stiffens and looks at me with an incandescent expression that sends chills up my spine, and I almost retreat, drawing back my actions, but my boiling wrath doesn't let me.

"I lost my baby too!" He points to his chest. "I don't get to be a father. I didn't get to know him or know what he would look like. If he was going to have your brown or my blue eyes. If he was going to have your black hair." His face flickers pools of affliction, his voice roaring with affliction. "I know I said fucked up things to you that one night and that will forever eat me alive." He drawls, stalking toward me, his steps loud and indignant.

"You're really blaming me for everything? Don't you dare act like I'm not a man at the end of the day. I've been grieving, too, but I handle my shit differently, Ari. I do my best to save who I can when I'm out there with my team. You don't know what you're talking about. You have no idea what it's like to watch a body get burned alive." Each word hits me like a bolt powered by resentment.

"When I told you I was pregnant with our baby, you couldn't even look at me, Danny." I sniffle, my voice crescendoing high and breathy as the memories of my announcement in his truck flood me like a hurricane of disappointment. "You crushed me. You broke my heart. You broke my heart over and over again this past year."

"Yeah...I did. Because all my life, I've been this man who couldn't feel anything unless I was drunk. I did react in such a fucked up way, and I'll be groveling for the rest of my life at your feet. There is no excuse for my reaction, but there is a reason why I didn't want children."

"What is that reason?" I wave my hands, awestruck, then cross them over my chest.

"Do you know what it's like to carry out dismembered children from an explosion from a fucking playground?" He quirks his brows, daring me to answer him.

I flinch, regretting my choice of words.

"To have a child bleed all over you while their parents beg you to save them, knowing damn well it's too late?" I flinch as he roars. "Children, Ari! Babies! Dead. Because of the level of evil these motherfuckers will go to, and with a smile on their face! Paul made a huge impact on my life, and you know that. I drank myself past dangerous limits all year because of it." He roars at me with cold, distant eyes. He deepens his tone, and I'm tempted to backpedal this conversation.

But I can't stop. Words spew out of my mouth like scorching lava, ready to swallow and burn anything in my path.

"All of this did happen because of you. I gave you all of me. Everything. *You* completely obliterated every moral I held so dear to me. If you hadn't started a war between you and Shane that night at El Devine, maybe he wouldn't have tried to kill me. Maybe our baby would still be here. Don't even get me started on Nora."

"So, I should have just let that coward abuse you?"

"Why didn't you? Because of the promise with Paul? That you refused to tell me about?"

"No, Ari, fuck the promise. This is more than that. I will always protect you. Look out for you and your mother because you are everything to me."

"I could have defended myself. I don't need your protection. I don't want it." My voice comes out high-pitched, and I'm yelling even louder. "Dammit, Danny! If it weren't for you, I wouldn't have these scars on me. Are you happy now? Are you happy that my body now carries scars just like yours?" I'm shaking, crying, and Danny holds his ground like I just obliterated his heart. He's listening to me, and his chest rises up and down from his heavy, angered breathing, or is it from his hurting?

Either way, I can't stop.

"You want to break me? Well, guess what, I'm broken. Mission accomplished! Do you want to hear me scream? Well, I'm screaming, and I don't know if I'll ever stop." I sob, my breaths rattled. "I should have never thought this could work. I fell for you so hard. Something about you captured my heart instantly, and yet you can't say the words I've felt about you since the first time you kissed me. You can't say those three words, can you? Are you even capable of that emotion?"

I narrow my eyes at him while he watches me fall apart, and my heart pounds. Every single vein boils with emptiness. "I knew our ending could never be a happy one." The words spit out of my mouth, full of heartache and resentment. I resent him. I can't stop myself. It just keeps pouring out of me like a broken dam, and the water flows without regard, destroying everything in its path.

"Well, I can say them." Raindrops fall down my cheek, and I push him from me, hitting his broad chest, but of course, he doesn't move, and through heavy salty tears, I shout, "I. Love. You."

He stares into me, nostrils flaring, but then he completes changes when I say it. The tension he holds inside shifts and diminishes when I say it.

"I love you," I repeat, shrugging. I say it like it is the easiest thing in the world for me because it is, and it's the truth.

"I love you!" I shout again. "I love you all the time, Danny. I've loved you since the day I met you. I love you *even when I shouldn't.* I worry about you because I love you. Every time you walk out that door, I'm scared you won't come back to me. I think these things because I love you. I love all of you...everything. All the parts of you that you consider dark? Every part of you that you deem unworthy? I think are beautiful...because I love you." My voice bleeds pure honesty, pleading with him to understand why I can't do this anymore.

It hurts to love him.

"But it hurts so much," I whimper, looking at the flowers and then back at him, my vision blurred with crushed tears. "It pains me to love you, Danny, and..." I sob, shaking my head, biting my lip, my teeth sinking until it throbs. "I don't think this life is for me."

I look at him, expecting to hear some type of response, or maybe those three haunting words.

Of course he can't say it back to me.

What was I expecting?

"If we have a family again, what am I supposed to do? Have them go through the same thing I do? Lonely nights and mornings? Missed birthdays, missed holidays, missed milestones like their first word or first steps?"

He doesn't respond. He stares at me, shutting me out like he always used to do when we first met. He's unpredictable again, and I don't like it.

I shake my head.

"No, Danny, I don't think I will allow that to happen if I want to start a family."

"That's not fair, Ari." He watches me, but he's quiet, and he looks away from me again, running his hand through his wet hair.

"Tell me, Danny, what the fuck are you?"

I've encapsulated his attention again.

He looks at me, his jaw closing right before he laughs, grinning, stressed. His mouth gapes open, amused as if I said something funny. He rubs his hands through his beard, grinning devilishly.

"Fucking tell me! I saw the way your eyes turned black. I dream of your tattoo every night. That's what I dream of. A freaking Grim Reaper haunts me every night since the day I almost died. So tell me, what the fuck are you?"

He shakes his head.

"What do you want me to tell you? You already know the answer to your own question."

"Tell me, dammit."

"You see him in your dreams, right? He talks to you, doesn't he?"

My shoulders slump and my eyes bulge because it feels like he's reading my thoughts.

"You know the answer. You know just how fucking real life can get, don't you? That's why you wake up screaming most nights?"

He's right, but I don't want to admit it. It sounds ridiculous.

When I fall asleep, he talks to me, only whispering the same words over again.

"Time waits for no one."

"You want to know? It's simple," he says. "He haunts me, too, and it started when your brother died." He looks away from me and looks up at the sky, letting out another sigh as white fog escapes from his body heat. The temperature drops even further.

"E-explain," I demand, my teeth chattering.

"There isn't much explanation, but just that. I only see him on missions or deployments. He's always there, like a fucking shadow. Talking to me."

Fuck, this all sounds so weird and crazy. It shouldn't make sense...but it does.

"When you died, I dared to talk back to it, begging it not to take you. I don't know how, but it let me save you. He gave me your soul back." Danny is transfixed on me as if he's staring into my soul, waiting for a reaction out of me, but all I can do is swallow as tears continuously fall, blending in with the freezing rain.

Then a massive gust of wind hits me, sending my hair flying, and another lightning strikes, but this time, it's close by, and I shudder when the crack of thunder jolts through me as if it struck me.

It all makes sense. Death possessed his body. The dreams, the nightmares with the Grim Reaper. Death has been here all along, trying to give me clues. He's a shadow stalking the living. Stalking Danny and me.

Stalking everyone, just waiting to grab us.

But this only makes me realize one thing. I should have died. I could've died, and all this suffering would have been avoided.

Danny robbed me of my chance to be with my baby and brother.

"I could have been with our son. I could have been with Paul. Why?! Why wouldn't you let me die?"

"Because, Ari..." He steps closer to me and I let him get close to me. So close I can feel his body heat, and he still clutches the tulips.

He leans down, so he's right in front of my face.

"I needed to save you...like you've saved me."

Some emotion flashes through his eyes, and I swear they're watering.

"You saved me, Ari, don't you get it?" He grabs my hand gently, holding it with his calloused hand. "I call you my *little angel* for a reason."

"You can't save everyone, Danny." I retract my hand from him. "You should have let me go."

"What about your mother, Ari?! Why would you want her to go through losing both of her only children?" He tucks the flowers into his jeans and cups my face into his hands aggressively. "*What about me?*"

I shake my head, sniffling.

"I could have been with our son. I could have been with my brother," I repeat. Am I so far gone? Is it such a horrible thing to want to follow my child into the afterlife?

He lets my face go, letting out a sarcastic scoff and smile. His face falls, but he still lingers close, not moving away.

His smile is anything but happy. It's wicked and sinister. Then he returns my gaze, his eyes piercing through me like a knife.

"Now, look, who's the selfish one?"

I slap him across the face, hard. I didn't even think twice about it. Something unusual came over me when he said it and I didn't hide from it.

He looks down, emotionless and unfazed by my outburst.

Internally, I'm apologizing. I step closer to him, but then I stop myself from palming his cheek when that's all I want to do. My hand falls back to my side. I can't believe I just did that. I didn't mean it.

"I'm sorry."

"I don't need your apology. What I need is for you to realize that I will never let you go. You're mine, Ari."

He cups my face into his big, rough hands again and kisses me. His eyebrows narrow in, and he shuts his eyes tight. His kiss deepens harder and harder, but it's not from lust... I swear it's from *love*.

Then he stops kissing me, barely moving away.

"Kane might leave the military for you, but... I would die for you," he breathes against my lips. He sighs, retracting away from me, shrugging his shoulders, stretching his back, and I can hear his bones pop.

A tear escapes me.

I swear, even though he hasn't said those three words specifically to me yet...it feels like he just did.

I'm stuck. I love them both, but in two different ways.

"I don't think I can live for myself," I whisper, my lips trembling as my dark confession unveils. I feel like I'm losing everything...even myself. I don't want to lose him, though.

"You need to be strong, Ari. Be strong for yourself. Not for me, not for your mother. Not even for Paul, but for yourself. Embrace your wounds. Embrace every single scar because they don't define who you are in the ways you think they do. It just means you can't be killed so easily. You don't go down without a fight. You're stronger than you think. Your wings may be bent, little angel, but they aren't broken. You're stronger than your scars. Because they'll fade away, but your soul won't."

I close my eyes, not wanting to face him anymore...it hurts too much. Everything hurts all the time.

Then he pries my hands open. I look down to find he placed the bouquet of tulips in my hand, covered in raindrops. He reaches into his other pocket and pulls out a sealed, small black envelope and drops it in my other hand.

"Merry Christmas, angel."

He forces my hand to close around them and walks away from me.

Then his phone rings, and I'm crying heavy tears in silence.

He looks at his phone intensely.

This is the part I hate. It can't be work calling again at this time. He just got back...no way. He can't leave me now. This is important.

He walks further away from me. A dreadful, long, sad silence between us stops us from talking.

"So this is what you want, right? Me, gone?" he recites my words back to me, spewing them with anger and frustration.

"I—" He interrupts me.

"I'm no good for you?"

"I—"

"I'm poison to you?" he shouts, the veins in his neck making a presence, and I'm growing desperate. I haven't seen him this hurt since the night he confessed everything.

"Danny, sto—" I try to interrupt him, but it doesn't work. This time, there's no stopping what's about to happen.

"We need time apart?" he growls.

"I don't know!" I shout, frustrated. I look into his eyes, my own searching back and forth vigorously for mercy and patience. I need him to wait for me, but...I can't say it. I don't think it'll change how I feel or how he feels.

He nods, defeated...and I swear the first time when I look at his blue eyes... He's the one that's broken, and I'm afraid Noel was right. I think I just broke Danny beyond repair.

"I'll make the decision for you, then. I'm leaving." He brushes his beard with his hand, looks at me, then back at his truck. "Goodbye, Ari."

It feels like my chest got defibrillated with pain.

Shit.

I never thought the word "goodbye" would hurt me with the devastation of an impact like it does now. A type of farewell that holds much more of a sting.

It feels like I took what we had built up these past few months, from when we first met, our journey of healing together, to his growth...and obliterated it. I depleted it like glass shattering on the floor into a trillion pieces with no repair in sight.

That's the first time he's ever said goodbye to me. It's always a "see you soon," but he didn't say it.

"You mean, see you soon, right, Danny?" I croak out. My whole body feels like it's going to fall over.

"I have to go." He looks at me through a tightened jaw.

He's really saying goodbye this time, and I'm full of regret.

He walks to his truck, but every step he takes breaks me more and more as I come to self-clarity.

"Say it!" I shout at him. My voice bleeds with sadness, pleading with him, like if he won't say it, I'll die. I walk after him, tripping over a rock, but I catch my balance, avoiding stumbling into the flooded lawn. My arms swing forward, and I see my reflection in a puddle, my wet hair falling into my face.

But he says nothing.

"Please say it! Say *see you soon*, please." Not one more word comes out of his mouth, and I know I went too far with my truth.

I stop walking when he gets into his truck and starts it. My chest heaves with desperation, sobbing against the freezing wind. I'm watching him through raindrops that blur my vision.

He's actually leaving.

His engine roars as he slowly pulls out of my driveway.

He's halfway down the road already, and I don't know what I just did. I'm full of remorse. I watch the rain in the sky, and I blink fast.

I run toward the road in the cold, freezing night. There's no more light. I reach the road in less than a minute, and I'm crying uncontrollably with each stride of despair.

"Danny!" I stomp my foot on the street and yell as loud as I can as if he could hear me, but he's already turned a corner to the main road.

He's gone. He's really gone.

"Danny..." I murmur through rapid breaths. I can see my breath in the air. My feet burn, and I feel like frostbite threatens my skin. My eyebrows furrow deeply. It makes me feel alone, and the only place that can make it better is going back in time.

I reach for the envelope, tearing the barrier open, and I bite my lip, shaking my head. My fingers tremble, and I do my best to shield it from the rain.

It's a drawing...

The photo of Paul and me as kids. The same one that I found torn to shreds in Iraq when someone had broken into my room and destroyed my things.

Danny hand-drew the picture, bringing back the memory of my favorite photo in pencil. It's incredibly detailed.

What have I done?

26

———

DANNY

The gates open to my property, and I grip the steering wheel tight in my hand to the point my palm gets pinched against the leather, and it twinges from friction.

I didn't want to leave her, but of course, I had to take a phone call regarding the current mission from the Admiral.

I'll continue to be the villain in her books if it means she stays protected. I won't let her in on the gruesome details that have been my life lately. It all began when I started work again after my leave of absence.

It's like I live two very different lives.

I tried to hide it from Ari. It was for a good reason. She doesn't need to worry about this, but alas, Kane can't keep his fucking mouth shut.

He keeps overstepping, and I've been a very, very patient man.

Ari has made me a more patient and forgiving man.

But this?

I didn't feel the need to act out and confront him because I knew once I did...it wouldn't be pretty. We have more serious matters in front of us. But I might have to show him what happens when someone crosses me regarding my girl.

The gates close behind my truck, and I loosen my grip on the wheel.

Ari's words stabbed me deep with no remorse.

A night that should've ended with her bent over, my cock deep inside of her while she screamed my name repeatedly, turned sour.

I wanted to fuck her mouth, cunt, and ass all in one night.

But instead, it ended with us...estranged in separate beds.

I park my truck in the driveway and pull out my cigarettes. The rain stopped pouring, and I could sense the old me poking at me, my favorite pick of poison sitting on my shelves in my kitchen, calling my name.

I step onto my front porch and reach for the pack of cigarettes in my pocket. My thumb brushes against the lighter two times before it lights up, and I inhale the cigarette.

The flavor burns onto my tongue, and I stare at the stars.

She loves me. She said it. She fucking said it.

But instead of pushing her away when she said it like I would have a few months ago, I wanted to carry her into her house and kiss her until her world only revolved around me. Fuck her over and over again in different positions, on her bed, tangled up in bed sheets until the sun came up.

I blow out the smoke and watch the bright reddish-orange fire crackle at the end of my cigarette.

She wanted me gone? I'm poison to her?

It pains her to love me?

I've been stabbed, sliced, beaten, *blown up*, but her words were worse than all of that combined when she said it.

Fuck.

It was cruel, but a part of me understands her.

It isn't fair to her after everything she's been through.

It feels like it's over.

She said it was over.

But even if she doesn't want me, she has me.

She has me wrapped around her pretty little soul, even if that means I don't get to kiss or hold her again.

I won't ever love another woman because she has me...she fucking has me.

A familiar darkness I've learned to push away twists violently in my chest, scratching at my sanity once again, and I crack.

I throw the cigarette to the floor, putting it out underneath my boot, and swing the door to my house open after unlocking it.

Swinging the door open frantically, pissed off even, and I'm met with silence.

It's dark, quiet and eerie.

I was born and molded by silence and cold-hearted parents from birth to adulthood. I thrive in quiet loneliness because of them...until Paul's death.

Until Ari.

After that, it's just been noise that I like to drown out with whiskey.

I haven't slept alone at home in a while. I've been with her every night, holding her, consumed by her scent, in her bed.

But now, I'm alone in my house like I used to be. Like the old me. Before I crossed paths with Ari, and I don't like it.

I walk toward my kitchen, not bothering to turn on any light.

I don't need to be guided towards a place I know too well. A place that used to be my favorite escape.

Throwing my keys on the counter without a care in the world, I grab a bottle of Jack Daniels off the bar. It's in my hand,

and I turn it until I read "Tennessee Whiskey". I stare at it long, getting lost in my thoughts. It feels like forever that I stand in my bar area.

I debate with myself.

Just one drink. One drink to take the edge off, the anger, the pain.

I twist the cap open, but this time, I take a couple of gulps from the top, not bothering with a whiskey glass. The familiar smooth, burning amber alcohol welcomes me back with open arms, and I sigh deeply, licking my lips after swallowing a reasonable amount.

I tighten my jaw over and over again, looking at it.

I have a few days back home, and now I'm going to spend them like this?

Fuck.

I slam the bottle back down on the counter and think long and hard before I make my next move.

I'm tempted to drive back to Ari's place, throw her over my lap and spank her until her ass is red and flaring raw.

I want to punish her for thinking such delusional ideas, like leaving me is an actual option.

Her soul is mine forever.

I'm almost entertained enough to crack a smile.

I already started to drink—shit.

I can't drive anywhere now, but I need to be alone, too, even though I want to be anywhere else but here.

I'll spend the night with the one thing I can always count on to make me forget things I don't want to remember.

Whiskey.

So why the fuck not? If she wants to leave me, one night of taking the edge off won't make a fucking difference.

I'm upstairs in my bedroom, throwing off my soaked shirt and pants, pulling off my belt, and kicking off my boots fast.

I change into my workout clothes, slipping into a dark navy blue shirt and shorts, and head to my basement. But I grab the bottle I left on the counter before I do.

Meanwhile, I try not to let my demons come back to me full circle.

I will work out until my body begs me to stop, and even then...I'll push more.

I will drink until I can only feel serenity.

I will forget that my life has hit this bottomless pit tonight... just tonight.

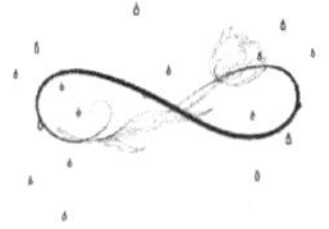

Push-up after push-up. Squat after squat. Bench press after bench press.

It's been three fucking hours, and I can't stop.

I'm breathing hard with each rep. My heart thunders against my rib cage as I push my body past incredible limits.

It's well into the night, around three in the morning, and I keep grinding hard until I can push the thoughts of Ari...our baby...and Paul's death out of my head.

Sweat profusely falls all over my skin, drenching through my clothes, and I still can't stop.

I'm still trying to digest everything Ari confessed. It hurts...this hurts more than I ever thought it would. She's stronger than she gives herself credit for. I know her well enough to know that she can get through this. Even if she shuts me out, I know my little angel will continue to thrive. But the selfish part of me wants to cheer her on every step of the way.

I've avoided taking another swallow of Jack for now. Instead, I've gotten lost in my workout, listening to Avenged Sevenfold and System of a Down blasting, the mirrors on my wall shaking from how loud the volume is.

My gym has about everything a regular one would have.

A treadmill and weights galore.

After my last rep of deadlifts, I drop the bar of weights, passing my personal best, and I grunt hard as I max them out.

The oversized plates on each side of the bar collide with the floor, bouncing, and the metal reverberates riotously.

Almost every single vein in my arms makes its dramatic presence known. I open and close my hands when I realize I've added more calloused texture.

No matter what I do, how much I try to forget our fight...

Ari is still in my head, along with her sweet scent.

I close my eyes, trying to catch my breath.

But I still see her.

Her smile glimmers in my mind. The same smile she gave me when I surprised her for her birthday. It dazzles in my head. Then I see her wide-eyed brown irises looking up at me, tears rolling down her face when she had my cock down her throat. Blood rushes down to my core when I remember how I had her against the hospital room wall, her beautiful tits bouncing each time I drove into her.

Her hard nipples should be in my mouth right now.

Fuck this.

I grab the whiskey bottle and take another drink, downing it quickly like water.

She should be in my arms right now, taking slow, peaceful breaths while she sleeps.

And if she has another night of terror, I should be there to promise her, assure her that she's okay.

We'll be okay.

I thought I was making the right choice by not informing her about the bounty I'm the center of.

Still, I don't regret not sharing it. I'm solid in my decision.

She's right, though. The evil won't stop.

She lost Paul and our son in one year. I don't want her to imagine me in a casket, too.

Something pulls at my heart, and the need to check on Ari consumes me. Breathing hard, sweaty palms, I check the cameras on my phone, ensuring she's safe and okay.

After a few swipes, I find my little angel. I can't see her face, but she's cuddled underneath the blankets in her room; on her side, the tulips I left her are on the nightstand.

I knew Kane stayed behind when I ordered them out of the building. He told me he needed to piss, and I told him to make it quick, but the asshole lied.

Our friendship ended the day he first overstepped. When he first aimed blame at me for Paul's death in Iraq. And then he asked Ari on a date right before.

It ended right then and there that day...and I don't feel shit about it.

The fact that he thinks he'll have Ari underneath him one day makes me laugh.

Over my dead body.

No one will ever touch her the way I do.

I stopped by her mother's early in the morning while Ari was at work. I wanted her and her mother to spend some time without me there, so I waited for her at her place after I showered and went to the store for her favorite flowers. I waited while they had dinner.

I shared a long, personal, one-on-one conversation with Mrs. Alvarez. We talked about Paul, and I asked her what Ari was like as a child. She told me she had always been intelligent, caring, and giving. Never selfish. Never disloyal.

But now, that same girl wants nothing to do with me or this military lifestyle.

I look at myself in the mirrors I have installed on the walls of my gym. I run my hand through my beard, my chest heaving.

Then I fidget and have both hands on my waist, pacing back and forth. My abdomen constricts as I breathe.

I'm tempted to finish the rest of the bottle of Jack, so I can pass out asleep without thinking of what Ari said.

But then a flash of red catches my eye.

I can feel something wet that's not my sweat, and I wipe the bottom of my nose to find blood smeared across my fingers.

I look at my reflection in the mirror, confused, narrowing my brows, and see more blood fall, and I swear my heart sinks with dread.

Because the last time I saw blood fall from someone's nose, it was the worst night of my life.

I feel the hairs on the back of my neck stand, cold breathing down on it, and it all feels too fucking painfully familiar.

The reaper laughs low and condescending into my head, and I tighten my jaw, watching the blood fall into my hands.

Drip, drip, drip.

It's demonic. My well-acquainted friend's voice sends me into nostalgia, and I'm transported back to the time I first met Death.

"Chop Suey" by System Of A Down begins to fade slowly

from my ears, as if the volume is being lowered to silence, and I'm back in Iraq.

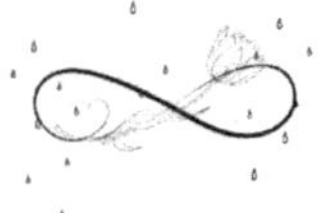

Adrenaline courses through my veins, and I'm burning despite the brutal cold conditions.

My molars grind against each other. My brows narrow in with aggression.

This is the stress I've been trained to handle. What I will handle.

Both teams are at each other's throats, arguing and going back and forth with each other, and I'm growing fucking tired of it, but I'll listen while I decide the next course of movement.

"Paul, if we go east, it gives us more cover! More time to retreat once Kane pulls the trigger," someone on his team hisses just loud enough we can hear him.

I'm sitting on a rock, bouncing my knee up and down while everyone stands, Paul's team and mine facing each other.

"If we go west, it'll make the best shot. We don't have anyone on this team that's made a shot that far before from the east. We can't risk it. We'll be letting Omar go if we choose your spot. A mission fucking failed, Aitu!" Paul snarls back.

Normally, I'd be the one taking the shot, but I've taken Kane underneath my wing, pressuring him to adapt under pressure so he'll be one to eliminate the threat.

This isn't going to be a topic of discussion. I'm in charge, and I know what I have to do. And it stops right now.

"Everyone, shut the fuck up," I snarl. All eyes are on me.

Everyone has their masks on, covered in black. Nothing but wide, frustrated eyes looking back at me.

"Executioners." I look at my team, pointing to the other side of the woods. "Re-group," I order them away from Paul's team. Rooker, Kane, and Lopez retreat with nods. All whispers come to a complete silence. Kane spits and chewing tobacco lands on the ground.

Paul stalks toward me as I clutch my rifle tighter. Even through the obsidian night, I can see the conflict brew in the air. Every single operator strained with apprehension.

Friction looms between the teams, and this needs to end.

"Grim, you know I'm right," Paul says, his breath leaving a white puff, his boots breaking more twigs on the ground with each step.

I look at him, my eyes narrowed, my mind running a thousand miles.

He is right, but his teammate is right, too.

"Just trust me, Grim. I know I'm making the right call," Paul pleads, standing next to me. "And if I'm wrong... Well, you can kill me yourself. But I think my little sister and Mom will be slightly disappointed."

I smirk underneath my mask, looking away from him and instead at my rifle.

I'm itching to grab a cigarette, but I decide against it.

"Are you sure about this?" I ask sternly, but my tone isn't friendly or brotherly. It comes out authoritative and stern. I'm not talking to him like he's my best friend, even though the decision I'm about to make says otherwise.

I need to get through his thick skull that this decision could not only mean a mission failed...it could mean our lives.

Killed in action.

"Yes." He doesn't stutter, he doesn't hesitate. He's confident, and my chest tightens. I inhale the cold, frozen air to ease the pressure, but it only returns with frost, making me feel worse.

I look at him, tormenting his brown eyes to see if he'll break or change his mind, testing him.

He doesn't break.

I look away and at every other SEAL in front of me.

"We're going west," I finalize.

Even when I say it, something tugs at my clarity. I am sure. I am always confident, but uncertainty tingles in the back of my mind for the first time.

We discussed a plan to execute the mission. We grouped up after I told them we were headed west and to follow Paul's orders.

So here we go, following my brother's plan, walking on the edge of a mountain, headed west with tension thick, and our minds set to kill.

We walked a couple more feet closer to Omar and his crew of followers.

I'm quiet as always, observing every little detail I can see through my night vision, and the aura rises with ominous anticipation.

We walk tactically, each step well accounted for. Paul and I lead our teams in the front. Every other operator trail behind us, and we're so close to our destination.

But then I catch something moving to my left, and I stop in my tracks on the side of the mountain, but Paul keeps walking in front of me.

It moved as fast as it came, and I glare at a tall tree where I last saw this dark shadow move like a figure.

Another deer?

Then I feel something touch my neck.

It couldn't be wind because nothing else moves when I study the landscape. No trees or leaves sway with it, but I feel something airy and wintry...like a breath, on my throat.

That's when I hear a familiar snap that echoes deep, the devastating sound bouncing off the mountains when it rang, howling like a ghost, and then it stops.

A shot was fired.

And then another shot rings out, sending Paul spinning, and then another one.

My soul shatters when I realize what the fuck just happened.

But the shooting doesn't stop, and everyone takes cover.

I drop to the ground, my chest hitting the floor to make sense of what's happening.

"They saw us coming! They have us pinned!" Lopez informs me before he starts radioing air support.

"Grim, get the fuck back, you're going to get shot!" It's Rooker.

"Is Alvarez okay? Where the fuck is he?" Kane shouts into the mic, panicking.

I want to cover my ears when every single man on this mission tonight screams into my ears with worried, shaky tones, demanding me to give them an answer.

Shut up. Shut up. Shut the fuck up, and let me think!

I dare to look forward, tilting my head off the dirt, and I see Paul on his back, wide-eyed to the sky, gasping for air.

"Don't do it, Grim. Don't you fucking do it," Rooker barks at me. He knows me too well. They are all a couple of feet away from us with cover. A luxury Paul and I don't have.

I jump off the floor, sprinting as bullets spray in our direction. Dirt and rocks explode into the air all around us. I pull him away from where he is lying. I drag him back behind a rock that sits nearby. He weighs nothing to me, when adrenaline lights me up and our lives on the line.

The boulder gives both him and I just enough cover.

I expect him to groan as I drag him to cover, but no...it's choking, I hear.

Another bullet is ricocheting off the floor by my foot but barely misses me, leaving my toes intact.

I make it to the only shield we have.

I sit behind the rock and kneel over Paul's body as my best friend's life gets drained away. I remove his mask so he can breathe better, and I do the same.

He's pale, his eyes watering, blood coming out of his neck, nose, chest, and mouth.

It's everywhere with no end in sight.

Bullets continue to spray all around me, but I focus on my brother. Then I hear the sounds of an Apache and a Black Hawk approaching in the distance. The blades whip the air, vibrating in a continuous loop.

"You better fucking hold on," I growl at him. "We have to do another fishing trip in Florida. You owe me a fishing pole, remember?" I joke with a smile, forcing it out through my jaw that threatens to lock up. I'm going into shock, disbelief possessing my body. Paul's team and mine fire back, gun shots from both sides vibrating our bones while I spew empty promises to my brother.

And I know...there's nothing I can do.

I'm in hell.

I do my best to stop the bleeding, but it's like trying to put tape on a leaking dam.

Nothing is going to stop this.

He trembles, and his bloody lips curve into a small smile because he knows his fate has been sealed, but I refuse to accept it.

"T-tell m-my s-sister—" he gurgles, his life draining to nothing, and there's nothing I can do but watch. "Tell m-my m-mom—" He swallows the blood again and again, continuing to try to croak out the words through it all, clawing at his wounds over my hands.

I shake my head.

"You'll tell them yourself, brother. Don't worry, just hang on. Air support is here already," I lie, repeatedly.

I lie, forcing him to believe he will return to his girls alive.

I need his last thoughts to be hopeful. He needs to know he's not alone and that I'm right fucking here.

"It's been one hell of a ride, brother." He trembles out.

Then he spits more blood to the side, the blood splattering across the dirt one last time before his eyes go flat, dull, and unsaturated.

His chest stops moving, and he goes motionless. He looks frozen in time, and I feel like my whole body is decimated. A sinking harsh sensation through my bones, and even through the night, I can see a black shadow swallowing us. The light from the moon goes away, and it's dark.

My eyes widen when I realize that my best friend has been KIA.

Paul Alvarez, Operator Slayer, gone.

No, no, no, no.

What the fuck.

Motherfuckers will pay.

But I don't cry, I don't move, I don't wail.

I'm composed while I continue to watch his body drain empty. My body grows numb. Paul is fucking gone, and it's my fault. For the first time in my career, I made the wrong decision that got my best friend killed.

I set his stone-cold body down on the mountain terrain as blood continues to leak out from his wounds, even after his last breath.

Even though I know there's no other way Paul would have wanted to go out, it still feels like a curse.

I clutch my rifle again, forcing myself to overcome the shock that threatens to possess me. My fingers grip my weapon tight, and I'm about to spiral deeper into my thoughts.

"Grim!" Kane shouts at me as his fingers touch the trigger repeatedly and his shoulder ricochets from the kickback each time.

I'm still in the fight. We all are.

I relax my shoulders, look into my crosshairs, and return fire.

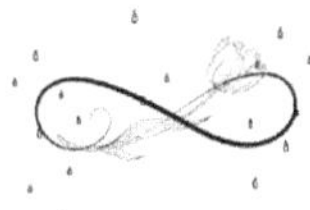

I don't know when it happened, while I was lost in thought, but I found myself with the whiskey bottle in my hands again. Staring at it while heavy metal music continues to play in my gym.

And then I see the future that I want for myself. The future I refuse to let slip away from me. The future I want with the one woman that consumes me every day just by existing. She has saved me in more ways than she'll ever fucking know. She makes me better.

I grit my teeth and smash the bottle on the floor, breaking the glass and little bits and pieces spread everywhere, and I walk away from the last bottle of whiskey I'll ever own.

27

KANE

Her breasts move up and down while she's on top of me. She moans, grinding her clit on me as she moves with my cock inside of her. It's the second time we fuck for the evening. The first time was twenty minutes ago on my couch. When I opened the door to my home, I found her, not expecting her to be there. She stood there, eyes radiating lust and need.

How could I say no?

The moonlight that shines through the bedroom illuminates her silhouette as she continues to ride me desperately.

My hands at her waist, barely touching her soft skin.

I close my eyes, and I can see her again.

Ari.

But when I open them, Meredith pants fast, biting her lip.

I don't know why I've let this go so far. I thought this would help me overcome my depressing attraction to my favorite nurse.

But no matter what I do. No matter how much time passes. It's always her that I see, even when I'm fucking someone else. I only want her, but Meredith makes me feel good. I know with time, if I keep giving our relationship a chance, I'll make it out on the other side.

She notices how hesitant I am and how badly my behavior has shifted.

"What's wrong?" She stops riding me. She places her palms on my abs, studying me through the dark. She drops her head, her hair falling down her face, and squints.

"Nothing, why?" I say, my hand palming her ass to make her believe I'm okay, even when I'm not.

"It's been a while since I've seen you. I thought you'd be more...*hungry.*"

I tilt my head apologetically.

Then I grab her hand, pulling her so that she's off my dick and on my chest.

I take a deep breath, snaking my hands through her hair, playing with the strands.

"I'm just stressed, that's all." It's not entirely the truth, but it's not a lie. There are people out there who want to kill us. And Paul's little sister, who I swore to watch over.

"Your job?" she murmurs against my cheek. I return with a nod. I let go of her and use my hands as a pillow instead. I rest the back of my head on my palms and stare at the ceiling.

We're at my townhome, downtown in Bloomings.

I like city life. I like the busy streets and the constant lively buildings with relentless traffic.

It makes me feel less alone.

I have siblings, but they're all spread out all over the country, and my parents don't live too far away. So, this place makes me feel less alone.

I had a girlfriend of a couple of months when Paul was still alive. It was getting serious, but of course…she couldn't handle my schedule or absence, so she ended things.

Meredith's fingers trail my chest hair down to my groin. She grabs my dick, stroking it again, determined to get me hard, and I wish it could be that simple right now.

I wish I could fuck her and forget everything, but the more I push myself into someone else, it backfires.

I'm tempted to call our relationship fun off because I like her. But maybe if I keep trying, I'll get over Ari.

"Mmm, I bet you taste good, Kane." Meredith shrinks down and crawls over my torso. She's about to suck me off but then my phone pings, and I internally thank whoever texted me.

Meredith stops feeling me, and I kiss her on the cheek before I reach over to my nightstand to answer.

I can feel Meredith grow disappointed when something else captures my attention. She lets her body fall on top of my bed sheets.

I look at the screen, and it's only one text with two unsurprising questions.

> Lopez: El Devine? Strip club after?

I hesitate before I reply. I stare at the words over and over again, tempted.

Meredith and I haven't made it official. We both agreed to a relationship of fun, and then we would see where it took us.

She's technically single, and so am I.

"Who is it?" Meredith asks behind me. I can feel her pull the blankets from underneath me. Probably to cover herself up.

"Lopez." My jaw ticks, and I swipe out of the chat and go straight for Ari's contact instead.

I'm not crossing any boundaries. I'm just keeping the promise I made to Paul. At least, that's what I tell myself as I type.

I've wanted to reach out, but how can I when she and Grim are together? I have to be careful with everything that I do or say because he's my best friend. But she's the woman I fell in love with before she met him.

I met her first.

I knew her first.

> Me: I'm sorry about last week. You deserved to know.

I tap send on the screen but don't expect a response. I need her to know I am sorry. She's been through a lot, but this can't get pushed underneath the rug. Ever since Ari started dating Grim, we don't text anymore.

"Why are you texting Ari?" Meredith asks me over my shoulder. I sensed her, but I didn't bother hiding. I don't answer right away. I run my hand through my dark hair and turn off my phone, setting it back on the nightstand and search for gray sweatpants.

"She's my friend. Paul was one of my best friends, and he's dead. Why wouldn't I check up on her?" I tell her calmly, pulling up my pants, tying the strings at my waist, and reaching for a shirt.

"Yeah, I get that, but—"

"But what?" I quirk a brow at her defensively. I hadn't meant for it to come out so territorial, but it rolled off my tongue naturally.

Because even if Ari doesn't feel the same way about me as I do, I will always be there for her. If she needs a friend, I'm there.

I'm the same way with my other friends.

If someone needs me, I'm there. No questions asked. It's just the way I was raised to be.

"I'm sorry if I'm being nosy, Kane. After not seeing you for a while, I thought I would have your full attention."

"We all made a promise to look after her. Paul's team and Grim's team. She just lost her baby, and—" I almost slip up and tell her that the people that killed Paul are after her and all of us.

"And what?" she snaps.

"Nothing." I close the drawer that stores all of my sweatpants and finish tying the knot at my waistband.

"But you're right, I guess...you should check on her. Last time Emilia, Ari, and I talked, she mentioned something about her and Danny not being together anymore."

A burst of a flame flows through me so seamlessly. I look over my shoulder for a split second.

"What?" My eyes light up like fireworks, and I clear my throat, trying to disguise my feelings.

"They're not together?" I ask, looking away from Meredith and instead at the city lights outside my window. Then I return my gaze to her to seem uninterested.

"I don't think so." Meredith shrugs.

She tears off the blankets from her nude, curvy body, grabbing the clothes she came here in.

I should stop her from leaving. Or maybe I should let her go entirely until I feel like I am officially ready to date again.

"I've gotta go, anyway. I promised my sister I'd babysit late tonight so she and her husband can go to the movies and catch the midnight premiere." She tosses her shirt over her curls and shoves her feet, one by one, into her wedges.

I guess that means I'll be spending my night at El Devine with Lopez and his new bed buddy of the week.

"Okay, but you're still my date to the ball, right?" I ask, walking toward her. She stiffens when I lift her chin, forcing her to look at me.

I smile as I lean down to give her a peck on the lips.

Even through the moonlight, I can see that she's blushing.

"Yup," she replies, giddy and high-pitched.

She pops the p in yup, and I chuckle at her flustered voice.

"Good night, Kane." She sighs, slipping out of my bedroom and closing the door behind her.

Another night of angst, regret, and uncertainty. My words I spilled with no remorse sicken me. My limit has fractured. It finally cracked from continuous trauma and worry. I love Danny, but his job is a lifestyle I would be signing up for, and...I don't love that part.

A part of me feels relieved, yet why do I feel destroyed?

Danny hasn't reached out to me. It's been a couple of days of long, lonely nights on the phone with Emilia and Meredith. I call them whenever I'm tempted to look for him instead. They stop me from running back to Danny when I crave him. I crave his scent, his arms...his everything.

It hurts so much.

So, I call my girlfriends.

Meredith is smitten by Kane. Every time we get on our girlfriends call, she goes on and on about how great he is in bed and how she doesn't want this fling with him to end.

I don't know what to say. He confessed he was in love with me a day before they started their relationship. And a part of me felt happy for her. And another small part of me felt weird about it and I was unsure of where it was coming from. There was a line drawn between Kane and I, and he made it hazy the night of our soccer game. I love Danny. But Kane...he's everything good. And Danny...he's the man I can't stop thinking about.

But here I am, another night of junk food, wine, ice cream, and horror movies binging them all until I cry myself to sleep, because I can't bring myself to pick up the phone and call him. I want to swear off ever dating a Special Operator again.

Tomorrow is the military ball. The thought of dancing the night away with my 6'6 man appears in my mind, like a fantasy that won't come true. He told me once that he doesn't dance but for some reason, I think if I asked him to dance the night away with me at the ball, he wouldn't say no.

I'm tucked underneath my velvet covers, watching *Scream*. It just started, and I'm rewatching it for the thousandth time. I take another swig from the wine bottle when I'm tempted to text Danny. I want to text him to come over when I hear three loud knocks on my door.

Drew Barrymore's house phone rings and knocks on my door send me into a jump scare. I flicker my gaze at the door, then back to the TV. I almost spill wine all over my lap, gripping the glass tight as my nerves jolt through me, and I curse out loud to myself.

I look at the time on my cell-phone when I see it's nearing midnight, and someone is at my door.

It has to be...Danny.

My heart skips a beat and my pulse awakens with hope.

I quickly fix my hair, tucking it behind my ears. Wiping away dried tears from my cheeks. I don't bother pausing the movie as I throw my blankets off me and stand from the couch.

As soon as I take one step forward, I slant to the side.

Whoa.

I may be a little tipsy. I'm two wine bottles down and on my third. The world is buzzing, and I'm not sure how I'll answer the door without slurring my words to my ex-boyfriend. Still, I have to try.

I stumble toward the door, ready to swing it open.

You can do this, you can face him.

I unlock my door, turning the lock sideways, and I'm prepared to meet light ocean eyes. But when the door opens, I see dashing, dark navy ones instead, on a beaming face.

Kane.

He's standing there, with a bruised eye that's slowly healing. His hands tucked into his pocket, shivering from the cold. I look around him, confused, searching for anyone else. I furrow my brows, my shoulders dropping when the reality hits that Danny still wants nothing from me after I said those horrid things to him.

"Oh, Kane? What? What're you doing?" I slur, tightening my drop on the door. The trees that surround my house sway behind him. There's a cold front that's rolling in, and the temperature has dropped into the thirties already.

He shrugs, smirking. He looks me up and down and he's suppressing a laugh, biting his knuckles. I'm in a Christmas onesie, with reindeer antlers on the hoodie.

"I came to see my favorite nurse...or should I say, my favorite reindeer?"

I cross my arms defensively. He's one of the reasons why I'm in this predicament with Danny, and I'm not sure letting him in will do any good. It'll make the lines more hazy...blurry. Tempting.

"Mr. Slaughter, at midnight?" Disappointment laced in my tone.

He shrugs again.

"Can I come in? It's cold out here." He motions toward the woods.

I bite my lip, looking at my living room TV, my messy couch, with a popcorn bowl and messy house. Usually, I clean like a neat maniac, and if there was one thing out of place, I go crazy, but lately, cleaning was the last thing I wanted to do.

"Sure...but my house is a mess." I cave in and walk away, waving to him over my shoulder. "Just like my life." I push open the door before I drag myself back to the living area.

I drop down on my couch, covering myself back up in blankets. Kane shuts the door behind him softly, following me to the couch. He sits at the other end. I inhale his risqué cologne as the air brushes in my direction, one cushion in between us.

"It's not a mess, don't say that. You could be me."

I scoff, taking another gulp of wine.

"What's so messy about yours?"

I swallow the sweet red wine down and glare at him.

But he doesn't answer me. He stares at my throat, and his jaw flexes while he pops his fingers nervously. I can't hold his gaze...my heart pounds and I turn back to the horror movie playing across the screen.

He follows my lead and watches the movie with me instead of answering me. A few minutes pass by before he breaks the silence.

"Shouldn't you be watching Christmas movies? And not a movie about a guy in a mask who kills people?" He reaches for the bowl of popcorn in the middle of us and takes a handful of it, snacking on it.

"Christmas is over. What're you doing here, Kane? Shouldn't you be with Meredith? Or at work?" I snap.

He stiffens at my aggression. He blinks at me, and I sink deeper into the couch with guilt.

"Sorry..."

"It's okay, Ari." He shifts in his seat, taking off his jacket. The way his triceps flex as he pulls it off himself has me clearing my throat and focusing on Drew Barrymore getting chased instead. I blink away, sneaking in one more glance, then I'm furrowing my brows at the TV.

"I heard what happened. Meredith told me you and Grim ended things. And I guess I wanted to make sure you're okay. I'm not leaving until you tell me you are. Is it true?" He folds his jacket over the couch arm. He arches a brow and my heart drops when he mentions him.

I nod, trying to fight the lump in my throat.

"Fuck...no wonder he hasn't been answering anyone's calls."

"He hasn't? Is he okay?" I rush out, sitting up.

Oh no. The last thing I want Danny to do is relapse and drink himself to the point of no return. I sit up, throwing the blankets off me once again.

I won't let him do that to himself. My mind travels to the worst. I'm picturing him passed out, somewhere with no one, with a crap ton of empty whiskey bottles. Because of me. Because of what I said.

"I need to make sure he's okay." I stand, ready to find my car keys. But then Kane grabs my hand, stopping me.

"He's fine. Rooker has been checking on him. He's good." he reassures me.

"Has he been getting...?" I can't form the last word, but Kane finishes it.

"Drunk? No."

I let out a sigh of relief.

I slouch back down the couch, my bangs get in my face and fear leaves my body.

"We all drink a lot...you know?" I turn to him as I hold my knees to my chin. "It's not just Grim. Rooker drinks when his old lady isn't around or when he's with us. Lopez is married to his beer, and Creature...well, he's just a maniac when it comes to whiskey, liquor or beer. Crazy ass was able to do the four horsemen at the bar without passing out or throwing up. It was impressive."

"That's insane."

"He is insane...but anyway, what I'm trying to say is sometimes, it's just easy for us to turn to it than to ask for help. Our jobs..."

"Your job isn't easy, I know...but it isn't right. Get help. There are programs, doctors, therapy. Lots of resources." Kane looks away from me, glancing at his hands, like I scolded him and maybe I kind of did, but that was not my intention. I would never judge Danny or his team for dealing with their lives the best way they know how. "But I get it. I can't imagine the things you've guys seen or had to do...I never want to see what you've witnessed or experienced. That's why I don't blame Danny for wanting to drink. Or if any of you guys want to let loose before missions or after them."

Kane purses his lips, still popping his fingers, but doesn't respond.

"Speaking of drinking, care to share?" he asks, grabbing the wine bottle from my hands, not bothering to wait for my answer. He eyes the label, looking at the brand and flavor, studying it and he licks his lips.

"Sweet red wine." He lifts the bottom, then puts it to his lips, smirking at me through a devilish grin. "My favorite."

I hadn't noticed how close I sat down next to him until his big hand brushes against my thigh. I look down at his gesture and I stop breathing, something ignites inside me and when I catch the veins on his hand standing out, and something pulls at my strings.

I clear my throat, breaking the tension. He reads the room and removes his hand, giving me back the wine bottle instead.

"I should go." He murmurs. He taps his finger on the arm of the couch and positions his feet to stand.

He should. He should go and stop showing up at my house like this. But...

Screw it. He's always been there for me and my mother when my brother passed. Why stop him now? He's doing what my big brother wanted him to do and I won't fault him for that...ever.

"You can stay." I give in to his need to watch over me. I guess I don't want to be alone tonight, after all. Even if this might blur lines. He's my friend, and this is what friends do.

I smile. "Just until the movie is over."

29

———

KANE

The entire time Ari rests her head on my shoulder, I have to control my dick that wants to come out of my jeans. She smells so good, and we're two more wine bottles down. The movie just finished, and I stopped drinking after a couple of swigs to watch over her. I stopped drinking when I realized just how inebriated she'd become. Her cheeks are rosy, she giggles at the smallest things and her eyes are glossy.

She's drunk but most of all, hurt.

I've never seen her drink like this. I can't imagine how Danny is feeling.

"Holy fuck. The boyfriend was the killer. I did not see that coming," I blurt out after the movie wrapped up.

"You really don't watch horror movies, do you?" she groans in a sleepy, drunken voice.

Dammit, it's cute. She's cute.

I can't try anything on her, I won't do it. She's vulnerable, the break-up is fresh, and that's not how I want to kiss her for the first time...*if* I ever get a first time with her.

I'm with Meredith. I'm with Meredith.

I repeat the reality in my head before I drift off into a delusion where I think it's okay to do more than just let her head rest on my shoulder.

I want to do more than this.

I need to go home before I do something crazy.

"I've seen enough horror that'll last a lifetime. I don't need to add to it." I laugh, looking down at her. Small flashes of past deployments run through my head like bombs going off. I shake my head out of those recollections and concentrate on the present.

I can't see much. I'm met with black strands of hair and her reindeer pajamas. Then she tilts her face up, and she's so damn close I feel her sultry breath on my mouth, and I'm tempted to taste.

She stares at me, not saying anything as the end credits flow down the screen like a backwards waterfall in front of us. Then a small curl of her lips turns, and a flash of sparks shines on her brown eyes and I can see she's searching for something.

"Your eyes are reaaaaalllllyyy pretty."

Yep, she's drunk.

"Alright, time to get you into bed. You are cut off, ma'am."

She breaks away and giggles into my chest. I feel her nose reverberating on it as she snorts.

She's snorting as she tries to catch her breath.

Too. Fucking. Cute.

Fuck me, man.

"Kane, you're no fun...but thanks for staying with me. Danny doesn't like horror movies either. But he would watch them with me, with no complaints. We had a scary movie marathon not too long ago since I spent the month of October in the hospital, and we weren't able to celebrate Halloween like we wanted to." She moves away from my chest and my arm that rested on hers retracts. But she doesn't stand. Instead, she looks back at me from the edge of the couch, over her shoulder. Her smile disappears, and a frown replaces the glow.

"What is it?" I quirk a brow, getting closer to her. I rest my forearms on my thighs.

"Maybe everything would have been easier..." She places her palm on my knee, and I watch her little fingers grip my pants.

What is she doing to me?

I want to stop her... I should stop her and ask what her intentions are. But the attraction for her is too much, it's too high.

Tonight was full of mixed signals. The way she laughed every time I criticized the movie. The way she leaned her head on my shoulder the entire time, I could feel every breath she took and how warm she was.

And now?

The way she's fucking looking at me, has me wanting to bend her over the couch, and confess the way I feel about her with my actions and no words. Just the sound of her taking it and me confessing the built-up craze with my...

I can't think straight.

"What would be easier?" I wonder what she's talking about. I lean in closer to her, temptation and desire running rampant. I'm sitting so close that our thighs are touching and I dare to look at those full pink lips, knowing the consequences. The havoc that will unleash on my body when I do.

Alas, a tear falls down her cheek, and like a moth to a flame, I rub it away with my thumb. I hate seeing her cry. I rub it until it turns into nothing, and she closes her eyes, as a small grin appears, followed by a soft, sweet hum like she's enjoying my touch.

Fuck.

Then she does something that has me questioning if I'm dreaming. My muscles tighten as she stops right in front of my face. She's about to kiss me, and she closes her eyes tight, sniffling. But I don't feel her come through. It's all in my head. She wasn't going to kiss me... I'm almost begging for it when I know it's morally wrong to.

"Kane...I'm tired," she whispers.

"You're tired? Let's get you to bed then because—" she stops me from continuing.

"Kane," she tells me again, choking up. "I'm tired of crying. I'm tired of everything." Then she opens her eyes again, wide with watery red eyes like she's begging me to take her pain away and her lips tremble.

I wish I could. I really do. It makes me ache to see her like this. I can't handle it.

I pull her into my chest, hugging her tight. She doesn't fight me. Instead, she holds on to me in return.

"I miss him, Kane. I love him... I love Danny so much." She chokes out and sobs, but they're soft and low, and I don't say anything. I can't do it. But what I can do is hold her like she needs to be held. And with each tear, with each innocent caress, time passes by with tortured emotions for the next hour as I rub her back until she falls asleep.

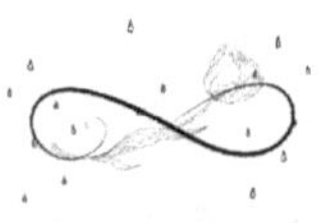

I carry Ari to bed when I feel like it is the right time. When all I wanted to do was stay like that with her in my arms until morning...or forever.

I'll take both.

I open the wrong doors twice before I finally find her bedroom. I don't turn on the light, afraid it'll wake her. It's not hard to find her bed in the darkness.

She groans in my arms, but she's in too deep to wake up. The wine has gotten to her system, so I make sure to position her on her stomach.

I cover her up after laying her down gently, tucking her in with her bedsheets. I make sure her cheek lays softly on the pillow and her hair falls over her face when I do. Before I turn around to leave, I spot the newborn shoes I bought for her and Grim's baby on the nightstand with the onesie he got. When I see it, it takes me back to the horrid day I watched her die.

This girl deserves better...and I want to give her that if she ever gave me the chance.

———

30

ARI

It's January. I should be happy. I shouldn't be at a fucking winter-themed military ball. But how could I turn down Violet's offer? If she needs me, I will always be there for her. This is our last night together before she's back in Texas.

I want to get so drunk that I can't walk or think straight anymore. I don't want to feel the grief I've been feeling all year—only the gratification of losing myself. I don't even want to think about the horrible things I said to my ex-boyfriend.

Shiny, glittering chandeliers hang from the ceiling as we walk toward the ballroom. The light brown colored walls have paintings of vintage couples in love. The lighting is warm yellow with candles everywhere.

It's beautiful. Like a European kingdom.

The ballroom is decorated with snow on the floor. A massive dark green winter tree so tall it almost touches the high ceilings. A star at the top shines bright, glimmering golden specks as it twirls in circles. Snowflakes bounce off the ceilings, floors, and walls.

Music plays loud and smooth. I smile as Violet hooks her arm with mine and smiles as well.

"I love military balls when they go out like this. They're usually shitty," Violet jokes into my ear before returning to Zeke's arm.

We take in our surroundings. Tables are set on either side of the dance floor.

Sailors in their blue dress uniform, everywhere.

They all look the same—it's comical.

Every man blends in with each other...except one.

Grim Reaper.

I stop breathing. My chest thuds unevenly rough, and I'm hot.

He stands with Rooker and Noel. Kane and Lopez are at the table next to them, and they're deep into light-hearted conversations. I can't hear them over the loud chatter and the music that drowns them out, but their body language tells me a lot.

They're all covered with medals and achievements, and Danny has the most out of them all.

We were supposed to come here together. Our official outing as a couple was supposed to be tonight.

He brings a glass to his lips and catches me. He looks my way for a split second and blinks. At first, he does a double take. He looks back at his glass and swallows the familiar dark amber poison.

Then I spot another pair of beautiful blue eyes looking my way.

Kane eyes me with pure shock and warmth. Danny, too.

My ex deadpans as he grits his teeth, staring into my soul as he always does, sending me to melt into a pool of serenity. My vision changes to the dark-haired Navy SEAL now.

Kane looks mesmerized with his mouth falling open, licking his lips. He closes it, swallowing. His Adam's apple bobs, and he shifts in his seat.

Meredith occupies his left, and she overlooks Violet and me. She's talking to Lopez, throwing her head back, laughing hard, smacking her thigh as she laughs at something he said. Lopez leans in close to her ear as they laugh.

Danny looks tense, and Kane seems the same. Danny doesn't budge. He won't break. He's so... intimidating. Kane is entrapping. They both are... It's like they can't believe I showed up.

Michael Bublé's Christmas music begins to play, and after what feels like an hour of holding these intense expressions, I break away.

This was a bad idea.

I clear my throat as Violet holds me closer. She notices my hesitation and quickly hovers over me protectively.

"Don't worry, we're not sitting with them. We're sitting with Zeke's team over here," Violet whispers as she guides me along. I nod, pursing my lips and forcing a small smile.

I clutch my small wallet as my breathing starts to pace evenly.

I'm wearing a long red dress ball gown that hugs my body. It's a see-through mesh embroidery that barely covers my chest. You can see cleavage, red rhinestones threaded carefully into the fabric along my chest and I'm embracing the new me. I'm showing off the body that Danny showed me how to love.

To love myself and to be unashamed of my body.

No.

I don't want to think of him. I don't want to think about the night we fought. The night I yelled and screamed at him. The night that ended things.

Zeke pulls my chair out first and then Violet's.

"Enjoy watching grown-ass adults act like children that get shit-faced," Violet says sarcastically, shrugging.

"Looking forward to it," I say as I turn to Zeke, tucking in the dress carefully as I shift in my chair. I want to avoid wrinkling the dress Danny bought me. He slides me a glass of sangria—my favorite.

31

—

ARI

The rest of the night, I stayed close to Violet. Meredith has been giving me a cold shoulder lately to the point where she didn't acknowledge me the entire time I was here.

I would sneak glances at my best friend every so often to see if she could sense my desperation to make amends for an unknown cause. I replayed every conversation and text with her, trying to figure out where I had gone wrong.

She hovered over Kane, kissing his neck and cheek with desperate need, with her hands constantly traveling all over his body and groin.

Kane looked amused and yet standoffish at the same time.

Occasionally, I looked for Danny. At one moment, I found three women walking up to him as the event went on, star-struck and flushed. The way they looked at him was apparent in their intention with him. But each time, he looked uninterested, and eventually, they got the message, leaving him alone. The last one put her hand on his biceps, wide-eyed and curious. I found myself hitching a breath and tore my eyes away from them, gripping my sangria tight in my hands. Seconds later, the woman stomped off, disappointed. I'm guessing whatever she was trying to do with Danny didn't go the way she wanted it to. He didn't even look their way, once.

Yet Kane and Danny continued to peer at me over their drinks or shoulders the entire night.

From what I could tell, he had only one glass of his favorite whiskey and didn't drink for the rest of the night. He sat beside Rooker and Noel the entire time, lost in conversation but looking relaxed.

And that made me feel good knowing he was okay.

"Oh no, here come the drunken toasts and awards," Violet whispers as everyone begins to riot excitedly, banging their fists on the table and whistling as Admiral Ravenmore wheels out a table.

It has a massive bowl with smoke lingering, hovering over it like a halo, hiding what's inside.

Dry ice.

"What's that?" I furrow my eyebrows, amused. I smirk as I watch everyone continue to yell out in anticipation.

Violet was not kidding about these men acting like children after several hours of drinking.

"It's a bowl full of different drinks from each service member's favorite. A different sailor gets called up, makes a speech, then dumps it in."

"That's funny. It *has* to taste bad." I scrunch my nose in playful disgust.

After about seven sailors make drunken speeches, Lopez walks up to the bowl, takes the cap off a bottle of tequila, and dumps it in.

"There isn't any other place I'd rather be but here, serving alongside my brothers." He takes a big gulp from the bottle and sighs, wiping off the rest from his lips, before he walks off from the center of the ballroom, retreating next to Kane and Meredith.

Short, simple, and thorough.

"Chief Petty Officer, Danny Rider. Get the fuck up here. The fearless, Grim fucking Reaper!"

Everyone chants, whistles, clapping their hands, some even banging their fists on the table.

"Grim Reaper!"

"Grim Reaper!"

From the side, Danny stands up from the table he shares with Rooker and heads for the center of the room. I dip my head at my cross necklace. Twirling it into my fingertips, trying my best not to rush out of the building. But the attraction I have for Danny will always prevail, no matter where we stand in our relationship. He will always be that magnetic force calling my name. I look back at him, my bottom lip trapped underneath my teeth as I try to let my bangs hide where my eyes are glued.

Danny twists the Jack Daniels' cap open. The Admiral handed his bottle to Danny so he could pour it in. He hangs it open on top of the bowl with hesitation, watching the smoke swirl around the bowl, and he smirks, shaking his head.

"Fearless..." he trails off. "That's where you're wrong, sir." His voice raises the Admiral's eyebrows, and everyone grows quiet as if they don't want to miss a word that Danny has to say.

"I'm not fearless." His jaw ticks off and on. "Last year, I wouldn't disagree with you." Admiral Ravenmore pats him on the shoulder with a hard smack in a brotherly fashion, and he looks at him with a softened gaze of understanding.

"But I just found something that scares the living shit out of me." His blue eyes search the crowd, and they land on me.

His hardened gaze stares into my soul intimidatingly, and I can't breathe.

"I'm scared of losing the ones I love most." His jaw bites down, twitching with narrowed eyes, and then he looks away and my heart chips.

Is he talking about me?

"At first, I didn't understand fear, didn't feel it, didn't care for it, and I was proud of that." He swallows.

"But someone taught me the realness behind an emotion I've managed to avoid my entire life." He looks at me again, licking his lips. "Now I know it's not a weakness, but a strength. It's a fucking strength to fear you might lose the ones you love most because it makes you want to fight that much harder."

"HOOYAH!" everyone roars in agreement.

"I'm not good at these things. I'm not good at words." He readjusts the bottle in his hand, watching the dry ice smoke flow out constantly.

"I'm surprised I even showed up tonight, if I'm being honest." Danny smiles.

"So here's to Paul Alvarez. Our fallen brother, my best friend." I blink through my blurred vision at the mention of my brother's name.

"And to fear. Here's to being scared. Because it is not a weakness..." He looks at me again before breaking his intense gaze and looking at his team instead. "But a fucking strength," he roars, emptying the whiskey into the bowl.

Everyone erupts in cheer and whistles while the Admiral throws his arm over Danny's shoulder.

Almost every sailor in this room stands up, and I've lost sight of Danny because of it.

I've been pushing away the madness that has overshadowed

everything good. I want everything to return to how it was when we were in Iraq. Everything was complicated, but he made it feel simple after we both caved in.

And now?

Will it ever go back to the way it was?

I want to go back in time. I want something simple.

"Ari, you okay?"

I freeze quickly, wiping away the tears that escaped me. Tears I didn't even know I was shedding. Violet places her hand on mine.

Zeke looks at me with curiosity flashing in his eyes before he grants me privacy, pretending he didn't just see me.

I refuse to let my emotions dampen her last night here.

Screw this.

"Yeah, I'm fine. Everything is good. I'm just going to get some fresh air. It's a little stuffy in here, but I'll be back." I wipe under my eyes, praying my mascara doesn't run.

"Okay, if you say so. Let me know if there's anything I can do."

"Of course." I nod with a lie of a smile.

I refuse to bother her with my problems. I want her to have a good time.

It's the best time to leave because everyone has stood up, gathering around the bowl, drinking, and howling like a bachelor/college party.

I sigh, trying to calm myself down, but Danny's speech, the flashback of Iraq, my brother in his coffin, *my baby,* makes it hard.

I'm having trouble.

I don't need anything complicated right now. *I shouldn't want* anything complicated.

Because I want Danny, all of him, but I need to see that he wants me back, with no secrets.

I stand, walking fast, bumping into sailor after sailor until I make it through a clearing.

Sweat begins to coat my chest, and I just need to *fucking breathe.*

I see a glass door giving me a clear view of a fenced-in porch with snow collecting on the pillars.

I push it open desperately, flinging it open. I stumble out, tripping over my heels.

My head is buzzing. My vision begins to blur.

Damn it, the alcohol has finally caught up. I'm a lightweight, so it doesn't surprise me when my whole body grows warm and slow.

The cold air hits me when I look at my surroundings. The night sky is littered with clouds, but it's a crescent moon that catches my attention. It glows, and I lose myself, letting my thoughts take over.

I need to go home. I don't want to be here if I'm going to be a downer.

I'm alone, just like I wanted. I should go home. Maybe I can sneak away and call an Uber. I twirl my cross necklace, as I watch the snow continue to fall around me. Thick patches of snow lay on top of the wood. I lean on my forearm...wondering why the hell I didn't grab my coat on the way out.

Then I hear the door open and slight music with drunken men's chatter escape, and I know I'm not alone anymore. Someone else or another couple has also stepped outside, trying to get away from the madness.

"Aren't you cold?"

I turn around to that familiar sunshine voice.

Kane.

I lean against the porch, palming it for balance.

I'm really drunk. This can't be good.

"Kane," I greet him with a soft smile before looking away. My heart sinks when I realize it's not Danny. "I think I just need to be alone. At least for a few minutes before I go back inside." I turn away, my open back facing him again, and I watch white clouds of air escape from my lips as I breathe.

"Is something wrong?" He steps closer, and I shake my head, closing my eyes, still not facing him. The only thing I feel is the snow that bites my fingers.

"No, I'm okay. I just need to be alone."

"No, something's wrong. I'm not leaving until you tell me." His deep voice rumbles with concern.

"I'm fine!" I look at the sunshine operator to my right, crossing my arms, growing colder by the second. I force a smile at him through teary eyes.

His black hair has loose strands that fall over his forehead, and his dark eyes look for mine, but I turn away from him, not wanting him to read me so quickly.

"Ari, I know you're not fine."

"Okay, you win. I'm not." I shrug aggressively, defeated. I still can't look at him because I'm tired of people seeing me like this.

Shivers run up my spine as a gush of crisp air hits my open back.

It's so fucking cold out here.

"I know something that might make you feel better. Maybe with the right person."

I roll my eyes, sighing before I turn to him.

"Right person? What? What could make me feel better after this fucked up year I've had?"

I stare at him with doubt, and I find him with his hands deep into the pockets of his uniform.

He's breathing fast, and his dark blue eyes soften with patience.

But he doesn't say anything as I wait.

Then he makes a move. A move I never expected someone like him to do.

"Fuck it," Kane closes the distance and kisses me aggressively, cupping my cheeks in both hands, forcing himself on me. My eyes bulge when I taste the vodka on his tongue as he kisses me. He must be drunk. Then he bites my lip harder than Danny ever has, cutting deep.

He's never overstepped. He's always been so gentlemanly. The type of man that always asks for consent.

I push him away hard. I can't believe he did that.

"Kane, no! Stop this! What has gotten into you?" I stumble backward, creating space between us. "You're with Meredith!" I yell, touching my bleeding lip. "This is wrong!"

"Fuck, Ari. I'm sorry. But I'm done hiding." He grips the railing tight, looking at me with determination, rocking on his feet. "I want you. I've wanted you since the day we met. I can't do this anymore. I know it's wrong. But fuck it, I don't care."

"You should care, Kane! Look. I love you—" His lips curve slightly with hope.

"I fucking love you, too."

"But..." I lick the blood off my lips, tasting metallic. "Thank you for last night. You've always been there, and I never truly saw *you before*. But I see you. I do. You're warm. You're good. You're safe. But I don't want safe. I want..." My head moves from side to side, unable to finish my sentence.

My unhinged, frustrating jerk.

Even though Danny also makes me feel safe, he pushes me to overcome every battle I fight on my own. He moves me beyond my limitations, and when I feel like I'm there, he'll push me even more.

"And now it's my turn to say this, and I'm only going to say it once." I touch my lips with my fingers.

I soften my gaze after closing my eyes tight.

"It'll always be Danny," I confess, and Kane's whole demeanor drops with disappointment.

"Maybe," he grits.

I open my mouth to say more, but my heart drops when someone clears their throat.

32

—

ARI

S hit.

Danny looks pissed. His blue eyes darken, with a pointed chin, and I feel like something terrible is about to happen. He rolls up one of his sleeves, slowly.

Kane looks guilty, but not enough to apologize or cower away.

Danny watches Kane wipe away my lipstick from his mouth.

"Danny..." I plead, stepping away from Kane before he makes any irrational decisions. I'm looking at the two men I care about so deeply, and still, I feel like I need to run away from the storm that's about to unfold. I can't even walk straight right now.

"Grim, it's no secret that I've always cared about her. She loves me, too."

Why is he speaking for me?

I turn to Danny, taking another step back until my ass collides with a railing. "That's not it at all—" Danny hushes me by raising his hand, with a glare of hurt. Still, he hasn't said anything, but he doesn't have to. I know what must be going through his head.

Danny rubs his beard, smirking devilishly.

"You're right, Kane. I did always know you cared about her. What I didn't know was how eager you are to die."

"Fuck this. I'm done hiding my feelings for her. She needs a man that's always going to be there for her. She needs stability, and you're always gone. I'm getting out soon."

"Don't talk about my girl like you know her." He snarls.

My girl.

"I knew her first. I think I know her better than you," Kane retorts.

Danny lets out a roar of sarcastic laughter.

"You know her, Kane? Do you really?" His smile curves on his thrilling face cruelly. Smirking like a devil.

He gets closer to Kane and they size each other up. Still, Danny is slightly taller.

He stops in front of Kane, grinning villainously. Danny looks down at him. He scoffs before he tells him with a vindictive, possessive tone, "Do you know whose name she screams when she comes?"

Oh shit.

Kane clenches his teeth hard. His dark blue eyes almost beamed black. I've never seen Kane like this.

"For now," Kane spits his words with fire.

Oh no.

Kane clenches his fist, and I just know they're going to kill each other. The door to the ballroom storms open and three men in their dress uniform stalk fast.

"That's enough! Walk away from each other," Rooker demands from a few feet away, with Lopez and a new guy I've never seen before next to him. He wears a black mask and pulls out a bullet from his hand, twirling it.

"What, Danny? If you can make her bleed, then so can I," Kane tests him further.

He did not just say that.

I shake my head disapprovingly and palm my mouth to stop the gasp from escaping.

This. Is. Bad.

A fast, strong punch sends Kane to the floor, and he hisses from the pain and anger. He rubs his nose before spitting out blood. He's on his knees, with one hand on the ground supporting his weight. He laughs wickedly, amused, and then charges Danny, pushing off the floor fast, and I feel my whole body grow even colder watching the two men I care about sincerely fight like this. I start shaking from fear. Every bit of me is stunned, and I can't look away.

Kane tries to push him against the wall, but Danny stands his ground, his feet rooted deep on the floor as if they were cemented and unwavering. Rooker shakes his head, disappointed. He's hesitant to step in, like he's afraid he'll be the one next on the floor fighting them both.

Kane swings at Danny, clocking him in the jaw, but Danny doesn't swing back; instead, he finishes the fight.

They're going to kill each other.

Suddenly, faster than I can blink, Danny grabs Kane by the arm, lifting him off the ground and into the air, sending his body flying over his shoulder before he slams Kane to the floor, making him land on his back hard.

Kane groans from the collision, moving slowly, and I cover my eyes.

This isn't happening. Maybe I'm just really drunk. Maybe I'm just seeing things.

So I blink, once...twice...but nope, they're still there. Both of them cross lines that will never again be mended.

Their brotherly friendship is wilted over, with no recovery in sight. The air we're all breathing feels like there's no more because it was all sucked away from their fighting and built-up feud.

Danny doesn't let Kane take a breather. He grabs Kane by his collar and stands him up, forcing him on his feet as Kane struggles to take in air. Danny swings at his face, making Kane's back stumble to the railing. He's a beast that's been awakened, and nothing and no one will be able to stop him...*not even me.*

"Danny, stop!" I plead. He's going to kill Kane. He ignores me, and he continues to punch Kane in the face with fury. His knuckles are coated with Kane's blood, and I wince. His lips are cut open, and his nose rains down red.

A deep chuckle of laughter distracts me for a split second, and I narrow my eyes at the masked man in the corner. He's tall, just like Danny. He has the same build as him, too, but I can tell he has dark hair with the lightest gray eyes I've ever seen. Scars on one eye. They start above one brow, like slashes, and go underneath his eye. He looks at me while crossing his arms over his chest and winks.

He thinks this is entertaining.

I shake my head at him disapprovingly. Kane doesn't get a chance to defend himself. Danny won't let it happen. Kane looks disoriented with every blow to his face. Danny won't stop, and I'm terrified of the outcome if someone doesn't step in.

Red...so much *red*. Kane might go unconscious.

Finally, Lopez and Rooker move.

Rooker immediately swings into action, getting between the two, his hands holding Danny back from further hurting Kane.

"That's enough. You guys are going to kill each other! This is fucked." He snarls at both of them.

"Motherfucker. We're done," Danny yells, rubbing his jaw and pushing Rooker's hand away from his chest, violently.

"Yeah, we are done! But I'll never be done with her." Kane holds onto the railing, readjusting his posture with a bleeding nose, breathing hard. "Tell him, Ari. Tell him that you love me. Tell him about last night."

My mouth pops open, glaring at him.

What does he want me to say? Nothing happened. We had a movie night as friends. *It was innocent* despite his confessions *to me.*

I never did anything to hurt Danny. I would never hurt Danny after everything that we've been through.

Kane has always been there for me since the day Paul died. The least I could do for him is be the ears to listen.

"Kane," I hiss, stuttering drunkenly over my words. My hands turn into fists, and I'm burning with frustration. I will not get into the middle of this. I refuse to be in their feud. I care about them deeply at the end of the day, both in different ways, but right now?

I choose *myself.*

Plus, I'm just too drunk for this. The world is spinning. I see about four Kanes and Dannys. I think it's best for me to slap them both and leave them here to deal with their own turmoil.

"I'll always love her," Kane shouts, and Danny takes another step forward, pissed off, like a bull, as if he's about to make him pay for saying he loves me.

I can't watch these two men fight it out all night.

"S-stop it...b-both of you! I'm going home alone," I shout, and every one of them looks at the shortest girl on the porch. I slur every single word out very slowly. The mysterious man with the mask chuckles darkly. I'm walking away like everything is in slow motion, and I'm going to regret drinking so many fucking Sangrias too fast.

Rooker raises his eyebrows when he hears my tone. This is the most out-of-character thing about me that I've ever done. He looks like he's impressed that such a loud voice can come from a small pair of lungs.

"The hell you are," Danny snarls as he strides toward me. Every step that he takes makes my eyes widen.

Uh-oh.

He grabs me like a doll and picks me up, throwing me over his shoulder before I can get away from them. His hands immediately protect my dress from going all the way up, and he pins me with his forearm, cupping my ass.

I thrash, but it's useless against his strong hold.

I look up through my hair, the strands covering most of my blurred vision, and the last thing I see is Kane trying to follow, but Rooker and Lopez push him back.

33

KANE

"The fuck is wrong with you, man? That's Grim's girl. You're lucky he only punched you." Lopez nudges me with his fist.

"Ari is not his girl. Not anymore," I seethe.

Rooker laughs at me mockingly. He pats my shoulder, then gives it a hard squeeze.

"Ari will *always be* Grim's girl."

I shake my head, wiping the blood off the tip of my nose. Motherfucker got me good.

"He granted you mercy," Rooker says, disappointed.

"Damn, did he break your nose?" Lopez smirks. He thinks everything is a fucking joke.

"Clean up your act. Admiral Ravenmore doesn't need to hear about this. As for your spot on the team, you'll be lucky if you're on the next mission with us. Danny will never work with you again."

"I don't give a fuck."

"Clean up your fucking act. I've never seen you act like this.

What the fuck is wrong with you? Risking your career for a girl? Stop thinking with your dick."

"She's not just any girl, and I loved her first," I spit with rage, trying to slow down the bleeding from my nose.

"You're right, she's not. She's Paul's sister. *And Grim's girl.* Know your place, son." Rooker squeezes my shoulder and I shrug him off.

"Dude, you're bleeding all over your uniform." Lopez hands me a napkin, and I clean myself up.

"By the way, Meredith is here. You're fucked, my dude," Lopez whispers while trying to suppress his laugh. His dimples appear as he steps away from me.

I look up, and sure enough, she's standing at the door. She's murdering me with her eyes.

Shit. I didn't want to hurt Meredith like this.

"Meredith," I call out for her. I throw the napkin at Lopez and run past a quiet Daegan who hasn't spoken since he saw Danny and me fight. He has his mask curled up just enough to expose his mouth and he inhales a cigarette in the corner of the porch, shaking his head.

Mother fucker never takes off his mask entirely, does he?

Creature catches me looking at him and blows smoke into the air.

"If I were Grim, I would have pulled out your teeth one by one so you could never bite again," he tells me, his devilish grin on display, as he puts out his cigarette underneath his shoe.

Psycho.

"Whatever." I scoff before chasing after a pissed-off Meredith. She's taken off already, stomping away. Her heels click on the floor with each step.

"Meredith, stop."

She keeps going, walking fast until we're outside.

Coming to the ball separately is working out in her favor and the guilt eats me alive each time she ignores my pleads.

We're in front of her car, and she scrambles for her keys. She lifts them from her purse, but they drop to the floor.

I grab her keys off the ground, holding them hostage, taking a step back. She leaps forward, trying to whisk them back out of my hands, but misses them completely.

"Give me my keys," she orders me through watery eyes.

"No. I want to talk."

"What's there to talk about, Kane? I saw everything clear as day."

"You shouldn't have seen that, and I'm a fucking dick for doing this to you. I'm sorry."

"Sorry for what, exactly? Are you sorry for kissing your best friend's girlfriend? Or are you sorry for using me to get to Ari? Which one are you exactly sorry about?"

I don't know what to say. I'm quiet. My nose throbs with pain. My back fucking hurts, and I'm choosing my next words carefully.

"I didn't use you to get to Ari." It's true...I didn't use Meredith as a tool to get Ari. I wanted to explore the possibility of a relationship with her, but now I know it's not going to work.

"Do you love her?"

That's an easy question, but does she expect me to tell her that?

I look at her, biting down, with my hands on my waist. She's livid but, most of all, *hurt*. And I feel like I just hit a new low. This isn't like me.

"Do you love Ari?" she repeats, stomping her heel on the ground once again.

I don't answer.

"Dammit, Kane, answer me. You owe me this. Was it all a lie with me?" Her voice cracks, and it breaks me to see that I hurt her.

"No, Meredith. I have enjoyed our time together. You're beautiful. You're perfect, even, but—"

"It's been her from the start, hasn't it?" she bites out.

I nod. "I owe you an explanation. I didn't mean for any of this to happen, it just did, and I know that's a shitty fucking reason. When Paul died, I promised to take care of her."

"Exactly. Take care of her, not fuck her."

She rolls her eyes, snatching the keys out of my hand.

"Good night, Kane."

My heart sinks when I realize what a fucking insensitive asshole I've become since coming back from Iraq.

I forced myself on Ari. Then I broke Meredith's heart.

I stand there in the freezing parking lot, alone. I kick a patch of snow, and flurries explode everywhere.

"Fuck," I curse to myself.

I need to make things right. I fucked up and I hope to God they all forgive me.

I'll reach out to Grim and Meredith when things are more stable and settled. I don't think they'll ever want to speak again, but I'll keep trying to mend the shit I've caused.

I watch the snow continue to fall on the ground, looking at the empty parking space where Meredith's car used to sit, and I pace back and forth.

I need Ari to forgive me...I can't lose her.

34

ARI

Danny threw me over his shoulder and stalked out of the military ballroom as if I weighed nothing; featherlight, a doll in his massive arms.

Every other sailor in the room started to whistle and chant immaturely as they watched us leave the building. They don't know Danny just beat the shit out of Kane for cutting my lip open.

I stop thrashing, and instead, I'm trying to focus on getting my world to stop spinning. I hope Kane is okay, and I'm hoping Danny doesn't go back there and kill him.

Everyone's chants die down, along with the music, as we get closer to the exit. We're outside, and I shout at him as I shake out of his arms, but it doesn't work. He tightens his hold.

"Let me go!"

He slaps my ass. "You only bleed for me," he snarls as he drops me into the passenger seat of his truck. He swings the door open explosively.

"Danny…" I complain, throwing my legs back outside, tempted to jump out of his vehicle. He stands there tall, holding the door open, ready to slam it shut.

"You're drunk. And I don't care that we're not together. I'll make sure you get to *your* bed, in your pajamas, in *your* house. You're also going to take Advil for the hangover you're about to have in the morning."

Of course, he knows what's going to happen to me. He's an expert in hangovers. "But my coat, my purse, my phone…"

I don't care if anyone can hear me complain. Very few people are in the parking lot because the ball hasn't ended yet. We're one of the first people to leave.

He grabs his phone and types away. I cross my arms over my chest like a petulant child being told no after having a tantrum.

"Zeke will take care of it," he says calmly before looking back at me, shoving his phone into his pants.

I glare daggers at him, but he stares back at me, holding my gaze unphased.

Fuck him for being so irresistibly handsome.

Because even though I'm angry, the hold he has on me is tattooed into my soul permanently, like the ink on his skin.

"Don't you have another mission to go on? Another deployment? Don't bother," I hiss, trying to jump out of his truck again. I look away from him and at the parking lot floor.

I grab onto the door handle for balance. The truck is lifted high, and there's no way I'll be able to hop out without holding on to something so I don't fall.

As soon as my hand touches the door handle, he grips my wrist tight, even painfully. He tightens his hold on me, and I look up to meet darkened, lustful eyes.

I wince at the sudden shock it sends down between my thighs. A familiar sensation that has me devastated, wanting more.

"Did you just sass me, little angel? You know what happens when you act out." His tone is anything but sweet. His deep, husky voice reverberates with a low growl.

I swallow nervously.

"Seat belt. On." I do as I say because the way he's looking at me has me frozen with obedience, and I'm lowkey afraid, *excited*... yet intrigued about what his punishment will be for me.

I settle back into my seat, securing myself in. The way Danny is so possessive of me has me melting with the reminder of who I fell for.

I haven't forgotten, but lately, he's shown me a side of him that I always knew he had. He's been patient, gentle, kind, but tonight?

He's grim like the Reaper.

The dark side of him creeps back in.

He's always been able to keep me in a chokehold with his unpredictable needs.

I'm about to be punished. I know it, and our interactions sober me up entirely. The engine roars after he climbs in and starts his truck.

We don't say a word to each other; instead, Avenged Sevenfold music fills the dark tension between us.

I don't ask if he's taking me to his place or mine. I wait as the throbbing between my thighs doesn't let up, but gets worse as he turns onto my street.

He's taking me back to my place, and I'm wishing he took me to his instead. I need to move on. I need to run away...and yet I'm silently hoping I end up in his bed tonight, holding him until his warmth replaces the emptiness. I look out his tinted windows to see the ground covered in only an inch or two of snow. It's not much, but it's enough to feel like winter.

The alcohol has worn off, and I'm desperate to run into my house, away from him. I can't give in to the temptations burning every resentful thought I hold toward him...even though I want to.

But it's not up to me whether I want to or not... I don't think I have a choice tonight.

Every single time I sass him, he delivers my "punishment." My clit pulsates as I wonder how the rest of the night will unfold.

What's he going to do this time?

He parks the truck, and we sit in silence beside the heavy metal music that plays, vibrating through the doors. It's completely dark inside his vehicle. The only light we get is from the dashboard. I bounce my leg anxiously as I glance at the handsome man beside me. I can barely catch his profile. He's looking straight at the woods surrounding my house, his hands relaxed. One is still at the bottom of the wheel, his fingers hooked over it and his other hand on the center console.

My heart is thrashing against my chest.

Maybe he forgot that I sassed him.

Either way, I must remind myself that I ended things. I don't want to be with a Navy SEAL who's always gone, even though he madly entrances me. I don't want a lifestyle where I have to watch him come and go, dreading those same traumatic knocks on my door when my brother passed. I grab the door handle.

My porch light is on. I can see the glow in the corner of my eyes, calling for me like a safehaven from the devil next to me.

"Did I say you can leave?" he asks, low and steady.

"Excuse me?"

Then he looks at me, but there's no emotion attached.

"You want to leave me? Fine. You want to get out of this truck? You will. But not until after you take your punishment like the bad girl you've been."

I glare at him daringly.

"We're not together," I remind him.

He smirks villainously, gives me a thrilling smile, and flashes me his perfect teeth with sharp canines. He looks at my widened, curious eyes before he trails his gaze over my lips, then down to my breasts.

He hums.

"Ari Natalia. You will always be mine." He clicks his seat belt open, freeing himself, and I watch his every move carefully. He pulls up the center console so there's nothing between us anymore. There is no wall or border to stop what he's about to do. "I'm going to punish you for thinking you could ever leave me. You drive me so fucking insane. Do you know what these past few days have been like? They've been worse than hell, baby."

I stop breathing when his large hand gets closer to my throat. My teeth sink hard into my bottom lip as he grabs my cross necklace.

"For having so much faith, you sure do love to sin."

He lets go of my cross necklace, and the cold chain drops between my collarbones at the center.

His fingers start trailing down the top of my dress. I squeeze my thighs tighter when I realize my body begins to betray me.

Then he yanks down the top of my dress hard with rough aggressive need. I gasp when my breasts pop out. I didn't wear a bra since the dress had built-in support.

My nipples are exposed, already hardened with salacity. Every hair on my body stands up, and goosebumps erupt everywhere.

"You love to break, don't you, Ari?" he taunts, palming one breast, and dammit, a moan escapes me when he squeezes it roughly over his calloused hands. Then he slaps my breasts hard, shaking them in response.

"What do you expect me to do when you look like that in the dress I bought you? You expect me not to touch you? Not to kiss you? Not to fuck you?"

I gulp down, closing my eyes, realizing he hasn't forgotten my drunken, angry outburst earlier.

He hasn't forgotten at all.

"I see your mouth is still as filthy as ever..." He grips my jaw, forcing my mouth to gape open. "Open wide, baby, because I'm about to cleanse it for you."

With his other hand, he unhooks his belt.

He holds me like a hostage with one hand on my jaw, still holding it tight. I wince at the pain, yet the skin between my thighs is soaked.

He leans over to me, his face so close I can smell the cigarettes and whiskey on his breath. I pucker my lips through his forceful grip on my jaw, and just when I think he's about to kiss me, he fixates himself on my tongue and spits into my mouth, then shuts my jaw tight.

"Swallow." He growls. My eyes bulge, and I do as he tells me. Swallowing his spit, I narrow my eyes at him, pissed off. His tone is dark and sinister, just like the night on the Black Hawk. "My cock and spit will be the only things that touch this dirty mouth of yours tonight. Not my come, not my lips. I won't even kiss you this time."

His degradation sends me fuming with resentment, but the throbbing doesn't let up.

I want him. I want his lips on mine.

He's not playing fair tonight, and it's killing me slowly.

He lets me go when his pants have dropped enough to expose his already hardened cock. He's fucking massive. Every time I see it, it feels like the first time. Fear creeps into every single vein inside me, igniting a fiery need to taste him...and to run from the pain he's about to inflict. My fingers curl hard at the seat, pissed off that he manages to get me flustered just by hearing his deep voice order me around.

Heavy metal music continues to blast into our ears, and I attempt to avoid getting sucked back into him like a black hole.

He's like quicksand, and I'm daring to jump back in. And once I do, I feel like I'm giving into this lifestyle... a lifestyle I don't think I want anymore.

"I'm not—" I want to tell him I'm not his anymore, but he cuts me off.

"Take your punishment, or I'll force it down your throat."

He doesn't have to tell me twice.

Maybe it's because I miss him...or perhaps it's because this is part of a dark fantasy I've always kept hidden beneath the shell he obliterated when we first met.

Either way, biting my lip, I reach over and get closer to him, inhaling his cologne that radiates sex and rebellion. The leather and his cigarettes are a mixture I never knew went together perfectly. Even his scent alone does everything to me; my heart is throbbing with need, and my drunken fog has completely faded away. Watching Kane and Danny fight sobered me up. And now?

Now, I get to remember my last goodbye to Danny before I

cut him off permanently. I hate myself for wanting to drown myself in him.

After everything we've been through, I hate the world.

But I want to forget my hate for the world and instead...*feel*.

I will treasure this moment because I'm determined to make it our last.

I want us both to feel our hatred, let it possess our spirits, and let our bodies do the talking instead.

35

———

DANNY

I'm the luckiest man in the world when I'm with her. When she entered the building at the start of the ball, I felt like my fucked-up world made sense again.

It's been torture these past few days without her.

I haven't been able to sleep since she left me. She destroyed me that day. Overthinking wasn't something I ever did in my life. I prided myself on the simplicity I built. But I found myself going crazy every minute I spent without her.

I promised her I wouldn't ever let her go, and I'm not.

I didn't expect her to come to the ball with Violet and Zeke. But when I saw her walk into the reception like the goddess that she is in the red dress that I bought her, I knew it wasn't completely over between us.

The promise Paul made us all take is the only reason why Kane still has a beating heart.

But now I want to make my little angel cry for me.

She gets close to me, her beautiful tits still outside her dress, and her hardened nipples fall to my lap, teasing me. She sits her curvy waist near me, and I can feel her lips at the head of my dick, breathing on me, the sensation making me hard, and I'm in pain if I don't feel her soon.

I grab the back of her black hair, holding it so rough she yelps when I tug the strands from her scalp.

This is the roughest I've been with her since Iraq, and I will not beg for forgiveness.

"You're going to take your punishment, Ari. You're going to bleed sweet tears for me, and you're going to hate it." I bring her face toward me, then I lick the bottom of her neck to her cheeks. She tastes so good, but it doesn't come close to the way she drips honey between her thighs. She's so enticing, so fucking addicting.

I'm obsessed with her.

"You like it when I force you, don't you?" I reach over, my hand snaking under her dress, and a low, sadistic grunt of a laugh escapes me when I realize she's not wearing any underwear. My fingers go between her folds, then I push two fingers inside her, and she trembles. So tight, so soft, so sweet. "Such a dirty angel." She's so wet, she's dripping down her thighs already, leaking all over my seat.

Fuck.

"Danny, I want—" I push my fingers into her mouth, not letting her finish.

"It's not about what you want tonight, Ari." Her brows wilt together, confused. "Taste what I do to you." She clamps her mouth down on my fingers, sucking them. "You're going to hate how much you'll enjoy this. Your pussy is already weeping," I coo in her ear mockingly. Then I bite down on her lobe gently, and she squeaks. "It will be screaming for me by the time I finish."

Her eyes widen, and her cheeks flare hot pink.

I will not let her come tonight. Maybe I'm jealous. Maybe I'm hurt. Or maybe I'm mad. Whatever it is, I'll apologize later.

Sin now, repent after.

Then I shove her stunned, open mouth on my cock. She gags on my length. My balls tighten, and I roar, satisfied.

"Change" by Deftones fills my truck, and I can barely hear her incoherent noises as she swallows me.

She wraps her tongue around me, licking every sensitive nerve, and I throw my head back on the leather seat as she gags, chokes, and sucks hard on me.

"Fuck, baby, such a good girl. *My* good girl."

I loosen my grip and watch her take control of her need to taste me. I still hold her hair, but she's doing it all.

I'm grinding my teeth so hard each time my cock hits the back of her throat. Tears glisten in the corners of her pretty brown eyes.

She keeps going, sucking, bobbing her head up and down, and I watch her so intensely, enjoying every fucking second. Then she pulls my cock out of her mouth and instead sucks on my balls. I groan, raising my brows when she swallows them. She's taking me by surprise. She puts each of them in her mouth, meanwhile wearing a sinful grin.

"Punish me harder, Danny."

My eyebrows raise. Her request has my dick jumping, but I'm hesitant.

"Careful what you ask for."

Because I will. I will punish her harder if that's what she wants, but giving me complete control? *Now, that is a dangerous thing.*

I snarl at her, warning her as she licks my length to the top of my cock, and she smiles as she does it. Then she takes the head of it, putting into her mouth, and gives it another world-shattering suck.

"I know exactly what I'm asking for. Punish. Me. Harder," she taunts.

I grin sadistically. She loves the pain.

I grab her by the throat, hard, rough, but this time, I put pressure on it. Bringing her face to mine, I tell her, "Give me your ass, Ari. I'm going to make your pussy weep for me as I fill your insides. You're going to be begging for me to stop, and when you do, I'll hurt you just a bit more." Then I trail my nose to her breasts, and she pushes her chest into my mouth.

I suck on her nipple hard, squeezing her tits with my other hand. My fingers pressed into her skin like a thirsty beast.

I close my eyes as I tease her. Her body stiffens when she realizes I'm about to unleash a taste of my darkest desires.

If she thinks this is it, she doesn't realize just how far I'll go to claim her as mine.

"You know what? No! I don't want to give you any part of me anymore. Let me fucking go."

"Let you go?" I hum sarcastically.

She nods, glaring daggers at me, and I laugh.

"You're not going anywhere. You don't have a fucking choice," I growl. Fuck, how I love to watch her hate me.

She tries to grind herself on me, probably to relieve the pain from not feeling me.

I could worship her tits all night. I bite her nipple right before I release her. "Fracture my boundaries like you promised me in Iraq, right?" she chokes out through my hold, testing me, still getting under my skin by sassing me. A deep snicker growls out of me.

I tighten my grip on her neck so it's harder for her to breathe. I'm going to physically take her breath away.

She struggles to breathe, but doesn't thrash against my hold. Her fingers are holding onto my hand that's wrapped around her throat. I dig into her skin, rough and tight, and she looks like she's about to pass out, but I won't let her...or maybe I will.

"This is what you do to me," I hiss into her ear angrily, my lips brushing against her ear. She yelps little moans through the chokehold I have her in, but I won't let her sneak in oxygen yet. "Feel my pain, Ari," I tell her as she struggles, tears in the corner of her eyes, crying like I wanted her to. She glares at me the entire time, letting me suffocate her.

"I can't fucking breathe when you're not with me. Just. Like. This," I growl, my voice husky and dark, while I give her one last tightened grip. Her eyes are about to roll back, and she almost passes out.

I let go of her, and she coughs, inhaling all the air I stole from her. She regains her composure, locking eyes with me. She doesn't have to say anything. She wants me to kiss her.

Not just yet.

Then she takes a deep breath and springs onto her knees over my seat, her ass in the air. I love seeing her in this position, but now she will regret her words.

She pants hard, looking over her shoulder to watch me.

"Such a dirty girl. You want to watch me destroy you?"

She nods, biting her lip.

I lift the dress just barely enough to expose her beautiful cunt. I smirk when I see that she's crying for me here, too.

Well, too fucking bad.

I tease her with my cock, hovering over her back, lubing myself up from the oil. It mimics the same lubrication as store-bought. I keep it in my truck. I also use the honey that drips from her. I also trail my cock at her clit, circling it, and she moans harshly.

"Still think you can handle me, little angel?" I position the head at her ass. The entrance is so tight. I know it will hurt her. I spank her ass hard. The loud slap rings out, and she winces away but repositions again.

"I'm not running," she bites out.

"What a shame. I would love to see you try…" I push myself into her ass, entering her slowly. She moans, clawing at my seat.

Fuck, she's tight here too.

Pleasure boils in every single nerve, and I'm in fucking euphoria as she clenches down on me. I already feel like I'm about to finish when she does that.

I'm not a total monster. I look over to make sure she's still okay. She looks at me over her shoulder, licking her red lips.

I circle her clit, playing with her, and she moans in response. Harsh breathing and her legs tremble. I'm going to help her chase her ending, but she won't cross the finish line.

I need to taste her.

I retract my finger from her clit and lick it.

"Sweet like a cherry."

"Oh fuck, Danny…" she begs and pleads through harsh breathing.

I thrust into her, every inch inside her ass, and she's screaming. But not from dread. She screams from pleasure.

"It hurts so fucking good," she breathes out over the heavy metal music that continues to play.

"Good, let me hear you scream."

I slap her ass again, then squeeze her cheeks as I rail her. I am marking more bruises and claiming her as mine again.

She plants her palm on the glass above the seat for balance. The way I'm fucking her, she has to reach for something because I'm not stopping. Her fingers twitch with each detrimental thrust I inflict on her.

"Your screams are like music to my ears, baby," I growl as I continue to pound her mercilessly. She takes it so well.

My truck starts to shake from how hard I'm giving it to her. Back and forth, swaying as I fuck her, and I increase the speed on her clit with my fingers, circling. My little angel wanted to fall from heaven tonight, and I'm the one to capture her. I let her clit go and I grab her hips. I know her body well, and she's about to come. Nope. No, she will not. Then I see her palm fall from the glass, leaving a handprint through the fog we've created on the window.

She reaches down to her clit, circling it, but I slap her hand away.

"You don't get to come tonight. That's your punishment."

She grunts in response, pissed off at me. She retracts her hand, going back to palming the window.

Fuck, she feels so good. It makes it just that much better to watch her hate me as she continuously begs me to wreck her body and her soul.

Every part of her body wrapped around my cock so perfectly I could bury myself inside of her round after round for the rest of my life, and it would never be enough.

As I continue to push myself in and out of her tight entrance, she moans and whimpers over the music and our skin slaps, my belt clanking joins the noise. Her eyebrows furrowed, *watching*. And with each detrimental thrust of sinful lust I rock her with, she has me ruined.

I feel the climax coming, and I'm a feral creature, and there's nothing stopping me from fucking her so deep because she feels too damn good like she always does.

I come so hard, and I pull out of her in time to spread all of my come on her perfect ass. Gripping my dick, stroking it all over my girl. I grab her hips so tight with my other hand I know I'll leave bruises on her. Marking her as mine, like I always do.

I grunt hard when I reach my climax and throw my head back from the intense serenity as I empty myself on her.

"Danny! Please don't do this to me. Let me come," she complains, but it's too late, and it's too bad for her because I'm still mad.

If this were any other night, I would have had her sit on my face so that she rode my tongue until she came so hard she couldn't remember her name, but only mine.

I ignore her pleas, breathing hard.

I reach for a towel that I have in a compartment. I always keep shit like this on hand. I clean her up, wiping away everything I shot on her back, and as soon as I finish, she escapes my hold. She pushes her dress down so that she's no longer exposed and read-justs the top of her dress so her breasts aren't out anymore.

She opens the door to my truck fast and jumps out, still with her heels on. She's angry. Well, so am I.

But if she thinks she's going to leave me again, she's sadly mistaken.

36

———

ARI

I slam the door to Danny's truck so hard his truck vibrates in response. I land on my heels, successfully landing without twisting an ankle on the frozen snowed lawn.

That was definitely hate fucking in there, and every second he buried his wrath inside of me, it only made me lust for him that much stronger.

My ass is sore, and my pussy throbs with pain because I only want to feel myself shatter one last time before I force myself to move on without him.

He wasn't lying about punishing me tonight.

I walk away with tears flowing down my cheeks, a fraction of me pissed off that he did that to me.

I'll never want to share what we have with someone else. He's the only man that makes me feel safe and scared at the same time.

But I loved every second of it, which makes me cry even harder. My chest tightens when I reach for my spare key hidden underneath a large red pot of plants I keep next to my front door.

All I want to do is erase the past few months. I want to erase the night I lost my brother and my baby. And maybe the only way to erase the pain is to leave any association with this military life...for good.

I'm stuck in between; *I'm hopelessly devoted,* and *I need to cut these ties from him for good*...if I want a chance at a normal life.

I am so lost in my thoughts, I don't hear Danny get out of his truck. I don't hear his footsteps behind me, and now all I feel is his big hand stopping me from entering my front door.

When I try to swing the door open, he holds my hand tight, and I try to wrestle it out of his grasp.

I turn around to see that he's only wearing a button up long sleeve and his slacks. He took off his top with all his medals, and now he's staring at me with eyes reflecting an emotion I'm not sure I'm seeing right. His dark, sandy blond hair is messy, making him more attractive.

"What are you doing, Ari?" His question catches me off guard, and another tear escapes me.

My lips trembling, I stare back at him.

"I hate you."

He grimaces when I spew out the words. He looks away from me, stunned, staring at the floor instead. He doesn't let me go, though.

He licks his lips. "No, you don't."

"I do actually. Don't you get it? I need you to leave me alone! I need to move on! And you're not letting me!"

Maybe if I say these words out loud to him and to myself, things will start to change. I'll manifest it into reality.

I'll free myself from this sorrow. It's everyone else's fault I'm feeling this way.

"Let me move on because the more we do this, the more I'll just fall back into you," I plead once again.

"I'm sorry, but no."

"Danny, let me go!" Finally, my hands are free, and I glare at him.

He's so beautiful, I can't look at him without feeling like I will melt away, even in intense moments like this.

"Someone taught me that instead of running from our problems, instead of letting them consume us, we have to learn to let go of the past."

I snort, trying to hide my sorrow, raising my brow sarcastically as my eyes water. A hateful smirk crosses my face.

"I'm sorry I couldn't save your brother. I'm sorry that you think of me as some fucking curse. I'm sorry I couldn't stop Shane from hurting you. I'm sorry I didn't tell you about the bullshit that continues to haunt us. I should've told you, and I'm sorry." He gets closer. I'm inches away from his chest. I can smell his intoxicating scent as I sniffle. I'm doing my damn hardest to keep myself standing when all I want to do is crumble to the floor. I tighten every single leg muscle to stay upright.

"I'm sorry. If you need to blame me for everything, if you need to burden me for all the horrible things that you've gone through so that you can live in peace again," he tucks a loose strand of hair behind my ear, "if it means my little angel can smile bright again," he forces a smile like he's begging me to return one with my own, still holding onto the strands behind my ear. Then I feel his thumb brush over my bottom lip gently.

"Then hate me," he states simply like it's easy for him. "Hate me because the love I have for you is enough to withstand all the pain we've endured together and the pain that we'll *continue* to go through."

My stomach swirls with magic as he continues to stare into my broken heart.

I'm crying even more grimly. I place my hands on his chest, and I'm about to embrace him because I think I know what's coming.

"Don't you fucking dare say it," I cry out.

His eyes flash with tranquility as he stares into mine. My heart beats harder, thrashing.

"Damn it, Ari Natalia, I knew it from the moment I met you. I was ruined." He clenches his jaw, cupping the back of my head, bringing me closer. "I lo—"

He freezes, and my eyebrows raise in confusion. My heart sinks like an anchor overcome by gravity when he stops talking. His eyes squint hard, and his whole demeanor tenses like a rock. He's not looking at me anymore. Instead, his gaze is *behind me*, looking inside my dark house like he's searching for something, on high alert. His eyes flash with worry.

"Wha—?" My lips start to move, confused, but then Danny's eyes widen.

"Baby, move!" he barks out. He throws me to the side so hard I fall to the ground in a split second. My hip collides with the ground, and I yelp from the sensation. He forced me away from him with extreme purpose. My hand burns when I fall. The collision scrapes my skin off in a split second.

It all happens like a fever dream because a gunshot ricochets, and my ears are in instant agony from the loud ringing. I look through my messy black hair strands to see my worst nightmare.

The blood drains from my face when I realize Danny's been shot. He falls to the floor, and I can't see him anymore.

I can't see where he was hit, but I know it's somewhere by his chest. *Maybe his heart.*

My whole soul decimates into a trillion pieces when I realize we're in trouble.

"DANNY!" The sound that comes out of my mouth bellows with hysteria. It echoes into the dreadful night, with nothing and no one to hear me. I scramble up, trying to find some balance and strength to move my way up from the floor, but I slip and fall, my knees colliding with the ground. I'm too fucking shaken, and I feel like I'm going into shock.

What the fuck is happening?

Footsteps surround us.

I turn to see the shadow that appears out of my house, and my eyes widen when I see a familiar face holding a gun.

"You?!" I gasp, and I can feel the hairs on the back of my neck stand up, my spirit leaving my body.

It's her.

It's—

Suddenly, my vision goes dark.

Danny can't die! He's been shot! He can't die!

I start to thrash against someone's hold; they're covering my eyes with no remorse, and I smell something strong as I begin to breathe hard.

Is this fucking chloroform?!

"We fucking got him! We killed him!" a male celebrates with a manic tone.

"NO!" I cry out.

I kick my heels hard against my porch. I scratch my attacker's arms and I know it's a man. He grunts in response and throws my body more arduously to the floor with revenge. His knee digs into my chest, pinning me to the icy floor, and he grabs my hair, pulling my head up off the wood, then smashing it back down so hard I'm seeing stars. I almost go unconscious. I groan through heavy breaths, and I feel like I'm moving in slow motion.

But then my adrenaline finally starts to kick in, and I shout again in excruciating pain.

"Help! Someone help!"

The closest neighbor I have is two miles away from here, but I'm hopeful by some miracle someone will hear me.

"Danny!" I scream for the love of my life. My protector. I hope I can hear his voice again, telling me that he's fine. But instead, the last thing I hear before I black out and succumb to the toxic fumes forced into my lungs, into dark shadows that have me traumatized...is another *gunshot*.

37

———

ARI

I hear my brother's guitar, but this time it sounds sad. He's not playing our favorite song anymore. Cody Jinks plays softly, and everything is hazy, blurry, and white.

I see Danny in the same uniform he wore when he got out of the truck, with dead tulips in his hands and blood pouring out of his chest as he sits on my porch in the cold rain like day of our fight. Except, there's no house. It's just my porch in a blanket of black shadows.

I open my mouth to scream for him, but nothing comes out. I try to move, but I'm chained down.

He hangs his head low, looking at the flowers in his hands. Blood continuously pours out of his chest.

I hear a demonic laugh. It sounds familiar...it sounds like the Grim Reaper.

I bolt awake and jerk my body as if someone had pushed me.

It was a dream. But why am I dreaming of Danny? I only started dreaming of Paul like this when he died.

A horrifying sensation anchors down through me, straight to the ground.

This can't mean he's dead?

Oh, God.

Oh, no.

No.

No.

No.

My body hurts as if I was run over by a train. I'm conscious again but can feel a cold, hard surface underneath me.

"Ohhh," I groan out loud in pain. The first thing I feel on one side of my body is burning pain. My eyes are closed, but I feel too tired to open them.

How did I get here?

My mind is still groggy, and I can't remember anything, but when I see my scraped hands after a few hard blinks, it feels like someone just hit me with a baseball bat.

The memories of Danny holding me when he was about to say those three words make me choke up, and I'm sobbing.

The military ball.

Our time in his truck.

Two gunshots.

Danny was shot.

Seeing him shot when we were both vulnerable was so calculated and planned. The people after us waited for this one moment of perfect opportunity, and they took it.

Kane warned me about them, but I was assured they wouldn't find us.

Then I remember a cloth with thick-scented drugs, causing me to pass out. I never got to see Danny again. He must be here, right? He has to be alive, right?

I can only hear footsteps as if I'm being circled like prey.

"Wakey, wakey," someone taunts me, and I already know who it is. The voice is too familiar.

I'm freezing, shaking, and wet. I'm finally able to open my eyes firmly, and I'm staring at the ceiling. My fingers twitch, trying to reach for my eyes because I feel the need to rub them. Maybe that will help me reach some clarity from this fog.

My vision is blurry, but as the seconds pass, after heavy breathing, I can see again clearly.

I look around, trying to pull away from the rope bound around my wrists that cut off my circulation, but it's no use.

I'm in a barn with horse stables. Except there aren't any horses, and I'm surrounded by a group of men in the dark, cold, empty night. Some of them wear white masks.

And her.

Ms. Salem.

The flashbacks of her standing in my front door after shooting Danny return, and I want to lunge for her throat.

She shot my Danny.

My heart pace accelerates with fear.

How could she do this? This doesn't make any fucking sense!

"I thought you couldn't walk," I accuse, rubbing my arms to help grow warm.

She ignores me.

"He's dead, you know...your boyfriend." She laughs wickedly, standing tall as if she was never injured or had a surgery.

I feel betrayed by a patient I cared for. What the hell?

She stands before me, dressed in all black, next to a man with a long beard going down to his chest, and he looks at me like I'm the scum of the Earth.

"Ms. Salem, but how? Why? Y-you." I shake my head as she looks at me like a game she's won.

"You're lying! He's not dead. I don't believe you. Why are you doing this to me?"

She walks slowly while I struggle to get out of the ropes. She bends down, getting into my face.

Her hair is tied up, slicked back perfectly, not one strand out of place. Her expression darkens with revenge.

Her lips curve villainously, and I'm shaking with anger. I will defend myself this time. Danny has taught me new tactics in self-defense, including using a gun. "I'm lying, huh?" She backhands me with her hand. My head tilts to the side from the hateful force she inflicted on me, but I stare back into her eyes.

She pulls out something from her pocket as she bends down, her elbows resting on her thighs, as she twirls a chain.

My eyes bulge when I realize what they are.

His dog tags.

Danny's dog tags.

With his name on it. The same dog tags he wears, always. But they're covered in blood. *I'm going to be sick.*

I feel like I was the one who was shot. I feel like I'm going to pass out again. The thought of Danny dead has me wanting to die, too.

"No!" I murmur, my voice shaking.

I cry harder and inhale sharply when I see them sway in her fingers, and she laughs again at my pain.

My Danny...he's gone?

"Death can be killed, after all." She stands back up, roaring with a giddy giggle. She throws the tags to the floor, far from me, in the opposite direction. I can only see the back of her as she meets up with the man again.

The dog tags sprawl out on the floor with a scraping noise.

"Why? Why would you kill him?!" I shout again, shaking my head as more gush of tears escapes me. I try to crawl toward Danny's dog tags.

I need to take care of them. Hold them in my hands.

He can't be gone. Please, God, no.

Then, a man pulls me back by my hair, and I shriek, kicking my legs. He drags me back into the passageway of the barn. I close my eyes right before the man lets go of me.

"A life for a life!" she yells, running toward me.

Then she stops and kicks me in my stomach.

I grunt in pain as my lungs feel obliterated to nothing.

I'm gasping for air, choking from the impact.

"Stop this! What the hell are you talking about?" I choke out. Danny doesn't tell me anything. I'm clueless as to what the fuck she's talking about. What has it got to do with me?

"That one thing we have in common, Ms. Alvarez. Don't you remember?!"

"Remember what?! What has this got to do with me?"

What the fuck is she talking about?

What did we have in common?

Then it hits me. Our brothers. But still, what does that have to do with me?

"For a nurse, you're fucking slow. He killed my only brother, you bitch." She thuds away again, and the man burns holes into me with demonic eyes.

"And now we killed him. Everyone that Mr. Death has managed to piss off will be thrilled to know he's dead. Especially his ex-girlfriend, Nora. She's the one who told us about you. We paid her a little visit in the jail. What did you do to piss her off that much?" she mocks me, grinning at me wickedly while the man who stands on her side has his arms folded across his chest.

"I told you...men are trash."

Fucking Nora. Of course.

"What do you mean, he killed him? You said your brother died in a car crash!"

"I lied. He died at the hands of your boyfriend. The night of Damon Hawk's execution. Someone had to get the job done, and my brother was in charge of it."

"His whole team will die alongside him, too. Everyone will pay if it's the last thing we ever do." She claps her hands once like a teacher who finished up at the end of the day.

"And now we have the one thing that Death loved, and that's you." She smirks, then moves her hands to her waist. "Don't worry, you'll join him soon."

"Hang her," the man orders, walking away from me.

"Don't kill me! Please!" I beg, trying to crawl away, but a man behind me stops me. He pulls me up from the floor by my hair. My heels are gone, and I'm only in my red dress.

My eyes close, wincing with pain, and I hiss.

"He killed my brother! My father's only son! And this is just the beginning. We won't stop until all of these so-called *executioners* are dead. We won't hang you if you tell us more about his team and their names. And about Creature."

Creature?

"I won't say anything. They're all good men."

I won't ever tell them anything. I wouldn't dare say anything about Kane.

Oh my god, *Kane* will find me.

I know it. Even Rooker, maybe. He and Danny are so close. He would most likely be next in charge.

"On second thought, don't hang her." The man paces around me, holding a philosopher's pose. He taps his jaw, his lips curve, grinning at me.

"We're going to make her scream as we torture her. Record it and send it to the executioners." He shrugs, getting into my face.

"They're all responsible for killing my son."

I start to sob harder, searching for Danny's dog tags on the floor. I don't want to die. I know I thought I did, but I can't leave this world like this.

I won't die without a fight. I won't let them get the satisfaction of scaring or hurting me on camera.

I won't be scared as they kill me.

My brother wouldn't want that. My mother taught me to be strong and have faith in my God, and I won't let them crack me.

38

ARI

I can't believe I'm in this spot where I'm treading life and death on a thin line like a rope.

They hadn't touched me after throwing me into a horse stable for the night. They questioned me repeatedly, but I kept quiet.

Ms. Salem slapped me several times, kicking me in my stomach so much so I feel like I have a cracked rib.

But I'll take it. After they killed my Danny, I'll take anything over, giving them what they want.

They asked about Bane, Cobra, Texas, and Creature.

They don't know their real names, only mine and Danny's. I will never tell them anything about them. I'd rather die than risk other people's lives, throwing them to the wolves that search for them.

They've barely given me food since they took me that night. I'm severely thirsty and feel like I'm becoming more disoriented as the hours go by.

Whenever I need to use the restroom, they take me into the woods behind the barn and force me to go in the dirt.

I overheard Ms. Salem and her father talk about their plans for me. They will kill me tonight since I haven't said one word to them.

My mouth is dry, my lips chapped, and I'm completely drained and tired.

I'm losing hope that Kane and his team will find me.

Every second, every minute of the day, I see Danny's face. My heart cracks repeatedly when I picture our last moments together.

He was shot.

He's really gone.

I start sniffling into my arms, hugging myself.

He's dead because of me and my stupidity.

I shouldn't have ended things with him. I shouldn't have told him those horrible things when we were in the rain. All he's wanted to do since we met was protect me, and I threw it in his face while telling him it *hurt me* to *love him.*

How could I have let my selfishness reach me like that?

I sob even harder.

And now he's gone?

Maybe I should let them kill me. I don't want to live without him.

Even if I make it out of this, I can't live without feeling his strong arms hold me like a safehaven. It'll hurt me to wake up every day knowing he won't walk through that door in his uniform after he gets home from work. I don't want to fall asleep again if I can't do it in his arms.

I won't be able to sleep knowing I'll turn around in the bed, and it'd be empty and cold.

I'll never love another man again. Danny Rider will always have my heart.

I lost my brother, my baby, and now Danny?

I'll join him in hell if it means I get to be with him forever. Our bodies will perish, but I love him so fucking much that I'm praying it's enough to have our spirits forever intertwined in the afterlife.

The thought of him in a casket like my brother makes me shrink into myself, and my stomach turns and my world goes dizzy for a minute. And I feel like I'm about to explode and scream. I feel like I'm already going crazy without him.

I don't want to see my beautiful, sinful man dead in a casket.

Even in his last moments, he sacrificed his life for me. He pushed me out of the way and shielded me at the last second when it meant his own life.

I hate myself.

My face is wet and flushed from the constant grief, and I'm not sure I can do this anymore.

I shift in the corner of the horse stable, my whole body sore, and I try my hardest to free myself from the rope. It's burned against my skin, and I've been bleeding slowly.

It's dark again, the night consuming me, and I feel myself going out again. My blood pressure is dropping to dangerous limits, and my muscles and eyes are fragile.

I'm no longer hungry. I'm no longer thirsty. I no longer crave these fundamentals to survive. That's how I know I'm in trouble.

"She's pale. Her lips are turning blue. She's dying," one of the kidnappers warns Ms. Salem.

I'm drifting in and out of sleep, my breathing slowing down, and all I want to do is go to sleep entirely and dream of Danny.

Maybe if I'll fall asleep, I'll get to see him. Maybe he'll talk to me. I dream of Paul even though he's dead...

Maybe I'll dream of the man I fell hopelessly in love with.

"Good. She can join her brother." She laughs wickedly.

I blink slowly, and Ms. Salem drinks her water in front of me. Then she throws the bottle to the floor by my feet. Water splatters everywhere, and my eyes widen. I gather the last fraction of energy I have stored and crawl to the water bottle.

My knees scrape against the cold ground. It's still freezing, and I'm the only one in this barn with hardly anything to keep warm.

Everyone else wears jackets, coats, and beanies.

I grab the water bottle and drink one gulp down. A few drops hit my tongue, and I'm shaking it desperately into my mouth.

"Hungry, too?" one of the kidnappers asks me in an evil tone.

I'm on my knees, the plastic water scrunched into my hands, and I look up at him.

He unzips his jeans and pulls out his hardened length.

I quickly start crawling back into the corner of the horse stable, covering my eyes with my shaky, cold hands.

"Death's little whore. I've got something you can snack on," he mocks me, stalking toward me.

I'm circled into a fetal position, dreading his presence, but he doesn't stop. I can hear the footsteps getting louder, and he pulls my hair upward.

I scream, clawing his hand, scratching the skin off.

He hisses in pain but holds his grip on my hair. He bends down, getting into my face.

"I always fuck our hostages before we kill them. Tonight is your execution, by the way. I've got the green light to have my fun with you before we hang you."

"Leave me alone, you piece of shit!"

He roars with laughter. This man is easily over six feet, covered in tattoos from his face down to his neck. He's overweight, and his double chin sticks out the more he tries to get in my face.

"I like her, Omar. Are you sure we have to kill her? I want to keep her as a toy."

"Are you sure?" Omar reaffirms from a few feet away.

"She'll be my new favorite shiny toy. Not a pet. A pet gets shelter, food, and water. You'll get nothing but my cock when I'm ready to play with you and when I'm done using you, fucking every single part of you so bad that the Grim Reaper will no longer want you by the time I'm done, I'm going to cut off your fingers, your toes, one digit at a time for every day that you're my toy."

I start screaming. This man is crazy. I'd rather die. The thought of me becoming some sex slave that gets dismembered slowly over time with this psychopath has me craving death over a life of torture.

"Kill me!"

I'm sorry, Danny. I'm sorry, Mom. I'm sorry, Paul.

He grabs a gun out of his pocket, pointing at me, shoving it into my mouth, and I scream harder.

"Oh, yeah?" He looks over to Omar and Ms. Salem, and they're amused, as if a sick show is entertaining them.

"We can hang the one they call Bane instead. We can shoot her. I'm getting annoyed by her cries. I don't want to hear your pets whimper at home," Omar tells him nonchalantly.

"Kill me!" I scream again through the gun, wailing uncontrollably. He forces it more down my throat, and I feel so helpless.

I'm going to die. At least it'll be quick and not torturous.

"I'm going to cut your fucking head off, bitch! Keep testing me!"

I scream again at the top of my lungs, howling with agony, the gun rattling back and forth against my teeth before he pulls the gun from my mouth. He strokes the tip of his length, and I cover my ears and eyes with my hands, but it's no use. He points his gun at me while he touches himself. Getting closer, he plants the weapon on the top of my head.

"Say hello to Death for us!" he snarls.

"Tell him yourself," a voice echoes through the barn.

I gasp, and everyone grows quiet. Then a shot rings out, and the man that held a gun to my head drops to the floor, his blood splattering all over my face and chest.

Danny.

39

———

KANE

You know when you fucked up so bad, and you realize it as soon as you commit your own heinous crime? And then you're desperate to right your wrongs? It doesn't matter that it's nearing midnight or the freezing temperature is biting my skin.

Or that the military ball is still thriving, and the night has just begun.

I have to apologize to Ari. And I need to apologize now. This can't wait. Even if she doesn't want me, I owe her an apology face-to-face for being an asshole. It isn't like me, and it'd be easier for me to blame it on liquor, but that's an easy out and I won't give her that excuse.

I love Ari. I'm so in love with her, but after what I did tonight, after I got my shit kicked in and broke Meredith's heart, I know I'm in the wrong.

I bit her lip because I knew that's what she liked. But that's not who I am. It isn't like me to overstep, and I had vowed to protect her. And if that means I'll be friend-zoned for the rest of

330

my life, I'll gladly take it because if I'm still in her life still, that's a privilege I don't want to risk letting go.

A part of me will always be in love with her.

I think I just lost my best friend for good, too. I pushed him too far this time.

I'm not drunk, but I'm acting like an insensitive ass.

I'm well under the driving limit. I can go to Ari's house, and even if Grim is there, I'm sure he wouldn't fight me if I apologized for disrespecting their relationship and Ari's boundaries.

It fucking hurt for her to tell me,

"It'll always be Danny."

But that was the closure I needed to move on finally.

There's just one more thing I need to do, and that's apologize.

My phone starts to ring, and I pull it out with one hand still on the steering wheel.

"Fucker, where the hell did you go?"

"I'm on my way to Ari's."

Lopez exhales, frustrated over the phone.

"*Pinche pendejo.* You really do have a death wish. She doesn't want you. *Ella no quiere tus ojos azules, quiero los de* Grim."

"First, I don't know what the fuck you just said, but fuck you, too. And I'm going there to apologize."

"Well, say less because I'm headed there too. Rooker's going home with his wife right now, and someone's gotta pull you guys apart."

"Not necessary."

"Yeah, yeah," he mocks me. "I'll meet you there."

Click.

I stop by the gas station to fill up the car. I'm standing there, holding the handle. The smell of fuel fills my nose, and I can see my reflection in the car door mirror.

My dark brown hair is a complete mess. My nose is bruised, and the black eye I received when I got into the bike accident is shockingly less dark and now lighter shades of purple and green.

I look like a fucking zombie.

This is what happens when you piss people off.

And the Grim Reaper.

My face is evidence of pissing off the wrong people.

After filling up a full gas tank at the closest gas station to Ari's place, I'm down her street in the next twenty minutes.

I've only been here three times, and I know it by memory.

I take a deep breath when I start driving onto the path leading to her home.

As soon as I enter her property, I know something is wrong. I see a group of people all over the front yard of Ari's house.

When my headlights flash across the men in white masks, I know something is going down, and it's not good. They look like the same men that tried to assassinate me, hadn't it been for Creature.

Then I see a familiar red dress, sprawled out in someone's arms, being dragged into a van ruthlessly.

A group of men, and I see a woman, but I can't make out her face or features when she closes the van's passenger door behind her.

My best friend lies unconscious on the floor with men hovering over him.

They're kidnapping Ari. Danny might be fucking dead...why isn't he moving?!

I reach for my pistol tucked into the center console; and going full send to hell, my foot hitting the pedal with no remorse as these men return with fire. They all shoot at my windshield, the glass shattering all over me, but I don't stop. I duck underneath the steering wheel. I barely miss Danny, and I run over two of the masked hitmen hard with my car, their bodies making the car jump as I floored.

There's no way they'll survive that.

Some of the hitmen crash against the hood of the car hard.

Then I realize the van has sped away with Ari because I hear it roar away, disappearing into the shadows.

Fuck!

Motherfuckers will all die for this.

Every. Single. One. Of. Them. Will die for putting their hands on her.

But four hitmen are left behind as they try to lift Danny and make a run for it in another van.

They're not going anywhere.

I raise my pistol, both hands on it, and shoot two in the head, granting them instant death. They drop to the ground.

The other two return fire on me, and I dodge every hit. They've got shit aim, thank God.

I jump out of the car on the opposite side, giving me cover to reload and reassess how to get to Grim.

He better not be fucking dead.

More gunshots ring out from another direction. My hands cover my face and I'm helplessly tensed up against the hood.

Not more of these fucking pieces of shits?!

I'm outnumbered.

I grab my cell phone, prepared to call in our team and the Admiral. My fingers tremble with adrenaline and shock as I try to unlock my phone, missing every number to my passcode, and I have to restart. But then I hear a familiar voice shout into the cruel, wintry sky.

"*Pinche cabron*, you alive over there?"

Operator Texas.

The cowboy from South Texas.

"Holy shit, I've never been happier to be called a *cabron* before," I shout back with gratitude and a smirk. I peek through the car windows to see Lopez sitting in his truck a couple of feet away from Grim, aiming his pistol at the men he just shot.

Fucker saved my life.

I forgot he was meeting me here even after I told him not to.

"I couldn't miss seeing Grim kick your ass again. Shit's better than the UFC," he jokes back, and I slump against the car door. The fiery tension in every single muscle of mine relaxes. And a short scoff of a laugh escapes me.

"Fuck you too." I snort.

I hadn't realized I was bleeding until blood splattered over my uniform. I touch my forehead and realize the shattered glass cut me.

Fucking hell, I will need a long-ass vacation after this to let my face heal. How much more can my face take?

"Is Grim alive?" I shout, still undercover.

Would if there's more of these assholes?

"I don't know, man, I don't like this. How the fuck did we not get alerted by this? Doesn't she have the best fucking security system installed? Where is she? Where's Ari?"

"Motherfuckers took her! They dragged her into the van. I couldn't get to her," I groan in pain, looking at my bloody hands. "I failed her," I murmur, knowing Lopez can't hear me. They have her...just like I've been worried about.

Fuck the Admiral.

That was one of my first thoughts. Why had the security system failed her?

How do they know where she lives?

"I'm calling it in."

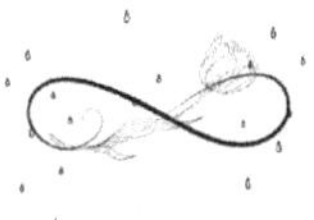

Spending time in hospitals is feeling like a new normal.

I watch the black coffee pour into the coffee cup. I'm at a nurse's station in the hallway. They granted me access to their coffee. It's around five in the morning, and Grim is stable.

Motherfucker is immortal, and I'm starting to question how the fuck he got on God's good side to escape death so many times. The man is anything but religious or holy.

"How's Grim?"

A deep burden of a voice rumbles behind me, and I almost drop my coffee cup in the hallway. I'm jumpy and on edge after I engaged in a shootout, so Creature's voice behind me made me want to return with a punch to his jaw.

I turn around to face the newest man on the team.

This man gives me the creeps. If I thought Danny held darkness, well, this guy bleeds poison, an aura that blurs the lines of what he holds morally right...*if* he has any.

"Damn it, Creature. Don't fucking sneak up on me like that, asshole." I seethe, glaring at him, seeing red. I didn't hear him come up behind me. Motherfucker is so quiet. Even his footsteps are complete silence.

"He's stable. That's all I know. Bullet went through his upper chest. No surgery is needed. They sedated him when he tried to wake up in the ambulance. He was going batshit crazy on the paramedics," I explain, sipping the burning coffee and holding the plastic rim to my mouth. "Admiral Ravenmore is on his way." Creature looks at me through his black mask with bored, unfazed eyes.

"We need to find the girl. Or we're all dead." Creature blinks slowly, leaning against the wall. He reaches into his pocket, pulling out the same bullet he always plays with. Twirling it in each finger, he breaks his gaze and stares at his hand.

"And I'm not talking about our enemies killing us, no. But Grim will." Then he looks straight into my eyes, and my stomach drops.

I know what he means. The whole world might be dead when Grim discovers Ari is gone, and we haven't been able to find her. It's only been a few hours, but it already feels like forever.

No leads. It's like they disappeared into thin air. Rooker and Lopez are in Danny's room, waiting for him to wake up.

Zeke explained to us that after he and his team did an initial investigation into the malfunctioning of the security system. He came up with the conclusion that Omar had hacked it.

We're not the only ones with incredible assets and technology.

They're well equipped too.

I love Ari. I'm still so fucking in love with her, but I'll never overstep again. Time will heal the hole I have in my heart because of her rejection. But it's not me. She told me that crystal clear, and it cut deep when she said those words.

Ari and I's relationship will always be unique, and I think a part of me will always wait for her. But for now, I'm letting her go.

"The girl's name is Ari Alvarez," I correct him with a snap before stalking away from him. "And we'll find her."

As I'm walking away, I check on Ari's mother with the police officer assigned to her. She's been in protective custody by local police until we handle this situation.

The closer I get to Grim's room, the more I hear shouting and muffled loud commotion.

I look up from the hospital floor tiles and look into the ICU room he's staying in through the glass doors. Rooker and Lopez surround him. They're trying to calm him down as he dresses into the uniform he was wearing when he got shot. The hospital gown is off him, torn to pieces on the floor.

Rooker's trying to calm him down, but Danny is gone, and the Reaper takes over. He flips the hospital bed to the side, and it crashes loudly to the floor as the realization of Ari's absence settles in.

Blood spills through his chest from where he was shot.

His IV was yanked out of his arm, and blood profusely pours down his forearm as he shouts in Rooker's face.

"I'm fine!" he growls at Rooker, and I know this is my cue to step in.

I open the door fast.

Hospital security comes rushing in as if ready to handcuff the patient wreaking havoc on the ICU floor. They reach for their handcuffs, but once they see it's us—SEAL Team Executioners—they stop midway. They backpedal into the hallway once they see it's Operator Grim Reaper unleashing his wrath.

"Grim," I call out to him, snapping him out of his thoughts. The space between his brows narrows with unforgiving intensity.

Fuck. He might kill me.

He pushes me, but I keep my ground, only stumbling one step.

"Where is she, Kane? Rooker told me you were the last to see her." He pushes me again, and I know he's blinded with wrath.

"Where's Ari? Where is she?" he repeats, yelling at me. The veins in his neck and hands are swollen with vengeance. He grabs me by my vest, and I swallow.

Everyone on the hospital floor stops, and it grows quiet. Tensions were so thick you couldn't slice through it. I look around and find the entire staff staring into the room. Lopez clears his throat with gloominess.

Rooker watches his best friend unleash his rage on me, and no one can stop Grim.

I turn back to Grim, and his chin is set high. I can see the heat that flushes his entire body. His breaths are long and cemented evenly. I can see that he's in devastation. He's broken. Not cool. Not collected. Not composed.

A man who has lost his reason to live.

His pain is infinite.

"I don't know, Grim, but Zeke is on it. He'll find her soon." I blink with determination. Zeke is good at his job, and Grim knows that. We'll find her quickly; I have no doubts.

He walks away from me, running his hands through his hair.

Rooker clears his throat as Creature walks in, not saying a word. He goes into a corner, crossing his arms and watching.

"They will find her, Danny. This isn't like any other mission. They might..." Rooker tells Danny, and he watches him like he's about to kill him just for saying it.

It's the elephant in the room no one wants to address.

We all know that Ari might be dead already. Nobody has the balls to say it, and Danny knows he can't disagree with him.

But I refuse to believe they've killed her. I don't want to believe it because I'll break too.

Then Grim flips his switch even more and looks at Rooker like he's about to kill him for saying it.

"Don't you fucking dare say anything more," Grim snarls, baring his teeth. "What do you mean, *they*, huh?"

Rooker's expression softens as he steps away from Grim until his back hits the wall. "You know this is out of our jurisdiction. It's not our place anymore. Let the police handle it."

Grim's jaw ticks as Rooker reminds him of protocols.

"If this was Noel..." I start and Rooker breaks away from Grim at the mention of his wife's name, but he needs to understand what Ari's disappearance is doing to Grim...to me. I've got his full attention now, and he just might beat the shit out of me for saying it.

"Look, all I'm saying is, we don't know that, Rooker. They might use her to lure us all," I argue. "And they'll leave her alive until they can draw Grim in. Isn't that what they want? So this makes everything more complicated and rules will be broken. Admiral Ravenmore will want us in on this, and the police will, too."

"Sir, please sit down." A nurse enters the room quickly and pleads with Grim. She points to the hospital bed, scolding him like a child.

She's scared and hesitant to come closer to a man whose entire world has been taken away from him. The heartache Danny is feeling is evident and crystal clear through wrath.

Her shoulders tense as she arches her brows, signaling him back to the hospital bed.

"Lori, I know you remember me," he says.

The nurse bites the inside of her cheek nervously.

"You have to discharge me. I have to find Ari." He walks toward her, and it looks like Lori wants to shrink away, but then quickly changes her demeanor.

"What the fuck do you mean? Where is she?! Wasn't she at

the ball with Violet?" She raises her voice, her chest rising and falling.

"I can't disclose anything," Grim mumbles.

"The hell you can't!" Lori screeches at him, stomping her foot on the ground.

"*Senorita hermosa*, you don't understand," Lopez chimes in. His southern accent clips through the tension in the room and slightly switches the mood.

I roll my eyes. Is he trying to flirt in a situation like this? *Asshole.*

"We have a job to do just like you do," he finishes, flashing her a dimpled smile, crossing his arms across his chest.

Lori glares at him, narrowing her eyes with annoyance at Lopez's flirtatious smile. "I'm gay." She scoffs before turning back to Grim.

Then she shifts to Creature, who stands in the corner of the room, flipping the same heavy bullet in his fingers.

"And who the fuck are you?" Lori snaps. She's unleashing hell at every single one of us, and it's justifiable.

Creature stops twirling the bullet in his fingers. He goes frozen for a couple of seconds. His gray eyes look at Lori through his black mask, a snicker of a laugh follows.

"No one. Just a ghost on the wall. Carry on."

What the hell. "Ignore him," Grim snarls. "Lori, you know damn well nothing will stop me from walking out of that room in the next five minutes. She's out there, and I can find her. I'm being courteous."

Lori sighs in defeat.

"You lost a lot of blood, Mr. Rider."

"And you gave me a blood transfusion, right? I'm good. I'm solid, Lori."

She purses her lips and looks at his arms that are covered in blood from him yanking out his own IV.

"I'll do what I can, but Doctor Reese is on shift tonight, and he's a bit of an asshole."

Grim eyes light up, and his eyebrows arch.

"Perfect."

40

DANNY

I grin wickedly, staring into my crosshairs, watching that fucker drop down to hell where he belongs.

Motherfucker got off easy but I couldn't watch him touch my girl anymore.

Son of a bitch.

As I suited up for tonight's mission, ready to unleash the deepest, darkest twisted ways of my mind against the men that took my angel... I sharpened my knife. And now we're here and the only way I'm leaving this ranch is with my girl in my arms and Omar branded with Death's scythe.

There's a big window on the roof. I broke it open and dropped in. The shadows of the night fade away my presence.

When I dropped in, I could hear my angel scream, begging for them to kill her. I'm about to send this whole fucking building to the ground.

My chest is fucking sore, and I'm in so much pain, but nothing could compare to the pain I felt to hear Ari beg them to kill her.

Fuck.

I will collect each and every one of these evil mother fuckers souls. The entire time my team and I were being transported by the police, I was contemplating which twisted way I would kill Omar, and I will.

Ari's on the ground in the stable with that piece of shit's body.

Kane, Lopez, and Rooker drop behind me. Zeke's team breaches the side of the barn, making an explosion of an entrance.

There's about an army of men in the barn and a hanging rope, as if they were setting up to hang her.

I hold my rifle tight against the shoulder that's been shot; I'll deal with those consequences later. My adrenaline powered by vengeance won't let me feel it right now. I will have Omar's body added to my long list of confirmed kills tonight.

Everything will come to an end tonight.

Paul's killer is in my sights and I will make sure this time he won't get away.

Our number one target on the most wanted list won't have a beating heart after I get a hold of him.

I pull the trigger, but one of his friends throws their body in front of him. He goes down instead of Omar. Fucking coward. But I'll make him beg for mercy...they all do when Grim Reaper is knocking on their door. Omar tries to reach for a weapon from one of his followers' belt, but I shoot another one down, preventing from arming himself.

Everyone draws their weapons, and I finally see my girl.

She stands, shaking and crying. She has her hands over her ears and her beautiful brown eyes meet mine like she's pleading for me to get to her. I swallow the pain in my throat. I will hold her again.

I just have to get through Omar's army first.

Easy.

"Run!" I shout at her and her watery eyes widen. She takes off running toward one of the doors in the back of the barn. As she opens it, a man chases after her. He's about to put his hand on her hair and I put a bullet in his head.

Then absolute chaos ensues. Everyone is exchanging fire. I take a few more out from behind cover, and the last thing I see is Omar and his daughter chasing after Ari into the woods behind the barn.

Over my fucking dead body.

"I need to get to her," I tell the team through the mic, reloading my rifle.

"Go! We'll cover you...get *our* girl," Kane responds and a part of me resents when he says "our," but he no longer means it in that way.

"Bane, don't make me put a fucking bullet in your head, too."

Paul trusted our team with his sister. And Kane will always be a part of Ari's life, just not the way I'll be and after a lengthy conversation these past three days, we've reached an understanding, but that doesn't mean we're close friends. He overstepped, and he's lucky I'm letting him live.

Our friendship is done, but he's still on my team, which means I'll always be professional.

"Do you need backup? I'll follow you out!" Rooker offers after taking down another from deep into the barn.

I hold my rifle up and shots are being sprayed all around us, but we're taking them all down one after one, avoiding getting hit. I aim for two men with AK-47s over a wall and pull the trigger. They fall to the floor.

"I got this. Just cover me. She ran into the woods, but Omar is mine," I roar. I need to get to her before they kill her.

I head for the breached explosion that Zeke created. My boots hit the frozen floor, there's still a few inches of snow, and I grimace when I remember my Ari is running barefoot on this.

I'm taking her to my house, and we will spend the next few nights by my fireplace after this is over. I will not let her out of my sight for the next fucking century.

The woods are thick behind the barn. We're in North Carolina, and I can see a glimpse of red glimmer in the moonlight. The dress I bought her has sequins and jewels and the night sky and stars reflect off her dress.

Omar, his daughter, and three men run after her. They're shooting at her as they chase. Gunshots ripple into the air and they sound like fireworks.

"Creature!" I yell at our most lethal sniper as I get closer to them. He knows I'm calling for him to take the shot. I know he's watching.

As if on cue, another bullet rings out by my ear, and the man chasing Ari falls to the floor.

His body falls against a rock and I take a quick glance as I run past his body, making sure he's dead.

Creature is fucking good at what he does. Admiral Ravenmore made a great decision, adding him to the team. The fucker never misses. This man was running full speed, and he still hit the target in the head.

"Good shit."

"I'll leave you the rest," he grumbles through the mic.

I lift my rifle now that I'm a few feet away from Ari. She's hit a dead end and there's a river flowing down hard. The sound of the river gets louder as I pull the trigger again.

I fire another shot, and that only leaves three men now. I have to reload my weapon, but I don't have enough time. I won't grant them quick deaths, anyway. I pull out my knife.

I can't see Ari anymore. Maybe she's hiding now that they are cornered towards the river.

My smart girl.

They don't know where I'm at. I'm Death's shadow tonight and I'm watching Omar call out for Ari.

"Spread out and find her. She couldn't have gotten far," Omar growls, ordering the few henchmen he has left.

"Dad! We have to run. He's after us, we can come back," his daughter pleads.

He slaps her on the face.

"We're not leaving until I have Death's head on a spike and his slut underground. Now fucking find them."

"Yes, sir!"

But his daughter rubs her cheek, glaring at her father. She looks like she had enough. She turns around, walking into the deep woods, abandoning them.

He's delusional. Even if he kills me, they're surrounded. They're not going anywhere. I watch his henchmen search around me. There are only a few left.

Don't they know the shadows are my friends? The Reaper calls out for them, and I will deliver.

I creep behind a tree and watch one of them step into my vision to the left of me.

He's short, but his frame is built…still an easy kill.

I grab him, palming my gloved hand over his mouth. I muffle his screams as I hug his body, twisting the gun out of his hand as I stab in the chest. Before he falls, I pull my silencer out and shoot him in the head, another one down.

I lay him down on the snow quietly.

One by one, they walk deeper into the cold, blackened night, and I assassinate them. Leaving only Omar.

He calls out for his henchmen and becomes frantic when he realizes he's alone. His voice echoes into the night with nothing in return. Death will take his soul; I can feel him dancing with joy, anticipation clawing hard. I can almost see him hover over him, licking his lips.

"Mr. Death, I know you're here," he mimics, and I smile.

I'm grinning from ear to ear as he searches for me.

"I might not make it out of here tonight,"

You sure as hell won't.

"I'll make sure to take your whore with me."

His tongue will be cut from his throat for talking about my girl like that.

He begins to shoot at random trees into the woods. He's desperate, and that's exactly what I want. I want him to know that his ending is near. No one escapes Death.

Sure enough. He stands in an open area and I'm done hiding.

I grip the handle, stepping out from the shadow, and the moon shines on me like a spotlight. Omar's eyes bulge, terrified. He's motionless. All that shit-talking, and look at him.

Fucking coward. They always are.

He raises his pistol at me, but I'm faster.

I throw the blade at his arm. His gun drops as soon as it collides with his flesh, and I stalk toward him.

I grab him as he pleads for his life, clawing at me, but my uniform stops him from succeeding.

He wails, flopping around to get out of my hold, but he's fucking weak and I'm having too much fun.

"Even if you kill me," I tighten my hold on his throat, but he keeps going, "It'll never be over Mr. Death. This is a war. And a war is never ending. I'll see you in hell."

A sinister grin spreads across my face with excitement. Chills run down my bones at the thought of getting to torture him in the afterlife. Sounds like a good fucking time to me.

"Looking forward to it." I snarl into his ear. "This is for Ari."

I do what I say and retract his tongue from his mouth, slicing it off. Cuts through like butter and blood begins to pour like a waterfall onto my hands and his body.

"And this is for Paul."

I slice his throat.

41
———

ARI

My feet burn, and the last bit of adrenaline in my system pulls through.

I don't know how I'm able to walk, let alone run, after two days with little to no water or food.

I'm running over snow, rocks, and branches, cutting myself as I try to flee.

I don't know where I'm going. All I know is Danny told me to run, so I'm running until I feel safe again.

I ran for the woods. It's the first thing I saw when I opened those doors. I feel weak, but I have to keep going.

It's dark, cold and freezing. It's a few days after Christmas, and the winter snow hasn't let up. That's rare in North Carolina. If it snows, it's very little, but for some reason, this winter, it snowed the most in years.

I hear footsteps thunder after me, leaves and rocks crunching underneath someone's boots.

"You're going to die now, bitch!" Ms. Salem screams after me.

I look around frantically through the dark and hear a river

flowing. I stop running and try to listen closely to it. Maybe I can cross the river, and they won't follow me. It has to be freezing, but I'm a good swimmer.

"When we get our hands on you, we're going to gut you!" her father roars from behind me.

I take off running when I get a good idea of where the river is. My feet ache, and the cold air burns every time I inhale. I can't feel my toes or fingers, but I must keep going.

Then I hear a gunshot ring loud. It hits the tree next to me, and I turn around to find them all after me... just a few feet away.

I whip around again and hide behind a tree. I watch the river; it looks peaceful, but the current is strong, and I hesitate to jump in.

They keep shooting at me from behind, and I'm shaking, trembling, and I silence my own whimpers with my hands. My fight-or-flight response kicks in, but I can't jump in the water. Instead, I try to curl up against myself, hoping I'll vanish into thin air.

I palm my mouth, biting down hard. I can't let them know where I am.

Then, another shot rings out, but it sounds different, like it came from a different weapon at a different angle.

I put my hands to my ears as more gunshots ring out, and I scream as if it's the last one I'll make. I feel like they're right behind the tree. I'm hiding behind it as more fire keeps going. It sounds like fireworks on steroids. Like small bombs going off, over and over again.

I'm going to die.

I'm going to die.

I'm going to die.

If the cold weather doesn't kill me, I'm going to get hit by the crossfire, or worse, they'll find me now that I've gone into shock, and I can't stop screaming.

Then it goes silent. No more gunshots…just the river. Keeping my hands on my ears, I'm praying to God I'll somehow walk out of this, unscarred.

Then a body drops next to me by the tree. It's the man who's been chasing me. A pistol drops from his lifeless hand, covering him in blood. Blood drops from his nose and into the snow.

The crimson coloration stands out against the white ice under the moonlight. The snow glimmers like glitter as I blink.

This is my chance to run again, but I need to take the gun from his hands. Danny taught me to use these weapons for self-defense.

I lean over, still crying and quivering with shock. I grab the metal gun. I'm hovering over the dead body and sneak a peek to my left.

I hear someone's voice, but my breathing over shadows their words but. I swear I hear Omar and Danny.

Immediately, I'm taken aback by what's unfolding in the middle of the woods. Danny towers over Omar and has the man restrained by his arms. Then he slits my captor's throat.

My eyes widen. I just watched him kill someone.

He's wearing his mask. But I'd know those ocean eyes anywhere.

Blood splatters all over Omar and onto the Snow White floor. Danny notices me watching, and he stiffens completely, letting Omar fall to the floor and choke on his own blood.

I whimper when I see him, biting my lip, and I'm tempted to start running toward him, but I can't move.

I feel intense pain in my chest, like my heart will stop from all the mayhem. No matter how much I breathe or cry, I'm devoured by terror, and it makes me lose any sense of movement.

Danny strides over the snow and dead bodies, and all I want to do is run, but my legs don't respond.

Then I see a shadowy figure pop up behind him, raising a gun to his back, and... I act.

I hold up my pistol like I learned from my safety training and pull the trigger.

It sends Ms. Salem to the floor, and my hand riddles from the power of the gun.

She falls to the floor, and I don't know where I shot her. But it worked because Danny looks behind him.

"Oh, my God. I killed her!" I drop the gun from my hand, and another anxiety attack ensues.

She was going to kill Danny if I hadn't pulled the trigger.

"Oh my God...she's dead, isn't she? What have I done?" I start stuttering over my words as Danny grabs my face with both of his hands as a panic attack holds me captive. I'm a murderer. I took someone's life.

"Baby, look at me!" He attempts to snap me out of my disarray. He plants a kiss on my forehead through his mask.

"Danny! I killed her! I shot her!"

I had to, right?

But still, I can't help but feel immediate and immense guilt. She's not facing me, she's on her side, but I can see her back.

"Ari, look at me!" he begs again in a deep, husky voice.

I finally look away from Ms. Salem, and through the blurry vision, I search for him.

"You're okay, Ari. It's okay." He holds my face tighter in his hand, and then he embraces me into a hold. "Are you hurt?"

I hug him back, crying into his chest.

"I'm freezing," I shiver through crying whispers, and he holds me tighter. "I'm thirsty...so thirsty."

I'm still in my red dress from the ball. It doesn't cover anything. I haven't had any type of warmth or coat since the dance. I'm getting hypothermic.

"I'll get you warmed up right now, baby."

"Danny, I killed her!"

Then he lets me go tactically fast, and I hear a loud grunt from a woman's voice behind him.

It's Ms. Salem.

She isn't dead even though I shot her.

She charges at him, screaming as if she has nothing to lose. Blood drips down her mouth, and she's stumbling while she runs at him. She is holding a knife over her shoulder with bulging dark eyes of revenge.

Everything happens in a split second.

Danny turns around, and he grabs a pistol from his belt. He shoots her in the forehead, and she goes down again.

"No, I killed her." He watches Ms. Salem for a few seconds longer. He reaches over and feels for a pulse. He bends down and then retracts his hand. I watch him nervously, looking around to see five dead bodies around us. Then he makes his way back to me.

He removes his top, leaving him only in a vest and camouflage top.

He throws it over my shoulder, and I slip my cold, frozen arms into the sleeves.

My teeth chatter, my feet burn, and I feel like I might become a human icicle.

I look into his light blue iris. The way he wears his disguise; he looks like the actual Grim Reaper with his mask on. A scythe symbol covers his mouth, and my wide-eyed man stares into my soul, so intimidatingly gorgeous.

"Danny, you're alive...you found me," I sob through chattering teeth. My shaky palm reaches to touch his face. I'm covered in blood and so is he. The blood is splattered all over his disguise and eyelids.

"You were never lost..." he breathes. "I told you, there's nowhere you could go where I couldn't find you." He lets me go, and I stumble back into a tree.

Tears fall down my face, and my heart pounds harder.

Even through his mask, I know he's smiling at me.

"Are you okay? Did they hurt you? Did they..." he clears his throat, "*touch* you?"

I shake my head.

"Now that you're here, I'm okay."

His hands reach underneath his shirt, by his collar bones, and he takes off his dog tags from his neck as my back is still pressed hard against the tree.

He places them over me, so I'm wearing them as another necklace on top of my cross one. The cold metal kisses my skin, and everything changes to slow motion.

"Marry me." He brushes my lips with his fingers, rigid with purpose.

A low whimper falls from my lips, but not from pain...from serenity.

"Baby, marry me." My mouth opens ever so slightly, not believing the words coming out of his mouth.

I stare at him, trying to figure out if this is a dream.

When I watch his stone-cold eyes search mine vehemently. I know it's real.

"Danny...I'm scared," I admit. "I'm scared the longer you're in the military—" I weep through heavy breaths, shaking my head.

I can't find the words. It's scary to think shit like this will continue for us. Maybe I'm ruining the moment, but I'm in a chokehold, unsure of what to do or say.

"I'm scared." I shrug, sobbing, and he watches me so intensely. I feel like I'll disappear into nothing the longer he stares at me like that. I can't handle it when he does this. I melt every single time. Even more so through his mask. Because even though I can't see his face, his eyes tell me everything.

They tell me what his soul needs and what he's feeling.

"It's okay to be scared. Fear isn't a weakness, angel. It means you're still alive."

I exhale through trembling lips and chattering teeth, and puffs of white follow, and I narrow my eyes at him with admiration. He's my haven.

"I promise you; I'll always find you. I will always protect you. You are mine forever, Ari Natalia. I will save you from the darkness that lives in this world and the darkness that troubles your soul. I love you, Ari. I'm so in love with you."

He said it.

And he's proposing.

Butterflies swarm and sparks fly into my throat. I sniffle and hold his dog tags tighter in my hands.

I look down at them. My fingertips trail blood, and I accidentally leave crimson traces with my fingers.

"This isn't a ring, but I can't wait any longer." He grabs the dog tags over my icy hand and holds it tight. "I'm proposing to you, Ari. Be my bride." He picks me up, and my feet no longer touch the ground. I'm straddling him as he pushes my back against the tree, and I hold on to him tighter.

A small bubble of laughter escapes me through the tears.

"Now you say it? We're covered in blood, and there are dead bodies right next to us. Now you say it?"

"I don't see the problem." He grabs my hair gently, pulling my head up so that I'm facing the night sky and twinkling stars.

"I'll get on my fucking knees and crawl to you if I have to, baby. I'll burn this whole world for you to be mine forever. Say it."

I exhale, biting my lips. It's like he's surrendering to me, unveiling every vulnerable factor about himself.

He kisses my neck through his mask. He lets go of my hair, sliding his hand underneath my dress and squeezing my breasts.

"Marry me." He moves my dress upward so that I'm exposed. My eyes close right when I know what's coming.

He unzips his pants, unbuckling his belt, and I'm growing more impatient to feel him.

We're both covered in blood from our chests up. Dead bodies surround us both, yet the feelings below my stomach crave him dangerously. I want him right here and right now.

Then he gets close, closing the distance, and I can feel his body heat. My gosh, he feels so warm. I want to smother myself against his massive body. All his muscles tense up against me when he positions himself at my entrance. He enters me, and I moan out loud.

"Yes, infinity times, yes," I breathe out.

Thrusting, he groans into my ear.

"I love you, Danny…"

His hard cock goes into me deeper. Over and over again, with desperation, everything I went through this past year disappears in this moment. I treasure Danny making love to me in this fucked up moment, because now that these people are dead, I feel like this is our new beginning. I know it.

He's fucking me passionately against the tree in the dark.

"I thought I lost you," I cry out as my back shifts with every pound he gives me.

"You're not going anywhere anymore. If I can make it happen, you'll have my last name first thing tomorrow."

He stretches me open and I hold on to his shoulders. His eyebrows narrow down at me, looking straight into my eyes. His face is covered in blood, and I'm clawing his shoulders from the pleasure I feel.

I'm going to come already. He knows how to hit that spot that drives me wild. I'm close, and he knows it.

He grunts, and I can't stop moaning.

With one hand, he squeezes my left thigh tight, pulling me closer so he can go deeper. He's devouring me like he always does. Fucking me roughly.

Then I climax all over his cock. My pussy grips down on his massive length, and I moan into his shoulders, clawing his shoulders harder.

I'm in complete bliss as relief washes over me like a hurricane.

"I can't control myself around you, fuck," he growls as he continues to thrust inside me.

"Danny, I haven't been on—" I croak as my breasts bounce faster each time he draws deeper and closer inside me, my whole body jolts against the tree.

I haven't been able to take my birth control pills since I was taken. A mini panic attack ensues, but Danny doesn't flinch, doesn't hesitate when I confess. Instead, he keeps moving like nothing can stop him from taking me completely. The thought of trying to have another baby sends swishes of hope through my heart.

I want to try again, but I don't know how he feels.

"I know," he growls. He picks up his speed fast, squeezing my thighs tight. I know there will be bruises to reflect what he's done. I whimper with pain and pleasure, and before I know it, he comes inside of me...answering my concerns with his actions.

He takes off his mask and pockets it.

It should be illegal for him to look this good. His dark blond hair ruffles out, and his cheeks reflect a reddish hue from the freezing night, and his beard hugs his sharp jawline.

"I need to kiss you."

He looks down at me like I'm the prettiest thing he's ever seen.

He looks forever tethered as he intertwines my hands in one of his hands, lifting them above my head as his lips crash against me. He's devouring me, deeper and deeper. Our lips brush against each other, his tongue finding mine, clashing together like two worlds finally becoming one.

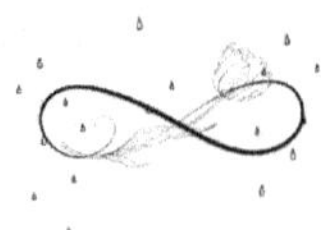

He carries my drained body in his arms. I cuddle deeper into his chest, crying and holding onto him for dear life. His vest and weapons make it uncomfortable, but his hands and scent compensate for it. He smells like home, and I never want to leave his side ever again.

I never want to let Danny go. I feel at complete peace knowing that the people responsible for killing my brother are dead and long gone. That chapter has finally closed because of him. He saved me again and avenged my brother at the same time.

As I drift in and out of sleep, as he carries me out of the woods, I dream of my brother. I can see flashes of Paul playing his guitar. It's a foggy, hazy dream, but I can see him. He looks up from his guitar and places his palms on the strings...this time, he stops playing.

He looks up at me with a huge, warm grin. I know he wants to say something. I know it. His dimples appear on each cheek, and a tear falls down my big brother's face.

I know he's at peace. And it's because Danny put an end to our misery.

Standing from his chair, throwing his guitar over his shoulder, he walks away deeper into black shadows, disappearing.

I smile against Danny's chest, and he holds me tighter as my dream fades out.

The last thing I hear before I'm overtaken by sleep is, "I'm done with this team. I'm taking her home."

42

———

ARI

My world feels like it finally makes sense again. The darkness doesn't feel lonely anymore, as long as I have Danny by my side. I kept telling myself I accepted everything about him this past year just to throw it in his face.

Being taken from him and my life made me realize I never want to live without him ever again.

He's the strongest man I've ever known, and I feel lucky every time he embraces me in his big arms.

He's my home. Wherever he goes, I will follow.

"Lie down."

We're both naked. As soon as we got home, it didn't take long for him to undress me as soon as we walked into his front door. All of my clothes are scattered across the hallway to the living room like a route.

He turned on his fireplace and undressed himself. He pulls off his belt, removes his uniform, and climbs on me.

"Mrs. Rider." He kisses my forehead as he hovers over me. I

stare at his chest where he's been shot. There's a massive bandage over it as he palms his hands on either side of my face.

"It feels weird to say it." I look at the diamond ring on my left hand as I brush my hands on the left side of his face.

I'm still wearing the same dog tags he gave me when he proposed. They fall over in my hair, and he plays with them for a couple of seconds before he lets them go.

It's late at night, and the fire from the fireplace keeps us warm. It stopped snowing, but it continues to freeze.

He grabs my hand and looks at the ring on my finger.

"You're never taking this off," he murmurs as he lets my hand go. He trails kisses all the way down my chest to my stomach. He stops when he sees the scar Nora and Shane gave me. I feel his beard skim over it before he plants a kiss on the fading scar, and my anguish falls into nothing.

Then, he pushes himself into me, slow at first. I moan loudly at the harsh intrusion. I was already wet and ready for him when we entered his house. The need to dominate me consumes him. He wants me to submit to him as always, and I will. But I'm not the only one submitting tonight, and I'll show him that.

I feel so full, and I scratch his back as he pushes himself deeper inside me.

I grab his ring finger. I pull it into my mouth, sucking on his black wedding band, earning a growl from him.

"My husband," I tell him.

After I was discharged from the hospital, Danny wasn't kidding about not wanting to wait any longer. He called the courthouse while I was being taken to the hospital for rehydration, and after, he let Lori finish treating his gunshot wound.

We got married when we were discharged. It wasn't easy

finding a judge to marry us, but then they saw who was asking, and they were suddenly available on a holiday.

My mom bought me a white dress from Target, and it was perfect. I didn't want a wedding. I wanted to be married to him. Finally start our lives intertwined, now that a huge chapter in our lives has closed.

My mother and Enzo Rooker were the only ones to attend our courthouse wedding.

But Danny promised me we would have a bigger one if I wanted.

He didn't want his parents there, and I don't blame him. They play a big part in his demons, but it's still not my place to tell him what to do about his estranged relationship with them.

We're on the same couch where we shared our first kiss.

The way he's moving, it's different. It's like he's savoring every second. He's moving into me slowly and deeply, and I can feel everything. I can feel the head of his dick move in and out of my entrance.

He groans every time he pulls out and then pushes himself in.

"You're so fucking tight...fuck," he whispers as he kisses down my neck. He trails his tongue down to my chest and then takes my right breast into his mouth. He sucks on it hard, humming, and then puts my other breast into his mouth.

His movements start to speed up, burying himself deeper and deeper inside of me. When he pulls my waist closer to him like he's starving, the way his fingers dig into my ass like he's greedy to have all of me until I'm consumed by him enlightens more and more.

"Baby, you smell so good...taste so fucking good." He breathes onto the skin of my neck, then he sucks on my nipple again as he moves inside me. Holding it tight in his palm, squeezing my chest, I throw my head back and close my eyes tight as his grip tightens.

The pain is world-shattering.

I'd let him do anything to me.

He keeps hitting the same spot deep inside of me, and I'm screaming, moaning at the top of my lungs every time he touches it, and my clit brushes against him.

He knows how to work my body every fucking time. He's so much taller than me, bigger than me, and yet he's careful not to *actually* hurt me.

Suddenly, he's pulling me up, keeping his cock deep inside me as he shifts positions. He sits on the couch, facing the fireplace and television like he's watching, and I'm on top.

I'm breathing heavenly, and he's looking at me intensely right before he pulls the back of my head closer to his. His big hand grips me with desperation.

His eyebrows furrow when I lift myself off of him to tease him.

"Jesus Christ, Ari..." he growls with lustrous need. "Get back down," he demands impatiently.

I smirk at his stunned anger.

His hands go to my waist, and he digs his fingers into my skin, forcing me to sit on his length, but I hold my ground.

"Promise me something?" I look at him, my lips curving into a soft smile. I can feel my cheeks heat, and the warmth from what I feel for Danny only spreads faster.

"Anything." One of his hands moves down to palm my ass, and he cups it, grasping it like he owns me.

He wants me to ride him.

"Promise me you won't ever hide the things you don't like about yourself to me? I want the vulnerability and the sadistic parts of you. You can be every variant of yourself with me. I hope you know that," I whisper. I reach out to feel his abs. Each of my fingers goes across his abs, down to his groin.

The veins near his lower stomach pop out, and I trace them with my fingers.

It's important that he knows this. I'm not sure if he ever had anyone to tell him that he's the most amazing man in this world, even with all of his scarred, haunted past.

I love all of him.

He swallows, and I can see his Adam's apple move as he does. His chest rising and falling. Sweat flows down his chest hair, and I can feel myself growing clammy.

I don't want him to treat me like I'm fragile. Ever since we got back to Iraq this past year, he hasn't belittled me like when we first met.

When he returned home after his deployment, he was the opposite. He looks at me like a queen. Especially after we lost our baby, I don't want to let Shane and Nora have this hold on me. I'm stronger than their hatred for me. I won't let them destroy my future with Danny or my mental health.

"I promise you." He moves his hand to my face, pushing my bangs behind my ear.

I bite my lip, and then I rock my hips into him, and he throws his head back onto the couch. I move my hips forward and back, and he tightens both ass cheeks, squeezing them hard.

I ride him, and all you can hear is moans and the fireplace crackling.

"Just don't run. Because I plan on destroying your ass while you wear my hands like a choker necklace until you black out."

He gave me a taste of that in his truck after the military ball. The thought of getting choked out was horrifying, but why am I so fucking intrigued? Why does it only turn me on, sparking a desire so hot inside me? If he thinks he can spook me, he's only heightening my curiosity.

"Choking me out completely?!" I squeak out and stop moving. He grins sinfully before he flips me over so that I'm no longer riding him. I'm facing the end of the couch, my ass in the air, and he pushes my head into the cushion. My cheek glides on the soft fabric, my teeth sink into my lip. "Let me see you come for me."

I think I gave him the green light to welcome his darkest desires. And I'm so ready.

He drives himself inside me, and instead of grabbing my waist for balance, he grips the back of my hair like a leash, and my head is the collar. His chest on my back.

"On second thought, maybe you should run. My ranch has lots of land, and I would love to see you try it. Because when I catch you." He pulls my hair harder, causing me to cry out in pain and lust. It drives my head to be pulled backward, and I hiss from the tug. He keeps thrusting himself inside me as he grips my hair.

"You'll pay the price, Mrs. Rider. You're my wife. And there's no escaping the devil, little angel. You're in my hell now." He picks up his pace, pulling my hair toward him so he can fuck my pussy ruthlessly with no regard for my threshold.

I'm whimpering, moaning into the air as he unleashes more strength onto my body as he rails me. My body shakes from his greed to fuck me rough.

Then I hear a loud grunt drift into the living room. He roars with satisfaction as he comes inside of me. He lets go of my hair as his last thrust moves in and out, emptying himself completely.

"I can't wait to see you carry my child again."

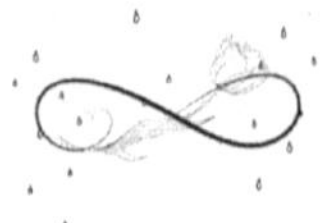

We're lying on his living room floor and Danny has me lying on top of his chest. My cheek lies on top of his hourglass tattoo. I touch the Latin words, trailing them like a puzzle.

My God, this man is too beautiful.

His hands play with my back, and he kisses my head.

We just finished round four, and it's nearing two in the morning. I'm exhausted, but this feels like paradise. It's a beautiful start to our honeymoon. Admiral Ravenmore granted his team a month of leave after taking out Omar.

Danny made him pay.

There's no one else I'd rather be married to.

I love Kane, but Danny owns my heart and soul.

As Kane pops into my head, our last moments together flash through.

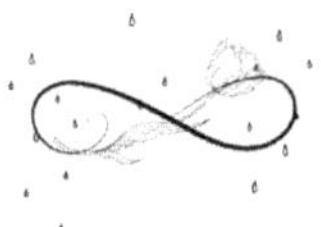

"My favorite nurse lies in a bed this time. I get to be the SEAL that impersonates one...this will be fun." Kane plops down on a chair next to me.

Danny left to get me new clothes and take care of our upcoming wedding. He's been the best fiancé I could ever ask for, but his friendship with Kane will never be the same. They like each other enough to stay on the same team, but they will never again hang out like they used to, and that sucks.

"What are you doing here?" I close my thriller book, placing it on my lap, and study him. He's dressed in a dark blue sweater with the same beanie he wore that night we played soccer together.

His warm smile disappears, and I glare at him. I love him...but my heart belongs to Danny.

He sighs, and I notice that he hasn't shaved in a while, leaving stubble over his sharpened chin.

He intertwines his hands, resting his forearms on his thighs that are spread apart. I cross my arms over my chest, hugging myself.

"I'm sorry, Ari. That's why I'm here. I'm here to let you know that I'm sorry."

I nod, giving him a cold expression. I don't know what to say... I'm scared I'll say the wrong things, and I'll hurt him further. I'm so in love with Danny, and if he didn't feel the same way for me...it would hurt. Words wouldn't be able to describe if our love ended...so I feel like I get an idea of what Kane is feeling.

"But I'm not sorry about being in love with you. I think I'll always be in love with you." I take a deep breath when he says it again. I break away from his gaze, and I do my best to refrain from blushing. I tense up because a part of me loves Kane too...just not like how he needs me to be with him in return.

"And that's okay, because at the end of the day, I just want..." He shakes his head. He licks his lips, and my heart skips. He grabs my hand, gripping it gently. "No, I need you to be happy."

I chew the inside of my lip before I let myself relax. He's always been there for me, and we'll always have a relationship. But I know my boundaries, and Danny will have no problem reminding Kane of his. He almost killed Kane at the military ball if it hadn't been for Rooker.

"Well, I am happy, Kane. Danny makes me happy, but so do you. Just in different ways." I squeeze his hand back before pulling my hand away...letting him go.

"I know." He clenches his jaw, and then his dark blue eyes flash with hope.

"Do you accept my apology?" he asks, smirking.

I chew the inside of my lip.

"Of course. Just don't bite me again, or I'll kick your ass," I threaten.

"Is that a promise?" he teases.

I roll my eyes playfully before laughing. I point to the door to my room, ordering him out.

"All right, get out, Mr. Slaughter."

He chuckles before pushing himself out of the chair, surrendering.

"Fine." He sighs sarcastically. He knows this will be the last time we'll ever be alone again together. He reaches for the door, and I grab my book, tempted to dive back in. It's nearing the end of the book, and I can feel a plot twist coming.

"Goodbye, Ari Alvarez." His soft voice flows like an airy rose, and I meet his dark cobalt blue pools.

His eyes are sad, but his smile is sunshine like it always is. He holds onto the doorknob, one foot in and one foot out of the exit to my room.

Nurses and doctors pass by him in the background, giving me a bit of déjà vu.

"Goodbye, Kane Slaughter," I tell him, returning his sunshine with my own.

My fingers track the edges of his hourglass tattoo. A skull sits at the bottom, and I repeat the Latin words repeatedly in my head, and a part of me feels like I'm back in Iraq with him the first time I saw it.

His fireplace continues to crackle. I'm finally at peace, and I didn't have to sleep or drink countless wine bottles to achieve it. I'm warm.

Danny is the fire I constantly keep burning myself with.

Usually, when you play with fire, you get burned and don't do it again. But Danny makes the pain feel good and normalized.

He holds me like I'll never shatter again, and if I do, he'll be there to find every piece and put me back together.

"You have a thing for cherries, don't you?" My eyebrows raise when I realize there's more to his first nickname for me.

"You caught that?"

"Tell me why."

He clears his throat, his hand palms the edges of his beard, and looks at the fire behind me as he continues to massage my shoulder blades.

"I had a v-very lonely childhood. No siblings. No cousins. Work on my dad's properties, mixed martial arts, and shooting ranges was all I knew growing up." He stops drawing circles on my shoulder blades, and I glance at him.

"My maternal grandmother was the only person that would make me feel...normal. Like it was okay to be a child and not grow up so fast. She passed away when I was in high school."

He sighs.

"Once a year, we would visit her. Every January, we would drive up to her house on the lake, and she would always have freshly baked cherry pie. She said it was for her favorite grandson. Granted, I was her only grandchild, but...it was the only glimpse of normalcy I had in my entire life... a cherry pie was the one thing that made me feel like I was deserving of love."

My throat constricts when he lifts my chin to meet his ocean eyes.

"Until you came along. You make me feel like I deserve more."

I blink fast, trying hard not to fall apart. "I wish I could have met her."

He pushes my hair back, stroking the side of my head repeatedly. "You were always there all these years..."

I reach over and tangle my hands in his hair, kissing him and he kisses me back softly while gripping my jaw hard.

"Danny?" I break our kiss. "Don't leave your team for me."

He goes rigid, and he stops holding me. I sit up so I'm now beside him, and I'm blocking his view to the fireplace. He merges onto his side, lifting his head onto his palm, looking at me intensely.

"If you're going to leave the Navy or whatever it is, do it because you feel like that's the best choice *for you*...not for me. Because I'm not going anywhere, my love. When I said yes, I meant it. I'm not going to lie, though. This life is frustrating and, most of all, terrifying, but I need you to know that no matter what you choose to do. I'm here. I'm not leaving you ever again, I promise."

"I don't need you worrying about me all the time. I don't want you in danger anymore because the longer I stay in the Navy, the more I put you at risk."

"I understand, and I've accepted it. But the military needs you. You help people just like I do. It's our job." I pull the blankets higher over my breasts. "Those children you saved... Violet...*me*." I point to myself, and his blue eyes soften. I have his full attention, and his jaw ticks.

Grabbing my hand, he brushes his finger over the giant diamond that sits on my hand. He stares at the ring on my finger, and then he scoffs. He crawls, moving his knees on either side of me, and pushes me back down on the pillow beside the coffee table.

"You're smart, too beautiful, you know that?" He pulls me in for another kiss before he rips the blanket off me. My nipples harden and graze against his chest when he closes the distance. His beard tickles my skin, and I moan when I feel him push into me again, and I claw at his back as he picks up his pace.

Oh, God.

He feels so damn good. Round number five, in less than twelve hours, takes off, and he grips my jaw, forcing my head off the pillow. He kisses me, whispering *I love yous* against my mouth the entire time.

EPILOGUE

DANNY

My dick stirs inside of my uniform when I see Ari in her maternity dress.

She's seven months pregnant with our twins and it's been a fucking blessing watching her grow what I left inside of her the night I rescued her from Omar.

She got pregnant that night I spilled all of my love inside of her against that tree. The night that was full of chaotic doom flashes in my head like it was yesterday. Her black hair glowed against the winter moonlight. Her breasts bounced over and over again as I drilled myself deep inside of her.

Women are beautiful creatures. Ari's small frame growing our twin babies amazes me every day when I wake up and see her stomach swollen so preciously perfect.

She's creating life.

I never thought I would be a man that believed in God after everything I've experienced in my career. But watching my angel come into my life in a time I needed her. She obliterated my demons by saving me from my fucking self.

If it weren't for her, I probably would continue the life of a selfish asshole, drinking and killing my life away.

And now she's cradling two innocent souls I'm committed to protect for as long as I live.

How could I not believe in heaven when Ari's existence is evidence of it all?

I was never a religious man, but that's changed. I've attended Sunday morning mass at our local Catholic church on base with Ari and her mother since we got married. I have a lot to learn but it's a start.

I'm about to leave on a deployment and she could give birth any day. There's a real possibility I might miss it.

"I could spend the rest of my days with my tongue inside your cunt and my hand wrapped around your ass."

Ari draws in a breath, her thighs quivering over my shoulders as I suck on her sensitive swollen clit.

My cock throbs in pain, and the need to feel her burns inside of me. The only thing that will extinguish this lustrous fire is her velvet insides.

And she will...but first I need to make my pregnant wife come.

Her hands tug at my hair strands on the top of my head as her soft weeping moans fill our bedroom.

"That's my good girl. You sound just as sweet as you taste, baby." Her cries make even more blood rush to the head of my cock, and I'm about to finish in my own pants, just getting off to the sounds she makes when my tongue fucks her perfect cunt.

"Danny... I'm about to—" She exhales another high-pitched moan, unable to finish her squeaks of ecstasy.

"I'm about to—" she repeats as my tongue flicks her clit repeatedly, up from her folds, tasting the honey she drips for me. I push three of my fingers, thrusting them over and over again. She buckles her thighs, tightening over my hand. Her soft skin presses against my cheeks and my angel is about to play me a symphony with her screams.

Then she's crying out for me. Her toes and feet curl in as her orgasm rips through her body and her heavy breathing echoes through our bedroom.

She's so intoxicating. I can't ever get enough of tasting her cherry lips.

"I want you to come again."

"What?" Her chest rises and falls. Looking at me, her whole body still trembling from coming all over my face and fingers.

"You heard me. I need to feel my pregnant wife come all over my cock."

I reach over and pull on her dress so that she's more exposed.

She wanted to take maternity photos before I left on the mission tonight. I'm not a person who takes photos. I fucking hate anything dealing with social media and taking pictures isn't something I do.

My camera has pictures of random shit. Most of it is work stuff. And if there are pictures of me, Ari's in them too.

Whatever my bride wants, she gets.

She rolls over to her side, her bump on display.

I throw off my uniform in seconds, determined to get inside her.

I lean on the bed next to her, the bed dipping underneath my knuckles. My weight makes Ari sink a little as I adjust my cock so that her ass is hugging it.

My hands go to palm the side of her stomach.

I trail my finger on her hips as I kiss her shoulder, then I bite down on her shoulder and she moans in response.

My fingers trail down onto her hips, my hard cock pressed between her ass cheeks, and I'm tempted to fuck her there too.

A few more months, and I'll be wrecking her ass. A few more months and I get to watch her bleed beautiful tears while she chokes on my cock.

Just a few. More. Months.

When my hand touches her purple stretch marks, she flinches, tensing up.

I raise my brows in confusion.

"I'm sorry. Is it bad that I don't like them?" she murmurs, tightening her grip on my fingers, wanting to push me away.

"Don't be ashamed of your body, baby. You have these because of me. Just another reminder that you're mine. These parts of you are my favorite."

She dips her head back, so she's resting more on my shoulder.

I take advantage of her arching her back into me. I take her swollen breast into my mouth, sucking and biting on her sensitive nipple over her shoulder, all the while fingering her.

I enter her slowly, and she hisses while I stretch her. I continue to suck on her breast as I rock my hips inside her.

I stop sucking on her breasts and my hand goes to palm her throat as I fuck her, savoring every second like it's my last. Because it might as well be. I never know if I'll be coming back alive from the mission, but Ari and our babies give me more of a reason to fight like hell.

"You'll always be beautiful to me, little angel."

She hasn't looked more beautiful to me, knowing that her stretch marks are there because of me.

I pick up my pace, pushing in and out of her.

Fuck, she just feels so damn good.

"I love you," she whispers as she grabs my hand and kisses each knuckle.

I suck on her neck, leaving her marks there too.

There's not a place on her skin where I haven't left a mark. I circle her clit as I pound inside of her.

"Oh, oh, oh," she whimpers from solace. Every flick makes a moan come out of her sweet tongue.

Then she clenches down on my dick and it sends me roaring behind her, in my own climax. I push myself deeper, tightening my muscles all over her body, yet careful not to harm her or her cervix. I don't need her entering early labor on me.

I'm coming hard, grunting while I bite down on her shoulder just enough to reflect my claim on her.

"I love you, Mrs. Rider," I tell her as I slow down my movements, emptying every single drop of my come inside her.

"I love you, infinitely."

I could listen to her say those words over and over again and I would die a happy, fulfilled man.

I grab a hold of her breast again and suck on it. Her hard nipple in between my teeth. I'm playing with it as she continues to recover from her orgasm.

I pull out of her, standing by the bed, headed for a last-minute shower before I'm on a C17 back to Iraq at around midnight. She doesn't know I'm going back there, but she understands the classification of the missions and hasn't asked.

She takes off her dress, slipping under the blankets.

Her long black hair has grown out tremendously and it goes all the way down past her breasts onto her bump, guarding her nipples.

I touch the doorknob to our bathroom, about to swing it open, but Ari's sniffles stop me.

I turn to face her. Tears all the way down her cheeks.

Shit.

"I don't want you to go. I'm about to give birth any day to our son and daughter. What if you miss it?" She holds onto her pregnancy pillow for comfort, squeezing it underneath her fingers. "What if...you don't come back? Forgive me for saying it, Danny, but I can't do this without you. You have to come back to us. Y-you have to." Her brown eyes, glistening with tears, plead with me.

I don't say anything at first. There's nothing I can say. After everything that's happened to us, I understand why she's having a moment like this.

I walk over to her, then plant a kiss on her forehead.

"I won't miss the birth. You're my home, Ari. I'll come back. I always have. I promise you." She grabs my hand, intertwining her soft fingers in mine.

"You know I've always thought of you as my ocean." I squeeze her hand.

She slaps my arm, snapping her teeth.

"Your ocean! I knew it, you think I'm a whale." She crosses her arms.

"No, Ari," I kiss her lips profoundly. God, I'm a lucky bastard with a wife like her. "You're my ocean because to me, an ocean has always been a place of tranquility, serenity, but most of all, natural beauty. Your waves represent patience, second chances, and ever since I met you, you've washed away all of my doubts...*my demons*. Our love is like an ocean, limitless and never-ending. Our story will always have more to explore."

I kiss her tummy once before standing. She watches me, biting her lip.

When I surprised her at her friends' wedding, watching her look out at sea, that's when I knew she truly was heaven-sent.

"And you're like Wrightsville Beach. Your love comes in different waves, fracturing my boundaries, pushing and pulling me past my limits in ways that transcend me further. You're relentless, unforgiving, and unpredictable, but smooth in the most remarkable ways, my love. Strong and unyielding. Your eyes are as blue as the water, especially during the summer when the sun shines on it just right. Your hair is as sandy as the beach, and when a sea breeze hits, I always get lost in the peaceful scent just like yours. And when the sun sets, it's my favorite. You know why?"

"Why?"

"When the sun sets, the sky turns orange, red, and gold, and it reminds me of the summer we fell in love in Iraq."

I look away from her, licking my lips, and I know the first thing I'm going to do when our kids can walk.

"Let's have our wedding there," I tell her, leaning on the wall.

Her brown eyes do that thing I love so much, and they sparkle.

"Wrightsville Beach? Where Emilia got married?"

"Yes. Our babies can watch their parents say, 'I Do.' Our little man can be my best man alongside Rooker, and our little lady can be the ring bearer."

"I would love that, Danny." She smiles, holding her bump. Then her smile fades, and she's lost in thought.

"What is it, angel?"

She shakes her head, and her eyes widen, but she's not looking at me. It's like she's still entranced by something on the wall.

"I just realized I have to give birth. I'm 5'1," She points to her chest, "you're 6'6!" she points to me. "I'm carrying your babies. *Two* babies."

I laugh, looking at the floor.

"God have mercy on my vagina."

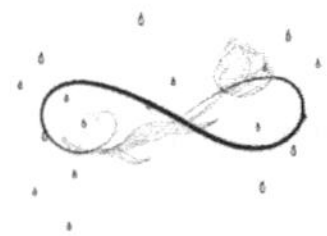

Ari

It's afternoon, and Danny wanted to say goodbye to my mother too before he left tonight. I've finished up dinner and he has to go in a few minutes.

"My love, just try it!" I beg him as I straddle his lap on the couch.

I dangle one of my favorite pieces of candy over his mouth, and he purses his lips, smirking handsomely. I arch my brows, opening my mouth so he can mimic my movements.

He shakes his head, gripping my waist tight, and I can feel his bulge harden as he forces me to rub more against him.

"Danny, my mother is outside. Behave." I laugh.

"Fine!" He grabs the candy from my hand and eyes the purple striped candy suspiciously. "What is this?"

"Try it! You'll love it. It's a Mexican candy. It's sweet and spicy." I giggle over his skeptical expression.

"Oh, so like you?"

I roll my eyes.

"Just eat it already!"

He raises it to his mouth and just when I think he's about to take a bite, he closes his mouth again. I let my hands fall to my side, frustrated.

"What's this called again?"

I cross my arms.

"Pulparindo."

"A what?"

"A Pulparindo!" I say, rolling the *r* on my tongue.

"A vulva-rindo?"

I sigh, frustrated, pushing his shoulder, and he chuckles.

"No! Stop!"

"Sounds like vulva." He studies the candy, flipping it.

"Just eat it before we have to say goodbye."

"Baby, it's never a goodbye."

He plants a kiss on my lips before letting himself fall back onto the couch again.

"It's a—"

"See you soon."

We say it together, and he smiles, flashing me that trillion dollar smile.

He takes a bite out of the candy, and I snatch it out of his hand before he can eat any more of it.

He chews on it, looking straight into my eyes. I'm watching him like a Hawk, anticipating his reaction to the taste.

"Wow, it's fucking good." He swallows before reaching back for it.

"Nope. Mine." I take off from his lap, and he groans.

"Ari, let me take these to where I'm going!" he calls out for me as I run toward the front porch where my mother is at.

"I guess you can't leave me now until you get more of these!" I shout over my shoulder. He stands from the couch, chasing after me. I wish I could say I was truly running from him, but it's more like waddling like a penguin. I swing the door open to the house and stop in my tracks. My smile fades away and confusion replaces the calmness in my chest.

A young woman stands in front of my mother. They're both in mid-conversation by her plants to the left of the porch. A baby girl that looks to be about a year or two hugs her like she's shy. She has brown hair and wide honey eyes.

My eyebrows furrow as I study the woman. She looks familiar.

"Oh, I'm sorry, who's this, Mom?" I ask politely. I feel big hands grip my shoulder and I peek a glance at Danny towering over me behind me, matching my expression. He stiffens and steps in front of me protectively. After what happened with Ms. Salem, he's been extra cautious.

"This is Paul's...friend." Mom looks at her dubiously.

The woman and child turn toward Danny and I. He steps in front of me, like my guardian knight, and places his hand on my baby bump.

When I see her brown eyes soften sadly, I remember where I've seen her before. She was in one of the photographs that Paul kept hidden in his nightstand.

The beautiful woman in the picture.

"Hi. I'm sorry I just showed up like this, but this can't wait any longer." She readjusts the baby on her hip.

"Okay?" I step out from behind Danny, furrowing my brows.

What could she possibly want this late at night? How does she know where we live?

"I'm Adriana and this is Celine, my daughter." She motions to her baby. Celine holds a stuffed bear in her hands, looking around the porch. "My husband isn't the father, which means the only other person it could have been..."

Husband? She's married? The baby isn't his? Does she mean what I think she means?

"Who are you?" Danny presses the woman in a grumpy tone.

I squeeze his hand, and he looks down at me protectively.

"I'm Paul's old friend...and I'm pretty sure your brother is my child's father."

What?

"Come again? What do you mean? He didn't have a girlfriend."

How?

I drop the candy, covering my mouth. The blood drains from my face while all types of emotions hit me like lightning.

"I, uh, had an affair. I'm not proud of it." Adriana murmurs like she's embarrassed.

Could this mean that a piece of Paul lives on? Is she telling the truth?

"We can talk about the details inside. Just please don't faint." Adriana begs.

My mother sobs, incoherent cries of happiness wiping them away as they fall.

"You mean—?" I whisper, tears falling down my cheeks. A blip of happiness and hope pulls at my heartstrings. Danny pulls me in closer to his body, holding me like he's afraid I'll pass out.

Is this possible?

"Celine is your niece and your mother's granddaughter."

My mom grabs the little girl's hand like she's holding onto a miracle, and Adriana smiles.

And that's when Paul's dimples curve onto Celine's face. Mom wipes away another tear before telling us, "I knew a part of him was always going to come back home. I knew he wasn't truly gone."

ALSO BY LEXIE AXELSON

Scarred Executioners Series

See You Soon

I Promise You

Pretend

WHAT'S NEXT IN THE SCARRED
EXECUTIONERS SERIES?

"Why does everyone call you Creature?"

"Want to find out?"

"Pretend" Coming Soon.

ACKNOWLEDGMENTS

To everyone who gave See You Soon a chance and fell in love with this story, thank you so much. It means the world to me. Thank you to my husband, my family, my friends, my beta readers, Becky, and my lovely book bestie, Dani. I couldn't have done this without you guys.

ABOUT THE AUTHOR

Lexie Axelson is a Hispanic author from South Texas. This is Lexie's second book. She is a military spouse and mother to two sons. She's a foodie, who loves traveling, spending time with her family, and binge-watching horror movies. If she's not in a bookstore browsing, she's reading a book. Her passion for reading and writing started a young age. And she hopes to bring more book boyfriends to your bookshelves!

 instagram.com/lexieaxelson

 tiktok.com/@lexieaxelson